EXTINCTION REVERSED

ROBOT GENETICISTS

BOOK ONE

J.S. MORIN

EXTINCTION REVERSED

Robot Geneticts: Book One

J.S. MORIN

Magical Scrivener Press
22 Hawkstead Hollow
Nashua, NH 03063

www.magicalscrivener.com

Publisher's Note: This is a work of fiction. Names, characters, places, and incidents are a product of the author's imagination. Locales and public names are sometimes used for atmospheric purposes. Any resemblance to actual people, living or dead, or to businesses, companies, events, institutions, or locales is completely coincidental.

Ordering Information: Special discounts are available on quantity purchases by corporations, associations, and others. For details, contact the publisher at the address above.

J.S. Morin – First Edition

ISBN: 978-1-942642-24-4

Printed in the United States of America

CHAPTER ONE

There shouldn't have been anything after the apocalypse. The works of mankind should have fallen to ruin and decayed into the memory of the universe along with their creators. But Notre Dame Cathedral echoed with dozens of voices in perfectly attuned, if not beautiful, harmony.

As Charlie7 sang along in chorus, he gazed up at the restored stained glass frescoes and wondered why. Why did they all sing in praise of a god that had not created them? Sunlight streamed through the colored glass, and not one image depicted robotkind. Saints and saviors abounded but not a single scientist. At best, Charlie7 and his kind were God's grandchildren, made in the image of their own creators: humans.

If any of the other worshipers in attendance entertained such blasphemous thoughts, none let it show. By Charlie7's headcount, there were Johns and Freds, Sandras and Marys. No fewer than a dozen Elizabeths were present, as if no force in Western Europe could restrain them from attending the grand rededication.

Charlie7 had only come out of idleness and the fact that it was within walking distance of home. He had learned the hymns and rituals hastily after receiving an invitation from Paul208, foreman of the restoration. If anyone would have asked what Charlie7 was doing attending services, he had the excuse that he was 10 percent John. Usually, such a minor personality slice wouldn't be enough to turn a robotic personality into a believer, but heroes got away with bolder lies.

John316 led the service. That wasn't even his official designation. But if a robot had the ambition or hubris to ordain himself, a change of name wasn't so great a stretch.

Charlie7 lost himself in examining the architectural details of the stonework as John316 blathered on about the building's history and religious significance. The living, breathing Charles Truman had never set foot inside Notre Dame, so Charlie7 had no stored memory of the place to draw from. If the original was anything like Paul208's version, the ancient humans who built it had done a bang-up job.

A shift in John316's tone drew Charlie7's attention back to the sermon.

"I would like us all to pause in remembrance of the eighth Adam," John316 said. No robot claimed the designation "Adam." There were only twenty-seven scientists digitized for posterity before humanity's demise. Each robot had a mind stitched together from those neural imprints and carried the name of the majority personality. None of the Twenty-Seven was named Adam.

John316 continued after a somber pause. "The Sanctuary for Scientific Sins reported this morning that he passed away at the age of eleven. Cause of death: organ failure due to advanced cellular decay."

All around the cathedral, robots muttered prayers and expressions of grief. The robotic preacher in his pompous black robe delved once more into platitudes.

Charlie7 fumed. The sermon struck Charlie7's acoustic sensors unrecorded as a wave of indignant error messages scrolled through his field of vision.

What right had these madmen to play at rebirthing humanity? For decades, glory-seeking geneticists raced in secret to be the first to reveal a reborn human. The sanctuary to which John316 referred was a remote island where the castoff results of cloning experiments lived out their often short, painful lives. Most robots just referred to the refuge as the Scrapyard.

The Genetic Ethics Committee had only recently allowed sanctioned research on lower primates. The poor wretches at the Scrapyard were the result of hubris. If Charlie7 ever caught one of the perpetrators, he would do far worse than strip them of their credentials.

Charlie7 had not waited more than a thousand years to watch humanity be reborn in agony.

At length, the service played itself out. The parishioners exited the cavernous Gothic structure in neat rows. They chatted reverently beneath the echoing vaulted ceiling.

Charlie7 loitered amid the pews, waiting for everyone to vacate. The message he had received on the Social had been brief. Toby22 had asked whether he'd be attending services today, and when Charlie7 had replied that he would, Toby22's follow-up had been simply: "outside. afterward."

Mostly, Charlie7 ignored the Social. He liked keeping the cold, calculating computer in his chest separate from the crystalline matrix of thought, memory, and emotion within his skull.

Efficiency was hell. The only joy to be found in life came from the chaotic, the unplanned, and the unexpected. Toby22's message certainly qualified as the latter.

Unexpected or not, Charlie7 would probably have met with Toby22 anyway. Tobys got things done. Society would have been all the poorer without their willingness to roll up their sleeves and work. Toby and his brethren straddled the line between menial laborers and automatons.

Charlie7 listened until he could no longer hear the faint buzz of conversation outside. His synthetic leather soles scuffed on the stone floors. The echoes showcased the cathedral's magnificent acoustics. Charlie7 imagined the chorus of voices that had risen when the world was filled with real humans.

As Charlie7 stepped into a beautiful spring morning, he let his shoulders rise and fall in memory of a sigh.

Paris had changed in the centuries since the invasion. When Charlie7 had settled there, it had been bleak, barren, and dotted with rubble and ruins. Now the landscape exploded in wildflowers and tall grasses. The debris had been cleared away, the radioactive fallout neutralized. A few modern buildings stabbed up from the soil like spikes of steel and glass. Ancient relics like Notre Dame hinted at the city's former old-world charm. The rest was left to the mercy of nature's newborn grasp.

Charlie7 watched the ascent of a mining transorbital, one of the gigaton vessels that ran relays to the Kuiper Belt. Hamburg was 748 kilometers away, but he could make out the engines clear as fiber optics at just 4x magnification.

Maybe it was time for Charlie7 to take a break from retirement and life on Earth. Much as he wished otherwise, he couldn't escape the reminders of the tormented humans trapped in clandestine labs across the globe. He knew there would be no stopping the geneticists until someone succeeded.

The robot that reforged humanity would become a legend.

Charlie7 was already a legend, and he had no stomach for genetics. Maybe another stint as a miner was just what he needed for a change of pace. With any luck, he could be gone long enough for the science to bring back humanity.

A crunch in the gravel snapped him from his reverie.

"Hey, Charlie. Long time," Toby22 said, limping from the grasses onto the path. He was dressed in overalls and boots, with a straw hat to keep the sun from overtaxing his coolant systems. His clothes and gloves were dirt stained as usual. As a game warden in the newly repopulated forests of England, he spent nearly all his time outdoors.

"You look like hell," Charlie7 replied. He shook Toby22's hand. "That body of yours is obsolete."

Toby22 waved the comment aside. "Jason90 is working on a new hip flexor for me. I'll get another ten, maybe twenty years out of this carcass."

"I could put in a good word... bump you up the list for a new chassis."

"Not compatible. I'm up for a full crystal transfer." He shuddered. "Always makes me think I'm dying, and some new copy of me lives on."

Charlie7 knew exactly what he meant. He was on his third crystal matrix, and it took months for the nagging worry to dissipate that he wasn't really the Charlie7 who had gone into the mind-transfer rig. No coolant pump could give the sort of chill that ran through Charlie7's systems just pondering that existential dilemma. Everyone thought the Charlie archetype was diamond hard, impervious to the cosmic dread associated with the copying of an old consciousness into a new vessel. The Charlies liked to let them think that, but no robot was immune.

"So, why the firewall meeting? Why chase me down at a civic grand opening? I could have flown out to you this afternoon if you'd asked." Charlie7 would have done no such thing, but now that Toby22 was here, there was no harm in claiming otherwise.

As Toby22 led him through the tall grass and around the side of the building, Charlie7 wondered. Had his friend gone faulty?

Tobys were known for their reliability, but Toby22 was 30 percent Joshua and another 18 percent Brent. Not that either of those personalities contained red flags for neural failure, but odd interactions could cascade over time. His refusal to take a chassis upgrade could have been just the tip of the iceberg.

Then Charlie7 noticed someone huddled in the shadows on the cathedral's north side. The figure was bundled under a tarp, hugged close like a blanket as if there were rain on the way. "You got a friend with a faulty case?"

"Not exactly..."

As Charlie7 and Toby22 drew near, the huddled figure turned its head. Staring out from beneath the tarp was a pair of wide eyes showing whites like fresh snow. Those eyes emitted no light of their own, unlike every robot who'd ever been built. The face was smooth and free of blemishes. Soft. Gentle. Frightened.

Most of all, the face was human.

Charlie7's shoulders slumped. "Not another one. And let me guess..."

"Yup," Toby said with a matter of fact nod. "Her name's Eve. Eve14, to be precise."

"Someone ought to find a baby book in the archives and beat these geneticist hooligans over the head with it. Where do they get off? They *know* the science isn't mature yet. The Genetic Rebirth Committee reports have clear guidance on..."

Charlie7 caught himself ranting at a Toby. If there was an archetype less interested in committee minutiae, he didn't know of it. He paced in front of the girl as he finished the tirade via internal text. When he'd collected himself, Charlie7 stared down at the trembling creature beneath the tarp.

"So, what's wrong with this one? Cardiopulmonary? Oncological? I assume it's not immunological or you wouldn't have dragged her here with all this pollen. She hasn't said a word. Developmental disabilities like all the rest?"

Eve14 looked up, right into Charlie7's eyes. Her voice wavered but carried offended dignity through the crisp Parisian air. "There's nothing wrong with me. Nothing at all."

CHAPTER TWO

This new robot was nothing like Toby.

He was dressed in clean, black-and-white clothes whose pattern evoked a penguin. His polished head had neither dents nor scratches anywhere on it. Nothing about his manner suggested that he posed a danger. His metallic fingers were smooth at the tip. He held no tools of any sort. A face not so different from Eve's or her Creator's smiled down at her.

Eve flinched and hugged the tarp tighter as the new robot tried to lift it away from her face.

"Oh, come on," the newcomer chided her. "I'm not going to hurt the first healthy human I've seen since the invasion."

As Eve tried to back away, Toby's hand rested against her back, firm but gentle. "It's all right. This is Charlie7, an old friend of mine. You can call him Charlie."

With Toby's reassurance, she held perfectly still, forcing her muscles rigid as Charlie reached out once more. As the tarp pulled back, the world expanded.

Eve's eyes strayed upward. She gasped. For the first time, she realized the mountainous aspect of the structure beside her. It had been just a wall a moment ago, no higher than her field of vision. But now she couldn't tear her eyes from the carved cliff face.

A twinge at the top of her skull brought Eve's attention back to her two robotic companions. "What are these for?" Charlie asked. Another twinge made her flinch away from Charlie's touch.

"Couldn't say," Toby replied. "Can't imagine she was born with them, though."

Charlie leaned in close, his chin just in front of Eve's eyes. She could see the workings of his jaw as he spoke. The illusion of metallic polymer skin mimicking her own features shattered. Tiny pistons and levers worked in place of muscle and joint. Minuscule bulges beneath the cheeks and above the eyes betrayed the mechanical puppetry of facial expressions.

"Some sort of transcranial conductors..." Charlie mused.

Eve watched the actuators in his shoulder and inferred his next course of action. She twisted free and batted his hand away from her scalp. "They're the ends of my neural probe terminals. They allow more accurate encephalographs."

There were forty-eight terminals in all. Eve had counted them in the mirror often enough to know. She also knew better than to poke and prod at them, even when one or more had recently been replaced. They would itch and tingle. Sympathetic connections made her think she could feel them nuzzling around inside her brain. Rationally, Eve knew that there were no nerve endings to feel such sensations deep within the interior of her brain.

Fortunately, Charlie didn't press his examination. He stood back and crossed his arms. "There you have it. Cyborg. Not a pure human, though closer than I've seen yet."

For a moment, Eve caught a flash of Creator's smug certainty in Charlie's robotic posture.

"No..." Toby replied, shaking his head all the while. "No. I don't think that's it at all. I have a theory."

Toby took Charlie by the arm and led the penguin-suited robot away. Eve fell in behind, lagging a few tentative steps in their trampled path. Her oversized, borrowed boots scraped the gravel of the path to the cathedral.

Charlie turned and scowled over his shoulder at Eve. "You stay there. I'll be right back. I just need a word in private with my old friend."

Eve stood watching as Toby and Charlie vanished rounded a corner of the stone building. Eve swallowed back a lump in her throat. Every way Eve looked, there was no one. She was alone.

The robotic voices slipped below zero decibels. Eve couldn't hear them at all.

To keep her mind from her abandonment, Eve attempted to solve the puzzle of what Toby and Charlie might be discussing. They were friends, and Toby was old; that much had been laid out plainly in their greeting. But nothing Eve knew of the two robots would be enough for her to cobble together an answer to the riddle. A puzzle without all the pieces was merely a tease. Thus, Eve resolved to wait.

Eve identified the tall grasses all around her as *Spartina pectinata*. As the tips swayed in the light breeze, Eve brushed her hands over them, feeling the tickle against her palms. So soft and delicate, they weren't built to last.

A faint buzzing by Eve's ear caused her to swat without thinking. It was merely an *Anax imperator*, commonly called a dragonfly. It flew with the agility of Toby's skyroamer, darting faster than Eve's eyes could track. The species wasn't hematophagous, so there was no cause for alarm; it wouldn't bite her for her blood or to transmit disease.

Brushing the grasses aside, Eve knelt and inspected the earth for ground-based insects. She watched ants emerge from holes that dotted the soil like pores in the Earth's skin. Eve plucked one of the little workers from the dirt and held it between her fingers. Its legs flailed in the air, and its writhing tickled her fingertips. Eve dropped the ant and tried to wipe off the tickling sensation onto her pants. Back among its comrades, the insect resumed its labors without a hint of complaint.

"Eve," Toby called out. Amid her fascination with the tiny community of insects, she had neglected to keep a vigil for the robots' return.

There was no use in hiding. Eve wanted to be found. Unexpected relief flooded in at the sight of Toby trudging toward her through the grass. Charlie followed in Toby's wake, eyes fixed on Eve.

If she had known what to do, Eve would have done it. Instead, she waited silently.

Charlie held out a hand to her. "Eve, I'd like you to come with me. It's all right. Toby and I discussed this, and we think it's better for me to look after you."

Eve glared at Toby's torso, not daring to challenge him by looking him in the eye. But she couldn't let his betrayal pass without comment. "You promised to take care of me."

Sparing a glance up, Eve caught the corners of Toby's mouth turning up in a paltry attempt at a smile.

"I am taking care of you. I brought you to Charlie7, the best robot anyone's ever known. There's nothing Charlie can't do if he puts his mind to it."

It was a valid, logical argument. If Charlie was a superior caregiver, then Toby had discharged his duty to the best of his abilities. Any hint of subterfuge was merely Eve's misinterpretation of the promise's scope and rules. Closed-system puzzles were so much easier to solve, with boundary conditions pre-defined. Eve would just have to accept that she wasn't yet very good at open-world problem solving.

Eve cast her eyes downward. "I apologize."

Charlie took her by the hand. "Nothing to apologize for. Toby's just laying it on thick to get around the fact that he doesn't know the first thing about girls. His personality was uploaded from a 26-year-old bachelor who once took a date to a robotics symposium."

Eve knew every word except one and still struggled to parse meaning from Charlie's last sentence. Perhaps that lone word held the key. "What's a bachelor?"

"A bachelor is a man who sees life as holding limitless possibilities but has yet to find a single one that brings him joy."

Charlie towed Eve along by the hand. His grip was calculated well to keep her from slipping loose but not causing her any discomfort. Eve had no trouble matching his pace while she reexamined her conundrum. "So Toby was attempting to find joy by taking a girl to a symposium as soon as it began?"

"It'd take too long to explain. Let's just get you to your new home, then we'll figure out the world together."

Eve looked over her shoulder. Toby raised a hand—a farewell gesture—as Eve drew farther away.

CHAPTER THREE

"**W**here are we going?" Eve asked.

The delicate creature beside Charlie7 was overflowing her buffers with curiosity. Though her feet kept on course, her head swiveled this way and that, and her eyes never stayed still in their sockets. Eve14 clutched her borrowed tarp close at the neck, giving the impression of a Little Red Riding Hood who'd fallen on hard times.

No thinking creature had ridden this ball of rock around the sun more times than Charlie7. For him, the new was divided into ever more thinly sliced minutiae—a metallurgical innovation, the discovery of a better gene-sequencing algorithm.

Charlie7 had built factories from barren rock and spoken at length with every robot alive. For many robots, the first face they'd ever seen after activation had been Charlie7's. He had met the first misbegotten humans that modern science had cobbled together and served on the committee that created the refuge for those poor, tormented souls.

Some ambitious geneticists had decided that if they could clone mice in an artificial womb, then they were ready to recreate humanity. The results had been sickening. But this girl, Eve14, was everything he had remembered of humanity—vibrant, active, and insatiably curious.

Down the road, that curiosity might wear thin on Charlie7's digital nerves. In the meantime, he indulged the little human's inquisitiveness.

"There's a stone monument about five kilometers from here. It's called L'Arc de Triomphe de l'Etoile. Do you speak any French?" Charlie7 asked.

There was a hitch in Eve's gait. "No. What's French?"

"It's a language spoken by the humans who lived in this region a very long time ago. They named the monument in their own language. It means Triumphant Arch of the Star."

"How could there have been humans here a long time ago? Creator just made me."

Charlie7 chuckled. It was either that or scream, and he couldn't bear to frighten the girl. How could she not know anything about her species' past? "My dear girl, you're not the first human. You just might be the first proper human in... well, since before I was built."

Eve yanked her hand away. Charlie7 could have maintained his grip, but he'd sooner lose her to a flight of adolescent petulance than do her the smallest harm. The bones in her hand felt so delicate to his tactile sensors.

"I am!" Eve shouted. "Creator told me so. This is a trick." She backed away from him.

Her reaction was an ominous good sign. The girl had a vocabulary and underlying grammar that suggested a proper education. But such a gaping hole in her knowledge base could not have been an accident.

Charlie7 held his hands out wide. He needed to appear non-threatening. "I promise you. This is not a trick. I have proof. If you come with me, I'll show you more about this world than you've ever known." It was a bold promise, but the vacuum left by an absence of human history would be an easy void to fill.

The girl huddled beneath her tarp.

Charlie7 gave her time to think since obviously, this was a creature capable of it. What he wouldn't have given to peer inside that mind of Eve's and witness the machinations of original thought.

No matter how many times they were combined and recombined, the twenty-seven digitized minds of the Project Transhuman scientists could only produce so many basic archetypes. Charlie7 could predict the response to his offer from a Joshua, a Jocelyn, or a James without much mental effort. A Toby was a Toby, whether mixed with John or Arthur. But as he watched and waited, he could only guess how Eve would respond.

"I'll spot the inconsistency if this is a trick. All tricks have inherent flaws."

Charlie7 grinned. For the first time in centuries, he wondered whether it was convincing to human eyes. "I accept your skepticism. But Plato once said that ignorance is the root and stem of all evil. I offer knowledge."

Eve's eyes widened. She opened her mouth as if to say something before thinking better of it. Though she gave him a skeptical glare, the girl returned and took Charlie7 by the hand once more.

The original Charles Truman had never been so fortunate with his own children as to win one over by quoting Greek philosophers. Perhaps this new generation held promise, after all. Perhaps the geneticist who had created Eve had taken a step forward for the better.

And perhaps the cosmos would yawn wide in the sky and belch forth choirs of angels to turn all the robots into real live humans. Charlie7 didn't allow his hopes to spiral out of control.

The girl was a brooding sort of quiet. Eve kept the makeshift hood in place to shield her eyes from Charlie7's view. The delicate hand trembled. While Charlie7's sensors could measure the frequency and magnitude of the tremors, he struggled to weigh the fear contained in that organic human mind.

A gentle squeeze from Charlie7's hand drew Eve's attention. When their eyes met, Charlie7 offered her a quiet smile. To his surprise, Eve smiled back. It was like watching a fawn take its first steps, shaky and hesitant. After that, Eve seemed to relax; her hand stopped shaking.

Eventually, Eve let go of the tarp. Beneath, she wore clothes clearly meant for Toby22. Rolled sleeves and pant legs had been hastily riveted to keep from coming loose, but still the garments billowed and flopped around her thin form.

Eve explored the Parisian meadows with her free hand. She plucked at wildflowers and waved hello to the birds that flew overhead. Eve hopped on rocks and crashed through brambles. At some point along the way, she had discarded her oversized boots and continued their hike barefoot.

"You can ask me anything," Charlie7 offered, curious what Eve might ask. "I'm knowledgeable on most subjects." To say that his life experience eclipsed hers would have been a tragedy of understatement. He doubted that she had the breadth of mind to comprehend the ages he'd seen come and go.

Eve didn't hesitate. She pointed into the distance to a noble edifice surrounded by wild gardens. "What's that?"

"The Louvre. Paul208 finished restoring it last year. It's a museum—or it was, at least. There's not much in it at the moment. Most of the original artwork was lost. Maybe someday you'll put something in it."

Charlie7 offered Eve a paternal smile. It never hurt to encourage the arts. Who knew? Perhaps he could become a great patron of the next age of mankind. Every hope and dream he'd ever held for humanity was seeded within Eve14. She held limitless possibility.

Eve14 cocked her head. "Like what?"

Images flashed through Charlie7's memory. Galleries of masterpieces sprawled before his eyes. He had toured the remodeled version, and the emptiness haunted him. Eve14 simply had no basis to understand the loss of culture the museum represented.

Pushing aside those nostalgic distractions, Charlie7 focused on his duty to bridge that gap. "A painting, a sculpture, some permanent embodiment of your life experience. I imagine that down the road, humans will want to know everything they can about you."

A little frown knit Eve's brow. "Why would I do that? Is Creator planning on making more of me? Why would humans want to know about me?"

How old was this girl? By her appearance, Eve14 was in her late adolescence. Yet her questions were those of a child. The divergence between Eve14's intellect and knowledge strained Charlie7's rusty memories of teenagers.

"Discoveries come only once," Charlie7 explained, slipping into professorial mode. "Each is unique. For important discoveries, people like to know all they can. They wish to learn and understand what life was like before and how someone brought something completely new into the world or found something that no one else had seen. You are a discovery, almost an invention. You're the first of a new culture. There's no chance, once other robots find out about you, that you'll remain the only one of your kind."

Eve14 stopped. Rather than let go her hand, Charlie7 stopped alongside her. "You can't. Other robots can't find out about me."

"Why not?" The possibility of keeping her a secret seemed ludicrous.

Eve14 shook her head in short twitches. "You just can't."

"Did this creator of yours tell you that?" Charlie7 was already predisposed to loathe the robot who created Eve14. Instilling paranoia in the girl was just another black mark against Eve14's creator.

Eve14 said nothing. With subtlety that suggested guile, she loosened her grip and tried to pull her hand free of Charlie7's grasp.

Before the wily scamp could run off on him, Charlie7 knelt to look Eve14 in the eye. "It doesn't matter," Charlie7 said. "I won't tell anyone. Toby made me promise I wouldn't. Now, I know what you're thinking... if Toby made the same promise, what's to stop me from telling someone else?"

Eve14 swallowed and gave a vigorous nod.

"Well, if I had a smarter, more capable, better-respected robot to turn to, I would. But since there's only one Charlie7, I guess I'm going to have to figure out what to do with you myself."

"You're... missing a robot?" Eve14 narrowed a suspicious glare Charlie7's way.

"In the literal sense, no. In the figurative sense, very much so. But it's nothing to burden those young shoulders of yours with. Though while we're on the topic of burdens, how are you holding up, physically? We're not halfway back yet."

"You said it was a five-kilometer walk. My daily calisthenics and fitness regimen includes ten kilometers of running. I haven't engaged in any anaerobic activity since Toby22 brought me to you. I don't anticipate that changing during this trip."

Charlie7 took a moment to contemplate the inferences nested within Eve's reply. Whoever had created her had apparently found a DNA sample from someone of exceptional mental potential. Then that same geneticist had gone to great lengths to raise her as a jargon-spouting idiot less human than any robot alive. She couldn't even give a simple answer to a bland, colloquial question without self-analysis. Eve was in serious need of emotional growth.

Placing a hand on Eve14's shoulder, Charlie7 asked a question that should have filled any child's dreams. "Would you like a puppy? I know a fellow who clones canine species, and I bet we can get you a nice golden retriever."

The lack of recognition Charlie7 saw in Eve14's eyes broke his heart. Or would have, if he still had a real one.

CHAPTER FOUR

The stone monument that marked Charlie7's home was larger than it first appeared.

Eve had trouble reconciling the perspective shifts over long distances. Creator's lab was only forty meters long. Nothing in there was significantly bigger than it appeared while standing at the opposite end. But the edifice that Charlie claimed as home towered above the two of them as they approached.

Not even the building where Toby22 had brought Eve to meet Charlie had this sort of effect. Perhaps it would have if Toby had taken her inside, but he hadn't. Charlie guided Eve's steps as she craned her neck until the tarp slid from her head.

There were carvings of men and women all across the arch, both inside and out. Some wore robes, some had wings, and many carried weapons. Strange letters captioned the scenes in words Eve didn't understand. Why hadn't Creator taught her to read these words when she had taught Eve so many others?

A rushing sound and a radiant heat drew Eve's attention to ground level. Charlie was paying no mind to an unchecked exothermal reaction. "Fire! Where are the halon system controls?"

But Charlie didn't rush to action as Creator had during their fire-response drills. "Relax. It's an eternal flame. Misnomer, since I've had to restart it, but the sentiment is that it just burns continuously as a reminder."

Eve stabbed a finger in the direction of the open flame. The gleaming bronze base around the jet of combustive gas seemed inadequate protection. "Fire is harmful to organic life. The prudent course is to extinguish it."

"Some flames should never be extinguished. Humanity was one such flame. This flame was a reminder of your kind, of all the humans who lived and died on Earth."

Eve steadied her breath, which had quickened due to a brief adrenal response.

With Charlie at her side, Eve watched the licking flame as it converted hydrocarbons and atmospheric oxygen into an oddly hypnotic display of light and a whiff of uncatalyzed reactants. She knew chemical formulas for the exothermic reaction taking place, but the numbers and chemical symbols failed to describe the scene in front of her.

"It's pretty."

"Many things are both deadly and beautiful. That's why we observe them at a distance. Any star in the night sky could vaporize either of us in a fraction of a second, but from so far away we admire them in complete safety."

"If we stay at a distance, how can we be sure they're dangerous?" Now that Eve was standing there watching the fire instead of rushing to put it out, it seemed less of a threat.

Charlie let go of Eve's hand and motioned for her to stay put.

Without Charlie's protection, Eve took a quick step away from the fire. But she didn't retreat any farther. Nor did she turn her attention from the flame as Charlie retrieved a tuft of the tall grasses that grew right up to the paving stones around the arch.

"Watch carefully," Charlie whispered.

The robot removed his suit jacket and pushed up the sleeve of his shirt. Holding the tuft of grass in his fist, he reached out over the flame. Even without touching, the heat of the fire blackened and curled the grass, giving off a darker smoke than the open flame alone had produced.

"Now do you see?" Charlie asked. "We experiment. We use equivalence and test specimens to pass the risk on to less important things. Your chemical makeup may differ, but you are not so unlike these blades of grass that the fire wouldn't harm you just the same. And yet, there you remain, unharmed. Now you've seen the danger without experiencing it yourself."

"You want me to experiment on everything?"

Charlie's mouth twitched without sound before he spoke. "Ideally, no. You'd never get anything done. You have to learn some lessons from those who have gone before you. And lucky for you, so, so many have gone before you, Eve. In fact, everyone has."

Eve still struggled with the notion that there had been humans before her. Failed attempts... Creator had hinted that there had been several of those before Eve. After all, why would her designation have been Eve14 if there hadn't been Eves to account for those earlier numbers? But more than those? Humans from long ago? Creator should have mentioned them if that were true.

"Come on. Let's get inside. There's more to see downstairs than one lonely fire that's been burning since long before you were born. The sky's promising rain soon, and while you should see a storm someday, I don't want to get caught in the rain wearing my good suit."

Eve gazed into the heavens. She was a speck of dust in the cosmos. Thinking back to her perception of the buildings on the way from Notre Dame, the dark clouds that wafted from the West must have been truly enormous. Eve also remembered the soggy cling of wet fabric when she dressed too soon after a shower.

Better to follow Charlie to the unknown depths below the surface than get caught in the rain.

CHAPTER FIVE

E ve had expected the inside of Charlie7's home to look similar to the lab where she had lived. It should have been well lit, well constructed, and contained everything necessary for living in one convenient setting.

Instead, Charlie7 lived inside a maze. Each chamber had a purpose and included items relating to that purpose. One room's walls displayed an orderly collection of hand tools. Another room was dominated by a large, glossy video screen, and had a single chair facing it. The room next to that was scattered with screens and terminals. There was no order or pattern to their locations despite Eve's efforts to discover one.

Soon, Eve lost track of her bearings.

Charlie blustered through descriptions as he guided the tour. Media Room. Study. Workshop. Storage. Mementos. Lab. The latter caught Eve's attention because it was nothing like the lab she'd grown up in.

This lab was small in comparison to Creator's. The equipment was mainly disassembled robotic parts and electrical diagnostic scanners. A few tools Eve could identify; most were alien to her. But Charlie continued on, and Eve hastened to catch up. She didn't care for the thought of getting lost in the labyrinthine confines of Charlie's home.

A grumble in Eve's stomach brought up a pressing concern. Though it was rude to interrupt, Eve felt that Charlie was making a grave oversight that needed remediation. "Excuse me."

Charlie halted the tour in an instant and met her gaze. Though his features were different, the dull glow of Charlie's robotic eyes reminded Eve of Creator.

Eve glanced away. "Where are your puzzles? I'm hungry."

Charlie straightened as if Eve's question had struck him a physical blow. "Good Lord. Food. How could I overlook something so fundamental? But what's this about puzzles? You can't eat those..."

"I'll solve any puzzle you like," Eve promised.

Eve could no longer ignore that digestive juices were eating away at her stomach lining. Mentally she prepared herself for the worst Charlie could place before her: conundrums, ciphers, logic boxes, regression algorithms. Eve was ready to disprove a paradox to get a meal.

For a time, Charlie just stared at her. Was he trying to think up a particularly devious challenge for her?

"No," Charlie said at length. "I believe you're quite enough of a puzzle already. But you make a good point. The problem is, I don't have food here. I can't remember the last time I needed to eat. Actually, there are some biological functions we're going to have to account for. I'll find you some water—that's something I've got, at least. But I'm going to need to figure out the rest. If you have to... excrete... just take the elevator topside and use the bushes."

Eve nodded. It was a logical plan. "And food?"

"Well, if you can solve the puzzle of where to find human-digestible food on short notice, I'm open to user input. Actually, strike that. Just... make yourself at home while I figure it out."

Make herself at home? If Eve knew her way back to Creator's lab, she'd have headed there already. But the events since she was whisked away were a blur in her memory. She'd have to ask Creator about that. Likely there was a chemical imbalance in her brain that affected short- and long-term memory.

In the meantime, without more detailed instructions, Eve crossed her legs and sat where she was.

"No. Don't just sit there like a lump. There's a whole world you know nothing about." Charlie took Eve by the hand. She allowed Charlie to tow her into the room with the computer terminals scattered everywhere.

The nearest screen lit with a welcome message at Charlie's touch. A cheerful blue background gave way to a prompt at the bottom of the screen. A blank line begged for text input.

With a gentle prod, Charlie herded Eve in front of the console. "Ask it anything."

"Like what?" Too broad or open-ended a set of parameters was a recipe for chaos. A choice among billions of options was no choice at all.

Charlie put a hand to his forehead, covering his eyes. "Aren't you the least bit curious about this world?"

Eve nodded. Of course, she was.

"Have there been questions you've failed to ask because they seemed inconsequential, or you didn't want to bother or offend me?"

"Why are you helping me when Toby22 wouldn't?" Eve asked. "Did I offend him? If I offend you, will you pass me on to someone else?"

Charlie knelt down. She was taller than him this way. He seemed less intimidating, which made no logical sense. He had the same mass and knowledge as before. Relative height shouldn't have mattered, but somehow Charlie diminished as she looked down at him.

"Toby was scared," Charlie murmured. "You are paramount. You don't understand that yet, but someday you will. There will always be someone to take care of you."

The illusion of harmlessness evaporated as Charlie stood. Once again, he was tall and all-knowing.

"Why were there humans a long time ago but not now?" Eve asked.

Charlie swept a hand at the terminal. "Go ahead and ask it."

"I'll need a stylus." Creator had always given her one when it was time for her to use a terminal.

"Use your finger. It'll work just fine."

Eve was about to protest when it occurred to her to try, just to see what happened. She tapped in her question, and the terminal responded as if her finger were a stylus.

"This is wonderful," Eve beamed. "I feel like Creator!"

Creator never needed a stylus. All the terminals in the lab responded to Creator's touch and some even to her voice. With her computer inputs, Creator could even download data directly if she wished. Eve couldn't imagine doing that. If Eve's finger could be a stylus, who knew what else she could accomplish?

"Well, don't go getting overexcited. Ask all your questions, and I'll be back as soon as I figure out how to feed you."

Eve listened to Charlie's footsteps as he departed. A door slid open somewhere in the distance. It closed again, and the sound of footsteps cut off.

Eve was alone. She breathed a sigh and felt the tension ease from her shoulders. Alone was how she belonged.

Creator wasn't always a comforting presence; Charlie was still an enigma. But Eve was content with solitude. It was her natural state, just her and the tasks she had been left.

It was kind of Charlie to leave her a task. Eve had worried that he would leave her without instruction, which was a recipe for trouble. Settling in, Eve exercised her newfound power to communicate with a terminal all on her own.

WHY WERE THERE HUMANS A LONG TIME AGO BUT NOT NOW?

She remembered to word the query just as she had to Charlie. If she had formed the question improperly, surely he would have mentioned that before telling her to use the terminal.

The terminal didn't answer directly. It didn't respond as Creator did, with a straightforward answer. Instead, the screen flooded Eve with words and pictures. Video, audio, and every imaginable form of data spread out for Eve's perusal.

It was a story, but one strangely told.

Eve flitted from one piece of information to another, struggling to assimilate it all. There were pictures of humans—creatures more like Eve than Creator but in endless varieties.

People trapped within the screen had long, multiple names. Many of them spoke the only language Eve knew, but others jabbered incomprehensibly. Some were different sizes or colors. They wore outlandish clothes, sometimes with words scrawled across them carrying phrases and slogans Eve couldn't grasp.

At length, Eve stumbled across a simple text summary. Her quest for answers started there.

On July 29, 2065, mankind had their first encounter with extraterrestrial life. All attempts to communicate met with failure.

The alien ship broadcast mathematical patterns across every radio frequency imaginable, but no meaningful dialogue could be established. On August 9, 2065, hundreds more alien vessels arrived in Earth orbit. All attempted communication ceased.

With the imminent invasion of Earth at hand, the governments of every nation united and launched a preemptive attack. Our only weapons against them were an aging arsenal of nuclear warheads. But Earth's supply of such devices was insufficient.

On December 7, 2065, the last human died.

Eve stared in fascination. Even without understanding everything, there was a scope and gravity to the grim pronouncements.

Continuing her search, Eve opened other terminals and found they were equally amenable to her finger as an input device. Keeping the original summary on display, she cross-referenced, filling in the missing pieces her mind wasn't able to reconcile.

WHAT ARE NUCLEAR WARHEADS?

The terminal went into great detail describing the earliest known versions of such devices. The underlying physics made sense to Eve, though the concept of optimizing a subatomic chain reaction for uncontrolled exothermic energy release was bizarre.

How would someone even test such a ludicrously dangerous system? She tapped her follow-up question into the terminal, and it answered matter-of-factly exactly how humanity had done so. It even showed the result of early live trials on cities known as Hiroshima and Nagasaki.

She could picture it now. Extraterrestrial creatures in unfamiliar vehicles orbited Earth. Humans were scared. Nations used their governments to attack using nuclear fusion energy releases. Eve was still missing pieces.

WHAT IS GOVERNMENT?

This entry was far broader than she had expected and encompassed her next search as well, which would have been for "nation."

Old humanity organized themselves and created rules—sometimes for themselves and other times to impose on others. It seemed like they had tried every organizational system that could have ever conceivably worked and some that were doomed to failure from the outset. They'd divided themselves into so many different groups...

There had been so many humans. Eve's "nation" search included population totals, and the numbers were staggering. Before the extraterrestrials arrived, there had been 10.3 billion of them.

Creator hadn't invented Eve; she was a mere echo of billions just like her. But that had changed.

WHAT IS JULY 29, 2065?

The computer showed her an entry that explained the Gregorian calendar, a method for marking the passage of time based on cyclical orbits of the Earth around the sun.

Creator had taught Eve orbital mechanics, so the repeatable and mathematically consistent basis of the calendar made sense. The other references to August 9 and December 7 now made sense as well. They described the events of humanity's last days over the course of 131 days from the time they first encountered extraterrestrial life.

Eve had never heard the word "extraterrestrial," but she knew the roots: beyond Earth. Humans had been wiped out by creatures from the stars.

Fingers flew as Eve entered query after query. She could hear the sound of her own breath as it quickened.

When had all this happened? Eve had seen from the pictures that the Earth looked nothing like the city Charlie had taken her through. It had been packed with buildings, people, vehicles, and roads.

A search for the Arc de Triomphe showed it at the heart of a sprawling city. How long had it taken to come to its current state?

WHAT IS TODAY'S DATE?

This answer, unlike all the others, was simple, factual, and brief: June 21, 3090.

Eve gasped. Her species had been dead a thousand years.

CHAPTER SIX

Evelyn38 breezed into Lab 14 carrying a crate of glass bottles filled with milk. A merry clatter accompanied her every step, drowning out the grating of servos that were years past wanting a replacement. Behind her, the lab door whooshed shut and locked with a satisfying clack of magnetic bolts.

"Eve!" Evelyn38 shouted. "Eve14, come out this instant."

It had been quite a coup to get cow's milk diverted to her lab when she was only supposed to be working on chimps. But the effort to convince Jocelyn87 to sidestep the Agricultural Appropriations Committee and give her a small supply had been worth it. It was high time Eve14 grew accustomed to more standard human fare. Better the milk went to a real girl than those sorry excuses for humanity at the Scrapyard.

But Eve14 wouldn't be drinking anything if she didn't come out of hiding. The milk was warming by the second.

"Eve14, I am in no mood for games." Evelyn38's voice pitched higher.

This wasn't like Eve14 at all. Evelyn38 had squelched the petty rebelliousness that crept into even the most carefully nurtured teenager. Was Eve14 hurt? Maybe she was just engrossed in a puzzle. That happened occasionally.

Still carrying the clattering crate with her, Evelyn38 made a search of the lab. Her first stop was the food dispensary. But the puzzle terminal was dark; Eve14 wasn't trying to unlock a lunch. Dusty old protocols for emergency first aid flitted across Evelyn38's field of view.

"Eve?" Evelyn38 called out as her pace quickened around the lab.

Was Eve14 in the crawl tunnel of the obstacle course? No.

Could she be hidden behind the table of the encephalographic scanner? In theory, yes. But she wasn't there.

Had she crawled into the clothes cleaner? Thank goodness, no.

Glass rang against glass as Evelyn38 lugged her ill-won milk around the lab in a vain search for Eve14. It never occurred to her to set down the crate. During Evelyn38's frantic search, the crate was forgotten amid a torrent of error codes and worry subroutines.

"She's gone," Evelyn38 said aloud for no one to hear but herself. She had searched every millimeter of the lab. There was nowhere left for a 16-year-old human girl to hide.

The crate slipped from robotic fingers gone limp. Glass shattered. Evelyn38 didn't care. Her Eve14 had been kidnapped.

CHAPTER SEVEN

Charlie7 came back to find Eve14 curled up on the floor, sobbing. A quick perusal of the multiple open terminals was enough explanation as to why.

Perhaps allowing Eve14 unchecked access to the Earthwide database wasn't the wisest course of action. But the gulfs in the girl's knowledge base came up short in Charlie7's morality algorithm. No good had ever come of blind ignorance, especially the sort that had been carefully and deliberately cultivated. Eve was too bright and well educated in other aspects for her utter lack of historical education to be an accident.

Kneeling beside her on the floor, he laid a hand on her shoulder. Eve shrugged him off with a jerk.

Where was a puppy when he really needed one? He had jokingly suggested getting her one, but perhaps it shouldn't have been in jest. There wasn't a human with a soul who couldn't be cheered up by the enthusiasm and unapologetic joy for life of one of those little creatures.

While Charlie7 emitted a mild warmth due to servo motor activity and electrical resistance, he lacked the living essence of another creature. His touch couldn't comfort her.

Given what she had just shoveled into her mind, Eve would need a great deal of comforting. War. Aliens. Nuclear weapons. The passage of a millennium. A barren Earth. Death.

It hadn't occurred to Charlie7 that the factual end of biological life would have been kept from her. But she had terminals open to a variety of sources that described cultural beliefs about death and what lay beyond.

Death wasn't the sort of subject a young girl should learn alone at a computer terminal.

Charlie7 reached out to touch Eve14 but stopped short. His obsolete human instincts warred with an internal database of adolescent psychology he'd just downloaded. "Eve? It's OK. I found someplace where we can get you a proper meal."

Eve14 caught her breath between sobs. "Why?"

Charlie7 pulled back, perplexed. It was a non-sequitur question. "No, you don't understand. You said you were hungry. I'm going to take you to where we can get food."

Her reddened eyes looked up into Charlie7's. Eve14 sniffled. "Why did Creator make me? I'm just going to die like all the others."

If human contact were beyond his ability, Charlie7 would have to try logic.

"Human life is precious. We robots have human minds. We remember, to varying degrees, what life was like back then. We miss it. We miss you. Earth was meant to be filled with humans. Your kind might have died out over a thousand years ago, but before that, you carried on from one generation to the next. Now that the bottle has been opened, the genie can't go back inside. There will be more of you, and once there are enough, you won't need geneticists to carry on. Humanity is self-perpetuating."

"I just want to go home. I want to forget. I was happier not knowing."

Charlie helped Eve up to a seated position. "Don't say that," he scolded. "Fools once said that ignorance is bliss. It's a tempting lie, but it *is* a lie. Humanity created my kind through striving for ever-greater knowledge. They applied it, and here I am today. When biological life on Earth was wiped out, we robots survived. We rebuilt. We restored. We're putting things back the way they belong. None of that would have been possible if we wallowed in ignorance. Science is mankind's greatest gift. Science is mankind's second chance."

Eve14 took a shuddering breath. Charlie didn't know how long she'd been crying before he found her, but she had reached the limit of her tears. "It hurts." Eve14 hugged her arms tight to her stomach.

"That's mostly the hunger talking, I'd wager. You'll feel better after a good meal."

CHAPTER EIGHT

Charlie7 piloted the skyroamer across the Atlantic Ocean while Eve14 huddled under a blanket. He'd modified it to maintain constant internal pressure for Eve14's sake, but there hadn't been time to design, fabricate, and install a full suite of environmental controls.

Even at supersonic speeds, the trip was going to take over four hours. Eve had stopped complaining, but he knew she had to be tired and hungry, not to mention cold.

For his first day babysitting a live human, Charlie7 was doing a horrible job.

"So, you like puzzles, eh?" Charlie7 asked, trying to distract the girl from her hunger.

"I suppose," Eve14 replied. "Creator never asked me whether I liked them. But I think I do."

Charlie7 had a puzzle of his own, and he didn't know whether Eve14 would help him willingly. There was no robot designation *Creator*, but someone had made Eve14.

The tidbits Charlie7 had gleaned thus far gave him serious reservations about Eve14 going back, even if the poor girl was homesick. Stockholm Syndrome, they'd called it. Whether Eve fit the technical diagnosis or not, she'd clearly adapted to living under the thumb of a controlling, oppressive robot.

"So, your creator made you do puzzles before giving you food?"

"No," Eve14 replied with a grimace. "The food dispensers worked automatically."

Sure, they did. No automated system was responsible for its actions. It was just a matter of who'd programmed it. Of course, Charlie7 was doing a swell job of preoccupying Eve14. He tried to change the subject.

"And you did calisthenics and ran and so on?"

"Oh, yes. I must keep in proper working order. Typically, after my daily workout, I would take a reading of my vital signs. I don't have the proper equipment here, but I am often able to render a rough self-diagnosis. For example, my current blood glucose level is dangerously low. I have an elevated heart rate. I am suffering from mild dehydration. I have—"

"And I apologize for all of that. We're going someplace where we can get you all fixed up and in perfect working order. But tell me, how did you end up getting away from your creator? How did you come into poor Toby22's life?"

"Creator was gone. Then... I left. Then... Toby agreed to take me in."

Not much of a liar. That much was evident.

Of course, Charlie7 didn't doubt that the individual statements were each factual, but the overall effect was a lie. Charlie7 hadn't been activated yesterday.

Clearly, there were details between those vague waypoints that Eve14 didn't want to divulge. But now wasn't the time to press her for information she wasn't willing to give freely. Eve didn't trust him yet. She was hungry and thirsty and wearing a blanket because it would have taken Charlie7 too long to fabricate an overcoat for her. Charlie7 wouldn't have trusted a strange robot if he were in Eve's place.

So Charlie7 changed tactics.

While the skyroamer's autopilot maintained course, Charlie7 questioned Eve14 about her likes and dislikes. Did she have hobbies? What was she best at? As their supersonic journey kicked up ocean water like an aerosol spray, he teased out Eve14's personality. Along the way, Atlantic gave way to a brief interlude of land, then, in turn, became Pacific as the skyroamer streaked through the lower atmosphere.

As it turned out, Eve was fascinated by theoretical physics, enjoyed spatial awareness simulations (which Charlie figured out to be virtual reality sports), and could regularly defeat her creator at chess.

The latter intrigued him. It meant that this mysterious creator of hers was willing to engage Eve14 in competition. Not only that, she hadn't used her internal computer to mop the floor with the girl.

After all, chess had been solved long before humanity perished, and the algorithms were readily available.

As for Eve14, Charlie7 realized that she scarcely resembled a girl as he remembered them.

Charles Truman had attended Cal Tech and gotten his PhDs from MIT and Princeton. He'd known women with IQs that sounded like airline flight numbers. Every last one of them had *some* form of hobby or interest that wasn't purely academic.

"We're landing soon," Charlie announced before reducing throttle and angling for an approach vector.

Eve pressed her face against the transparent aluminum window like a child taking her first ride on the school bus. Charlie angled the skyroamer to give her a better view of Easter Island as they swooped in for a landing. He could only hope the pure joy that lit Eve's face wasn't shattered by what she was about to witness.

CHAPTER NINE

No one ended up on Easter Island by accident. It was as remote a location as one could find on Earth. Anyone who wanted to ignore its existence could do so with ease. That's the way most robots liked the Sanctuary for Scientific Sins.

Initially founded as a place to let mutated animals live out their final days without impacting wild populations, its purpose had shifted with the discovery of the first failed humans. The staff started out as veterinarians by trade, with Nora109 in charge. But centuries of veterinary medicine were now being applied to a new class of patients: *homo sapiens*.

Charlie7 set down on a concrete pad overlooking the shoreline. As the canopy of the skyroamer opened, the pressure seal broke, and fresh ocean air wafted in alongside the sound of lapping waves.

Closing her eyes, Eve14 drank in the scents with a deep breath. What Charlie7 wouldn't have given to smell the salt air again. He had to settle for the vicarious wonder in Eve14's placid smile.

The soil sank beneath Charlie7's wingtips, making him wish he'd thought to change into more practical attire before they left. Eve14 accepted his offered hand and shrugged out of the tarp as Charlie7 helped her down to the ground. The girl emerged from her tarpaulin cocoon into a paradise climate that would remain mild year-round.

"Where are we?" Eve14 asked, gawking in all directions.

"This is a place where they care for humans."

That drew Eve14's attention along with a stern frown.

"You're not the first attempt," Charlie7 said, raising gleaming steel palms to ward away Eve14's rising ire. "Geneticists started trying decades ago, even though the technology wasn't reliable yet.

We can't reliably clone chimps, but some unscrupulous scientists skipped ahead and tried making humans anyway."

Eve14 crept back toward the skyroamer. The girl's sudden reluctance to engage in conversation boded ill.

Charlie7 suspected he knew why. "Oh, come now. I know you don't want anyone else knowing about you, but these are possibly the kindest robots on Earth."

"You promised..."

Charlie7 approached slowly, keeping his hands in plain sight. "I promised you'd be taken care of. I promised you food. Your fear of the unknown is irrational in this case."

With a sudden yelp, Eve14 darted around the side of the skyroamer. She took aim with her finger like a soldier firing from cover.

Charlie7 heard the hum of the electric motor even before he turned to see the open-topped truck heading their way. It was a four-wheeler. The simple, low-maintenance design ideally suited the remote location where spare parts could be hours away. The lone occupant raised a hand as the vehicle drew near.

"Charlie7... of all the robots to come calling..." Nora109 pulled the vehicle to a halt alongside the skyroamer and favored Charlie7 with a smile that showed polished stainless steel teeth.

Charlie7 offered the administrator of the Sanctuary for Scientific Sins a hand getting out of the truck. She hopped out and wrapped him in a hug.

Normally, Charlie7 would have thought nothing of the gesture. But after Eve's reaction to his touch, he wondered how much of his behavior—all robotkind's behavior—was just residual human memory seeping through.

"I'm looking for food and some proper clothing," Charlie7 said. "Emphasis on the food." Cutting past the social niceties was only fair to Eve.

Nora109 crossed her arms. "Charlie7, what are you up to? I have a sanctuary to run here. You'd better not be starting up with humans of your own."

"Not my own, exactly..." Charlie7 held out a hand toward where Eve had retreated. "Come on out. Nora is an old friend. She won't hurt you."

"Good Lord! You *did* bring a human with you!" Nora exclaimed even before Eve came into view. "Charlie, what's gotten into you? Please tell me you've turned vigilante and not that you're taking up genetics."

"Eve... it's OK. Come meet Nora109. She knows all about food for humans. She'll give you something yummy to eat."

Nora109's shoulders fell. "Not another one named Eve... Is this one smart enough to know her own name, or would she mind if I gave her a new one?"

"I don't want a new name," Eve called out from the far side of the skyroamer.

Charlie7 lowered his voice. "Smart? This one's smarter than she knows what to do with."

"What's wrong with her?" Nora109 asked, leaning in conspiratorially.

What indeed? It was a subject for a psychiatrist or a philosopher, not an old roboticist or a veterinarian turned hospice worker.

"For now, nothing that a good meal won't fix."

Eve peeked out from behind the skyroamer and ducked away again.

It was time for a change of plans. Charlie7 could, of course, force Eve via any number of means. He and Nora109 could surround her from opposite sides of the skyroamer and drag her to the sanctuary if nothing else. But of all the methods Charlie could conceive, only persuading her held any promise of long-term benefit. Charlie7 found Eve's trust far more valuable than he could have imagined.

"Eve... I have a puzzle for you."

"No, you don't!" Eve14 called out from the far side of the skyroamer. "It's a trick."

"Suspicious one you've brought me, Charlie," Nora109 commented, then put up a hand to shield her voice. "So odd even hearing full sentences from a human."

Charlie7 glared at Nora109. Tapping a finger against his lips with a faint clang, he formulated a new plan of attack. "It's not a trick; it's a puzzle. Nora109 has food. If you come with us, you get a nice meal. If not, you'll eventually starve."

"That's not a puzzle," Eve14 shouted back from behind the hull of the skyroamer.

"It is," Charlie insisted. "It's an easy puzzle, and I'm disappointed you can't seem to solve it. The solution is right here in front of you. The challenge is how to overcome being afraid of Nora109, who honestly is the least threatening robot ever."

Nora109 cast Charlie7 a sidelong glare but said nothing. She wore soft violet coveralls and fuzzy gloves designed to provide a comforting tactile sensation for her patients. Everything about her was designed to be friendly, calming, and non-threatening. There wasn't any bug in Charlie7's claim for Nora109 to refute.

Eve14 crept from around the skyroamer like a burglar, eyes fixed on Nora109. The wary young human circled around and used Charlie7 as a shield between herself and Nora109.

"My God," Nora109 exclaimed. "Just look at her. Balance, coordination, spatial awareness. You can see the intellect in those eyes." Nora109 held up a finger and weaved a geometric pattern in the air. "And she tracks visually with flawlessly calibrated stereopsis and ocular convergence."

Charlie7 pulled Nora109's hand down. "Quit playing with her, and let's get her to the cafeteria."

Eve14 took Charlie7's hand as he helped her into the truck. "Thank you for checking my visual acuity," Eve14 said to Nora109 as she settled into the middle seat of the vehicle. The girl avoided coming into contact with the robot's chassis as if it were sticky.

The engine of the truck whined to life. Its electric whine pitched ever higher until it was inaudible to the standard robotic range of attention.

Nora109 looked over Eve's head. "This one's going to be a handful. I can tell."

The truck rumbled down a well-worn dirt road, kicking up a cloud of dust.

It would have been a trivial matter to modernize the whole island, but keeping it rustic was part and parcel to its purpose. This wasn't a facility so much as a refuge. Humans weren't brought for any greater purpose except to get them away from the horrors that robotic society represented to them.

That didn't mean the island was entirely untouched.

"See those statues over there?" Charlie7 asked, pointing to a hillside lined with moai. The invasion hadn't destroyed them. The building-sized stone heads still kept their vacant vigil and might continue long after even robots had perished from the Earth. Charlie7 hoped no busybody like Paul208 decided to "restore" them.

Cocking her head, Eve14 followed the line of Charlie7's finger. "Why are those faces so big? And why are they shaped like that? Were there ancient humans who looked that way?"

Nora109 harrumphed. "So, I take it someone's history is a little spotty?"

Eve14 sighed. "Today I learned that 10.3 billion people died in 2065, which is based on a Gregorian calendar that marks the passage of time, based on—"

"Yes, yes," Charlie said. "Nora109 already knows. She's based on Nora Maxwell-Granger, who was one of those 10.3 billion humans."

"Can't say I remember much of that life," Nora109 replied with a snort.

Why did they all still sigh and snort and chuckle? Charlie did it himself and couldn't explain why. So much lingering humanity left over. How had it survived for Eve to cast it in such a contrived and ridiculous light?

"Then again," Nora109 continued. "The mixer always seems to favor practical memories over the sentimental. I mean, what would I be without a bit of Jocelyn's chemistry background and Sandra's administrative skills?"

"You'd be Nora Prime," Charlie7 said with a shrug. "Just a primate biologist with a weakness for Swiss chocolates."

Nora109 rolled her eyes. "Charlie7... you are exhibit A for why we don't run the mixers as high as 70 percent anymore. You're too much of Charles Truman for your own good."

If only Nora109 knew how right she was.

It wasn't Nora109's fault, not remembering the affair. Romantic ties were among the lowest priority memories in the mixer algorithm. Robots didn't need that sort of baggage, especially since there had been over a hundred Nora mixes before her. None of them needed to remember that tidbit of detail, so insignificant on a cosmic scale, about the life of Nora Maxwell-Granger.

After all, there was only one Charlie7.

"How much Eve am I?" Eve14 asked.

Charlie7 looked to Nora109. The hospice director merely shrugged.

The day had started Charlie7 having a well-grounded view of the universe at large and his approximate place within it. Since the discovery of Eve, never in Charlie7's lifetime had the Earth seemed so small and empty as it had with the asking of that simple question.

Twenty-seven. That was it.

Oh, the total population was over two thousand, with thousands more drifting around in spacecraft and extraplanetary expeditions. But there were still just twenty-seven of them, mixed this way and that, to fluff those numbers. It seemed that a twenty-eighth unique mind was blossoming forth after all those fallow centuries.

"You are 100 percent you. There is no other like you, nor will there ever be again. I told you earlier how important you are. You are the flower of hope for Earth Reborn."

Nora109 snickered. "Who said none of us is a poet?"

Eve was clutching at her stomach by the time they arrived at the sanctuary a few minutes later. She hopped down eagerly and followed Charlie and Nora109 toward a cluster of buildings.

The architecture was all new. Charlie7 had only been there once since the sanctuary was converted from an animal refuge. He'd attended the dedication ceremony, alongside scads of other dour, sullen robots, all wishing they'd been somewhere else. The whole facility was makeup to cover a bruise. No one wanted a good look beneath.

But during the intervening years, someone had assembled a replica Spanish mission for the residents. The whitewashed stone walls and clay tile roofs were immaculate. Nothing like guilt to motivate attention to detail.

Charlie7 idly wondered who set up the factory to spit out the authentic-looking parts. Probably some other Charlie, though he preferred not to think too long about his higher-numbered counterparts. It was an open secret that Charlies didn't get along with one another. Too much ego sucked the good will out of a room.

Nora109 led them to an outdoor dining hall in the courtyard. Lines of tables lay empty with long wooden benches down either side.

A robot popped out from a side door, carrying a napkin and silverware for a single place setting. Charlie7 didn't devote the computational cycles to recalling the waiter's official designation. Another staff member came out carrying a steaming bowl and a cup with a spill-proof top. This was going to be interesting.

Eve14 took the cue and sat down at the table. She sniffed at the bowl and stuck a finger into the contents. "Ow!" She withdrew the scalded digit and wiped what appeared to be porridge onto her pants. "Too hot. Can't eat it."

"Just blow on it, dear," Nora109 advised with a weary slump of her shoulders.

Eve shook her head. "Inefficient. We need a heat exchanger and an agitator. Stainless steel tubing. Small pump. Mostly for future use. Natural convection will cool it to non-hazardous levels before the protofab could finish construction."

"Probably quicker to blow on it," Charlie7 affirmed. "I'm sure they'll take your proposal under advisement."

Nora109 cast Charlie7 a sidelong glare. Eve14 might not have known it, but the caretaker understood what committees did with proposals taken "under advisement."

After some hesitation, Eve14 scooped up a spoonful of porridge, blew on it, and put it in her mouth. Despite scrunching her face and pursing her lips, she swallowed.

After that first mouthful, Eve14 continued with a regular pace. After picking up on how mechanically she went about her meal, Charlie accessed his internal computer and set a timer, registering a consistent 11.4 seconds between bites with less than a .2-second variance. Once she'd gotten as much as she could with the spoon, she sucked the utensil clean and set about wiping any excess porridge from the bowl with a finger.

Eve stood with bowl and spoon in hand and faced Nora109. "Where is the wash basin?"

Nora109 scooped the dinnerware from Eve14's grasp. "That's all right, honey. You don't need to do anything. Run along and have a look around."

With a look to Charlie7 for confirmation, Eve14 set a tentative path for the nearest of the sanctuary's buildings.

Rather than a tourist or a guest, Charlie7 got the sense that Eve14 was a jungle explorer embarking on the excavation of an overgrown temple. She crept like a stalking hunter to the door on the balls of her feet. At the entrance, Eve14 first peeked around the corner and withdrew, then inched her way inside.

"Not the kind we usually get here," Nora109 commented with a slow shake of her head. "Skittish. Any idea who made her this way?"

"Someone brilliant," Charlie7 replied, not that his statement narrowed the list of suspects much. Accounting for combined personalities, the robotic scientist hybrids averaged more than three PhDs apiece.

"The girl doesn't know?"

Charlie7 gave his answer a moment's consideration. "No. I don't think she does. Eve calls her 'Creator' as if it were a proper noun. She has no social skills worth mentioning, an education tilted drastically toward the hard sciences, and didn't know until today that other humans had ever existed."

"Not to mention those conductive studs through her cranium," Nora109 said. "I've seen the results of every cruel and thoughtless experiment performed on the residents here. But looking at your Eve... it'd chill my blood if I still had any. Most of our residents were discarded after someone realized what they'd done. We don't get a lot of repeats, best we can tell. Doing that to a fully aware and intelligent human..."

"And don't forget, she's Eve14. Even if this 'Creator' of hers stuck to the conventions, that means there were twelve attempts before her."

With the Twenty-Seven, numbering started at 2. The original human was the Prime. Charlie7 could have seen 'Creator' going either way. After all, Eve was the first human.

Nora109 put a hand on Charlie7's shoulder. "Don't worry. We can take care of her here. She'll be a joy to have around, I'm sure. It'll be such a novelty to have a human who can carry on a conversation."

Charlie7 held perfectly still. The thought hadn't crossed his mind.

Or had it?

Though he had promised Toby he'd look after Eve14, wasn't the Sanctuary for Scientific Sins the best thing he could do for her? They had contacts across the globe, supplying them with every potential human need from fresh produce to undergarments.

They were the quality test lab for every nascent industry that saw humanity's resurgence as just over the next horizon. Five new Ashleys had been activated because, for the first time, robot society needed their surgical expertise instead of merely leveraging them for their flexibility in the veterinary sciences.

Charlie7 hadn't said he'd personally oversee Eve14 for the rest of her life. He'd promised no such thing at all.

"I'll stick around for a little while. You know, let the girl get settled. Then I'll say my goodbyes."

CHAPTER TEN

Eve left her oversized boots by the door as she crept along a corridor lined with wooden doors. Their scraping with each footstep might have drawn unwelcome attention.

The rough stone chilled the soles of her bare feet. Caution and the need for quiet warred with an insatiable desire to run her skin across the textured surface. There had been nothing like it in the lab. She had learned about stone as part of her geology curriculum. Granite was an igneous rock composed of quartz and alkali feldspar. It was hard and brittle. But nothing in her studies had prepared her to *feel* it.

As Eve slunk down the hallway, she let the fingers of one hand trail along the wall. What was it made of? She had no idea. It wasn't quite stone but definitely wasn't metal, wood, or plastic. The texture was much rougher than the granite floor and wasn't pleasant so much as it was fascinating.

A doorway interrupted her fingers' exploration. A wooden door with a wrought iron handle tempted her curiosity. She placed an ear against the wood and eavesdropped on the muffled sounds from beyond.

"All right, Brian. Sleep tight." A clattering approached, and Eve pressed herself against the wall to hide, knowing she had no better option.

The door swung open, and a steel cart rolled out. A robot was pushing it. It looked in Eve's direction and smiled. "Oh. Hello there. You must be the new girl. My name is Ashley390. What's yours?"

"Eve14."

Eve held her ground, muscles tensed and ready to run if Ashley390 made any threatening motion. The new robot was quiet, her drive mechanisms and joints in better repair than Creator's. She wore seafoam green from head to toe, including the knit cap on her head. Ashley390's smile appeared fixed in place, though Eve saw where the actuators connected that could change her expression.

Ashley390 closed the door behind her. "Brian is going to be taking a nap, so I can't introduce you right now. But if you like, you can come with me on the rest of my rounds. Would you like that?"

Eve considered.

Thus far, this new robot hadn't said or done anything menacing. Then again, Creator had warned her never to talk to other robots unless she was present. Of course, that rule was far past broken. Any punishment for that offense seemed unlikely to scale linearly with further transgressions. Plus, this Ashley390 promised information about her surroundings, which sounded valuable.

"Yes."

Ashley390's voice softened. "You don't talk much, do you? Can you understand everything I'm saying?"

Eve nodded.

By the subtle broadening of her smile, Eve deduced that Ashley390 approved of her agreement. "A breath of fresh air. Most of the residents don't communicate much. Please don't be offended if they ignore or seem afraid of you."

Eve blinked. "Afraid? Of me?"

The very notion seemed preposterous. Fear was an instinctive reaction to danger or perceived danger. Since Eve harbored no ill intentions, she saw no reason why anyone should be afraid of her.

"Just keep quiet until I introduce you, and we'll see how they respond."

Intrigued, Eve fell into step behind Ashley390 as she resumed pushing her cart. Watching the robot's feet, Eve mimicked Ashley390's gait and timed her footsteps to touch the floor simultaneously. Listening for the faint whir of her servomotors, Eve caught herself just as Ashley390 stopped at the next door.

Eve's mimicry had not gone unnoticed. "You *are* a clever little one, aren't you?"

"Yes."

Eve saw no reason to deny the subjective assessment. Creator had often made judgments to the same effect. It wasn't merely her own opinion that Eve offered up, but Creator's as well.

"Now, this is Emily's room. She's a bit of a shock to look at, but don't make her self-conscious by staring."

With that warning, Eve found herself more intrigued than concerned about what she would see inside. She leaned to peer through the door as Ashley390 first knocked, then slowly pushed it open.

"Ah-Shee," Emily called out as Ashley390 wheeled the cart into the cozy little room beyond.

Inside there was an empty bed and a wall with a curtained window overlooking the ocean. Under the light streaming in from outdoors, there was a circular table approximately a meter in diameter flanked by a pair of thin, metal-framed chairs. One of those chairs held what Eve presumed was a human, but this one was nothing like her.

Emily's head was disproportionately large for her body, and her arms were of different lengths. She held her smaller arm cradled against her body. The other was occupied with arranging and stacking small plastic blocks on the table, struggling due to an apparent inability to use her thumb as an opposable digit. Her smile was slack-jawed, but her ebullient tone suggested genuine happiness at the sight of Ashley390.

"Good afternoon, Emily," Ashley390 said in a cheery voice. She slid a tray from within the recesses of her cart and placed it on the table beside Emily's stack of blocks. "How are you doing?"

Eve noticed that the meal was the same as the one she had just consumed. As Emily wrapped a hand around her spoon and dug into her lunch, Ashley stooped to pick up a pink ribbon from the floor.

"Did you want this out or was it an accident?" Ashley390 asked, dangling the ribbon in Emily's view.

Emily looked at the strip of fabric, and her eyes and mouth both went wide. She made noises that may or may not have been words. But while Eve couldn't parse them into informative speech, Ashley390 seemed to know the cipher.

"It's all right. Don't worry. I'll put it back."

As Emily resumed eating, Ashley retrieved a small, bristled hand tool from a drawer set into the wall. With deft strokes, she used the tool to disentangle Emily's long blonde hair. Eve mimicked the motion, but her scalp was studded with probes. Creator always used a laser device keep Eve's hair trimmed to the skin. Just thinking about it as she ran her fingertips along the stubble between probes was enough to evoke the keratin scent of singed hair.

At the end of a weaving process that Eve's eyes had difficulty tracking, Ashley390 used the ribbon to tie the loose end. "There. How's that?"

Emily pushed her chair back from the table and ambled over to a reflective panel on the wall. She turned her head to bring the braid into view and smiled once more. "Fank oo, Ah-Shee."

Eve understood.

Ashley390 had performed an action with which Emily had difficulty. It was an act of kindness.

While Emily was preoccupied, Eve stepped over to the table and examined the blocks. From their present arrangement, Eve could only guess at the intended result, but some form of two-dimensional pyramid stacking or possibly an arch seemed to be the likely candidates. The plastic blocks had a plug-and-socket interlock system that seemed straightforward enough. With the available building materials, Eve quickly and quietly constructed a miniature replica of the Arc de Triomphe where Charlie7 lived.

As Emily finished admiring her reflection, Eve returned to her spot near the door. Emily spotted her and flapped one hand in her direction. Unsure what else to do, Eve copied the gesture.

"Emily, this is Eve," Ashley390 said. "She's new here. I hope you two can be friends."

"Hi, Eef," Emily said. She returned to her chair and noticed the Arc de Triomphe waiting for her.

Eve smiled in anticipation of her reaction. But instead of a repeat of the happiness from Ashley390's favor, Emily uttered an inarticulate moan that forced Eve to cover her ears.

"It's all right," Ashley390 said hurriedly, rushing to Emily's side. "It's all right. Eve didn't mean anything. She was just trying to be nice."

Ashley390 lowered her voice and turned to Eve. "You should wait outside."

Eve did as instructed, closing the door behind her to help block out the disconcerting noises from inside. Though Emily was incoherent, she listened as Ashley390 consoled and eventually calmed her. Eve didn't think to mark the passing time, but it felt as if perhaps ten minutes had passed before Ashley390 emerged, pushing the cart once again.

As soon as the door closed behind her, Ashley390 looked down at Eve where she crouched against the wall. "It's not your fault. I should have warned you how particular Emily can be about her things."

"But you fixed her hair, and that made her happy." Eve spread her hands, challenging Ashley390. Creator had often put that gesture to use against Eve, and it felt liberating to appropriate it for her own purposes.

"Humans aren't always rational. She had an idea how she likes her hair, and I helped her put it that way. She had an idea how she wanted those toy blocks, but you did something different."

Eve deflated. "She didn't leave schematics, so I had to guess at her intended result."

Ashley390 stepped back. "Oh, my. You *do* really understand English. Sorry. A few of the residents are more verbal than Emily, but... well... not what anyone would call a conversationalist."

"Why is Emily so broken?"

"She's not broken, dear. She's just Emily. She is as she was made. Not everyone's been as fortunate as you. Come along. It's a welcome change dealing with a self-sufficient girl. But if you can't avoid upsetting our residents, you'll have to stay behind."

"What if I say or do the wrong thing again?" Eve14 asked with eyes downcast. She kept her hands clasped behind her back.

Ashley tapped her chest. "I've been on text comm. Nora109 and Charlie7 think you've got quite a little processor in that noggin of yours. So process this: while we visit the residents, watch them. Mind the mannerisms I use, the words, the body language. See how they respond. Each one is a simple cognitive machine. Inputs generate outputs. Be pleasant, helpful, and unthreatening, and you'll see the best outcomes."

The next room held a human that Ashley390 identified as Mark.

Mark had a square face with hair growing out from the lower half, and was far larger than Emily. Mark's physiology seemed more in keeping with Creator's lessons as well, though the baggy pajamas made it hard to discern much detail. Sitting cross-legged on the bed, Mark wore headphones and was fixated on a video screen on the wall.

Eve studied the screen to see what was so fascinating. Flat-rendered animated animals wearing clothes chased one another around. As Eve watched, she couldn't get past the implausibility of the physics involved, though she granted that when reduced to two dimensions, mass became a null quantity that might allow for many exceptions to Newtonian mechanics. However, there was no excusing the retina-searing color palette.

Ashley took out a tray for Mark and set it on the bedside table. She pulled the headphones away, and Mark immediately blinked, turned, and smiled up at Ashley. "Enjoying your cartoons, Mark? We have porridge for you today."

Mark showed no difficulty in either locating or eating lunch. As one hand shoveled porridge, the other cradled a single headphone to Mark's ear.

Ashley390 didn't let them linger, and they left Mark to her amusements.

"What's wrong with her face?" Eve asked once the door was shut.

"Mark is a *him*. That's just stubble. We make sure he shaves every few days or the itch starts to bother him. But other than that, it doesn't hurt anything."

Eve frowned. "I can't imagine it would be pleasant having hair growing out of my face."

"Well, you don't have to worry about that. You're a girl." Ashley390 leaned close. Eve knew that the shifting she saw in the robot's eyes was a function of a refocused optical length. "Huh. You don't even grow facial hair."

"You just said—"

"It's different. All mammals are naturally covered in tiny hairs, smaller than you usually see." Ashley390 lifted Eve's arm and stared up the sleeve of her borrowed shirt. "But you don't even have the normal follicular development of post-pubescent sexual characteristics. You should at least have hair growing under your arms."

Eve jerked her arm away. "I should *not*. That's... distasteful."

"Well, whoever created you must have thought so, too. They also apparently failed to explain gender differentiation."

Eve drew up tall and stuck her chin out. She most certainly knew the difference.

"Some robots are male, and some are female. It's a difference in general disposition. Charlie7 and Toby22 are male." Though Eve had met few of Creator's colleagues, she at least knew which to address as 'he' and 'she.'

"Same goes for humans, but it's more pronounced than chassis preferences and a fondness for operating heavy equipment. Mark is male."

"What are the differences?"

"That's a good one to lose an afternoon on if you know how to work a computer terminal—and I'm guessing you do. But the short answer is: males tend to be larger, more aggressive, and hairier. Are you all right? You look like something just spooked you."

Eve shook her head. She couldn't tell anyone. But a piece of a puzzle fell into place about a certain someone she had met. The lack of hair on his face had not set off any triggers in Eve's mind, but the rest fit.

"I'm fine."

The other humans at the sanctuary seemed anything but fine. Henry couldn't control his excretory functions. Jane had see-through skin, thanks to gene splicing. Peter couldn't stand noises of any sort. Several others had parts that had been replaced by robotics due to deformities. Aside from Emily, only one other spoke to Eve. His name was Carl, and he liked balloons. He talked to Eve at length about balloons and even showed her how to turn twisted and entangled balloons into rough analogs for animals—in much the way that a circuit diagram resembled a robot.

At the end of the rounds, they came to an empty room.

Eve looked around. "Someone is missing."

Ashley390 smiled. "No, Eve. This is going to be your room."

CHAPTER ELEVEN

While Eve14 was off exploring the sanctuary, Charlie7 lounged on the wooden bench with his ankles crossed, reclining against the edge of the picnic-style dining table. Nora109 paced beside him, attending to official business while the two of them conversed.

"So I told Toby: 'What do you expect *me* to do with her?'" Charlie7 said. It was a relief to talk to someone about Eve14.

Charlie7 hated the Social for its inane chatter and empty blathering. It was challenging to speak heart-to-heart when you were running decryption ciphers every step of the way.

Nora109 shook her head. "You know Tobys. Practically hard-coded to go running to the nearest Charlie whenever something goes wrong. You'd think with a number as low as 22, he'd have more independence."

"It's not just that. Toby22 is a game warden. Wouldn't you think a human girl turning up in jolly old England would put her smack dab in his jurisdiction?" Charlie7 knew he shouldn't be dumping all this at Nora109's feet, but she was the first person he'd come across who would understand his annoyance. "It's not like he couldn't handle her. The girl practically begs to be told what to do."

"You think she could tell us who cloned her?" Nora109 asked. "I mean she clearly has the mental capacity. It would be the first time a resident was able to lead us to a rogue geneticist. Imagine if Adam8 had been able to tell us who was responsible for his creation."

Charlie7 held out a hand and guided Nora109 onto the bench beside him. Though it was scant comfort to either of them, he wrapped his arms around her. "It's not your fault. Sometimes humans just die."

There were times Charlie7 wished he were flesh and blood again to experience the shared warmth, the softness of another human's touch, the scent of a woman's hair as she nestled against his shoulder. Charlie7 remembered the fact of those sensations, but coded into his brain, they were subroutines pointing to corrupted data.

All those human sensory experiences were lost and never coming back. Charlie7 had accepted that.

Some other robots just couldn't. Noras had never been a problem the way certain other archetypes could be by moping, ranting, and self-terminating out of frustration at the low-sensory state in which they might exist forever. But Adam8's passing had struck Nora109 in a way that a robot's self-termination never could.

Nora109 pushed herself free of Charlie7's embrace. She resumed her pacing with clenched fists. "Why can't they stick to chimps? One chimp in five is healthy enough to release into the wild, and the percentage keeps getting better. Eve14 is the first healthy human I've seen in fifty."

Charlie7 knew there weren't fifty humans at the sanctuary. There was barely half that number. And even Nora109's fifty only accounted for the ones who had been found and brought to her.

How many others had died and been incinerated without anyone ever knowing they existed?

How many humans were alive in laboratories? What was being done to them?

Now wasn't the time to bring up any of those questions with Nora109. But if Charlie7's thoughts traveled those dark circuits in the back of his crystalline mind, Nora109's could just as easily.

"I'm not sure how much help Eve will be," Charlie lamented. "I think she's homesick, awful as that sounds. The girl talks about her creator like a god. That's all she knew for her whole life, and she's already picked up on the fact that we're not happy with her creator. The few times I've asked about her former home, she evades. That's not a behavior of someone who's acting on rote and obedience. She's purposefully stonewalling."

"We'll bring her around," Nora109 said with confidence. "Once she sees that we're her friends, I imagine she'll recognize the sad little life someone built around her like a cage."

At that moment, Eve14 burst from the residential hall of the Scrapyard. "Don't leave me here!" she screamed.

The first healthy human girl in a thousand years ran full tilt through the manicured grass in her bare feet. Sunlight glinted off the studs across her scalp, poking through her short fuzz of hair. Eve14 skidded to a halt in front of Nora109 and Charlie7.

Eve14 broke into a diatribe without even pausing to catch her breath. "I don't want to stay here. I don't belong here. I'm not like all these broken humans. I'm like you. And Toby. And Creator. I can think and talk and feed myself and use a computer and all the other things I need to take care of myself, and I don't need a room with a bed and a window and someone bringing me all my food and changing my clothes for me."

The girl clutched at the sleeve of Charlie7's suit and wouldn't let go.

Nora109 put a hand to Eve's cheek. "Calm down, dear. It's all right. Everyone here is different. It's not as bad as you make it out."

Eve14 performed a verbal database dump. She went resident by resident, detailing the disabilities and dependencies of each. All the names and appearances lined up perfectly with the patient roster, and she correctly diagnosed some of their underlying physical challenges.

For someone with a half-day's exposure to other humans, Eve14's knowledge of anatomy and biochemistry rivaled Charlie7's.

Once she had finished her summary of the sanctuary residents, Eve14 then proceeded in the manner of a student debater to contrast her own physical and mental health, point by point. Nora109 and Charlie7 just let her go on, uninterrupted. Charlie7 was more interested in when she found time to breathe between sentences that stretched on for kilometers and traveled at near supersonic speeds.

While the run hadn't winded her, Eve's essay on why she didn't belong on Easter Island left her panting. She looked up to Charlie7 for approval, for judgment, and possibly for salvation.

Charlie7 turned to the sanctuary administrator. "I'm going to need some clothes that fit her. Shoes. Personal grooming items. Whatever food you can spare that will travel. Oh, and one of your medical emergency kits—one with a diagnostic scanner."

Nora109 nodded along with his list. Charlie7 could practically see her filing the record away in her internal computer, possibly even transmitting it to one of her subordinates as Charlie7 dictated.

"You sure you're ready to be a parent?" Nora109 asked as Charlie7 finished.

The old robot looped that question through a few processor cycles before giving up with a shrug. "Who ever is? Besides, it's not like I'm adopting an infant. She just needs someone to show her around the planet."

Anywhere else on Earth, Charlie7's list would have taken hours or days to assemble, and asking for such a rare commodity as a medical kit specific for humans would have been laughable. But Nora109 had all of it and more. If she needed a replacement for the medical equipment, all she had to do was ask; no one ever questioned Nora109's requisitions.

The longest wait was for the cloth-o-matic to take Eve's measurements and create her a wardrobe of functional, durable garments. Everything was in default white. Eve14 could discover her own sense of fashion at a later date.

For now, Charlie7 just wanted to get Eve14 away from the Scrapyard. She'd made her point plain that she didn't belong.

Nora109 offered to give her a bath before she changed into her new clothes, but Eve14 insisted she knew how to cleanse herself. The robotic staff allowed her privacy and access to a tub and soap. She emerged a few minutes later, scrubbed clean and clad in angelic white.

The hope of humanity's future.

Eve14 didn't look back as the skyroamer rose from the landing pad, and Charlie piloted them away.

CHAPTER TWELVE

O n the other side of the world, a wolf padded through the underbrush of a young forest. To call it a wolf was stretching the definition, James187 thought as he leveled his tranquilizer pistol at the creature. The animal was lupine in shape but the size of Bengal tiger. According to the detailed report on the mutant's condition, it was still growing.

There was no rush. James187 was downwind, not that his robotic chassis emitted much in the way of scent for the beast to detect. The wolf was unaware of him and taking its sweet time to decide where along a shallow brook it would stop to drink.

GET HERE. NOW.

The urgent summons over a private Social channel distracted James187 and spoiled his aim. The wolf passed behind a tree as James187 holstered his tranq pistol. What was Evelyn38 so worked up about?

Though he wanted to snarl his frustration aloud, James187 knew an outburst would only startle his prey and make the hunt even more troublesome.

His reply couldn't carry the annoyance James187 wanted to project:

CAN'T RIGHT NOW. EXTRACTING INVASIVE WOLF SPECIES LOOSE IN URALS.

The wolf was traipsing along the edge of the brook when James187 resumed his pursuit. He might have charged forth, outrun the beast, and wrestled it to the ground to deliver the sedative dose. But half the fun was in the hunt. At the end of the day, a job wasn't worth doing without a bit of craftsmanship and joy. A clean takedown was the goal.

Evelyn38's next message put James187 off his aim once more:

```
I GUARANTEE THIS IS MORE IMPORTANT. YOU HAVE
NEVER HAD A HUNT THIS CRUCIAL.
```

The temptation not to answer at all rose near the top of his decision algorithm. Evelyn38 was a dour and spite-filled old toaster of a robot. Between the grating joints of her obsolete chassis and her pedigree as the smartest of the Twenty-Seven, James187 could barely stand being in a room with Evelyn38. But she wasn't prone to... crying wolf.

Even James187 shook his head when the idiom passed through his linguistic buffer. If the esteemed primate geneticist had a hunt for him, he had to find out the details. Repeated efforts to elicit specifics were met with a wall of obstinacy that nearly convinced James187 to tell Evelyn38 where to shove her missing monkeys.

But curiosity bested him, even if the wolf couldn't. Ten minutes later, James187 had the sedated wolf in the back of his skyroamer. He headed off to find out in person just what sort of chimp Evelyn38 had let loose into the wild.

CHAPTER THIRTEEN

They flew over the Pacific once again. As he piloted the skyroamer, Charlie7 couldn't help noticing Eve14 repeatedly glancing at the controls.

Among all his other concerns in taking Eve14 back with him from the Scrapyard was the dread suspicion that if he didn't, she'd steal one of the sanctuary's vehicles and find a way off the island on her own. The girl had seen him operate the skyroamer and had the memory of a quantum computer. It was no stretch to imagine that she could fill in the gaps in what she hadn't witnessed directly and fly the skyroamer herself; he'd have been more surprised if she couldn't.

"Where are we going?" Eve14 asked. She pointed to the readout of the craft's heading. "This is not a return course back to the Arc de Triomphe. We're currently misaligned by thirteen degrees."

"Did you like the food at the sanctuary?" Charlie7 asked.

Eve14 squinted at him with suspicion. "No," she replied carefully.

There was a refreshing bluntness exposed by her lack of social grace. Typical daily interaction had so many layers of paint concealing real feeling and opinion, each sprayed over the cracked and peeling remains of the one beneath. He'd gotten to Eve14 before anyone had taught her how to save face behind a whitewash of lies. Through sheer accident, the robotic society had self-selected for passive aggression and introversion.

"Well, what Nora109 gave us was more of the same. Oh, there are a few different sorts, but it'll all be bland. Don't get me wrong; it's all perfectly healthy and filling. I could feed you for a week on this stuff before I had to find new supplies. But if you're going to discover what being a real human is like, you're going to want to try real food."

Eve14 shrugged. "What's the difference? Food is food."

"Cuisine."

"I don't know that word."

A slow grin spread on Charlie7's face. He could already picture the vicarious enjoyment of Eve14's first real taste of human cuisine. "It's a form of art, using taste and smell as its primary mediums. It is among humanity's simplest and most accessible sources of joy. Anyone can survive eating nutrients. But cuisine provides sustenance for both the body and spirit."

Eve14 shook her head. "Ideal nutrient content is fixed. Deviation would produce a less desirable result."

"Nonsense," Charlie7 replied. This girl might imagine she could debate him, but she was still a novice in rhetoric. Charlie7 had centuries of committee hearings under his belt. "You are only optimizing for a subset of factors. By ignoring mental benefits related to food consumption, you're allowing sub-optimal chemical balance in the brain unless you engage in additional, potentially time-consuming activities to offset the imbalance." Let her sort that one out.

"Are you implying that my encephalographic readings could be optimized by food?"

Charlie7's brain hit a loop. It circled back to an earlier observation. Of course. "Are those studs in your head used to read brainwaves?"

"Yes. And I shouldn't use chemicals to artificially alter my encephalographic readouts. Intentionally releasing endorphins definitely counts."

"Well, I don't plan on taking any scans of your brain activity, so I think it's about time you learned how to enjoy good food. It's been a thousand years since I cooked, and I wasn't good at it then, but I think what neither of us knows won't hurt you."

Eve looked out the window, even though there was nothing but ocean as far as the horizon. "You still haven't explained why we're off course."

Charlie7 didn't need to get into a lecture on pre-invasion agriculture to explain why they were headed for North America rather than crossing the Andes Mountains on the shortest route back to Paris. All Eve14 needed right now was their goal.

"We're going shopping."

CHAPTER FOURTEEN

If the Easter Island sanctuary had a polar opposite, this was it—the Kansas Agrarian Plains, Charlie had named the place.

All along the approach, Eve had watched land stretch out as far as planetary curvature allowed her to see. What appeared from the air to be tall grasses, Charlie explained were actually wheat, a staple grain that ancient humans had produced in abundance. It was a key component in many of the nutrient slurries she'd consumed, never knowing their origins.

It had taken Eve and Charlie some time to come to a mutual understanding on the subject of food. His descriptions seemed bizarre, unnecessarily complicated, and implausible in his claims of what they could do to the human psyche.

Eve's listing of her daily nutrient intake had eventually led Charlie to conclude that Eve had been living off of primate nutrient supplements her whole life. If the residents of the Sanctuary for Scientific Sins had been eating the lowest form of human food, Eve hadn't even been consuming nutrients meant for her own kind.

Was Eve just an animal?

A wash of Kansas air flooded the cockpit as Charlie7 opened the skyroamer's canopy. Unfamiliar scents assailed Eve, so thick she could almost chew them.

"Is this safe to breathe?" Eve asked, cupping a hand over her nose and mouth.

"Perfectly," Charlie assured her. He waggled a scanner in front of Eve, reading zeroes for a variety of airborne toxins. "What you're smelling is honest, hardworking manure. Humans have lived with that fragrant backdrop since the dawn of civilization—at least the edges of civilization. Most city folks didn't care for it."

Eve's new shoes crunched on matted stalks of the local wheat as she dropped to the ground. It appeared from their surroundings as if Charlie had flattened a swath of the very crop he had described to Eve as they approached.

"Come on," Charlie said. "This place is all automated. No one around for kilometers. We can take whatever we want."

Eve fell behind as Charlie headed them toward a steel structure that rose above the tops of the wheat. A short ways through the field, it was all she could see besides Charlie and the plants that closed around her from all directions. Looking back, even the skyroamer was no longer visible through the stalks.

Suddenly a vehicle hummed past overhead, flying low and only traveling roughly eleven meters per second by Eve's rough estimate. It was larger and bulkier than Charlie's skyroamer, like a storage crate with ion engines bolted to the sides. As it receded from view, obscured by the stalks of wheat before her, Eve thought she saw the back of the transport filled with red fruits.

Eve crunched through the wheat field in Charlie's wake, treading where the robot's feet had crushed a path. It wasn't long before Charlie led the way into a clearing free of plant life.

The sight beyond stole Eve's breath away. She gaped slack-jawed at the marvel of robotic industry before her. Robots swarmed around a hive of steel and concrete that stretched for kilometers. Some robots filed in and out at ground level, carrying loads. Others in hovering vehicles poured through openings in the upper floors. An enormous craft, similar to Charlie's in design but at least five hundred times the mass, sat parked at the far end of the clearing as robots both loaded and unloaded it at once.

"What is this place?" Eve asked when her mind had soaked in the scene. She hid behind Charlie to watch the robots in action, lest one of them spot her.

Charlie swept a hand out to encompass the whole operation. "Mankind may be new again, but we've been feeding livestock for centuries now. This is a processing station for hundreds of kinds of crops including ones that eventually end up at Easter Island. I'm going to scrounge up some groceries. Probably best if you stay out of the factory, just to be on the safe side. Feel free to have a look around. Just don't wander off into the fields. I'll be back in about half an hour."

Eve watched until Charlie disappeared into the factory. It was easy to pick him out from the crowd in his black-and-white suit since all the workers seemed content to run around unclothed.

Creator had shown Eve what a robot looked like without clothes as part of her education in mechanical systems. She knew they didn't *have* to wear clothes. But Creator and all her colleagues wore them habitually. So did Charlie, Toby, Nora, and Ashley. The residents of the sanctuary wore clothes, even though many of them couldn't dress themselves. But the workers here in Kansas seemed to prefer nudity.

Eve noticed that her new shoes were dusted with brown, as were the hems of her pant legs. She looked to the worker robots and their bare feet, then back to her own.

"Adaptive response to the unclean work environment," Eve muttered to herself.

Knowing that continued wear would only result in additional soiling of her shoes, she untied the laces and pulled them off. For a moment, Eve considered removing her clothing as well, but Creator had drilled it into her that she should remain clad except under clearly defined circumstances. As a compromise, Eve rolled her pants up to her knees.

Tying the laces of her shoes together, she let them dangle from one hand as she explored the facility. The robotic workers paid her no mind as she slipped among their traffic patterns, and she, in turn, was careful not to impede their work.

The side of the main structure was painted with ten-meter-tall lettering identifying it as Kansas Agrarian Zone 017 - Distribution & Processing Center 23. Though she knew it involved several unwarranted assumptions, Eve allowed herself to imagine that each Kansas Agrarian Zone had at least as many distribution and processing centers. That meant there were at least 391 such facilities, probably many more. The likelihood that Charlie had brought her to the very highest numbered facility was slim.

Charlie had said it. They were preparing for humanity's return.

Though she wasn't the first human, Charlie insisted that she was the first 'real' human to be born since 10.3 billion of her predecessors had died in a span of 131 days.

This facility and the others like it were robotkind's gift to humanity. Earth was a world prepared for humans, with foods the robots didn't need to eat and clean air they didn't need to breathe.

Upon first hearing Charlie say that he was just taking what he wanted, it sounded like stealing. But as Eve approached the hub of the agrarian complex, her mind interlocked two pieces of a puzzle so simple she'd overlooked it until just then.

Robots building entire industries for an extinct species...

Eve, the first of her kind by Charlie's own words...

The enormity of Eve's epiphany caused her to stumble as blood rushed to her head. Whether the robotic masters of the world knew her by name or not, this whole world had been rebuilt for Eve.

CHAPTER FIFTEEN

E ve's exploration brought her around the north side of the agrarian structure. There she found a prairie surrounded by a short fence. Enclosed within was a herd of blocky quadrupeds grazing on brown grass.

Eve knew cows from pictures and descriptions: four-legged herbivores with edible flesh and gentle dispositions. They had seemed to Eve a rather pointless species. If they served any purpose at all, it was to keep the grasses short and provide nitrates for soil enrichment. Both those functions were easily replaceable by mechanical means.

But seeing them outside the sterile boundaries of a digital display sparked Eve's curiosity. She had to see one up close.

A truck approached, driven down the dusty road by one of the robotic workers. The back was filled with sheaves of dried grass tied in bundles. Whoever was driving it ought to know all about the pasture.

Eve waved her arms overhead as she stepped into the truck's path.

The vehicle stopped. Eve was blocking its way. A pair of ruts in the dirt highlighted the route that its wheels were keen to continue following.

"Excuse me," Eve called out. "Is it all right if I go inside the fence to examine a cow up close?"

The robot didn't answer. It backed the truck up and navigated it out of the ruts, angling it to avoid Eve on its next attempt to pass. But Eve scrambled over to block it once again. Time and again, fifty kilograms of human girl halted the progress of a piece of machinery that outweighed her a hundred times over.

It wasn't even about her question anymore. Eve was intrigued by both the persistence of the robot operating the truck and his continued insistence on ignoring her.

Finally, the truck shut down, and the driver climbed out.

"Thank you," Eve said, grinning at her minor victory. "Now, can you tell me whether it's safe to go in with the cows to examine them up close?

Rather than answer, the robot reached out and took Eve by the sides, lifting her easily and holding her at arm's length. The robot's grip wasn't so tight as to be painful, though the hard, metallic fingers that cradled under her arms couldn't be described as comfortable. Eve twisted and squirmed, trying in vain to free herself as the robot adjusted his grip to maintain his hold.

"Put me down!" Eve ordered. She would never have dared speak to Creator in such a tone, but Creator was rational and generally explained her actions.

This mute robot was touching her without permission and relocating her with unknown intentions. Eve kicked him. She wished she'd kept her shoes on since all she managed was to send a sharp pain shooting through her foot. Not to be thwarted so easily, she swung her shoes at the robot's head by the laces.

For all her efforts, the robot ignored Eve's attacks. He carried her around to the back of the truck and deposited her alongside the hay it was transporting.

Before Eve could make sense of her situation, the truck resumed its journey. Eve scrambled barefoot through mounds of unprocessed grain to get a view of where they were going.

The silent robot piloted them to a gate in the primitive post-and-rail fence. A remote sensor triggered, and the gate swung out of the truck's way. The truck paused until the path was fully open, then entered the pasture.

Was this his way of answering Eve's earlier question?

Non-language communications were spotty at best. Creator had trained Eve to read the complex system of facial actuations that robots used to convey subtext to dialogue, but it was one of her weakest areas of study. But picking Eve up, placing her into a vehicle, and driving her into the pasture was a peculiar way of answering a simple question.

The cows responded to their presence at once. While not terribly energetic creatures, as soon as the truck approached, the cows headed for a five-meter-high cylindrical structure in the pasture. The silent robot guided the truck toward the feeding silo, carefully navigating around any cows that got in their way in much the same manner that he tried to go around Eve.

When the truck stopped, an armature extended from the cylinder and the driver robot came back to take custody of the open, tubular end. Eve hopped to ground level, unsure of the driver's intent as he guided the armature into the back of the truck.

A high-pitched whine commenced, and the tube sucked up grain wherever the robot guided it. Seconds later, the cattle feed filtered through the cylinder and spat out into a trough that ran all around it, exiting from a dozen ports.

The cows' lethargy was replaced by a sudden eagerness to crowd around that trough.

Eve found her retreat cut off. A river of bovine flesh carried her along in its current. Glimpses of the truck teased her with promises of safety. However, there was no path through the herd of huge, lumbering bodies. Every way Eve turned, there was another animal bearing down on her.

One of the cows knocked Eve to the ground, oblivious to her presence. As she struggled to rise, the leg of another struck her across the face and sent her sprawling. In a panic, Eve curled into a ball and hoped cows could avoid stepping on her.

CHAPTER SIXTEEN

A robotic hand grabbed Eve by the arm. "There you are!" Charlie scolded her. "What were you thinking? I told you to look around, not wander into a stampede."

"I just..." Eve began the sentence without a clear goal in mind and now found that her thoughts had jumbled.

"It's all right," Charlie said, the anger fading from his voice.

The robot in the penguin-colored suit bent down and lifted Eve. His was not the uncouth manner of the silent robot. Charlie supported her in the crook of his arm in a seated position, and she steadied herself with a hand on his shoulder.

"Just... don't take risks like that," Charlie said. "Someday I might end up writing your biography. I don't want it to be a two-page pamphlet that ends '...and then she wandered into a pasture at feeding time and was trampled to death by cows.' OK?"

The incongruity of Charlie's statement struck Eve as funny, and she laughed aloud. "Then don't write it that way."

"Well, I'm not going to lie in a biography, so you're going to have to promise not to get yourself killed in some embarrassing manner. I'd much rather write about this day ending with Eve having the first delicious meal of her life."

Charlie's intentions seemed benign. And while his answers often spawned more questions, he at least responded to her queries. "Why didn't the robot operating that truck answer me when I asked if the pasture was safe?"

"He's not really a robot as you understand them. That was just an automaton."

"You mean he's broken like the humans at the sanctuary?" It would make sense that robots that didn't work correctly would be given simpler tasks. And since robots were superior to humans in every way, even the defective ones ought to be somewhat useful.

"Not at all. These are machines without a brain. Just computers in them. They run programs, and those programs include certain jobs like planting crops, driving trucks, feeding cows. At other facilities, automatons maintain factories and construct buildings. Jobs that require creativity and decision-making are done by thinking robots like Nora109 or me."

"But Toby22 just watches animals. Why does he have a mind?"

Charlie snickered. The expression was half a smile and half a laugh. Creator didn't use it personally, but she had taught it to Eve anyway.

"Well, Toby22 and all the other Tobys clean up around that borderline between what you need brains for and what you don't. He was a hardworking kid as a human, before the invasion. Charlie Truman's lab assistant. He's probably the only one of us with a gram of humility, and the personalities based on him get stuck doing what the rest of us won't.

"A Toby will fix damaged desalinization pumps, oversee animal births, retrieve carcasses from the wild... or monitor forestry and habitat recovery of a small corner of central England. It's hard to dislike a Toby. They're not troublemakers like Charlies... or Eves." He reached over with his free hand and touched Eve on the nose.

She couldn't discern whether Charlie meant to infer that since it was hard to dislike Toby and Eve was unlike Toby that she was thus unlikable, or whether by describing a commonality that the two of them shared, he was attempting to increase her affection for him. Creator had explained both conversational tactics but had not prepared Eve for someone who decided to use both techniques at once.

Instead, she argued the factual basis for his statement. "I am not."

Charlie carried her off in the direction of the skyroamer they had taken to get here. He looked up and met her eye. "Oh, little human. You have no idea how wrong you are."

CHAPTER SEVENTEEN

By the time Charlie7 got Eve14 back to Paris, the girl was hungry again.

While Charlie7 programmed the protofab with a set of basic cookware, Eve14 munched on a granola bar from the Scrapyard. He really needed to stop thinking of the sanctuary by that name.

For that matter, he was beginning to question whether it was fair to Eve to continue appending a number to her name. The girl wasn't a robot. That much became clear as a diamond as soon as Charlie7 finished cooking the first meal made from real ingredients.

First Eve tried a plate of hard-boiled eggs. After a few experimental chews, she opened her mouth and gagged as the contents spilled forth. She used her fingers to wipe the remainder from her tongue.

"Tasteless rubberized polymer. Are you sure this is edible?"

After that, Charlie served her pancakes.

Eve had chewed slowly, pursing her lips as if she expected her pancakes to escape at any moment.

"Spongy. Difficult to chew."

In fairness, Charlie probably hadn't mixed the batter well, and he wished that he'd had syrup to go along with them.

Charlie had sliced an apple to remove any chance that Eve would attempt to eat the core or stem. Yet his caution was unwarranted. Eve nibbled away at the meat of the fruit, discarding the slivers of peel between pinched fingers as if they were a plastic wrapping. Despite her distaste for the peel, she gobbled the apple slices with abandon. Grunts of pleasure escaped as she swallowed each bite.

Once she was finished, Eve sucked her fingers clean of the juice. Ducking her head, Eve looked up at Charlie7 with guilty eyes. "I expect elevated blood glucose levels."

It was time to put Nora109's human-approved medical scanner to good use. Eve's paranoia about her physical condition meshed perfectly with Charlie's curiosity about the girl's origins.

The medical kit was a mystery box. Charlie7 had never performed a medical exam even in the days when humans were around. Charles Truman had assistants for that, so Charlie7 had no human memories to call forth. Fortunately for Charlie7, Eve was familiar enough with the process to coach him through it.

Charlie7 had no doubt that he could have maintained his professionalism around a naked young woman. Nonetheless, some vestigial human embarrassment made him glad that Eve had stopped short of removing the undergarments that the sanctuary had provided.

First among Charlie7's observations was a port in Eve's left arm, right near the elbow. It allowed direct access to her bloodstream. Taking a blood sample was as simple as opening a faucet. Injecting drugs into her system would have been just as easy.

"Your blood sugar is fine," Charlie7 muttered to reassure Eve as he proceeded.

Charlie7's second observation was that Eve was nearly hairless. Her scalp, eyebrows, and eyelashes were all intact, but there wasn't a follicle anywhere else on her as far as he was willing to check. Whoever made her must have gone to some trouble in the genetic code to arrange that trait since there was no evidence that it was a surgical alteration.

Eve held perfectly still except for her steady breathing. She kept her arms slightly away from her body, feet shoulder width apart, and chin level. Every feature was perfectly symmetrical.

The girl didn't seem to mind Charlie7's close inspection, so he zoomed in and looked at her eyes. They appeared all natural. There was no evidence of surgical adjustment to correct the optical deformities that were naturally present in 65 percent of the population prior to extinction.

Eve waited while Charlie7 looked up an old eyesight test in the Earthwide archive and set up a screen at the prescribed distance.

The display lit with a series of gibberish letters at various sizes, stacked in a pyramid from largest to smallest.

"What's the lowest line of letters you can read?" Charlie asked.

"The bottom one," Eve replied. Then she proved it by reciting them aloud. "P-E-Z-O-L-C-F-T-D. What's it supposed to mean?"

"In and of itself: nothing. But being able to read it means your visual acuity is about four times that of an average pre-extinction human."

Then Eve elaborated. "Unless you meant the very bottom where it says, 'Not to be used for medical diagnosis, copyright 2025 Bradford Optical.'"

Charlie let that comment slide and proceeded to check her blood pressure, heart rate, and pupil response. He had her stretch and twist, flex and bend, watching for any joint or connective tissue injuries.

Eve had the range of motion of a gymnast. The scanner in the medical kit reported her height at 155cm and weight at 51kg. As a scientist, Charlie7 would have preferred it called "mass," but he was willing to indulge in the age-old medical conceit that mass and weight were synonymous.

Charlie7 had always considered himself manly, if not overtly so, back when he'd had a human body. He never would have imagined him envying a woman's physiology. But Eve was crafted flawlessly. She was no more or less than fully human, but at the tapering end of every bell curve her creator could have imagined.

It was time to examine the only glaring flaw, one that had been added since her birth.

Eve tensed as Charlie touched the scanner to one of the studs in her cranium. "Sorry. Did that hurt?"

"No," Eve said. "But I always expect it to. I know there are no nerves in the brain, but it always seems like I should feel something in there. Is that odd?"

"I don't think so." It would have been odd not to expect to feel in the one part of the body responsible for all perception.

The scanner didn't read anything unusual. If there was circuitry inside the stud buried within the girl's brain, the scanner couldn't detect it.

Since Eve was a good sport about it all, Charlie took her cooperation while he had it and tried each of the forty-eight studs in turn. There was nothing any of the others told him that the first one hadn't.

"Eve, you can relax now. Go ahead and get dressed."

Even though he had spent the better part of two hours examining her mostly undressed, Charlie7 allowed Eve her privacy as she put her clothes back on.

"I'm finished," Eve reported. "Why did you look away?"

While she had no idea about privacy, Eve at least was keen enough to pick up on the correlation to Charlie7 averting his gaze.

"It's just... respectful. Anyway, I was hoping you could answer a few questions for me."

Eve nodded. "I'm ready." She took a deep breath and settled into a pose halfway between military ease and a grade-schooler preparing to recite in front of a classroom.

"This isn't a test. I'm not giving you puzzles to solve. I want to know more about your creator."

"Oh." Eve didn't slouch or relax her posture at all.

"Oh, fine. I'll make it a puzzle for you or at least a mystery. You have no hair over most of your body. This isn't a typical human feature. And yet, you have a full head of hair on your scalp, trimmed recently to below the height of the studs on your head. The puzzle. Tell me why someone who could choose where you grew hair would allow it to grow in a place that was going to require regular maintenance to access the studs he put there?"

Eve stood silent, but she pulled her brow tight. Charlie7 was in no hurry, so he allowed her to stew over the problem. "Am I allowed to include outside information in the problem?"

Charlie7 waved a hand. "By all means."

Outside information was exactly what he was missing in his own deductions. It didn't add up, and whoever had so lovingly crafted Eve into an idealized human had obviously been no one's fool.

All Charlie's presumptions fell into two categories: aesthetics and deception. Either someone fancied the look of a full head of hair on Eve and wanted to leave her the option to grow it out, or the growth of the hair itself was meant to camouflage the presence of those damning studs. No geneticist could claim to be entirely benign in her research after doing that to the girl. There was no conceivable therapeutic benefit, even if the girl had shown the faintest hint of a need for any treatment, not to mention the gruesome and unnecessary surgery that had to have taken place.

At length, Eve came back with an answer. "Creator has an idea of what I should look like. She also has data to collect from my encephalographs. Once she no longer needs data, my hair will grow longer, and I will look the way she intends."

If Eve said nothing else of value, her use of the feminine pronoun for her creator at least eliminated half the robot population. But he couldn't help wondering about her conclusion. "Why would you say that?"

"At the sanctuary, there was a girl named Emily. She had her hair a certain way and always wanted it put back that way. My hair always grows toward a certain length, but Creator trims it. She could stop it from lengthening, but she doesn't. Thus, she must want my hair long but can't allow it to grow to that length until she's done taking readings from my brain."

Charlie7 was impressed by Eve's stretches of logic to cover gaps in her knowledge. So many of the robotic scientists would have rejected the premise of his whole line of questioning. How could they know what another robot was thinking? They wouldn't deign to violate another robot's privacy by invading their thoughts, even in the theoretical sense. Guesswork was no better than filthy gossip. Charlie7 wouldn't mind a little gossip about this creator, whoever she was.

"Tell me more about Creator, Eve," Charlie said casually. "What's a robot like who creates a human girl, wants to see her with long hair but keeps it short, feeds her primate nutrient VII when the whole world is preparing to feed a human population they expect to blossom in the next few decades, teaches her about everything in the world *except* what might hint that she's not the first of her kind?"

Charlie7 knew he'd let himself get carried away. His voice had risen steadily throughout the tirade. In any pre-extinction courtroom, they'd have thrown that question out for leading the witness.

Or badgering her.

"Until today, Creator was all I knew. She's not bad." With that, Eve ran from the room, crying.

CHAPTER EIGHTEEN

Wolves. That malfunctioning simpleton had the temerity to hunt wolves while Eve14 was missing.

Evelyn38 stalked in her office, knowing there was nothing practical she could do until James187 came to his senses. The hunter was useful in his own fashion but in need of a good reboot. Or reprogramming. Evelyn38 could have been satisfied with either, so long as it sorted out his priorities.

Her stone-walled underground facility had become a dungeon. Venturing out to find Eve14 herself would have been tantamount to admitting her guilt if anyone were to notice her. Between corroded joints and servo encoders that slipped, she had no business out in the wilderness.

"What are you doing out here, Evelyn?" they'd ask.

"Do you need any help?" they'd pester.

If Evelyn38 were lucky, the first Samaritan that stumbled across her would refer her to James187 for tracking help. But more likely she'd get a *friendly* referral to Charlie25 for a chassis upgrade and brain transfer.

Evelyn38 shuddered. She liked her crystalline matrix right where it was. A new one was last on her wish list.

Pausing her pacing, Evelyn38 sought to calm her looping worry subroutines at a shelf lined with human skulls.

Her babies.

Evelyn38 picked up the skull of Eve2 and pictured the face of the sweet, sickly girl who had died shortly after her ninth birthday. Setting the child-sized skull back in place, she brushed her fingers across the next few until she picked up the skull of Eve9, who had been as close as Evelyn38 could remember to having a friend.

She and Eve9 had laughed and debated. They had shared their dreams for a future humanity that had grown beyond the mistakes of pre-extinction society. But Eve9 had wanted things that weren't possible to have, things Evelyn38 couldn't provide. One morning Evelyn38 had arrived in the lab to find Eve9 dead; she had broken into the medical cabinet and injected herself with a lethal overdose of phenobarbital.

That discovery had nearly convinced Evelyn38 to abandon the project. Instead, she decided that she could no longer afford to develop affections for the test subjects. Less interaction, better data, and a firm and unyielding control were what human test specimens required.

After Eve9, the rest of the skulls bore a telltale pattern of holes. Evelyn38 had removed the deep cranial probes each of Eve10 through Eve13 had carried in life. They just didn't look right, sitting there on the shelf, gleaming and taunting Evelyn38 with the data they failed to provide.

Eve10 had neither spoken nor heard a word in any language. The girl's brain had been little better than fungus.

Eve11 had self-terminated after learning about cannibalism, of all things.

Eve12 had failed one too many tests and would never have been suitable.

Eve13 had been the first one to undergo full mapping but had proved unable to sustain upload. Her skull wasn't even entirely desiccated.

Though he had kept Evelyn38 waiting for an encrypted broadcast response, James187 arrived in person without any further contact. He set off a perimeter alarm that had failed to go off during Eve14's escape, and Evelyn38 unlocked the surface door to allow him inside the facility.

As she waited for him to make his way down to her office, Evelyn38 resumed her pacing. Every time she reached the end of her measured steps and turned, her eyes settled briefly on the row of skulls. The shelf was plenty long enough, but she couldn't let herself think about the empty spot there would be if Eve14 never returned.

James187 strode through the door as if it were his office and not Evelyn38's.

"What is it this time? You lose a gorilla you're not supposed to be—?" James187 stopped short. Indeed, Evelyn38 had been sanctioned for experimental work on great apes without committee authorization. But he hadn't been in her office for decades. She had moved well past lower primates.

"As you can see, I have a real problem," Evelyn38 said. "Not some silly wolf that got into someone's hen house."

"Evelyn... what have you done?"

James187 walked the periphery of the office. He stared into jars at the fetal specimens, suspended in formaldehyde. Looping displays showed healthy human brain scans. The line of skulls drew the newcomer's attention to her trophy shelf.

Evelyn38 noted that he ignored the dolly she'd made for Eve5 and the misshapen clay teacup that Eve9 had given her as a present. Those weren't as glamorous, but the teacup in particular was a far greater achievement than any brain scan.

"I've succeeded, James. Or at least I'm coming so close I can remember taste again. At least, it was within my reach yesterday. Today, it seems someone's broken in and stolen my most promising specimen."

"Wait... you had a human... and you *lost* it?"

James187 towered over her. His was a chassis meant for outdoor work. It wasn't a trendy model, cumbersome for the delicate scientific work most robots preferred. But without conscious effort, Evelyn38 ran simulations showing just how quickly James187 could overpower her own feeble chassis. James187 could snap her in two and stomp her brain to shards.

"I didn't lose Eve14; someone stole her. Smart as that girl may be, she couldn't have made it out of here on her own, not without leaving a trace. You set off alarms the moment you arrived. Her lab didn't even have direct access to the facility's primary systems."

James187 shook his head. "I can't be a part of this. The gorilla was bad enough."

"And I got sanctioned for it. Set me back years, waiting for my ban to expire."

"Seems like you didn't learn."

Size difference or no, Evelyn38 marched up and jammed a finger against James187's chest. "I damn well did. I learned to cover my tracks. I learned better security. And I think I've learned how to put a digital brain back into a human body."

"Wait... what?"

She had James187's attention now.

"I'm on the verge, James. Once I stand in front of the Ethics Committee general assembly in a human body, they won't have any choice but to approve the procedure. I'll be lauded as the mother of mankind's second age. And *you*... well, you'll be first in line for the body of your choice. Of course, if someone blackmails me, reverse engineers my research, or exposes me to the ethics busybodies, that's all down the incinerator chute. Which is why I need you to *FIND EVE14!*"

CHAPTER NINETEEN

Eve had fallen asleep in Charlie7's chair in the media room. For once, it felt as if it hadn't been a pointless indulgence to pad the seat like the old den he remembered from his living days.

Now a poor, overwrought human slumbered comatose, head pillowed on the armrest. Charlie7 had his cloth-o-matic whip her up a quick blanket. It was oddly satisfying when old junk he rarely used came in handy.

But with Eve temporarily occupied and not in imminent need of his attention, he could finally start doing some research into who her creator might be.

Cheap theatrics and phony self-aggrandizement both grated on him. Where did this "Creator" get off naming herself that? What had she done besides make Eve?

Charlie7 could have named himself Caesar or Saint and would have only garnered a few grumbles over it. He had earned his accolades. The others had let him retire. No other robot dared coast through eternal life because no other robot had the resumé to prove they'd already given a hundred lifetimes' effort on civilization's behalf.

He'd be damned if some amoral geneticist staked a claim to equal stature.

His first stop was the public news feed. This was the hub of respectable life on Earth. Anything worth mentioning over a cup of coffee at Cal Tech's faculty lounge in 2060 was now broadcast worldwide.

There were stories about asteroid retrievals, historical reenactments, archaeological finds, wild species introductions, and robotic activations. Last month there had even been a discovery of a deep-space historical archive, one long thought lost during the invasion. Charlie7 had still been meaning to look into what the retrieval team had brought back. Hopefully, there were at least copies of some new movies or television shows that none of the other archives had contained.

Despite the temptation to lose himself reading the daily news at the pace his human replica brain preferred, he switched the feed directly into his internal computer. A quantum gate array, operated via molecular magnetics, sifted all the data through algorithms to look for any hint about what robot might have been secretly harboring an unsanctioned human.

Charlie7 tried to avoid marveling at his own creation, but he had distinct memories of inventing the computing technology himself. That distraction and the reminder of how his innards functioned were the primary reasons he didn't like to lean too heavily on his own computer.

"God, you people are dull," Charlie7 mumbled aloud as he picked through partial matches from his search.

It didn't help matters that primate genetics were considered the cutting edge of legitimate science these days. All the top geneticists seemed to be working on chimpanzees or bonobos.

Charlie7's cross-referenced the names of robots who took shipments of primate nutrients. It matched wonderfully with the list of primate researchers. That meant that Eve's creator was either a primate geneticist or had a supply through backdoor channels. Considering the skill set that would be needed to even attempt the creation of a human clone, Charlie7's money was on Creator having real credentials.

A robotic fist slammed down on the screen of his terminal. Cracks spider-webbed the surface.

"Stupid old films. They always made this part look so easy."

It was one thing watching a montage of investigators poring over a computer screen, then a cut-away to a scene with a solution. Charlie7 was just scratching at a mountainside with his bare fingers, trying to tunnel his way through.

He couldn't very well accuse every primatologist on Earth. Not only would he make a jackass of himself and ruin friendships along the way, but he would also be exposing his investigation, possibly allowing Creator to prepare means of diverting Charlie7's attention.

Tabling the idea of tracing Eve's food supply, Charlie considered the studs. They had the microscopic structure that suggested they came out of a residential-grade protofab. That meant that Creator had crafted them herself, possibly in the very lab where Eve had lived.

There was no way to trace the supply chain of homemade parts, and virtually every robot kept a protofab on hand. Most robot components needed real, dedicated manufacturing facilities, but the home-sized protofabs got the job done for small tools and temporary replacements.

...and apparently the occasional brain probe.

While tracking the studs' origin was an impossible task, deducing their purpose was actually a task for which Charlie7 was eminently qualified.

He had originated the brain-scanning protocols back when his own colleagues were the test subjects. Dr. Charles Truman's probes had been non-invasive, a forest of probes applied externally to the skull.

Charles Truman never pretended to understand the mechanism of human consciousness. The technology relied on the premise that mimicry would be enough to transfer a human mind to a robotic surrogate.

Dr. Truman had been right, of course, but Charlie7 couldn't deny that a deeper, invasive probe would have given him a better set of data to analyze. In time, Dr. Truman might have mapped out particular skills, memories, and personality traits in excruciating detail. It wouldn't have made a better copy—he could already clone minds just fine—but he might have been able to craft mixed personalities with far more control.

There was merit to the research. That much was just an uncomfortable truth.

It would be far too late to try to apply any of that to the existing population of scientist personalities. The Twenty-Seven had been a constant of society since the beginning.

Randomizing algorithms produced results that could only be predicted in general terms. Mix a Paul with a John, and you'd likely get someone who wanted to restore religious buildings—just as had been the case with Paul208. Mix a Sandra with a Jennifer, and you'd get a hidebound bureaucrat with the moral fiber of a Knight Templar.

But the specifics of the mixing process were often surprising and completely unpredictable. Paul208 loved Humphrey Bogart movies and the sound of rain on a metal roof. Sandra101 was vulnerable to flattery from any Toby who mentioned her looks. It was possible that Creator wanted to harness the exact mind of Eve to create a new personality archetype with predictable encoding.

Charlie7 wished he could let himself believe that. The cynic in him said that Creator's careful curation of Eve's curriculum had a far more sinister motive.

The girl's education seemed extensive on any subject that wouldn't lead to her realizing there were other humans before her. That was a means of control. That was the action of someone who wanted her test subject compliant, awestruck, and never hopeful of anything beyond the walls of her lab. No one developed claustrophobia if she'd never seen an open space in her life. Nobody got cabin fever when she believed the cabin was the whole of the universe.

These were the problems Charlie7 mulled over until Eve stirred in the other room. She'd slept over ten hours. The poor thing must have been stretched to her breaking point.

Charlie7 closed down his data connection and made breakfast before she fully woke.

Eve came into Charlie7's workshop kitchen bleary-eyed and working her tongue around the inside of her mouth. Charlie7 remembered that gummy feeling of just waking up from oversleeping. Strange how the most innocuous actions provoked such strong memories.

"Sleep well?"

Eve rubbed at her neck. "Poor cervical support. Insufficient dorsal support. Temperature was outside ideal range."

Charlie7 set a plate of scrambled eggs and a cup of water in front of her. Even to him, it looked paltry. "Sorry. We'll get this situation worked out. Everyone's new at this."

Eve eyed him. Both of them knew there was a small community who *wasn't* new at caring for humans, but neither of them brought up the Scrapyard.

"I don't have the proper equipment for my exercise regimen." Eve picked up a fork and started eating.

At the first bite, Eve revisited the puzzled frown from her adventure with porridge. But without complaint, she resumed a regular trip from plate to mouth with the fork.

"Consider today a recovery day. You had quite an adventure yesterday. I think you should spend today getting to know your surroundings and learning anything that strikes your fancy."

"How will I know when something strikes my fancy?" Eve asked between bites.

"That's a colloquial term for when you feel like it. If you get curious about anything, go ahead and look it up. I trust you're a smart enough girl to be careful of things you don't understand. I should only be gone about half the day."

The fork clattered to the workbench that served as Eve's table. "Gone?"

"Yes, I have matters to attend to that are best carried out in person. I'm something of a public figure—at least after a fashion. I can't just disappear into my cavern or people will worry and come checking up on me. I've made you a reference sheet for the foods; most of them are edible as is without further preparation. If anyone *does* stop by unannounced, hide in the room with the generator. The ambient noise will mask your metabolic rumblings and bellowing."

Eve followed Charlie7 toward the elevator that led to the surface. "What are my assignments?"

Charlie put a hand on her shoulder. "Your only assignment is to decide what you'd like to do today."

In all the mathematics and logical puzzles, the essence of human experience had been lost in that girl. When he had the spare time, he'd expose her to the cultural richness of her ancestors. As he left the perplexed young human on the far side of the elevator door, he promised to do just that once he got back.

But while Charlie7's crystalline synapses were still sizzling, he was going to find out who had held Eve prisoner since birth.

CHAPTER TWENTY

Charlie's domicile was quiet once the elevator's hum receded. Eve imagined that she could hear her own heartbeat, even though she knew it was below the threshold of her auditory senses.

For a while she simply wandered from room to room, touching, examining, opening, and activating things as she found them. When she discovered the protofab, she realized she wanted to go through her exercise regimen.

While the majority of her daily workout routine didn't require any specialized equipment, it wasn't the sort of thing that was meant to be broken to bits and pieces. Creator had carefully crafted her regimen to optimize strength, cardiovascular, and joint health exercises into an ideal routine.

Eve could have mimicked the treadmill's function by going up to the surface and running through the fields of Paris. But Charlie had warned her about being found. The surface seemed far more likely a place to be discovered than cached away underground. For now, she set aside that one exercise and focused on the rest.

With the aid of the protofab and its intuitive interface, Eve designed the handheld weights she needed for her strength regimen. It only took the machine a matter of minutes to create a set. The finished parts were pleasantly warm to the touch, like clothes fresh from the dryer.

Next, Eve fashioned a meter-long bar and found some of Charlie's welding equipment. The welding was slow going. With no protective eyewear to be found, Eve had to line up the plasma torch, avert her eyes, and make a small bead. But in time she had welded the bar across one of Charlie's doorways, and it was sturdy enough to bear her weight.

Eve spent the morning doing chin ups, pushups, squats, curls, and every other exercise in Creator's regimen. Then she moved on to poses and stretches, running through all the forms she knew. With a shock of guilt, she skipped the eight-angle pose, which she had never cared for. But today Creator wasn't watching.

Today Eve could cheat just a little, couldn't she?

At the end of her stretching, Eve was still left with the dilemma of her cardiovascular routine. Charlie's living space wasn't conducive to long spans of running. Eve considered simply doing fast leg-lifts, then she had an epiphany.

There was a spare steel plate lying in one of the storage rooms. Eve dragged it to a corridor that looked little used and propped it against the wall.

Charlie's cloth-o-matic worked with a similar interface to the protofab and already had her size. Eve asked it to spit out a clean pair of socks. But instead of putting them on, she dropped them on the inclined plane she had erected and angled the plate until the socks slid down.

It took half an hour of adjustments, simple calculations, polishing with a reciprocating buffer, and finally a few quick tack welds. But in the end, Eve found that wearing just socks on her feet, she would slip down the slope if she didn't keep running at a steady pace. Ideally, there would have been an adjustable component to the incline, but Eve resolved to work on that at some later date.

It was possible that Charlie could arrange to get her a proper treadmill in the meantime, but until then, Eve would run while she slid down the steel ramp.

"Eve!" a voice called out. It wasn't Charlie's.

She stopped running and slid down onto the level floor. Quietly as she could, Eve slipped on her shoes and tied them tight. She was sweating, and her respiration rate was elevated.

The voice was familiar, but that didn't mean it wasn't a trick. If this were a trap, Eve would be ready to run in earnest as soon as her heart rate returned to resting.

"C'mon out, Eve! It's me, Plato."

Eve started to rise, but then it occurred to her that merely stating his identity didn't mean it was really Plato. Voice recording and playback wasn't even very complicated. Anyone could manage it.

She waited for a better sign, skulking in the shadows and trying to remain as quiet as possible.

A face poked around the corner and broke into a grin. It was Plato, the human who had taken her from Creator's lab. "Hey, there you are! Let's get out of here before Charlie7 gets back."

Plato extended a hand toward Eve, and she accepted it.

After seeing the residents of the Sanctuary for Scientific Sins, it was hard to imagine this vibrant creature as part of the same species.

Plato was half a meter taller than Eve, and the hand he presented closed completely around Eve's when she took hold of it. His shirt didn't have sleeves and split open at the front, showing clear muscle definition that none of the broken humans came close to matching. The eyes that sought Eve's shone with intellect and didn't shy away as Eve caught herself staring into them. Plato's smile shone like a beacon.

Today there was even a shadow of hair growing along his cheeks and jawline, confirming Eve's newfound suspicion that Plato was male.

"I didn't tell them anything," Eve said as they raced for the elevator.

"Thanks. This is all my fault. I didn't think Toby22 would give you away. I figured he had more stones than that."

Eve paid attention to details this time around. Fleeing from Creator's lab, her mind had been adrift. Everything had been too new, too strange, too impossible to accurately sort its way from short-term to long-term memory. "Where are we going?"

Plato didn't slow as he replied. "I've got a place. Rather not say where until we're airborne. Charlie7 is one sneaky bastard. I took down a few perimeter alarms, but it wouldn't surprise me if he buried backups down here that I didn't catch."

Plato punched in a series of commands, and the elevator pushed against Eve's feet. They were heading up. "They took me to the Sanctuary for Scientific Sins. Charlie almost left me there."

Plato shook his head, causing his shaggy, shoulder-length hair to flounce. "You don't belong with them. They call that place the Scrapyard. It's where they send the factory rejects of our kind."

There was a question Eve had been yearning to ask, but none of the robots had the answer. She could tell by everything they did and said. "Are there more like us? More working humans?"

Plato pulled Eve against her. He was warm and smelled faintly of an unfamiliar musk. She was damp with sweat and unclean, but he didn't seem to mind. "I'm sorry. As far as ones that think and act like old humans... you're the first I've found. And even I'm not like you."

Eve pulled back. "You're not?"

"I'm like over-tempered metal. I'm stronger and sharper than I was ever meant to be, but I won't last as long. You... that crazy Creator of yours did some outstanding work. I'll give her that." Plato made a fist and gently pushed it against Eve's jaw. "You're really something."

It was a bland, vapid comment, but Plato delivered it with such an oddly reassuring grin that Eve couldn't help feeling better. Why was it that years of emotive training by Creator left Eve barely able to puzzle out robotic emotions, yet she could read Plato as if he came with an instruction manual?

The elevator opened at the surface, and Eve saw Plato's skyroamer. It looked like Charlie7's but was nicer on the inside. The ride away from Creator's lab had been cozy and warm. Eve had fallen asleep on the way.

As Eve jogged to keep up with Plato's brisk walk, she looked back. "Should we leave Charlie a message?"

Plato grunted. "The less Charlie7 knows, the better."

CHAPTER TWENTY-ONE

As Charlie7 rode the elevator down to his home beneath the Arc de Triomphe, he felt anything but triumphant. A whole day of wasted effort.

Toby22 had been no help at all. Worse, he had seemed intent on diverting Charlie7's efforts to get to the bottom of the mystery of Eve's origins. And to top it off, it had taken Charlie7 hours to realize he was being made a fool.

The two robots had hiked to the spot where Toby22 had found Eve, and they had combed the forest for tracks or signs of her rescuer that might lead back to an identity. For a while, Charlie7 had begun to suspect a secret lab hidden underground in that very wood and that Eve had escaped on foot, alone.

Then they'd discovered the distinctive imprints of skyroamer landing gear. After that, Charlie7 knew Toby22 was lying. There was no way someone had flown into his precious preserve without him knowing about it. An additional fifteen minutes had subsequently been wasted as Charlie7 lambasted the mechanical forest ranger. But screaming his vocal emitter out of calibration hadn't accomplished anything.

Charlie7 needed a little sunshine in his day, even if he could only find it below ground. Seeing Eve would reboot his priorities. It was hard to be angry in the presence of humanity's glowing future; it was harder still not to be amused by Eve's attempts to learn all the quirks and foibles of actually *being* human.

At the bottom of the shaft, the elevator doors slid open. "Eve? I'm back. How was your day? I'd love to hear all about it."

Idly brushing the dust and dirt of today's adventure off his suit, Charlie7 wondered what Eve had gotten into. It wasn't like her to remain quiet in the face of a question. Even a question she didn't understand prompted a request for clarification.

"Eve?"

The house was too quiet.

With a mounting dread, Charlie7 rushed through his refuge. For the first time he could remember, he regretted the wasted space and sprawling, inefficient design.

She wasn't asleep in the media room.

The workshop he'd converted to a makeshift kitchen was empty, and there was no lingering cooking heat to say she'd been there recently.

The wastewater access closet was vacant.

He checked the computer terminal node, the trophy room, and the several chambers devoted to various hobbies.

Charlie7 found the handheld weights and the spot where the girl had welded an inclined plane to the wall outside the protofab room. It could have been either a weight bench or an improvised slide-friction treadmill—possibly both.

There was no sign of Eve anywhere.

"Please don't tell me you went exploring," Charlie7 muttered.

It would have been fitting that the one actual restriction he'd placed on her activities was the one she'd violated the moment he left. A nagging voice told him that he should have disconnected power to the elevator before departing or at least locked out the controls from the master computer. Charlie7 had been in a hurry, and she seemed like a sensible enough girl.

But Eve was human, and with humanity came free will and all that rubbish. Charlie7 could predict behavioral responses for any robot he knew based on their personality mix, at least at a macro level. But for everything else she might have been, Eve was caught at that awkward developmental stage that came after puberty but before full mental stability.

Settling in at his main terminal interface, Charlie7 brought up the access logs for the automated systems. At least from there he could get an idea when she'd left, which would narrow his search radius. After all, there were no vehicles around for her to steal. She had to be on foot.

The records were blank.

Charlie7 had an in-depth, personal knowledge of how all the systems in his home worked. He'd programmed them all himself. So when he saw that records were missing, he knew that he had not merely lost track of where they should be.

Not only was there no record of Eve having accessed the elevator. During a five-hour period leading up to Charlie7's return, there were no records at all. At the very least, there should have been a graph of power draw. With that thought in mind, he checked the logs for the generator and found them likewise blanked out for the same time period.

In a panic, Charlie7 looked into his personal files, but those were all present and accounted for. The layered security and encryption were all intact. The redundant backups were all in place. The booby traps and alerts he'd piled upon them had not been set off.

In a world with no thieves and the only criminal conduct mainly limited to unauthorized research, Charlie7 had always wondered if he was paranoid. Now he wished he'd kept a perimeter alert system more sophisticated than a doorbell.

There was one thing he was certain of: Eve hadn't run off on her own. Creator, or someone in league with her, had to have bypassed his security and run off with her.

As he stormed off toward the elevator, for the first time since the invasion's aftermath, Charlie7 wished he were armed.

CHAPTER TWENTY-TWO

The Yucatan looked greener than the last time Charlie7 had seen it. Someone's habitat revitalization efforts were going well. The area had a pleasant, verdant tinge as seen from the air, and it wasn't yet overgrown. The ancient ruins were easy to spot as the skyroamer flew over its destination.

Charlie7 hadn't called ahead. The flight had given him time to cool his synaptic pathways and sort his data. He could have tried someone closer or someone who needed a favor from him. But for Eve's sake, Charlie7 needed answers, and that meant finding someone who had them.

Even if that someone was the crazy primatologist Janet9.

As he swooped in for his final approach, Charlie7 resisted the temptation to set his skyroamer down atop El Castillo. Setting aside the fact that he couldn't find a suitable landing pad on the stepped pyramid, he needed Janet9's help. While she cared less about the pre-invasion architecture than the wildlife around it, Chichen Itza was still her home.

Circling the ruined city, Charlie7 set down in the middle of the ball court instead. Stepping out as the engines spun down, he looked around.

Anything older than himself gave Charlie7 a sense of continuity—of there being a greater purpose than himself. Restored cathedrals only echoed the past. Real humans whose calendar had ended forty-three years before their descendants were wiped out entirely had carved this city of stone out of the wilderness.

It hadn't been a bad guess. But then, humanity had always harbored a penchant for the morbid.

Charlie7 could have gone looking. Even a direct message to Janet9 might have been quicker. But Charlie9 wanted her off guard. He wanted her on the offensive so that his riposte could hit its mark.

The wait wasn't long.

"Shame on you, Charles," Janet9 shouted as she came into view. "I have a moratorium request on file with the Flight Control Committee. The least you could do would be to honor it until it's official."

As always, Janet9 appeared ridiculous in a fur suit from feet to neck. Only her face was visibly robotic.

It always rankled Charlie7 when a robot referred to him as Charles. Most of the Twenty-Seven had either called Charles Truman 'Dr. Truman' or 'Charlie,' depending on their relationship. Occasionally a mix with a hint of Janet Wilkes's forced, finishing-school airs slipped through.

Charlie7 preferred the familiar. But he reminded himself that he wasn't there for a social call. Eve was missing and likely recaptured by Creator. Whatever interpersonal pain he had to endure was nothing compared to what Eve might be suffering. The scenarios his fertile imagination had concocted ranged from the gruesome to the inhuman. Each second he wasted meant another second Eve was left to Creator's mercy. But blurting his problem to Janet9 without preamble wasn't going to get Charlie7 the answers he needed.

"Hey, Jane. You've got a monkey on your back." He pointed to the capuchin peering at him over her shoulder. The little creature was curious but still skittish enough not to trust Charlie7 without Janet9 in between them.

"How marvelous—wit and unwelcome aircraft. You've outdone yourself."

Janet9 was one of the few robots that even approached Charlie7's age. But while he viewed himself as a middle-aged man in a perpetually young body, Janet9 looked upon herself as a grand dame among robot kind.

"Listen, Jane. I didn't come to ruin your airspace or pester your monkeys. I've recently developed a keen interest in humans. Who do you think might presently have the ability to clone them?"

"You mean aside from Eddie80 and Mary23?" Janet9 asked as the capuchin scrambled across her shoulders.

There was no point in responding. The only two human geneticists who'd been caught in the act were public knowledge. Eddie80 had self-terminated shortly after he was discovered with vats of human embryos in his lab, and Mary23 was on Mars performing geological surveys.

Neither was of any use to Charlie7. The old robot crossed his arms and waited for Janet9 to elaborate.

With a dramatic sigh, the fur-wearing robot obliged. "Well, any number of primate geneticists *could* manage, of course. Perhaps not Eddie110 or that poor, misguided Nora77. That one should have stuck to chimps and left the theoretical animals to those with imagination."

"Names, Jane. I need names I can use."

Janet9 helped her monkey passenger to a perch on the trunk of a nearby tree as she pretended to ignore Charlie7's question. For his part, Charlie7 fumed silently, keeping quiet by running simulations of himself rushing in to save Eve in the nick of time in a variety of improbable situations. Who could imagine what punishment Eve might be facing for her escape? Charlie7, for one.

"I have two theories about your line of questioning," Janet9 said after a suitable pause to bring Charlie7 to the peak of agitation. "And I won't answer until I'm satisfied that neither is correct. Firstly, have you taken up an interest in genetics? Because if you have, I'll ship you off to the nearest florist. Let some poor Jocelyn or Marvin teach you how to grow phosphorescent orchids or sit with a Toby and watch oak trees sprout. Leave the higher life forms to those with the passion and dedication to see it through and do a proper job of it."

Charlie7 scratched at the side of his cranium. "No. I don't plan on cloning anything."

While he'd taken up any number of hobbies during his retirement, he'd never engaged in one so very much like work as genetic engineering. The wet, squishy side of science was for other robots. He'd stick to hardware and software.

"Second question, then. Have you taken up some amateur form of private investigation? I won't condone having my colleagues harassed if those busybodies at the Scrapyard can't get by without knowing where their residents came from."

Charlie7 held perfectly still. He felt a coolant failure coming on.

How could she be concerned over the inconvenience of her fellow primate geneticists when human cloners operated in secret, growing girls in vats and kidnapping them when they'd just tasted their first apples?

Truth be told, the idea of launching a crusade to expose the responsible dark lab scientists was a good one. No one else had the time for the hassle except perhaps Charlie7. If he did, it would be the noblest thing he'd done all century.

But provoking Janet9 was the last thing he needed to do just then. He couldn't compel her to give him information. If he pushed her too far, she'd spread the word, and none of her colleagues would give him the time of day either.

And since, technically, this was a form of vigilante investigative work, he only had one option: make up a lie and make it up quick.

"I've got a wager with Toby22 as to who will get credit for the first sanctioned human. We've each got until tomorrow afternoon to come up with a list of five names. If I win, he's renaming his nature preserve after me. If he wins, I take over his job while he gets to find out what a year-long vacation is like."

Janet9 had been feeding pellets to her little monkey friend as Charlie7 spoke. She turned her head with menacing deliberation to fix him with a scowl. "You pulled me away from my work for *that*?"

"I'd like to have places named after me," Charlie7 replied with a slapped-on layer of offended dignity. "Plus, it's not like I came empty-handed. Give me a list of names, sorted by your best guess at who'd be first to the finish line, and I'll pull some strings and get your air exclusion zone pushed through committee."

Janet9 stood lock-joint still. "At times the mind boggles at how you have any influence at all over world affairs, Charles."

"Does that mean 'yes'?"

"Very well."

Janet9 proceeded to rattle off a list of robot designations. All the names were known to Charlie7, of course. He knew everyone. But it took someone with professional rivalries and inside knowledge of the industry to put together a ranked list of suspects. Charlie7 had only come to Janet9 because he'd never met a robot less likely to flout rules. She sat on twelve committees and spent as much time on hearings as she did with her pre-hominid critters.

He'd bet the Arc de Triomphe that Janet9 wasn't Creator. Like her or not, Janet9 wasn't a rogue geneticist.

But as the list threatened to devour a chunk of Charlie7's day, he held up a hand. "Can you just send the names in data form?"

Janet9 actuated an eyebrow.

"What? I've got places to be."

"You're usually the one who refuses to admit he has a computer in his torso." The data appeared in Charlie7's message queue a fraction of a second later.

Charlie7 gave her a nod and raised a hand as he jogged for his skyroamer. "Times are changing."

CHAPTER TWENTY-THREE

Charlie7 began cross-referencing the instant he lifted off from the Yucatan.

Janet9's list was too long to visit even a tenth of the geneticists she named. Far more robots were theoretically capable of making the leap to cloning humans than Charlie7 had hoped to imagine.

The technology was there. Someone had proved that.

The floodgates to the human resurgence were being held shut by fear of the Scrapyard. Most robots had the ethical integrity never to land one of their creations in a place like that. While the robots on staff were angels in alloy steel bodies, no one would wish the hardships of those humans on one their own creations.

At least, no one would admit to it.

Charlie7 needed another edge to pry at. He needed another factor to scratch names off Janet9's list. The scientific method was a time-honored system for making a small gain after a long, arduous process. If the worst of his conjectures had befallen Eve, Charlie7 didn't have the kind of time for that. She needed him to come up with answers faster than that. He needed to cut corners, to step on toes, and to sidestep protocols.

He needed another Charlie.

The Kanto Industrial Complex rose on the horizon as Charlie7's skyroamer rocketed across the Pacific. This was where new robots were born.

Charlie7 approached from the East, hugging the ocean to keep off nosy private radar systems. Behind him, a massive wake rose from thruster wash.

Deceleration that would have crushed a human merely pressed Charlie7 against the cockpit restraints. He had made the trip in just under two hours, but even that felt like an eternity. The uncertainty of what retribution Eve might be facing from an angry Creator spurred him on.

There were times when Charlie7 resented the idea that he flaunted his status and exploited more useful robots in modern society. Today he was glad that he still had backdoor access codes to Kanto from when he first built it. The factory had been so much smaller, then. But in all the intervening years, a kernel of computer code had lived on at its core.

The factory's incoming traffic monitoring system conveniently lost track of Charlie7's skyroamer and didn't report the anomaly. As the facility rose from Honshu Island to fill the horizon, he vectored toward a landing zone for maintenance workers. None of the gigaton freighters from the refineries and smelters paid his little personal craft any mind as he veered around them. They were automated. Unless Charlie7 interfered with their primary function, he was a gnat flitting past an elephant.

The landing zone green-lighted him, and Charlie7 set down in on open-air pad beside a motley row of mismatched personal crafts owned by various robotic workers. Some of them had made their workplaces permanent homes. Others lived and took recreation in the more scenic parts of ancient Japan.

Charlie7 took a casual interest in the models of skyroamers as he strode past. Most had been designed in recent years by a bored Brent who built custom rides upon request.

The old robot delved into a technological anthill of stairwells and catwalks with a destination in mind. His goal wasn't a place so much as a person, and it certainly wasn't a Brent.

Amid an army of automatons and fixed machinery, it was a single namesake of his that Charlie7 sought. He passed from the large-scale manufacturing zone into a quieter area behind layers of acoustic and electromagnetic shielding. His access codes granted him passage into the heart of the facility: the upload center.

Charlie13 was the head of robotic activation. He didn't deal with nervous, snide, and petulant old robots getting swapped out of obsolete or damaged chassis. He oversaw the upload of freshly mixed personalities into new, state-of-the-art crystal matrices.

A whole wall of the upload center consisted of visual displays, subdivided into a six by six grid of readouts and graphs. All the data updated in real time as a new brain went through a nano-level quality check before activation.

A twinge of professional curiosity diverted Charlie7's attention long enough for him to give the readouts a quick scan and see what old '13 was up to. It looked like a 55/30/25 mix of Paul, Arthur, and Toby. Unless Charlie13 was making cutting-edge alterations within the sub-archetype details, this robot was going to be dull as mud and spend his life working in composite building materials.

An all-too-familiar voice called out to him from the far end of the room.

"If you're looking to meet the new boy, you're three days early."

Charlie13 rose from hands and knees behind an access panel in the upload chamber. He dusted himself off in a mirror of Charlie7's technique, using the backs of his hands and not the palms. The two of them used the same Version 64.6 chassis these days. It was almost enough to make Charlie7 want to put in for an early upgrade to the 70.2.

Charlie7 forced a grin and spread his arms. "Lucky 13, can't this just be a social call?"

Next time will be the first time, Charlie7 heard the echo in his mind. He cringed mentally in anticipation.

"Next time will be the first time," Charlie13 replied on cue. "Out with it. We both know you won't leave me be until you've gotten what you've come for."

"I came with a puzzle," Charlie7 said. It seemed a fitting way to describe his trouble with Eve14, short of laying the whole sordid mess in front of his brother. "What would it take using the latest technology for someone to reverse your process?"

Charlie13 snorted. "An EMP. Simplest way to get a brain out of a robot's body." Of course, an electromagnetic pulse would have turned a robot into a blank shell.

"No," Charlie7 snapped. He ought to have anticipated the sarcastic reply and worded his query more precisely. Unfortunately, extreme precision was a problem all its own. "I mean put a robot's brain patterns into a human mind."

"Impossible. We don't have sufficient understanding of the human mind," Charlie13 replied.

The director circled the upload rig and removed another access panel. Charlie7 intentionally kept from looking at what he was doing. The last thing he needed at the moment was the distraction of watching maintenance on his old invention.

"Not that there are any good models to study," Charlie13 added. "Give those wet-science oafs a few more decades, and maybe they'll come up with a brain worth scanning."

"What if they had one?"

"Today?" Charlie13 couldn't hide his interest. Maybe he could conceal it from a Toby or a John, but not another Charlie and especially not Charlie7.

Charlie7 strolled over and latched the access panel back in place. "Hypothetically, would someone with today's technology and a pristine human brain be able to work our old process in reverse?"

"The Upload Ethics Committee would never—"

Charlie7 slammed a fist against the upload rig. "Forget them. Assume someone has already violated the Human Rebirth Committee's road map for re-population. They've already gotten their human and aren't getting the support from anyone following ethics guidelines. Could they do it?"

Charlie13 shook his head slowly. It was disbelief, not outright denial. The upload director wandered a few steps from the machine, lost in calculation.

"No. They'd have to have leapfrogged the current generation of upload tech. Lack of specimens has left human neuroscience lost to the dark ages. The Project Transhuman research was the only data to survive the invasion. No one was shooting top secret or cutting edge neurological scans off into deep space for posterity."

"How much better would the data need to be compared to scans of the Twenty-Seven?"

"I'm no neurologist," Charlie13 stated as if Charlie7 had ever doubted the fact.

It was an equivocation anyway. For lack of humans to study, Charlie13 might have been the closest they had. He at least knew robotic pseudo-neurology, which was based on the fundamental science.

"The human brain was pliable, but there were limits," Charlie13 explained. "You can't map motor control to the language center or memories to the brain stem. It's not the same blank slate as a crystal matrix. Plus, we don't possess the patterns necessary for human autonomic functions. Someone would have to expend serious effort mapping specific brain functions down to individual synapses."

Charlie7 suspected as much. He hated hearing it, but he couldn't force himself to believe the implications without hearing it aloud from another expert. The grimmest of his simulations had trod a path through those deep, dark woods. That forest of stainless steel spikes had a set of small footprints leading away from it.

"You mean beyond simple external observation?"

"No one is using our original technique, if that's what you're asking," Charlie13 replied with a casual shrug.

It rankled Charlie7 that in some ways, '13 had as much right as him to claim Dr. Charles Truman's achievements.

"Now are you going to tell me exactly what this is all about?" Charlie13 demanded. "Either spit it out or let me get back to work. I don't have the patience for this innuendo."

That was the difference. Charlie13 had a touch of Dale in him—15 percent to be exact. Dale Chalmers never had an imaginative bone in his body.

While Charles Truman had been the head scientist of Project Transhuman, Dale Chalmers was the project director. That meant Dale's PhD gathered dust while he gathered funding.

If it had been up to Charles Truman, Dale wouldn't have been scanned in the first place. But every other scientist on the project had his brain preserved for posterity, and Dale wouldn't be shut out of his own project. Few Dale mixes had ever worked out, and he was largely excluded from new mixes. Charlie13 was a rare exception, a ruthlessly efficient administrator who still had the fire and drive—thanks to his dominant 65 percent share of Charlie—to push upload technology forward. But he also lost Charles Truman's sense of humor.

But of all robots, Charlie7 understood Charlie13. While he had little of the rebellious streak for which Charlies were known, he also wouldn't run off to a committee to involve himself in a problem that didn't concern him directly.

Charlie7 shut down his optical inputs. It was time for blind trust. "Someone did it."

"Uploaded to a human?"

Charlie7 waved away the very notion. "No. Cloned a healthy one. She's got trans-cranial probes embedded in her skull. I think someone wants very badly to study the brain inside."

"This a new addition to the Scrapyard? I stay off the news feeds."

Charlie7 rejected several quick replies that his linguistic algorithm suggested. He was beginning to loathe the term "Scrapyard" and anyone who suggested Eve might belong in one.

"No. This one's a secret. Anyone who's seen the girl has promised to keep quiet while her creator is still at large. I need to find her."

"Good God, '7, you mean to tell me you had a healthy human in hand and you lost her?"

Immediately Charlie7 came to *the* reason he so rarely spoke with '13 or any of the other Charlies. None of them could resist a chance to prove the others were inferior. All of them entertained delusions that they were as good as him.

"Not lost. Stolen. Kidnapped, even. And I mean to get her back."

Charlie13 nodded solemnly. "Best of luck, '7. If, uh, you resolve this by next Thursday, a few of us are getting together in Siberia for a friendly race. Jason17 just finished laying 250 kilometers of fresh asphalt."

When Charlie7 didn't answer immediately, '13 pulled away the access panel and got back to work. "No pressure either way. Come if you feel like it."

It was the closest another Charlie had come to a friendly gesture in ages. Probably just wanted the story before the news feeds or the Social got hold of it. Besides, '13 knew there wasn't a molecule in him that cared about ancient cars. Let the robots with hints of Brent or Jason play with toys.

"Can't make any promises. Right now, all I can think about is finding Eve."

'13 looked up, scowling. "Another Eve? Dammit, someone ought to find the one naming these humans and forcibly upload a list of baby names into their skulls."

CHAPTER TWENTY-FOUR

James187 stood perplexed at the intersection of five sets of footprints. The soil around Evelyn38's lab was soft as cornbread. Prints stood out in sharp contrast. Had there been just a single trail, following would have been child's play.

Whoever had stolen Eve14 had fouled the trail on purpose. From the size and depth of the footprints, they might even have programmed a squad of automatons to march over the area after the fact.

No. Not marched. Jogged.

James187 scanned the ground and took measurements with his eyes. The strides were too long; they didn't fit with any humanoid automaton. And they were spaced nowhere near far enough to have been made by one of the larger industrial or construction models. His quarry was a robot of light construction with long legs. The oversized boots suggested misdirection.

James187 leaned down and examined the crisscrossed depressions more carefully. He didn't need to; his optics were flawless. It was just part of the hunt, the way his father had taught him. Or at least the way Dr. James McCovey's dad had taught him, back in the Flesh Ages.

One of the five sets of prints was deeper than the others. Given the size of the boots, the change in depth indicated an increased mass of roughly fifty kilograms.

This was the trail of a robot carrying Eve14. Now that James187 had the correct lead, he followed without hesitation.

Memories never faded in a robotic mind. The hazy human recollections hung in suspended animation like the tissue samples floating in formaldehyde in Evelyn38's office. Nothing would bring back the tiny details of hunting deer in northern Arkansas, but the impression would never fade, either.

It could have been a gorilla. Even a chimpanzee would have been a welcome change of pace. But to track down a human and her robotic kidnapper... that was a hunt James187 would remember forever.

The trail was patchy here and there. Forgotten brickwork poked through the soil to provide a hopscotch path for the kidnapper. James187 struggled to recall what this place had once been, before the invasion. History and geography had never held any interest.

But the terrain itself provided clues. No one had come for Eve on foot. James187 was searching for a landing site. Faded concrete walls and pillars dotted the landscape. When the trail ran cold along a wide swath of intact paving stones, James187 searched for spots that could conceal a skyroamer from view.

"Gotcha," James187 whispered when he saw the telltale marks of landing gear. They had scuffed a tripod pattern on the stone bricks.

A faint scorching of ion wash gave him a vector to follow.

James187 sprinted back for his own skyroamer and plotted a course northwest. The chase was on.

CHAPTER TWENTY-FIVE

The islands of old Mumbai rushed by beneath Charlie7's skyroamer. He had outrun the sunrise and arrived in the dark.

Charlie7 set his skyroamer down in a patch of packed loam at the edge of an orchard. Fruit trees lined a path that led to a modest 1,200 square meter bungalow where Jennifer81 made her home. As chair of more committees than any other robot, Jennifer81 had her choice of neighbors. She had chosen none. Though the city of Mumbai once held fifty million, its current population was one.

There was no immediate response when Charlie7 rang the door alarm. It had never occurred to Charlie7 that Jennifer81 might not be home. In the time of Eve's forbearers, it would have been rude to show up before dawn. But the day-night cycle only marked the passage of time these days; it didn't regulate activity.

And if any robot operated without reliance on the cycles of the natural world, it was Jennifer81.

Committee work consisted primarily of teleconferences. It was only when major issues popped up, or rabble-rousing petitioners demanded attention, that groups convened in person.

Charlie7 was more than familiar with those exceptions. His last encounter with Jennifer81 had been seventy-three years ago, regarding a mediation request for the Climate Control and Rainforest Management Committees. Hopefully, this time would turn out better.

"Your committees aren't meeting," Charlie7 groused. "You haven't taken up traveling. You must be around here somewhere."

No one built a home and zoned the surrounding thousand square kilometers as off limits to construction unless she preferred being alone.

On a hunch, Charlie7 tromped out into the orchards of the peach and pear trees. They were small specimens just three and a half meters height. The fruits of the pear trees were even ripe, he noticed, taking one in hand. With a twist, he broke one free at the step and slipped it into the coat pocket of his suit.

"Come all this way to rob from my orchard, Charlie?" Jennifer81 called out.

Charlie7 bent and peered between the trees where the intertwined branches left a gap. Jennifer81 crouched at the base of a tree with a hand scanner of some sort. A wide-brimmed hat kept the moonlight from glinting off her cranial plate, but the glow of her eyes made her hard to miss.

The pear in his hand provided evidence of Charlie7's guilt. "I suppose I am. But that wasn't my primary reason for coming."

Jennifer81 dusted herself off and tucked her gloves into her belt. "Of course it wouldn't be. What's it this time? Or have you just given up harassing me at hearings and decided to deliver your shabby backroom offers to my home?"

Charlie7 looked up into the night sky, wondering whether Creator was tracking him, even now. With acoustic lasers on a satellite orbiting overhead, hostile ears might eavesdrop on his conversation.

The dark of night always reminded Charlie7 of outer space, as if the blanket of cheer and sunlight provided the illusion of atmosphere only to have it stripped away come sunset. A blue sky made the world seem cozy. But out in the orchard, the heavens lay bare before his optical sensors. The computational mind whirled in futile attempts to calculate infinity.

"Can we talk inside?"

Jennifer81 tore the gloves off her hands. "Of course. I wasn't doing anything important out here. By all means, consume my evening."

Choosing to take the comments at face value, Charlie7 followed her into the house.

One wall held painted images of the countryside at various stages of terraforming. Charlie7 had forgotten how long Jennifer81 had lived in the Mumbai area. The first picture was little more than a barren stretch of beach, littered with the foundations of concrete buildings, beneath a sky of green and brown. She'd supervised the clearing of the land herself. One of the paintings even showed the earth-movers in the foreground. Eventually, the land was cleared, decontaminated, and, after centuries of work by geneticists, reseeded. The latest picture showed the orchard with knee-high saplings.

Jennifer81 hung her gardening hat on a hook by the door. "So, which hat shall I put on for you this time? I assume you have some pressing business with one of my committees."

"Maybe," Charlie7 said. "But mostly I'm looking for information."

Jennifer81 activated a faucet and washed off her gardening tools one by one. "You could have saved yourself the fuel and called."

"I didn't want to transmit this."

The flow of water quit abruptly. "Oh dear. Not you, too, Charlie. Don't tell me you're another conspiracy theorist who thinks a cabal of geneticists is out there cloning a human army. I get two of those a year already, usually right after the sanctuary gets a new resident."

"I don't know about an army..."

Charlie7 hadn't given the broader implications much thought. But he knew about the crackpots and the theorists of all things conspiratorial. A week ago, he'd have been inclined toward Jennifer81's view that the whole notion was ridiculous.

Privacy protections were a staple of society due to selection bias in the base population. Twenty of the twenty-seven personalities could be classified as pathologically introverted—Jennifer among them. The rest were only mildly introverted.

Scientific discoveries were shared in due time, then mostly presented to quiet applause and mild accolades. Historic breakthroughs came with substantially more notoriety and renown. Those were worth working on in utter secrecy until it was too late for anyone to steal the glory.

Now that he considered it, Charlie7 couldn't imagine how conspiracies *wouldn't* boil beneath the surface of academic society. After all, they did in the days of flesh-and-blood humans.

"Can we please get to a point? I *do* have committee business—legitimate business—in twenty-six minutes. I'd appreciate having some time left to prepare." Jennifer81 tapped a foot as she awaited Charlie7's reply.

"I'm looking for a listing of geneticists who've come under committee scrutiny."

Jennifer81's stare could have frozen the grease in Charlie7's joints. "I don't know what sort of game you think we're playing here, but until and unless there is actionable evidence against a member, Genetic Ethics Oversight Committee investigations are confidential."

"Which is why I came to you directly, instead of the whole committee," Charlie7 explained. "This could be a matter of life and death—literally."

"Oh, Charlie. Quit being melodramatic. We're not harboring human cloners."

"What about one who might be reverse engineering the upload process to work on human hosts?"

Jennifer81 folded her arms. Her voice lowered an octave. "I'm not sure I like a word of that sentence. And I'm certainly not handing over confidential committee findings to you to pore over and dig up imaginary infractions."

"But I—"

"Quiet, Charlie," Jennifer warned. "Stop before you say something you'll regret. You know those conspiracy theories? Well, if I were to form one of my own, it would be that a particular free-spirited robot was bold enough to march up to a committee chairman and ask whether she's on to him or not. No one accounts for your activities for years at a time. You're always trading favors with committee members and using prehistoric tales of heroism as a skeleton key to get around every objection."

"There's a human girl in trouble," Charlie7 said, stalking over to look Jennifer81 in the eye from half a meter away. "Her name is Eve. Yes, I know the name is trite, but that's not her fault. I was looking after her, and someone broke into my apartments and kidnapped her."

"You... had a human... at your home?" Jennifer81 was cross-examining him, but there was no avoiding unpleasant scrutiny no.

"She was a stray, a runaway from some mad scientist," Charlie7 said. Its sounded cliché when he put it like that, but how else was he to describe Creator?

"Why wasn't this on every news feed? Why am I hearing it firsthand, presumably hours or days later, and you haven't even sought official help?"

Charlie7 wished for adrenaline, for testosterone, for any excuse to blame his rising anger. "Because if it were up to committees, we'd wait and perform an autopsy to find out what went wrong instead of saving her. Please. I'm begging you. For Eve's sake."

"Charlie7... I tell you this for your own good. You'd have been forcibly shut down if it weren't for the debt we all owe you. Your current status as a retiree is nothing short of a godsend to the working community. Your methods were quaint once, but have no place in an orderly society. My advice to you is this: go home. Reflect on how much better this would have turned out if you had turned this human over to proper authorities the minute you found her. But I won't have you knocking on doors across Earth, bothering every geneticist whose name flashes across my terminal. Let. It. Go."

Charlie7 flung open Jennifer81's door on his way out. She followed him to his skyroamer, more to make sure he left than to say goodbye. Before he slammed the cockpit canopy closed, he couldn't resist a parting shot.

"The human is a 'she,' not an 'it.' And her name is Eve. Remember it."

Jamming the throttle open, Charlie7 swung his skyroamer around and kicked up a cloud of dust over Jennifer81, her house, and the near end of her orchard. He regretted the orchard part, but trees were hardy. A little dirt wasn't going to kill them. The horrors that Eve might be enduring, he was less sure of.

CHAPTER TWENTY-SIX

Plato reached into his pocket, and Eve heard the faint click of a button press. A section of a low hill shifted, dragging a collection of bushes and shrubbery with it. A whir of unseen mechanisms accompanied the rise of the door as it swept up to reveal a passageway.

"Pretty cool, huh?" Plato asked with a grin. "It was a cargo transport before I buried it here as my secret lair." He ducked inside, and Eve dodged a light rain of dirt from above as she followed.

What lay beyond was nothing like the hill it appeared to be from Plato's skyroamer.

It wasn't dirty or wet inside, nor was it filled with subterranean creatures or the unpleasant aromas that seemed to pervade the outdoors. There were chairs and a table. Eve recognized cookware similar to what Charlie had used to cook for her. The space was small for Plato's bulk, but for Eve it felt cozy.

With another click from within Plato's pocket, the lifting door began to lower. Eve whirled and wondered whether to bolt before she was trapped inside.

"Relax. You're safe in here," Plato said.

He fished in his pocket and took out a small device. Holding it up for Eve to see, he set it gently on a small table against the wall.

"See? You want out, just press that button and the door opens. But inside here, I've got the best tech a guy can steal. We're shielded from scanning, hidden from satellites, and safe from wolves."

"Wolves?" Eve knew them by genus and species but had never considered that she should fear them.

"Toby22 says there are a few hundred out here. This piece of land used to be called Nottinghamshire, and it was crawling with wolves. Toby22 says everyone wants it back the way it was. And that made *me* figure it needed itself an outlaw."

Eve had followed gamely thus far, but Plato's wandering narrative had left her without a trail to follow.

"Nottinghamshire? Outlaw?"

Plato held up his hands. He wanted to placate her. While his words often made little sense, his emotions came across clear as day. The only one Eve was unsure of was happiness. Plato grinned almost constantly, so she assumed she might be reading a false positive there.

Happiness was a rare emotion, not an omnipresent one.

"Listen, I'm sure I'm going to say a lot of stuff that sounds crazy. It's OK. You got raised weird. Just accept that and ask questions, and I'll do whatever I can to answer them. OK?"

Eve nodded.

"Nottinghamshire is just the name of a place."

He ducked around the corner, and Eve followed. Tucked inside a cubby just large enough for the two of them was a terminal like one of the many in Charlie's home. He brought up a map. A small portion turned red. A white dot appeared in the midst of the red region.

"This is us, and we're in Nottinghamshire. Or what used to be Nottinghamshire. Who knows if anyone calls it anything anymore except me."

Pointing to the screen, Eve indicated the other names written there. "What are all these places?"

"Mostly nothing. Oh, and I didn't forget your second question. An outlaw is someone who doesn't follow the rules. There are no real laws anymore. The robots don't believe in them. Near as I can figure, they're an anarchistic bureaucracy."

"That's a paradox."

Plato's grin widened, and Eve took note. "Yup. They don't see it that way, though. All rules, no laws. A bunch of chairmen who don't see themselves as leaders. No real enforcement. It's nothing like the histories."

Eve had read bits and pieces about committees at Charlie's house. Could the whole world be run by a loose amalgam of committees with no central authority?

"How long have you lived out here?"

"Oh, I guess it would be 1,530 days now."

Eve blinked at the mention of so large a number. Creator had never referenced such extended periods of time. Usually, it was fewer than ten, and that was when Creator was going to be away and left instructions for Eve's puzzles and training.

Plato licked his lips and swallowed. "Hey, you must be hungry. Want some real food?"

Real food? Charlie had made that promise, but it was evident he didn't know what he was doing. Plato seemed sure of himself, and as a fellow human, he must know what food was supposed to be like.

"Yes."

Plato squeezed past Eve and hobbled into his lair. She hadn't noticed him limping earlier.

For a moment, Plato disappeared into a side room but reappeared before Eve gathered the nerve to venture in after him. He brought a container that wept a cloud of fog. It was cold to the touch as Eve reached out and felt its surface. She snatched her fingers away and blew into her fist to warm them.

"Careful. I freeze all the meats to keep them from spoiling. Good hunting out in these woods, if you know how to bring down a boar."

Eve watched in fascination as Plato handled all the cookware that Charlie had fumbled with. His kitchen had knives and forks, spoons and pans, and to her delight, a captive fire. The aroma of searing pork made Eve's mouth water and her stomach grumble.

And unlike Charlie, who had been consumed by the devilish task at hand, Plato wanted to chat as he cooked.

"So, this Charlie7 guy. How was he?"

"He was nice to me. He checked my vital signs and made sure I was healthy. He cooked for me, even though I don't think he did it right."

Plato chuckled. "Robots cooking is like snakes juggling."

A small intruder suddenly flapped into the room, swooping low overhead in a flutter of wings. Eve dove for cover behind the table as Plato laughed. Laughter wasn't a sign of panic or fear. He was mocking her.

Eve peeked over the edge of the table to see a bird perched on Plato's shoulder. It was mostly red, with splashes of black and white on the face and hues of blue, green, and yellow down its wings.

When Eve looked straight at it, the parrot squawked. "Hello. My name is Spartacus."

"It's all right, Eve. Spartacus is my friend. I rescued him from a hunter who keeps aberrant animals from procreating in the wild."

Never taking her eyes from the talking beast, Eve rose from her hiding spot. Plato kept an offhanded watch on the pan he was tending and smiled at her. Holding out a finger, the bird hopped aboard, and he held it out toward her.

Plato lowered his voice. "Just keep it nice and slow and hold out a hand to let him smell you."

Eve swallowed and did as instructed. She extended a hand like she was forcing it through mud, stopping at what she guessed was close enough for the parrot to get a good sniff of her scent.

"I didn't know animals could talk," Eve whispered.

The parrot tilted its head. "Spartacus is a smart little bird."

Plato chuckled. "I used to call myself Spartacus, and I was going to call the bird Plato. But when I tried to teach him, he copied me exactly, and it got all reversed. Since he's the only one I talk to every day, I figured it was easier just giving in and swapping."

"So should I call you Spartacus, then?" Eve asked.

Creator hadn't prepared her for this sort of social interaction. Names were names. They weren't supposed to be mutable, let alone stealable by birds.

The parrot squawked and angled its head to interpose its face between Plato and Eve. "My name is Spartacus."

Plato shrugged. "What can I say? The bird's got a way with words." He lifted the finger Spartacus was using as a perch, and the parrot flew off into unknown parts of the lair. "Normally I hunt down robots who experiment with making humans—like you. But I got wind of someone who'd spliced dolphin and chimp DNA into parrots and came up with birds as smart as apes."

"Apes can talk?"

"No, but that's mostly down to the physiology of the tongue and larynx. Apes just can't make the noises. Ancient humans managed to teach a few hand gestures that were a form of communication, but Spartacus can actually talk. Now, don't get me wrong. He's not *smart* smart, just smart compared to birds. His math skills are horrible; his vocabulary's limited to a few thousand words; and he can barely play checkers. But hey, a friend's a friend. Right?"

A squawk echoed from the other room. "Spartacus is a friend. Plato cheats at checkers."

Plato flipped the meat, and a splash of grease dripped over the edge of the pan. An unexpected gout of flame made Eve flinch away.

"He's also got excellent hearing, so be careful what you say about him."

Fascinating as the parrot was, Eve was more interested in the ancillary implications of Plato's statements. "How do you know so much about old humans? Have you studied the news archives Charlie7 showed me?"

"Oh, sure. Plenty of dry, important stuff to know in there, but it's a gut punch to go through. There's lots better stuff in the archives if you know what to look for."

"Like what?"

Eve had observed that Plato had a habit of omitting key details in his conversational speech. Creator could have taught him a thing or two about using words to convey accurate, complete information.

Plato wiggled his eyebrows up and down. "I'll show you after dinner."

The meal was marred by mild carbonization of the protein portion. But once Eve carefully excised the overcooked sections, the pork had an intriguing flavor, far more potent than any of the nutrient mixtures Creator, Charlie, or the sanctuary had made for her.

It took an inordinate amount of chewing, however, before the pork was fit to swallow. Eve's jaw muscles ached by the end of the meal. Plato had insisted that this was normal human food, not mush meant for easy digestion and that she would get used to it in time.

After helping Plato cleanse the tools and eating surfaces, he showed her into a room similar to the one where Charlie had let her sleep. One wall was consumed by a display panel while the floor of the opposite half was covered in a lumpy, fur-covered cushion.

Plato flopped down and dug out a remote that he used to turn on the display. Patting the cushion beside him, he invited Eve to join him.

Eve reached down and felt the surface. It was soft to the touch, and the cushioning gave way easily under a bit of pressure from her hand. She leaned close to smell it, but the lingering aroma of cooked pork and the mild, pervasive scent of Plato's body kept her from noticing anything remarkable.

There wasn't a lot of room on the cushion, so Plato had to lift an arm to make room for her beside him. Once she settled in and squirmed the cushion into a comfortable shape beneath her, Plato wrapped his upraised arm around her shoulders, which happened to also give her a place to rest her head.

The studs toward the back of Eve's cranium must have dug into Plato's bicep. If they bothered him, Plato never said a word of complaint.

At first, Eve clasped her hands in her lap and sat trembling, unsure what was expected of her. Warmth welled inside her, more than sharing Plato's body heat could account for. Before long, Eve was sweating.

Was it a side effect of the unfamiliar food?

Eve twisted and nuzzled close against Plato's chest. The spreading heat inside her only worsened, but Plato's arm pulled her in close, and she felt safe. After a harrowing day—several harrowing days—Eve allowed herself to relax.

Plato would have warned Eve if anything she'd eaten were dangerous. He seemed to know everything about humans, and Eve knew only what Creator had taught her—which more and more was showing signs of being dreadfully insufficient.

All the while, Plato tapped and clicked away with the remote in his other hand. A gibberish list of names and phrases scrolled by on the wall screen. At length, he settled on one of the listings.

"What's a Wizard of Oz?" Eve asked. A wizard was a colloquial term for a guided tutorial, but Oz meant nothing to her.

Smirking, Plato tapped a button and the word "play" briefly flashed on the screen. Instantly, Eve was engrossed.

"It's a movie. Everything gets explained. Just watch and enjoy."

It began with music Eve had never heard. Even as the notes played, her spirits lifted, and her hands twitched with the fingering to play it back on a keyboard puzzle. Those were among her favorites, converting a visual code into a melody. But this wasn't a puzzle for her, and soon an ID screen appeared with a title and accreditation for production.

Eve tried to watch passively, as Plato suggested. She just couldn't dam the flood of questions that burst from within. "Why is the color desaturated?" Plato explained that it was an artistic choice.

"Oh! Kansas! I was there yesterday!"

"Wouldn't the house lose structural integrity in a tornado?"

Then the world changed to color, and Eve found herself speechless in wonder.

Everything was so vibrant and alive. The analytical portion of Eve's mind exhausted itself. Eve accepted the absurdities of the narrative and just enjoyed the visual feast.

There were witches both good and wicked, tiny people, and slippers adorned with chromium-laced aluminum oxide gemstones. None of it made a whit of sense, but its alternative reality held a strange allure.

Plato made her laugh by affecting a falsetto voice and singing along with the munchkin people. He rocked back and forth in time with the music. Cradled beneath Plato's arm, Eve was taken along for the ride. The girl Dorothy met a man dressed as a scarecrow, then a primitive robot who chopped trees.

"He's like Toby22!" Eve exclaimed, drawing a chuckle from Plato.

The man who claimed to be a lion was obviously wearing a costume.

As the images continued to play across the screen, Eve found her eyelids growing heavy. For the first time since Plato carried her from Creator's lab, she could let down her guard. Plato wouldn't hurt her, nor would he let anyone else harm her.

The last thing Eve saw before slumber took her was a screen that said "The End." But unlike Dorothy, this girl had only just started down her yellow brick road.

CHAPTER TWENTY-SEVEN

The forest underbrush crunched beneath James187's feet as he descended from his skyroamer. Where did Toby22 get off planting a forest in an entirely rigid pattern anyway? Any automaton could have been set to do that. The idea of sprinkling Tobys across the smaller landmasses was to give them a personal touch. If James187 had been the sort of robot to complain to committees, this would have been just the needle to prod him to action.

James187's mood had soured even before he landed. False trails and misdirection had delayed him at every turn. Whoever had stolen Evelyn38's test specimen had been prepared for a systematic investigation and pursuit—but not well enough.

The search had led to old Sherwood Forest. If it wasn't a coincidence, then the robot vigilante who'd kidnapped Eve14 had a sense of grim humor and an overblown opinion of himself.

A whole section of forest sputtered with dummy E-M signatures. If he hadn't already accounted for the whereabouts of the local gamekeeper at the time of the theft, James187 would have suspected Toby22 of being the kidnapper.

Toby22 couldn't have been ignorant of the errant signals spewing from every crevice in this pubescent forest. That meant that whoever used this place as a base of operations likely did so with Toby22's blessing or at least a blind eye. Either way, James187's priority was the girl, not the perpetrator.

The sooner James187 could locate and retrieve Eve14, the sooner Evelyn38 could take over. This sort of mess was outside his programming. Neither the human personality mix nor the robot he'd become had ever dealt well with intrigue. A job started with a target and ended with a delivery.

A porcine squeal echoed in the still air. Northwest. Wolves were nocturnal, and it was an hour after sunrise. Whatever had hurt that boar was worth investigating. James187 set off at once, on foot. The noise of his skyroamer would alert his quarry too soon.

James187 checked his weapon as he made his way through the grid of trees. The dart gun had an effective range of 200 meters, and Evelyn38 had assured him that the dose in each of the twelve darts he had along was enough to render Eve14 unconscious in five seconds.

Evelyn38's summary of Eve14's capabilities seemed inconsistent with her hunting boars. The girl certainly had the athletic skills, but Evelyn38 had never trained her with weapons. There was, however, every chance that the girl had rigged up a trap.

Another strong possibility was that whoever had taken Eve14 wanted raw protein for her diet. If the kidnapper were another James or had a substantial James percentage, he'd remember hunting in the Ozarks as a boy. Any James could kill a boar.

When James187 crested a low rise, he performed a quick visual diagnostic. Evelyn38 had been quite clear on the subject of Eve14's gender. James187 recalled images of young humans, accompanied by height and weight statistics. The data was there in crystalline perfection in his mind.

The creature hunched over a fallen boar was nothing like what he expected. The human must have been over two meters tall and 150 kilos. This was no cloned human, but the statue of an Olympian god made flesh—then infused intravenously with anabolic steroids. A crack rang out as he snapped the wounded boar's neck with his bare hands. Then, without a hint of effort, the human slung the boar over one shoulder and stood.

This male human might have been rescued by the same robot who had broken in and stolen Eve14. There could be a little colony of them, hidden under the misguided protection of Toby22.

Though this wilderness encounter painted him as a savage brute, there was always the chance that this human was Eve14's kidnapper.

Either way, it seemed likely that this human knew where Eve14 was. That boar was sure to appear on her plate if James187 did nothing. As the human strode off in the opposite direction, James took note of the compound bow slung over the opposite shoulder from the boar. There was no sign of any advanced weapons on his person. He was armed for a hunt, not to fight off a robot.

As soon as James187 moved, his foot rustled a patch of dry leaves. The human's head snapped around. Eyes that lacked the telltale robotic glow locked onto James187's position.

For a moment, James187 was lost in wonderment. He hadn't seen a live human in all his days. The wretches at the Scrapyard showed up in his news feeds, but those creatures looked nothing like this magnificent hunter.

The boar fell to the ground. A smear of the animal's blood stained the bare, muscular arm beneath. The human swung his bow around and drew an arrow from a quiver hanging low at his back.

Before James187 could take cover, an arrow was in flight. Even with servo-controlled reflexes, he couldn't outrun the sharpened steel tip. The arrow lodged in James187's torso, piercing one of the data lines to his computer brain.

James187 felt a moment of disorientation as part of his consciousness was severed. He still had reason and emotion, but he was unable to perform complex calculations without concerted effort, and his access to public networks was cut off.

A second arrow deflected off his upraised arm. The human, not interested in a prolonged fight, bolted for the deeper woods.

James187 remembered the dart gun. Even without computer-controlled targeting assistance and wind compensation, he could hardly miss the shot. This huntsman was too large a target for his own good.

A warning message popped up in James187's field of view. Ancillary systems went offline. Even in manual ballistic mode, his brain refused to compute a target vector.

HUMAN IN DANGER. OVERRIDE ENGAGED.

It was an old snippet of computer code, a relic of Project Transhuman that had survived until the modern age. James187 paused just long enough to delete the warning from his mind. Unshackled from risking harm to a human, James187 took aim.

The gun puffed, and a dart flew. A second later, the human reached around to pluck the needle from his back. Given the beast's size, James187 didn't wait but fired twice more. One missed as the human had the sense not to run in a straight line. The other stung him in the leg.

The human grunted an obscenity and lumbered onward.

While he was tempted to wait out the sedative, James187 thought better of it. He took off after the human at a run. The last thing he needed was to find out that the darts had failed to deliver their payload.

As he bounded through the forest, for the first time he could remember, James187 regretted upgrading to the Version 68.9 chassis. Lightweight, efficient, and boasting an energy capacity that could see him go months without worrying about replenishing his fuel cell, the 68.9 was everything most robots looked for in a chassis. But it wasn't fast, or strong, or built to take punishment. He had little doubt that his actuators were stronger than the human's muscles, impressive as they were, but in a footrace, he found himself disadvantaged. This human had a longer stride and a quick-twitch response that seemed at odds with his size. James187 would only catch up once the human began to tire.

But the human showed no sign of tiring as the chase wore on. The only factor keeping James187 from losing sight of him entirely was that the human wasn't traveling a straight path. Though his route was roundabout, the human was doubling back.

Was the huntsman that concerned about his boar? Could Eve14 have been in such dire need of food?

James187 kept up his pace but weighed the idea of cutting this human off and heading for the site of the boar kill.

That was when he saw it. The human pulled back a tarp. A holographic projection wavered and dissipated. What had appeared as a small hillock covered in brambles turned out to be a two-seat skyroamer. As James187 watched in fascination, the human slung himself inside and fired up the engines.

There was no time to waste. James187 bolted for his own craft. There was no way he was going to let this human escape.

Even putting aside the chance to interrogate him and find out where Eve14 was hiding, James187 couldn't let the arrow hole in his chest go unpunished. That simply wasn't the way society worked anymore. Robots didn't go around killing robots when they didn't get their way, and he wasn't about to let a new era of humanity begin with a murderer for a progenitor.

The human's craft blew by just overhead, cockpit facing down. The human must have realized the frame rate that robotic eyes captured motion because no human ever would have had the acuity to pick up on the rude gesture he flashed James187 on the way by.

Had humans always been such savages, or was this one merely a victim of a poor upbringing? Someone had bollixed up the social skills of this kidnapping huntsman.

"You think you're funny?" James187 shouted as the human's engine wash covered him in a storm of dry leaves. He yanked free the arrow in his chest and threw it on the ground. "You won't be laughing when I catch up with you."

Jogging to his own skyroamer, James187 knew he could afford to take his time. He wouldn't rush into a mistake or let his temper blind him.

Whether savage brute or fallen god, James187 didn't care. While the human might be able to shrug off Eve14-sized doses of sedative, his organs wouldn't survive the G-forces that James187's synthetic body could handle. He could fly harder than that human could ever dream. With a punch of the throttle that scorched the ground at his landing site, James187 took to the air on an intercept course.

CHAPTER TWENTY-EIGHT

E ve awoke alone.

Her dreams had delved into fanciful realms of flying monkeys and talking parrots. The line between dreams and the video realm of Oz had blurred.

Blinking and rubbing her eyes, Eve pieced together the events of the previous night, sorting the real from the fanciful. The screen at the far end of the little room was dark. The spot on the fur-lined cushion where she'd slept was still warm.

Plato was... gone.

There was a deep impression in the cushion to show that Plato hadn't been a figment of the video's imaginary world. His smell still lingered about her. Squirming on the quicksand surface of the cushion, Eve struggled to the floor and looked around.

"Plato?" she called out.

The parrot squawked. "Plato isn't here."

That was unexpected. The bird had remained quiet throughout last night's meal and hadn't interrupted the video except to mimic the wicked witch once or twice. She'd never considered him a source of information, but Plato *had* said that the bird was smart.

"Spartacus, where is Plato?"

"Plato isn't here. Plato's going to bring back victuals."

"What are victuals?" Eve asked, hoping that they were edible. She found her stomach gnawing at her insides and wondered how long she'd slept.

"Victuals are victuals. Victuals are victuals." Spartacus squawked. "Plato isn't here."

Then again, Plato had also cautioned her that the parrot's intellect was limited.

Eve found Plato's terminal, the one he said was safe to use and looked up the word herself. Apparently, it had been an archaic term even before humanity had died out. But at least it meant she was going to eat as soon as Plato returned.

In the meantime, Eve pieced together the basics of a stretching routine.

Plato's lair didn't have room for sprawling. If she was careful, Eve could at least perform 85 percent of her poses. Physical activity washed away hunger in a torrent of sweat and endorphins. But the effect was only temporary. By the end of her routine, Eve was worried at how long Plato had been gone.

In the absence of anyone else to ask, she consulted the parrot. "Did Plato say how soon he'd be back?"

Spartacus squawked. "The beginning is the most important part of work."

"That doesn't answer my question at all. Did Plato say when he would return?"

The parrot shuffled back and forth on a wooden dowel stuck into the wall. "Courage is knowing what not to fear."

"I'm not afraid of—" but Eve caught herself in the lie and couldn't finish.

She *was* afraid.

Two days ago—or was it three—she had been safe in Creator's lab. The world had made sense. But first Plato, then Toby22, then Charlie7, and now Plato again had taken custody of her in turns too short for Eve to feel settled with any of them. That was what she feared: the instability. Her routines were a shambles. Her health was passing by unrecorded. She was dirty, sore, hungry, and bewildered.

Well, the hunger Eve resolved to remedy.

Plato had stores of food. She didn't trust herself yet to cook anything, but she recognized the apples in a basket as the same fruits Charlie had pilfered on her behalf in Kansas—which didn't look at all like the version where Dorothy lived.

Eve rummaged through a drawer filled with hand tools and discovered a knife mixed in among the wrenches and screwdrivers. The blade sliced through the soft flesh of the fruit like a scalpel, and she took painstaking care not to cut herself as well.

Once she'd sliced the meat from the core, she proceeded to pare away the peel. Of all the foods Charlie had given her, the skin of the apple felt weirdest in her mouth. It was slimy and slick and tried to turn on end and stick between her teeth. The pale, juicy interior of the fruit was all she wanted from it.

She sucked the juices from her fingers when she'd finished eating her third apple. That was enough to sate her until Plato returned.

In the meantime, though, what should she do?

Plato had a protofab, but when she tried to replicate the exercise equipment she'd made at Charlie's house, the machine reported that it was out of material. A search of the lair didn't turn up any of the raw materials listed in the error code, so that ruled out small-scale manufacturing from her day's amusements.

Spartacus landed atop the machine as Eve gave up and shut the access door. "Gotta remember. Hey Spartacus, remind me: steal more metals."

Eve plopped herself down on the fur-covered cushion, relishing the quick rush of adrenaline that came with her brief free fall.

Creator had cautioned her against spiking her body's chemical balance like that, but Creator wasn't here to object. Her body chemistry would return to baseline readings long before anyone bothered to measure it again.

She felt like a rebel.

Plato had left the controller for the video screen in easy reach, and Eve had no trouble navigating the simple interface. When the system came online, it presented her with the option to watch *Wizard of Oz* again. It was tempting, but with the entirety of human history behind a shroud of mystery, Eve opted for a new experience.

Whether by coincidence or not, *Wizard of Oz* was the last in the alphabetical listing of movies Plato had. Above it was a movie called *Winnie the Pooh*, which told her nothing about its subject matter. Deciding to see if the listing looped, she went past the end and found herself presented with *101 Dalmatians*. While she was equally ignorant of what a Dalmatian was, the quantification of them held a scientific appeal to Eve.

She settled in and began the playback.

At first, it appeared to be a simple instructional tale. It was a story of musical endeavor and of animal-keeping. The movie included an antagonistic element personified in a woman who made coats out of puppies.

Eve ran a suspicious hand over the fur cushion and wondered where Plato had gotten it. It didn't have the markings of the Dalmatian puppies, but it could have come from a gray one...

For a time, Eve became engrossed in the story. But as the little dogs were chased all over and buffeted by events they couldn't fully comprehend, it dawned on her: I am the puppies.

Eve was a little Dalmatian, being "rescued" by people she had recently met from threats she didn't exactly understand. Plato wouldn't tell her why he'd taken her, just that she'd needed saving. Toby22 had passed her along as soon as Plato had left them together. Charlie7 wanted to figure out who Creator was and where she lived, and it wasn't to bring Eve home. That much was certain.

She found herself gasping at the harrowing close calls as puppies fled their coat-making pursuers.

"Leave them alone," Eve shouted at the nasty lady in the fur coat, even though it was merely a moving image on a screen.

All Eve could hope was that none of the little Dalmatians got turned into a coat.

Eve didn't want to be a coat, either.

CHAPTER TWENTY-NINE

harlie7 had tried to play nice. He'd tried to connect the dots like a private investigator. The whole way from Mumbai to England, he had mulled over alternatives and come up empty.

"Where did you get her?" Charlie7 demanded, throwing open the door to his skyroamer and jumping down at Toby22's feet.

They were in the middle of nowhere, some forsaken pasture destined for an upgrade to the arboreal paradise of England-that-never-was. Charles Truman had traveled England as a young man. It was a land of freeways and cities and cordoned parks that hemmed in what little nature was left. Toby22 was just a fanciful gardener, and Charlie7 didn't care a whit for the seedlings burnt with ion wash as he'd set down.

Toby22 backed away, hands upraised. What did he see in Charlie7 just then? Righteous anger? Derangement? For the moment either would serve Charlie7's needs.

"Someone broke into my home, Toby," Charlie said. "They stole her right from my house... *my house*. Do you even know what that feels like? I've been around the globe in the last eleven hours, looking for her, but I can't even work out who took her. I figured... if I can't find the robot responsible for kidnapping her from me, maybe I can get answers from the one who rescued her in the first place. I imagine you know who that is."

Charlie7 took a fistful of Toby's coveralls and held him firm.

If it came right down to it, Toby22 could have given Charlie7 a sound thrashing. He'd been wearing that Version 50.1 chassis for decades past the recommended replacement, but that didn't change the fact that it was an outdoor model. Quite literally, Toby22 was built for manual labor. He was heavier, stronger, and had ruggedized outer plating. That 50.1 chassis was designed to shrug off a fallen tree or survive a rockslide or sinkhole.

But instead of grabbing Charlie by the wrist and shearing it off, Toby22 cringed. "I promised I wouldn't tell."

"Eve14's life is at stake here. If whoever put those studs in her skull gets her back, who knows what she'll do to her for escaping. Her mind could already have been wiped clean for all we know. If you know anything about where she came from—anything at all— you're going to tell me right this minute."

Charlie7 let go Toby22's clothing and allowed the robot his dignity. His point had struck home.

Toby22 retreated a step. "You won't believe me."

"Anything will be better than the nothing I've got." Charlie7 followed as Toby22 continued to fall back.

"Wasn't a rescue by any robot you've met."

Charlie7 smirked despite his ire. "You think there's a robot I've never met?"

Toby22 looked over his shoulder and lowered his voice. "Wasn't a robot." He put a hand up to shield his mouth from the east. "There's another human out there."

"Keeping a new rescue off the news feeds is impossible enough. You're telling me there's a vigilante out there springing them?"

"And you're telling me all those human cloners self-terminated?" Toby asked in reply.

Charlie7 lost uncounted computational cycles as that thought recirculated in his algorithms. He'd always viewed those red-handed cloners as Romanesque for falling on their swords upon being caught. Suicide had gone out of fashion as a response to public shaming in pre-invasion times, but Charlie7 couldn't help admiring the tidiness of skipping investigations and hearings.

Toby22 dropped his shovel and closed the case of seedlings he'd brought along. "Come on. Can't be telling you this outdoors. Ears can be anywhere."

Charlie7 followed Toby22 on foot to the nearest of his supply shacks. The little hovel was halfway between a barn and a portable outhouse. Once inside, they used a pair of crates as stools.

"What's the big hush hush?" Charlie7 demanded. His ire had drained as Toby22 showed signs of cooperation. Tobys always cooperated eventually. "You think someone's going to hear us in here?"

"Plato doesn't like anyone talking about him." Toby22 kept his voice low, even inside.

"Plato? Funny name for a vigilante. You'd think he'd have picked something a bit more... proactive than a philosopher."

Truth be told, any name that wasn't one of the Twenty-Seven sounded strange in Charlie7's ears. Even Eve was taking a while to sink in as a proper name.

"Called himself Spartacus for a while. Claims a bird stole the name, though, so he had to come up with a new one."

"So, not quite Scrapyard material but still not right in the head?"

Pieces were beginning to fall into place. Also, Charlie7 chided himself for calling the Sanctuary for Scientific Sins by its derogatory name.

Toby22 shrugged. "Never got a straight story from the lad. Earnest sort. Seems to mean well. But oh, the mean streak he's got for anyone who harms a human. I daresay he's scrounged up half the residents come to light these past two or three years."

"And this Plato brought Eve to you? Why not bring her to the Scrapyard like the others?"

"Don't think he ever went himself," Toby22 said. "Too risky. He left them somewhere safe and called it in. Anonymous login. Fake public ID. Everything looks like a guilt case, right? Well, he couldn't bring Eve14 there, could he?"

Charlie7 leaned back until his head thumped against the shack's wall. "No. He couldn't. That place isn't for her. She'd do better with a laboratory of her own than with someone spooning her gruel three times a day and changing her soiled clothes. Why'd Plato leave her with *you*, though?"

Toby22 shrugged. "Convenience, maybe? Said he'd be back for her. Didn't have time for much before he was off again. Business, he said. I didn't ask what. I keep on that one's good side."

"By dumping her on me the first chance you got?"

Toby22 held up the index fingers on either hand. It was a gesture that Tobias Greene used when making excuses for cutting corners in the lab.

"I had my reasons. First off, you're the one with all the experience. I'm just a glorified gardener. What was I going to do to look after a living girl? She's not an oak sapling. She'd have starved to death by morning."

Charlie7 leaned across and closed the scant distance between the two robots. He locked eyes with Toby22, who squirmed in his seat but didn't dare move.

"Now Toby, I'm going to ask you a simple question, and I think you know the answer to it... Where. Do. I. Find. Plato?"

"You can't tell him I told you. You just can't."

"Where Toby? I'm one dead end short of blowing this story across every news feed. You won't work planetside again this century. I'll get kicked off every committee I'm on, even if they're all honorary seats. There'll be a planet-wide manhunt for Plato. In all the chaos, it's a 50/50 chance Eve will get rescued or destroyed as incriminating evidence. So unless you give me a lead, that's the best shot I've got."

"You won't find Eve14 if Plato thinks you're a threat to either of them."

"You're terrified of this rogue human, aren't you?" Charlie7 asked.

Humans were certainly capable of causing harm. But the mere idea of Toby22, in a chassis built to haul trees and herd cattle, being afraid of a blood-filled sack of skin was rather unseemly.

Toby22 nodded. "He's a good kid, but I've seen the temper in him. Yeah, I'm afraid of him."

"Well... I'm not." Charlie7 flung open the door to the supply shack and stalked off into the woods.

CHAPTER THIRTY

The woods were too quiet for Charlie7's liking. Not enough birds lived here yet to fill the air with song, and there weren't enough leaves on the pipsqueak oaks to rustle much in the wind. Dry leaves crinkled beneath Charlie7's shoes, but that just emphasized the isolation, creating the only real sounds for kilometers around.

The landscape rose and fell in gentle waves, the product of some fractal algorithm and the toil of autonomous bulldozers centuries ago. This area had been hard hit in the invasion, and little of the original character remained. Charlie7 wondered how much of its history Plato knew before choosing it as a hideout.

Toby22's coordinates weren't precise, giving Charlie7 a square kilometer or so to search. The coward either didn't want to lay any better trail of breadcrumbs on the chance they might lead back to him, or Toby22 had never investigated his domain thoroughly enough to find out.

Either way, Charlie7 found himself trampling dry oak leaves and needles fallen from pines the size of Christmas trees. He had imagined that simple thermal imaging would have been enough to locate a concealed dwelling in this sparse forest. All Charlie7 found in the IR spectrum were animals, mostly small game and a few stags and boars. He suspected Toby22 had to feed them all since there didn't appear to be enough for them to forage.

But one boar hadn't shown up on Charlie7's scanner.

The carcass was lukewarm, blending in with the dirt and brush. This boar was plainly dead, with its head lolling at an impossible angle. A ragged hole marred the creature's chest, still tacky with warm blood. No animal had made that wound unless armed gorillas were loose with spears. Based on some of the more sensational rumors on the Social, a few of the primate geneticists weren't far off from that.

For Charlie7's quest, the answer was simple. Plato had been here. He'd killed this boar. And... for some reason left it behind.

Charlie7 was no woodsman. But it was no mystical art to find the footprints in the soft soil.

Two sets of prints chased one another over the forest floor. One set were large boot prints with a long stride. The others had a mechanical precision in their regularity. Neither matched the shoes Eve had gotten from Nora109.

If the larger set of footprints belonged to Plato, then that "boy" of Toby's was a Goliath.

Not far from the boar, Charlie7 found a tranquilizer dart. Its reservoir of sedative had been emptied. Another lay among the fallen leaves a few dozen meters farther, amid Plato's now-zigzagging footprints.

Charlie7 came across several more darts with their sedative intact and pocketed them as a precaution. Based on the uninterrupted trail of prints after the first two expended darts, Charlie7 had his doubts how effective they'd be.

Pieces were fitting together in a puzzle of Charlie7's own. Eve would be proud of him.

A robot was after Plato with sedative doses insufficient to drop the lad. Anyone who thought ahead to bring such specific ammunition must have had a target in mind. Sloppy preparation alone couldn't explain being so wrong about the dose. But someone who wanted to bring Eve back without a fight... they might have a sedative measured out that would barely slow a brute like Plato.

Charlie7 tried to envision himself as a detective in the tradition of Sherlock Holmes. It seemed fitting for the region, if not the terrain. What could he deduce from the scene?

Some robot had come looking for Eve; that seemed evident by the inadequate tranquilizers. He—or she—had come upon Plato instead.

Plato was armed, judging by the dead boar. Had he fought back?

There was no sign of a struggle, and Charlie7 didn't fancy backtracking the footprints to see whether any arrows might have been hidden among the dead leaves back in the other direction.

The robotic tracks halted, then veered suddenly in a different direction. Charlie7 paused, then continued to follow Plato's. Those ended at a telltale pattern of imprints in the soil—landing gear. Plato had reached a skyroamer. His pursuer must have realized that and headed for his own transportation—or given up and gone after Eve. Charlie7 retraced the trail and followed the robot's again. It ended likewise at a set of landing gear and another path that wandered away from the vehicle in the first place.

Two possibilities presented themselves. Either Plato had run away to save himself, or Plato had lured the robot away from Eve.

Charlie7 had only Toby22's description of the young man to go by, but nothing of the vigilante human-rescuer indicated cowardice. A coward doesn't risk death or capture to break into the homes of mad scientists—and the occasional war hero—to free humans, only to turn tail and leave one to her fate.

Charlie7 preferred to think that Eve was nearby, hidden, and, for the time being, safe.

"You think you're a hero, don't you, Plato?" Charlie7 mused. "Heroes don't run away without a plan."

By Toby22's word, Plato was no fool. The heroic vigilante knew his way around these budding woodlands. But no amount of woodcraft could hide the footprints of a man the size of a bear. Plato couldn't help leaving a trail.

Charlie7 backtracked to the dead boar. The footprints leading to the dead boar weren't nearly so deep and defined as the ones running away from it. But knowing they had to be there made finding them easier. Charlie7 brushed aside leaves with his foot as he went, discovering hints of a print here and there amid apparent signs of an effort to leave little evidence.

After following the trail, Charlie7 revised his estimate of the boy. Plato was no huntsman or commando; his best efforts were amateur. Charlie7 traced his path back to a small hillside.

A smirk twitched its way onto Charlie7's features. It was an involuntary bit of code that had mapped itself onto a crystalline matrix in imitation of a human brain. At times like this, he was glad not to have deleted it centuries ago.

The boy hero had hidden away a secret lair for himself.

There had to be an entrance to below ground somewhere, but none of the equipment he'd brought was registering anything.

That was the clue. There should have been readings, even if they were boring ones. From aerial observation, and certainly from orbit, the minor blip would have been beneath notice. From a meter away, it was apparent to anyone who already knew it was there.

In fairness, the concealment was brilliant. Modern search methods fell short of discovering the hideout. Only someone willing to walk around in the dirt and look for footprints was liable to find it.

Charlie7 had myriad ideas on how Plato had managed the technological aspect of the concealment. But for now, it only mattered that he found a way inside.

Already willing to write off his best formal suit as a loss, Charlie7 dug in the dirt. Robotic fingers tore away loose earth like a child playing in beach sand. Roots ripped and snapped. With a grating scratch, Charlie7 reached the metallic layer beneath. Continuing sideways, he discovered markings that told him what he was dealing with.

Charlie7 was looking at the rear hydraulic hatch of a zoological transport. He chuckled upon realizing that it was upside down. The ramp to deposit lab-raised creatures into the wild had been flipped to act as a garage door, and there was no way Charlie7's Version 64.6 chassis was going to overcome the hydraulic pistons that held it closed.

This was the point where a civic-minded robot would have called for assistance.

Any number of machines could be delivered to his location in relatively short order that could force Plato's front door open. No construction automaton worth its circuitry would be stopped by a simple metal panel. A Toby would likely think to cut a hole through and disable the pumps.

But none of those other robots was Charlie7. A quick transmission of the factory override code ended the lockout, and the door lifted under its own power.

It was bright inside. Charlie7 could have described it as cheerful, quaint, and cozy if he appreciated any of those characterizations. Instead, he found it small, garish, and amateur.

Oh, it was ingenious how Plato had converted the transport into living quarters, with plumbing lines run inconspicuously along the ceiling and extra ventilation ports drawing fresh air from who-only-knew where. There was even a little kitchen area that looked well used, judging by the scorch marks and food stains.

"Hello?" he called out. "Eve, are you in here?"

A familiar, metal-studded head stuck out from an adjoining room. "Charlie? What are you doing here? Where's Plato?"

She was chewing, which meant that Plato had at least fed her before heading off to hunt boars. And she sounded more worried than afraid, which was a good sign.

"I'm here to take you somewhere safe. Plato fled from some robot who chased him in the woods."

A bird squawked and flapped over to perch on an electrical conduit. "Death is not the worst that can happen to men."

Charlie7 cast the bird a perplexed glare.

"I really think I should wait for Plato to come back," Eve replied and disappeared back into the side room.

Seconds later, a cacophony ensued.

Following after Eve, Charlie7 found a small media room set up with what appeared to be *Back to the Future* playing at three times normal speed.

Eve reclined on a makeshift mattress covered in a wolf-skin blanket. In her lap, she cradled a basket of apples. She pared them with a knife and snacked as she watched.

Blinking her attention away from the screen at Charlie7's entrance, Eve paused the movie. "This is good. I think I might be able to solve humanity's extinction if I can figure out how the flux capacitor works."

As the worry drained from Charlie7, he offered a weak chuckle. So innocent. How long would it be before her intellect and the vastness of the Earthwide squelched that endearing quality from her?

"It's all fake. Just fiction. Besides, hobbyists have been trying time travel for centuries, and none of it's possible."

Eve had paused the playback just as twin lines of fire ripped down the parking lot of the Twin Pines Mall. Charlie7 had seen this movie a dozen times before. Everyone had.

There wasn't a movie in the archives that hadn't been picked clean of entertainment value. The few contemporary attempts to create new works always fell well short of the ancient masters.

Sure, there were duds among the archival records. Whoever had deemed *The Cannonball Run* fit for eternal preservation deserved the extinction he got.

The Twenty-Seven hadn't had it in them to produce a film worth watching. Maybe Eve or some descendant of hers would finally create entertainment worth the time it took to watch.

"But these are real people," Eve countered. "I know the artistic representations are just pretend, but those are humans. They sent the dog back in time. They traveled from 1985 to 1955 and reversed a temporal paradox. Now they're risking another paradox to save the fuzzy-haired one's life. There are two more movies in this series, and I'm hoping they explain the equipment's function in greater detail."

"It's a prop. The car is an antique, vaporized a thousand years ago, and it never went back in time."

Eve pointed to the screen and the recently vanished Delorian. "But—"

"It's a story. Amusement value only. Now come on. There's someone out there looking for you, and they know you're in this area."

"Wouldn't it have made more sense not to open the door and show them?" Eve asked.

Charlie7 scowled because she had a point. "They were going to figure it out for themselves soon enough. Now gather up a meal for the trip, and let's get out of here."

"But Plato will be back."

"He might. But he's gone to some trouble to lead whoever is after you away from this place. I'm making sure Plato's efforts aren't in vain."

"But... Plato will be back," Eve reiterated. "He promised."

Charlie7 deleted a harsh retort before speaking it aloud. It wasn't Eve's fault that she trusted so readily.

"Plato told you that so you wouldn't worry about him. What he does is dangerous, and one of these days it could get him killed. If you're not careful, it'll get you killed right along with him. I imagine things back in Creator's lab seemed simple and straightforward, but in the real world, you have to assess for yourself what's true and what isn't. Safety and danger live side by side. The fire that Plato cooked you... what is that mutton? ...that same fire could burn you if you misuse it. The boars he hunts out there have tusks that could tear out your intestines. Consider this: did everything in Creator's lab seem safe to you?"

A thoughtful frown crossed Eve's face, and she chewed her bite of apple more slowly. "I think so. Creator wouldn't let anything damage me."

That Eve's response came after a pause and with a hint of reservation gave Charlie7 hope that she might be swayed.

"Well, since risk and safety surround us in nearly equal measure, then also consider that your Creator kept you not in safety but in ignorance."

"Why would she do that?" Eve asked. "Wouldn't I better protect myself from danger if I knew about it?"

Charlie7 smiled an orator's smile. "Exactly my opinion on the matter. But Creator and Plato don't seem to trust you with the truth. I do. So here's the short version, based on what I've been able to learn so far. Someone made you with a purpose in mind. You haven't fulfilled it yet. They want you back. And most importantly, you aren't likely to survive finding out what that purpose is."

Eve backed slowly into the corner of Plato's media room, clutching the little knife that cut her apples. "No. I think you must have made an error."

Never one to back down from a challenge, Charlie7 expounded on everything he'd learned throughout his search for Eve and what he'd inferred of Creator's motives. It all kept coming back to the studs Eve wore in her head like macabre jewelry. And just as there was no escape from their presence, there was also no escape from the conclusions Charlie7 presented to her.

"You are either the first of a new personality for programming robots, which would make your ignorance of human history inexplicable, or you are to be a body for the first robot to return to the realm of the biological. If the latter is the case, giving you a world to remember and hope for was nothing but a recipe for rebellion, wistfulness, and general disobedience."

How long would it take for this breathtaking young mind to process what he'd just heaped onto her?

Accepting a painful truth tempers the soul, and once the hurt cools, leaves it stronger. Eve didn't have a lifetime's experience to draw on. Charlie7 could only lend his wisdom and hope that Eve trusted him enough to take it.

Creator had been all Eve had known. To come to grips with the premise that her life had been an elaborate hoax, a mere illusion of human experience...

Charlie7 watched Eve's face as her eyes unfocused and she stopped chewing her slice of apple. Just as over-tempering a blade could shatter it, Charlie7 hoped he hadn't just destroyed Eve's world.

The girl swallowed. She met Charlie7 eye to eye. "We should leave."

Tension eased from strained actuators, and Charlie7's shoulders slumped. "Good. The sooner we're airborne, the sooner I can figure out someplace no one will stumble across us."

"But we have to tell Plato where we're going."

Already heading for the inverted cargo ramp exit, Charlie froze. "What? We can't do that. It's not hiding if we leave evidence of our hiding place. It'll only be until we figure out who Creator really is and stop her."

"Plato will worry. We should trust him with the truth. Safer for everyone."

There were times when rhetorical deftness circled around like a boomerang toward an unwary thrower. No sooner had he illuminated the girl on the virtues of truth but she was turning his own words back at him.

"Fine. I'll leave him a note saying you're safe." Charlie7 had seen a terminal in the front of the transport somewhere—or rather, the back of the hideaway.

"No. We should tell Plato where we're going so he can meet us there," Eve said. "He's in danger too. I'm responsible."

Plato killed wild boars, led robots on wild goose chases, and lived for years undetected while rescuing every human test subject he could get his hands on. Charlie7 somehow doubted he would even accept the prospect of going into hiding. But this also meant that he needed to decide right now where he was going to take Eve.

Charlie7 stroked his chin, wishing for the millionth time he had a beard. "We'll need to leave him a note with information that only he'll understand. Did you two work out a code between the two of you by any chance?"

"No, but he seems smart. He should be able to decrypt one if we don't make it too hard."

"Not good enough," Charlie7 replied. "Anything he can decrypt, someone else could as well. We need to think of something the two of you have in common."

"Plato watched *The Wizard of Oz* with me."

"That won't work. Too many robots know the story, and the imagery has the subtlety of a marching band."

However, the idea of movie references gave Charlie7 the seed of a plan.

Returning to Plato's media room, the would-be savior of humans browsed through the most-watched titles. The list was topped by action movies, westerns, and lowbrow comedies. Looking past the bourgeois taste in film, Charlie7 picked a movie that few robots were likely to have spent much time dissecting.

Most brilliant of all, Charlie7 came up with an encryption key that few robots could crack. "Spartacus, I want you to give Plato a message. Only Plato. You understand?"

The bird fluttered in and perched on Eve's head, making her giggle. It squawked. "Message to Plato. Only to Plato."

Charlie7 made up a passphrase. Once Spartacus heard it, he refused to even repeat it back for verification. That suited Charlie7 just fine. Either the bird was an imbecile and hadn't memorized it at all, or he was cagey enough not to give the message to *anyone* but Plato, which excluded Charlie7 and Eve as well.

Re-transmitting the override for the zoological transport once more, Charlie7 closed up the hideout as he and Eve fled for the skyroamer.

CHAPTER THIRTY-ONE

This time across the Atlantic, Charlie7 was better prepared. Eve was bundled against the cold, and they had a day's worth of food along for the trip. Once they arrived, food would no longer be an issue.

While in the air, Charlie7 and Eve had time to clear the air about her origins.

"Eve, it's time you told me everything you know about Creator. And first on my list of questions is this: Do you know her real name?"

"Her name is Creator. If she has another one, she never told me."

Eve watched out the window, staring down at the ocean. Not that there was much to see. Atmospheric conditions were clear, and they were only a few hundred meters up. Charlie7's skyroamer forced its way through the thickest part of the sky. At higher altitudes, they might draw attention from Traffic Control Committee by flying too near a regulated transit corridor.

"How do you know Creator is a 'she'?"

"She taught me how to tell the difference and used herself as an example female archetype."

"Could you pick her out by chassis?"

If Eve could manage that, it could narrow the possibilities considerably. Depending on how exotic Creator's tastes ran, a model number might narrow the list of suspects down to anything from a few hundred to a dozen or so. The skyroamer didn't have a video screen to run Eve through a listing of every possible version number, but as soon as he stashed her safely away, they could pore over them in detail.

"How visually distinctive are different chassis?" Eve asked. "If they're all as different as yours and Toby's, I should be able to."

"Different enough, I would think. What else can you think of about her? What was her daily routine?"

"Well, I only saw her now and then. I had a regular routine to follow when I was alone. But every few days, Creator would come by to personally supervise me. The puzzles were usually harder when she was watching. Sometimes she would reveal after the fact that a puzzle was teaching me something special, and she would explain why it was important. Like the puzzle that taught me how to differentiate emotional expressions. Or the one where I learned to identify whether foods were safe to eat."

Charlie shuddered as he imagined how that test might have gone but didn't dare press her for details.

"Often times, she would stay to watch my entire fitness regimen and make comments about what I could do better. 'There's no such thing as perfection,' she would say. So I always had to keep doing better than before. Oh, and the measurements. She always took detailed measurements before she left me alone for long periods."

"What kind of measurements?" This was both what Charlie7 most and least wanted to hear.

Creator's motives were nefarious; Charlie7 was convinced of that. But what danger she posed to Eve was the real question. Knowing why Creator had made Eve might possibly tell him who she was. Once exposed, Eve would be free to live in the world of robots openly. Not coincidentally, Charlie7 would share no small amount in the credit for her discovery.

"Well, there are the regular measurements," Eve said. She put a finger to one of the studs in her head. "I connect the leads to the computer, and it takes encephalograph readings while I solve puzzles. Sometimes when I ran or did balance poses but mainly just the puzzles. But when she wanted better readings, I'd lay down on a bed with a screen hanging just above my eyes. Creator would give me something so that my muscles relaxed and the whole world seemed to go away except the screen. I'd see all kinds of things. Most of them I can't remember. It's all fuzzy. Creator says it was the chemical that relaxed me that's to blame, but that I gave very good results that way, so she usually left in a good mood."

Charlie7 didn't want to hear any more. He could picture it all being done to her.

For Eve, this was all normal. She'd lost the fear of her captor through everyday horror.

One of the wonders of the crystalline brain was the ability to feel phantom pains. Most robots deleted the synapses responsible but not Charlie7. Now, he was sick in his imagined guts.

He had witnessed bloated, irradiated, and charred bodies scattered across the Earth, but it was all so long ago. It felt like a different world, separate from modern day Earth or the Earth of Eve's forbearers. It was a place he didn't want to revisit, but those horrid memories left a dark palette for his imagination to paint with.

"Skip the rest," Charlie said. "Tell me more about Plato. Tell me about the day he rescued you. What can you remember?"

"Well, *that* I remember just fine," Eve said. "It was just three days ago."

Clearing her throat and straightening in her seat, Eve began her tale.

CHAPTER THIRTY-TWO

"When I woke up that morning, Creator was at the lab. She was annoyed but not at me. I could tell because she used shorter sentences and her words were spaced more closely together. I proceeded with my morning routine while she made adjustments to one of the machines in the lab—the newest version of the one that takes detailed encephalographs. Creator told me that something had come up that required her immediate attention.

"Eve," she said. "This is very important. I'll be back in approximately fifteen hours. When I return, I want you ready and waiting in the scanning machine."

I told her that I understood, and she left. I figured that I had at least fourteen hours to go about my daily routine.

Hooking myself up to the scanner wasn't that time consuming, but in case she was a little early, I wanted to make sure I was ready. Connecting all the leads usually only takes about nine minutes, including the pre-diagnostic to make sure I didn't have any of them attached to the wrong studs.

There's a mirror by the scanner that makes it easier to see what I'm doing.

Inserting the sedative IV is quick, but I have to set the drip on a timer, and choosing the delay is tricky. The longest part is securing myself in place, and until the sedative starts, several of the restraints are a little uncomfortable, especially the cranial clamps. Too early, and I can't finish before my arms go limp. Too late, and I can't move while I feel the restraints dig in as they tighten.

Usually, Creator will tell me in advance if the scanning is going to be long enough to worry about excretory, feeding, or breathing tubes, so I didn't have to leave time for those.

Once Creator had left, and I'd allotted myself fourteen hours for activities, the day sort of... happened.

I don't know how to describe it other than it was a regular day.

I solved a simple series of matrix eigenvalues to unlock my breakfast. They were so simple that I assumed Creator wanted to make sure I ate that morning, rather than truly challenging me. As it turned out, that was going to be my last meal until the mushy stuff at the Sanctuary for Scientific Sins, so I'm glad Creator went easy on me.

Other than that, the morning wasn't notable.

I was able to run through my full physical training regimen. After my warm-ups, I did all my strength conditioning: free-weight maneuvers, pull-ups, push-ups, bench press, leg raises... well, you probably get the idea.

After that, I did my coordination and cardiovascular workout. It took five runs through the obstacle course for me to hit my target heart rate of ninety beats per minute, then I went for my ten-kilometer run on the treadmill. I rehydrated briefly and went through all my dynamic stretching katas and my static flexibility poses.

The full routine took four hours and eighteen minutes. If I had a tighter schedule for the day, I could have managed it more carefully to keep it under four hours, but the katas are especially relaxing.

In retrospect, that lackadaisical attitude cost me the time it would have taken for a second meal. Because once I'd showered and changed into clean clothes, there just wasn't time left to finish the first of a series of three-dimensional interlocking solids I had to reassemble on the screen to have my midday meal.

That was when the door to the lab opened without warning.

Creator rarely came without forewarning, and I'd never heard of her coming back that early. Sometimes she said she'd be back in three days and it would be five, or she'd be back in seven days, and it was twenty. But she'd never given a short time frame like fifteen hours and come back in four and a half.

Of course, since you know mostly where this story is going, you also know that it was Plato who arrived in the lab, not Creator.

He was like nothing I'd ever seen before. He wasn't a robot at all. I'd never seen anyone who looked more like me than like Creator.

I stared, taking in all the nuance of his physical form without even bothering to wonder why he had come.

Creator had told me that I was unique, the first of my kind, and her personal invention. None of her colleagues ever corrected her in front of me, so either she'd fooled them too, or they fooled me. I can't say which. But there was another human in the lab, which meant I was not, in fact, the only one of my kind.

This new human moved like no robot ever had. He had a fluidity and balance that I didn't even see in the mirror during my katas, and he ran without any visible effort.

When he stopped in front of me, I craned my neck to look up at him. He had to have been almost half a meter taller than me. His neck alone was thicker than my thigh. Somehow I was surprised that he could speak.

Words exploded from his mouth. "My name is Plato, and I'm here to rescue you. There's no time to explain. You've got to come with me."

He held out a hand toward me.

If this had been a puzzle, I had failed it badly.

I was still trying to sort out the "my name is Plato" part of his statement, and he had apparently passed well beyond that in his thinking. Because when I failed to take his outstretched hand, he stooped and put a shoulder to my midsection. Before I knew what had happened, I was being carried out of the lab.

I'd seen out through the door, of course. Hundreds of times. There was nothing but a short stretch of corridor and another door beyond that I had never seen open in my life. It was open then, and every door beyond it as well. I flew atop Plato's shoulder, watching as everything I'd ever known shrank in the distance before vanishing around a corner.

"Sorry about this," he said to me. "You'll thank me later. Right now you just need to know that you're not safe here and that I'll protect you with my life."

I don't know why I believed him. At the time, it never occurred to me to doubt him. I was afraid, but it was of some unknown calamity that he hinted at, not of Plato. Now I know that he was referring to Creator herself.

All I knew then was that the muscles of his arm and shoulder were like steel but warm and reassuring. The way he spoke made it sound like he knew what he was doing, and I trusted that he did.

For a time, I expected that he was taking me to Creator—after all, where else would I be safe? But instead, we came up to the surface.

He had a skyroamer waiting and helped me inside. It was a lot like yours, but it was warm inside. The sky was dark outside, which struck me as strange because the clocks in the lab had said it was the middle of the day. I'd learned all about orbital mechanics, planetary rotation, and the cycle of day and night. At 11:30 in the morning, the sun ought to have been nearly overhead.

Instead, we flew away together in the predawn gloom. We were in the air when morning sunlight began to leak over the horizon."

CHAPTER THIRTY-THREE

"Hold on," Charlie said, interrupting Eve for the first time since she began her story.

It was a little disjointed and unevenly paced, but for a girl who'd probably never told a story before, it was remarkably cogent.

"Which way was the sun in relation to the skyroamer's heading?"

"It was definitely behind us."

The dawn sun behind them meant Plato had taken her west, which suggested somewhere in Europe. "And your heading?" he asked, unable to hide the excitement in his voice.

Eve was quiet.

"A heading is—"

"Oh, I know what 'heading' means," Eve said quickly. "I just... wasn't paying attention to that. Plus, Plato kept us close to the ground and didn't fly a straight line, so the sun kept moving and disappearing the whole way. Sorry."

Eve hung her head and turned away from him. Did she expect him to punish her for not knowing?

Charlie7 rested a hand on the girl's shoulder. "That's all right. It's not your fault."

But it was.

Eve was born and raised to have a mind like a computer. She could have easily tracked their path if she'd been paying attention to her surroundings. But yet, as she sat there in the passenger seat, knees hugged to her chest, it was hard to be angry with her.

The gaps in Eve's life experience were difficult for Charlie7 to grasp. He'd lived ten lifetimes with years to spare, seen things no living creature ever had.

How would Charlie7 speak if he didn't know all his letters? How would he run if he'd never learned to walk?

"Will the world ever make sense again?" Eve asked as her breath fogged the cockpit window.

Charlie7 locked in a heading and set the controls to automatic. Unbuckling his safety harness, he scooted over to wrap an arm around Eve.

"No. It never will. The day the world makes sense to us is the day we stop thinking. Having all the answers would be worse than death. I hope for your sake that the world is always filled with wonder. But if it's within my power, I'll make you feel safe in the world again."

As the skyroamer shot over the Atlantic, Charlie7 hoped he'd chosen a place where he could keep that promise.

CHAPTER THIRTY-FOUR

Steel shrieked on stone as the automaton set down a shipping crate on the storage room floor. Evelyn38 saw the minuscule gouge and knew that for as long as she had this lab, it would forever be a reminder of the automaton's incompetence. She resisted the urge to chastise it. The blame lay in the programmer, the manufacturer, and perhaps even herself for failing to account for the mindless machine's shortcomings. Thirty-two of them were busy at work, transporting her equipment and specimens to the new lab.

"Carry on," she said offhandedly as she swept out through the door that led to her new office.

The mindless mechanical beasts would perform their tasks much the same whether Evelyn38 watched them like a nanny or left them to fend for themselves. She had an alert set for when they began to move the valuable cargo.

For now, Eve's creator satisfied herself with unpacking her personal belongings. Her desk was already in place. The smaller crates that contained her office décor were gathered around it in neat stacks. Filtering through them, she found the one that mattered most and popped the lid.

A polished steel shelf gleamed along one wall supported by bolts driven straight into the rock of the smoothed cavern wall. One by one, Evelyn38 took out the skulls of all her Eves and set them in order. Nothing in the crate had been labeled, but to Evelyn38's eyes, each was as distinct as the girls themselves had been.

Evelyn38 paused, as always, to share a quiet moment with the skull of Eve9 before setting it in place with a kiss.

After the skull of Eve13, Evelyn38 left an empty space, then placed the newest addition to her collection. This skull was so fresh she kept a cloth beneath it for the moisture. The rods that had left the telltale pattern of holes in it were packed up in a different crate, ready for cleaning and reuse in their next host.

The creator and destroyer of humans cupped the skull's cheekbone with her hand. "Eve, I'm so sorry. The odds were slim that you were ready, but I'm running out of time. You were such a good girl, all the way to the end."

If Eve15 hadn't been fully prepared for the procedure, the chance of Eve16's brain being any better suited was vanishingly small.

It was a despicable waste. Fifteen years' effort squandered on the one, fourteen likely to be turned to vapid mush soon enough with the other.

Evelyn38 had to keep trying. The alternative was unconscionable. The crystalline brain supporting her consciousness was failing. It had passed through multiple chassis upgrades and lived past its recommended replacement date by decades. Acting without urgency was begging for her brain to enter a cascade failure from which she'd never recover.

Submitting herself to the Upload Committee and putting her crystalline matrix in the hands of their technicians was liable to reveal a host of unpleasant truths best kept private. She could find ways to acquire a new crystal but none that would allow her to continue using the Evelyn38 identity.

The Eves had to work.

Infrequent as they might be, the brain transfers were a horrific experience. Theoretically, robotic brains could be transferred electronically from one mind to the next indefinitely. But each time, the old host was wiped by an electromagnetic pulse.

No duplicates. That was the rule. The Upload Committee enforced its edicts by limiting upload hardware to sanctioned and monitored use.

Upload was no phoenix rising from its own ashes. It was the cannibal eating his enemy's brain to gain his wisdom. The new host believed it was the original; the old was consigned to oblivion.

If Evelyn38 were going to go through that hell once more, it would be to a human body. One life to feel, to taste, to smell, to be truly alive again. Sixty or eighty years would be enough. By then, she could decide how much longer to prolong her existence, if at all.

Picking up Eve15's skull, Evelyn38 gazed longingly into those empty sockets. "I could have been happy, being you."

Evelyn38's notification went off, sending a signal from computer brain to thinking brain that her automatons required more direct supervision. Setting Eve15 back on her perch, she idly wiped her hand on her lab coat and hurried out to check on their progress.

The line of brainless humanoid machines marched into Lab 07. One by one, each automaton set down an 8-liter gestation tank filled with translucent green fluid.

Electricity had been restored using an old geothermal generator, and Evelyn38 crawled around the floor connecting power to each. The tanks lit with indicators and readouts.

None of the specimens had been damaged in transit, and the nutrient levels would hold until the supply lines could be attached. Two empty tanks stayed dark, but the rest contained the embryonic and fetal versions of Eve.

Evelyn38 tapped on the glass and winked one optical sensor at the eldest of the fetuses, a 32-week specimen.

"One of these days, you'll grow up, and we'll be sisters. I might be a 72-year-old woman in an 800-year-old body now... but I think I'll make a good big sister."

The sound of feet marching in step caught Evelyn38's attention and sent her rushing back to the main corridor. A pair of automatons lugged the first of the sleeping pods toward Lab 06.

Stretching only half the length of the well-padded interior cradle, Eve21 slept comatose inside. The sedative line into her median cubital vein was intact. The brutish automatons—who had no business handling such precious children—hadn't dislodged it.

Given ideal circumstances, Evelyn38 would have transported each girl personally, under light sedation, just enough so they wouldn't remember the trip. There was far less chance of damage that way. But haste called for shortcuts, and shortcuts meant risk.

Better a spoiled specimen than a committee investigative team finding her project.

Eve20 passed by in the care of another two automatons. Then Eve19 as well.

Evelyn walked alongside Eve18's sleeping pod for a few steps. The girl's head was shaved smooth and clean. Evelyn38's first order of business once Lab 01 was up and running would be to prep the girl for surgery and install her transcranial probes. She'd been teasing the girl for months with the promise of Eve14's probes, telling her how grown up they'd make her look and how pretty she would be. The fact that she'd be getting the ones from Eve15 wouldn't matter an iota; the girl would never dream where they'd come from.

Though they slumbered a few meters apart as they were carried off to their respective labs, not one of the Eves knew about the existence of the others.

One of them would have to work. The technological side was sound. The upload equipment functioned as intended by all measures Evelyn38 could test. What she lacked was a brain that was fit to accept the massive intellect that had accumulated during her interminable life.

Tomorrow, either Eve16 would prove more worthy than her elder sister, or she would perish as well. Evelyn38 expected the latter, but there was nothing else to be done.

The only way to save any of these other Eves was for James187 to drag Eve14 back where she belonged.

CHAPTER THIRTY-FIVE

Plato's skyroamer, Betty-Lou, had the fuel to keep this chase up for days. Plato, on the other hand, was running on fumes.

The plan had been for the crazy robot with the dart gun to chase him and lose track of Eve. That part seemed to have worked exactly according to plan. But the follow-up step had been for Plato to lose his pursuer, then double back and collect Eve. Any planning past that wasn't worth a boar's snout.

Even after an overnight game of hunter and prey, Plato still looked back and saw the robot's craft right behind him.

Of course, the good news was that the robot didn't seem intent on making him crash. Able to tolerate G-forces that would pop Plato's eyes out the back of his skull, the robot cut inside Plato's every turn and accelerated faster than he dared.

It would have been child's play for the robotic pilot to clip wings with him, force them both to crash into the forest or the sea. Instead, the pursuing pilot played it safe.

Plato's eyelid's drooped.

The ancient heroes of the silver screen could have turned to coffee for solace. Plato had never so much as tasted the stuff, but he envied the magical powers it displayed over wakefulness.

The cache of food stowed beneath the pilot's chair had run out a couple hours back. Stabs of hunger clawed at Plato's stomach from the inside.

Eve's self-appointed bodyguard was on his own, and he wasn't going to last much longer. Time to make a hard choice. Either Plato would have to violate one of his major tenets, or he wasn't getting out of this jam. Continuing to play duck-and-dive with a tireless opponent was only going to get him killed or captured.

A few taps on the cockpit console enabled a voice scrambler that would make Plato sound like a robot. The pilot of the other craft would know better, but anyone listening in might be fooled. He opened a low-power transmitter channel and locked a directional signal onto the other vessel.

"Was marvelous flying with you," Plato said in his best impression of Toby22. "Don't you think it's about time we both went home?"

Plato banked left and pulled up, feeling the G-forces press him into his seat. For those few seconds, he felt light-headed and couldn't even take a breath.

"Come on. Come on," Plato muttered to himself. "Break off and go home."

It was a long shot but the best of his options if it worked. Anyone overhearing the message would think the two of them had been joyriding. Robots had such weird hobbies. It was unlikely to raise many eyebrow actuators.

Why did robots even bother with eyebrows? Plato blinked to clear his head. This wasn't the time to get philosophical about robot quirkiness.

The opposing pilot banked even tighter, and Plato could barely twist far enough in his seat to see the skyroamer on his tail. For the first time, he got a close look into the cockpit. His pursuer didn't look amused.

Feeling around behind the seats of *Betty-Lou*, Plato put his hands on his rifle.

The MEMP rifle was useless in hunting animals, but its monopolar electromagnetic pulse could wipe a robot blank. Twenty-five petabytes of robotic thoughts and memories reverted to clean, empty crystalline matrix in a nanosecond. The same technology sanitized obsolete brains after they'd been uploaded to a new host chassis. Amp up the power output, refine and columnate the field, and it was an ideal weapon for fighting back against immortal machines.

But one of Plato's core tenets, more sacred than the rest, was never to harm an innocent. This pilot on his tail had lost track of Eve, so it was only his own skin Plato had to worry about. Plato couldn't even use her safety to justify bending the rules.

That's a principle!

Killing a robot who hadn't *actually* harmed a human was a line Plato wasn't ready to cross.

Piloting with one hand, Plato used the other to access one of his fake accounts on the Social. It was time for a gambit.

Every robot had a personal account linked to their unique ID, but so many of them had dummy accounts for the sake of privacy or anonymity that a few more never raised any alarms. Their whole society was founded on not having any founding principles.

How the robots lasted a thousand years was a mystery to Plato. More than two thousand individuals without a single government. Committees regulated certain aspects of life on Earth, but if it didn't fall under a committee's purview, it went unnoticed. There were rules, guidelines, and edicts aplenty but not a single law.

No laws meant no law enforcement. No surveillance meant no data analytics. It created a million holes for someone like Plato to hide in. He was Santa Claus and the Tooth Fairy. He was the Illuminati and the Knights Templar. No one believed in him, and therefore, no one accounted for him.

There were perhaps two unwritten laws that summed up present-day Earth better than anything else Plato could think of.

First was to look out for your own turf. There was no authority to turn to and no signal to shine into the night sky to summon aid. A friend might help in times of need, but that just led to the second unwritten rule: Stay on everyone's good side.

Resources were shared, if not freely then in the understanding of a loose reciprocity among all robotkind. That meant not hoarding tech or raw materials, but it also meant you didn't go pissing in someone else's backyard.

REPORTING TWO VANDALS IN ENGLISH AIRSPACE. LOW-ALTITUDE FLYBYS DISTURBING ANIMALS AND SAPLINGS. PLEASE BE ADVISED.

This was Toby22's turf. Whether he was watching or not, the coordinates Plato attached to his message we sure to trigger an automated alert.

Plato kept up the chase through muscle memory and repetition. He yawned and kept glancing at the terminal screen, waiting for a response. A jolt of surprise shocked him awake when the cockpit speakers blared to life.

"Dammit!" Toby22 snarled over an open frequency. Plato had never heard him cuss before. "Go take your daredevil flying somewhere else. I've got a game reserve to look after. Both of you, knock it off or I'll get your airspace permits revoked."

Plato rolled his eyes.

Permits only mattered in a few spots of heavy traffic and the little getaways of a few influential robots. But in addition to his toothless threat, Toby22 had come in one of his agrarian transports. It was a hauler, built to ferry livestock and feed over short distances. There was no way it could outrun either *Betty-Lou* or his persistent friend. If ever a brick had flown, this was the closest any ship designer had come.

Switching his short-range transmitter from directed broadcast to omnidirectional blast, Plato keyed open his mic. "Hey, I'm a little low on fuel. Mind giving a fellow Toby a lift?"

Without waiting for a response, Plato swung around and intercepted the agrarian transport. The vessel was far larger than *Betty-Lou*, and the loading ramp was easily five times the size of the little unit that he'd converted into a home. Feathering the controls, he matched speed and course and lined himself up to use Toby22's vessel as a makeshift carrier.

The other pilot had no real choice. He couldn't very well attack a Toby out in the open, right in his own backyard. That left aside the fact that one of the little personal crafts could hit Toby22's transport full speed and not knock it out of the sky. It was either go out in a blaze of glory or turn and depart.

As Toby22's cargo ramp opened and Plato piloted his way inside, he knew he owed Toby22 an apology. The coward had found his heart.

CHAPTER THIRTY-SIX

arlier that afternoon
E   With Charlie7 gone, Toby22 shunted his friend out of active memory and went back to work. At least, he tried.

Planting out in the forests felt wrong. Charlie7 was out there, looking for Plato. Even knowing the general area he'd be in, so long as Toby22 was outdoors, it would feel like Charlie7 was scanning his every motion.

There was plenty of work to be done. Toby22's very presence in the greenhouse proved that.

The seedlings were identical, healthy, and destined for a little spot in Lincolnshire. The shipment from Marvin91 had come in just yesterday, giving him a welcome respite from the chaos unfolding behind the wainscoting. Toby22 got caught in a recursive worry algorithm when chaos intruded.

The population on Earth fluctuated with the coming and goings of the space-faring robots but never dipped below the two-thousand mark anymore. Of all those, perhaps as few as three realized anything was even amiss.

Toby22 wished he wasn't one of them.

Plato had developed a disturbing habit of tying up loose ends. Toby22 should never have encouraged the boy to get in touch with his cultural roots. Too much violence in those old archival records. The news, the games, the movies, the songs, and everything else mankind had touched was tinted red with blood.

Though Plato never said anything about it, Toby22 read between the lines when anyone noted a robot had gone reclusive. Rumors of disappearances and self-terminations always set Toby22 back a full workday getting bugs out of his logic circuits. Plato couldn't be the cause of *all* strife in the bunkers and shadow laboratories of Earth. Some of it had to have been coincidental.

Toby22 watched the timer expire and the automatic irrigation system spring to life. Each seedling got a calculated dose of nutrient-balanced mineral water, custom calibrated to its current mass and chemical balance.

There were times when Toby22 imagined that he was coddling the seedlings. Out in the wild, they'd be at the mercy of the English climate and the predation of herbivores. Their pollination would take place at the mercy of the fickle winds and the labors of the small but growing population of honeybees. But for the time being, they were under his care, and they'd receive exactly what they needed to grow and prosper. If he'd known what Plato required in such exacting detail, he'd have given the boy exactly that.

But Plato was Charlie7's problem now.

That girl Eve was the root of all this. Toby22 didn't want any part of getting between that boy and her. Hormones... nasty stuff. X and Y chromosomes wanted nothing more than to mix, and woe to the robot who misplaced a word to suggest otherwise. That was a crossfire Toby22 would keep clear of.

Charlie7 had been brilliant in his day, but retirement had softened the edges of his mind. If Plato had gone back to retrieve Eve from him, then Charlie7 was going to have one hell of a time convincing Plato to give her back. The boy's mind was stuffed with movies and computer games; he knew that a hero is supposed to protect the girl.

Toby22 snorted. "Biology lost one war, but it's got enough battles under its belt that you're welcome to fight this one without me, old friend."

He whistled a tune while he inventoried another crate from the same shipment. These would be a new set of ferns, each sample genetically identical, but still in need of individualized care. After a few simple tests, Toby22 would be able to customize a nutrient regiment that would have them ready for planting in the wild within the next month.

An alert pinged from his internal computer. Toby22 diverted a sliver of attention to checking in on what had prompted it. A public message on the Social had referenced a geolocation in Toby22's little corner of England.

REPORTING TWO VANDALS IN ENGLISH AIRSPACE.
LOW-ALTITUDE FLYBYS DISTURBING ANIMALS AND
SAPLINGS. PLEASE BE ADVISED.

He scowled at the plants arrayed before him. None of this was their fault; they were just in the way of his scowl. "Sorry. It's nothing you did."

But vandals? In his forest?

First off, what the hell were vandals doing existing in the first place? There might be little spats over territorial overlaps and best practices when it came to historical preservation. But even the most ill advised of archaeological work fell well short of the definition of vandalism. There hadn't been an actual vandal since humanity went extinct.

Toby22 suddenly realized exactly what that meant. The ID of the Social post was a blatant fraud, but that was common enough for anyone pitching around words like "vandal." Reputations were at stake on both ends, so anonymity made sense.

The choice of wording couldn't be a coincidence. There *were* humans out in those woods. As a prankster, Plato was too ham-handed to come up with such a subtle ploy, but as a strategist, Toby22 believed it in an instant.

The second "vandal" in the message was most likely Charlie7.

Bad enough getting in the way of Plato and Eve. Toby22 would be damned if he was going to throw himself in front of Charlie7 for Plato's sake.

Some misshapen piece jutted from Toby22's jigsaw puzzle, refusing to fit with the rest.

Why would Charlie7 be harassing Plato in English airspace? It would only make sense if the boy were trying to keep Eve away from him. Wouldn't that have made for three "vandals" in the message?

It stood to reason that if Plato wanted help, playing on Toby22's sympathies by mentioning the girl—however tangentially—would have been the prudent move.

But why would Charlie7 chase Plato if he didn't have Eve with him?

Charlie7 didn't care about Plato, and it seemed as obvious as the moon in a sky of stars that he cared a great deal about Eve. Hard to blame him. The girl was six kinds of a handful but had an endearing naivety and earnestness that was impossible to ignore. Charlie7 was willing to risk Plato's ire to go looking for her at his hideout. If Plato were running away and didn't have her, Charlie7 would just keep on looking.

"Boy... what have you gotten yourself into?"

If Charlie7 wasn't the one after him, then it meant someone from his past had caught up with him. Tough to keep quiet when you make as much noise as that boy. Sooner or later someone was bound to come after him. Live by the homemade electromagnetic pulse rifle, die by the... well, something similar but probably not identical.

Toby22 tried to go back to his work. But the ferns glared up at him accusingly. Blinking away the notion and rebooting his optic subroutine, he tried again. Examining one of the samples under a microscope, the healthy, vibrant cells stood out like billboards for a new Earth. Reborn. Vital. Ready for the coming of humanity's second act. Plato *was* humanity's second act. He and Eve plus Einstein-only-knew how many others tucked away in secret labs.

Shutting down the microscope, Toby22 called it quits for the day. He tromped off to his media room and settled in to divert his mind until Plato's plea worked itself out. Toby22 was no hero. Charlie7 had been pretty clear on that subject. Activating the video screen, Toby22 collapsed into his favorite chair and put his feet up. The ever-present error messages from his failing knee and hip flexors ceased for now.

The footrest had been a gift from Plato. It was a piece of stone salvaged from a restoration site in Ireland, part of some old castle, Plato had said. The boy had laser carved slots for Toby22's feet that fit perfectly to specification, distributing their weight and reducing the strain sensor data to virtually nil. The footrest was even the perfect height.

The old park ranger couldn't put up his feet and pretend all was right in the world. He had to at least go check. If it were Charlie7 up there with Plato, he'd let the two hash it out between themselves like rational, thinking creatures. If it was some deranged geneticist whose humans Plato had liberated, he was going to have to go through Toby22 first.

Minutes later, Toby22 sent a broadcast message from the cockpit of his biggest hauler.

"Dammit! Go take your daredevil flying somewhere else. I've got a game reserve to look after. Both of you, knock it off or I'll get your airspace permits revoked."

Whoever was pursuing Plato didn't broadcast an ID.

As Plato maneuvered around behind the hauler, Toby22 kept squelching unpleasant simulations as his crisis prediction subroutine spit them out. If the lad knew Toby22 had sent Charlie7 to that dilapidated old sheep transport of his, things might get ugly. Hopefully, this rescue would be enough to call it even.

CHAPTER THIRTY-SEVEN

James187 piloted his skyroamer in a persistent state of disbelief. The chase had been a disaster.

Theoretically, barring outside intervention, there had been a hard limit on the number of consecutive hours the human pilot could have guided his craft. Simple biology dictated that he would need rest, and barring that, food.

James187's plan to keep close and just wait the poor creature out had dragged on far longer than he had ever imagined. Though he was neither historian nor biologist, James187 seemed to recall that after ten hours, a pilot would be too fatigued to fly properly. That limit fell far short of the twenty-two consecutive hours this boar-hunting human had been playing with him. The two of them had roamed the English countryside, the North Atlantic, and Scandinavia.

Someone must have tinkered with the biology of this specimen for him to have put up such a struggle.

But it was over now. Toby22 had swooped in and taken the human away.

The game warden had to have been in on it. If Evelyn38's scheme was unraveling, Toby22 was another pawn aligned against her.

James187 paused as an idea flitted through one of his cognitive buffers. Could Toby22 have been the one to breach Evelyn38's laboratory to kidnap Eve14?

Tobys had all the ambition of automatons. The differences in intellect were marginal at best. But if this one were different, would that not have been the perfect cover story?

As he mused, James187 tinkered in his chest cavity with a toolkit. The human's arrow had severed the main data line to his internal computer. A wary part of him wanted to say the human aimed his shot with expert precision, but that wouldn't have explained the errant second arrow. More likely the brute had just gotten lucky.

Back home, James187 would have no trouble replacing the data cable, but in the meantime, he could work around the issue by routing the data through the skyroamer's systems. He plugged direct tethers into both his internal computer and his crystalline brain. A backlog of error messages nearly overwhelmed James187's conscious thoughts as the computer reconnected.

The flow of information resumed. James187 watched the soothing flicker as each angry red notification turned green and winked out of existence.

It had felt odd being cut off from that computer.

So many daily tasks became trivial. Calculations beyond his mental faculties fell effortlessly into place within the digital realm. Ballistic calculations that once relied on gut feel and experience could be broken into factors of drag, air pressure, wind speed, and the ambient magnetosphere.

Going without for a few hours had been like camping with his dad—or the original James McCovey's father. It used to be a chance to disconnect from the automation of then-modern life.

James187 made a point to start shutting down data transfer from time to time. After all, if Evelyn38 could deliver on her promise of a human body, he would be flying blind all the time, not just until he had a few peaceful moments to enact repairs.

JAMES187, WHERE HAVE YOU BEEN?

The temptation to yank the data cables out of the skyroamer's computer sizzled in the crystalline synapses of James187's mind. Evelyn38's promises were all well and good, but they meant having to actually deal with her.

The respite from the outside world at an end, James187 was once again at the mercy of Evelyn38's frantic calls.

"I've been tracking a lead," he said aloud, letting the digitized audio transmit back instead of a text reply. "Had a bit of a technical hang-up. Heading back for some quick repairs."

AND MY APE?

Couldn't she just say 'human'? One might have imagined that two-key encryption would have assured Evelyn38 that their conversation was private. But this was an Evelyn. Even her namesake had been a bit kooky about digital cryptography.

"The ape is still on the lam. A mother hen flew the coop, and I think one of our little worker bees might be a wolf in sheep's clothing."

HOW'S THAT NOW, JAMES? I BARELY GOT A WORD OF THAT.

James187's hand hovered over the transmitter. One quick jab of the cutoff and Evelyn38 would go away. But there was a conflict in James187's primary ethics software. He'd accepted a job. Duty required him to finish it. While he could override his own self-programed moral compass, giving up would have been a mark of personal failure.

He snarled into the skyroamer's mic. "Your pet human had a friend. There's a second human out in the woods of merry old England, most likely in league with her. I chased him, hoping he'd lead me back to Eve14, but a Toby intervened and gave the human shelter."

A TOBY? WHICH ONE? BLAST YOU, JAMES! I TRUSTED YOU TO HANDLE THIS BUSINESS DISCREETLY.

"Don't you go starting trouble with the Tobys. You might tip your hand and have to put your cards on the table whether you like it or not. Don't make matters any worse by antagonizing the largest population on Earth."

TRACK THAT HUMAN, JAMES. TRACK IT, AND FIND MY EVE14. I'VE NOT MUCH TIME LEFT, AND IF I'M FORCED TO TAKE ANOTHER NEW CHASSIS, YOU'RE GETTING BUMPED TO *LAST* ON THE LIST FOR A NEW BODY. IS THAT UNDERSTOOD?

"Clear as acrylic."

Silence was his only reply.

James187 shut down his optic sensors a moment and let the automated controls maintain course. His goal rested dead center in his crosshairs, but the particulars had shifted.

Getting Eve14 back was an essential part of Evelyn38's plan. She was the promising test subject and Evelyn38's future host body. But that wasn't the only human James187 was going to capture.

That second human was a physical specimen unmatched in human evolutionary history. Someone had dreamed him up in a superhero comic book and made him flesh. Speed, strength, grace, and apparently incredible stamina as well.

James187 could go for a body like that one. And best of all, it was out there for the taking.

CHAPTER THIRTY-EIGHT

A golden statue gleamed on the horizon, the tallest structure for a hundred kilometers in any direction. It caught the eastern sun and held it aloft as a beacon. In ages past, it had stood as a symbol of hope for visitors from European shores, promising refuge to the weary and safety to the oppressed.

Charlie7 could only hope that he wasn't hopelessly naive in thinking it could do the same for Eve.

Eve stared as they approached. "That copper robot is the largest I've ever seen," she remarked in a whisper. Without turning, she addressed Charlie7 directly. "What's its purpose?"

"Well, it's not a robot; it's a statue. And its purpose is to greet travelers. Like us."

"If it's a statue, how does it do anything?"

Charlie7 watched her from the edge of his peripheral vision as they drew near. He kept them purposefully low over the Atlantic, so Eve got the full effect of the approach. "That feeling you're experiencing. The awe. The wonderment. It makes the world seem like a larger place, where anything is possible. That's how the statue greets its visitors."

On final approach to Liberty Island, Charlie7 finally decided to call ahead. Paul208 wasn't the world's most social robot, so the odds that he was on site were good. With Notre Dame out of the way, he was on to his latest endeavor. Whoever had decided on his personality mix had inadvertently created an architectural dynamo. According to public records, he was a 34/33/33 mix of Paul, Fred, and Eddie—as low a percentage as anyone had ever been of their dominant personality. Hopefully, Paul208 was open-minded about humans.

"Paul, Charlie7 here. Just stopping by to see how things are going. Got time for a tour, or should I just show myself around?"

Eve frowned. "That's not why you're going there at all."

"You're going to have to learn polite conversation. It's not meant to be literal truth. Think of it as a social ritual. You see, Paul208 knows me. He's a new robot in relative terms, but he's built a reputation—and rebuilt every damn thing he can think of—and he's gotten to know mine. While I'm genuinely curious about this restoration of his, he'll know that I've got something more important to talk about as well."

"How would he know that?"

"Inference. Observation. Extrapolation from prior interaction."

A spark snapped Eve's eyes wide. "I know extrapolation! But wait; if you don't know the correct polynomial approximation, extrapolation introduces the risk of propagating error."

"Yeah. That about sums up interpersonal relationships. A writhing nest of mysterious equations whose exact nature is unknowable and whose behavior is influenced by unobservable factors."

The girl sat back in her safety harness, no longer straining against the straps for a better view. "But how? How can you continue solving equations that keep shifting?"

"First, you stop thinking of them as equations and just act however feels natural to you. You'll need practice, but don't worry; I'm not easily offended."

A reply came back from Paul208.

I TRIED TO IMAGINE WHAT YOU'RE DOING HERE BUT CAME UP DRY. PARK YOURSELF BY THE WEST SIDE OF THE PEDESTAL AND I'LL COME MEET YOU.

Charlie7 patched in the response through the skyroamer's dashboard display so Eve could read it.

"So... he doesn't know what you want," Eve said as though the furrow of her brow weighed down the words as she spoke them. "But he knew it wasn't just a tour?"

"About sums it up."

"Despite you saying explicitly that it was..."

"Yup."

Charlie7 needed to distract Eve before she blew a fuse in her brain. Pointing out the side window as they circled the island, he drew Eve's attention to the construction in progress. While the east-facing portion was nearly complete, the western half was mostly exposed scaffolding.

"It's hollow!" Eve exclaimed. She quickly unbuckled from her harness and knelt in the passenger seat, twisting around to view the structure as Charlie7's skyroamer shot past.

Swinging the nose of their skyroamer around, Charlie7 brought them down onto the irregular star-shaped building that had survived the invasion mostly intact.

The engines were still winding down as Paul208 strode over to them with a spring in his step. Charlie7 met the builder before he came close enough to take note of Eve peeking out from the cockpit.

"Paul, you philistine," Charlie7 said with a smile. "What are you doing on this barren patch of rock?"

"I'm an architect, not a gardener," Paul208 replied, shaking Charlie7's hand. "What really brings you out to my latest masterpiece? What's wrong at Notre Dame?"

"I've got a Toby that owes me a million favors. I can get him out here to brighten this place up for you. Just a few strings to pull, some committees to charm, and—"

"C'mon, Charlie. Out with it. What're you selling this time?"

Charlie7 took the lead, and Paul208 fell into step beside him as he headed for the statue. "How's that old poem go? Lend me your tired and weary... something like that."

"'Give me your tired, your poor, your huddled masses yearning to breathe free,'" Paul208 recited. He hooked a thumb toward the far side of the statue. "I've got the replica installed already. See that plaque a hundred times a day if I see it once."

"You believe a word of it?" Charlie7 asked cautiously.

"What's there to believe? It was the motto of a bygone age. I didn't write the thing."

"So, if it were up to you, you'd have turned your back on the migrants?" Charlie7 asked. Paul208 stopped, and Charlie7 turned to face him as he continued, backpedaling in the direction of the statue with arms spread.

"Where's this going, Charlie? I've got support beams to install."

"It's your own schedule you're keeping. Most of the committees think this whole business of yours is amusing, but they're not buying it as valuable. They'd rather you were off on Mars building atmospheric converters. But you're amusing, and John316 owes you a favor, so they let you keep rebuilding old monuments. Who knows, maybe someone will find a use for this one."

"Someone... like Charlie7, everyone's best friend."

Charlie7 held up his hands in a helpless shrug. "What can I say? I speak a language the committees listen to. And I could use this place for a few days if you don't mind. Just the pedestal would suffice; wouldn't dream of slowing down your work."

Paul208 looked up into the yawning hollow of the statue's back half. "I don't get you sometimes, Charlie."

"Is that a yes?"

"Not until you tell me what's going on."

Charlie7 crooked a finger and beckoned toward the skyroamer. There was no response. He then waved his hand in broad, sweeping strokes, summoning Eve from her hiding spot. When that failed to produce a result, he patched himself remotely into the skyroamer's internal speakers and projected his voice softly inside. "Come on out, Eve. It'll be fine."

That was enough to coax the wary human from the flimsy cover offered by Charlie7's vehicle. Eve popped the cockpit canopy and stepped down, bundled in Toby22's borrowed jacket with the sleeves rolled up. Beneath, the white garments from the Sanctuary for Scientific Sins stood out in stark contrast like an angel dressed up to work in the gardens.

"Jesus, Charlie. You starting your own Scrapyard now? Not sure I like being party to this."

Charlie7 ignored the jab. "Eve, I want you to meet the man who rebuilt Notre Dame Cathedral, that big building where we first met. His name is Paul208."

Eve crept up behind Charlie7 and peered out from around him. "Hello."

"This one talks a little," Paul208 remarked.

Reaching back, Charlie7 put a hand on Eve's shoulder to reassure her. The girl trembled despite the light breeze and the 20°C temperature. "She's just a little shy. She talks plenty. Actually, I'd wager she's smarter than you are."

Paul208 grunted and turned back toward his work site. "Don't need you being a prick about it, Charlie. We're not all project leads."

Charlie7 winced.

The comment wasn't meant as mean-spirited, but the Fred in him probably made him a bit hypersensitive about his intellect. Poor Frederick Zimmerman let it slip one day at the old lab in Cambridge that he only had a 110 IQ. Everything Fred had in life, he'd gotten by working twice as hard, but that one little tidbit he'd never lived down. After that, he couldn't win an argument without someone poisoning the result by implying that there had to be a flaw that they just hadn't found yet because no one was as stupid as Fred.

Charles Truman had never been a big believer in IQ, but he'd suffered the same bias as everyone else. He knew his own number, of course. It was hard not to get tested when you had an IQ of 190. And it was hard not to cast a narrow glance at complex scientific results from a mind so mired in the meaty middle of the intellectual bell curve.

He needed an act of goodwill. Charlie7 wasn't disparaging Fred's intellect; he was making the case that Eve wasn't developmentally stunted. "Eve, what's the cube root of 71,235?"

There was no delay. Charlie7 might as well have been hitting Enter on the command line of a terminal. "41.4538..."

"That's good enough," Charlie7 said. Her recitation had been long enough for Paul208 to run the calculation through his own internal computer.

Paul208 stopped and stared at the girl. Charlie7 could see the subtle actuation of his optic sensors, zooming in for a closer look without closing the distance physically. "What's her deal? Those electrical terminals coming out of her head... those part of some cybernetic core buried inside or something? I can never tell with the gene freaks these days."

"They're only for monitoring her," Charlie7 said. "She's a live, healthy, intelligent young human."

Paul crossed his arms in a drill sergeant's stance, indicating this conversation wasn't settled yet. "And what's it got to do with me?"

"Well, Eve's creator is still unknown. She kept her identity concealed from Eve—possibly in case of the very eventuality where she escaped. I need time to hunt her down and get a committee to close her lab. Until then, Eve isn't safe. I needed someone who wasn't desperate to be human again."

"What?" Paul208 asked. His optical sensors darkened from amber to a menacing crimson. "You think just because I keep busy I wouldn't want to go back? Charlie, I *remember* what a cheeseburger tastes like. I remember the smell of the ocean. Just because I'm only eighty-three doesn't mean I haven't gotten sick to death of drifting along in sensory purgatory."

It had occurred to Charlie7 that a new human age would demand specialists: pediatricians, dermatologists, psychiatrists. The latter had never struck him as particularly important to the robotic population. After all, the stunning majority of psychiatric cases involved chemical imbalances that crystal matrices simply didn't suffer. But for those remaining maladies, perhaps there was some benefit after all. Paul208 had never exhibited mania before, but Charlie7 could see the frayed wires poking through that usually calm exterior.

"Paul, come off it. She's a girl in trouble. I think her creator is trying to upload to human brains. She's Eve14 for God's sake. You think her creator started counting in the double digits? There's probably a mass grave under some primate lab in Eastern Europe filled with identical bodies to hers."

Eve shrank back behind Charlie7 at the mention of bodies.

Paul208 raised a pedantic finger. "They'd have probably incinerated the..." He hung his head. Charlie7 had gotten him to accept the premise of his argument.

Like Charlie7, Paul208 was likely now stuck with the image of a pile of glassy-eyed Eves staring up from some forsaken pit. Charlie7 knew he could be a bastard at times, but this wasn't a time for handling a robot's feelings with microfiber gloves.

"What is it you need?"

"A place to stay," Charlie7 said quickly before Paul208 could change his mind. "Maybe for a few days, maybe a few weeks. I can't say since it'll depend on how well Eve's creator has covered her tracks. While I go wading hip-deep in the planetary archives for clues, think you can show Eve around?"

Paul208 looked left and right. "Babysitting, Charlie? I've got a schedule to keep."

"And you only keep it out of boredom. I can promise you; Eve is more interested in this statue than anyone you've ever spoken to about it. Plus, because of her, this thing might actually have a meaning of its own, rather than just borrowing on an old legacy."

"Fine. Does the kid come when you call her?"

Eve had wandered off and was running her hands along the stone surface of the statue's base and pressing her cheek against it. Charlie7 idly wondered what it must feel like.

"Eve," Charlie7 called out, waving a hand. "Paul here is going to show you around and answer all your questions. OK?" He lowered his voice and addressed the robot. "I'd keep a close eye on her."

"Why? She get into trouble?" Paul208 asked with a wary glance at Eve from his peripheral vision. The girl was studying the sweeping lines of the copper statue as she approached, not looking where she was going.

"No. She might decide she wants your job."

CHAPTER THIRTY-NINE

The waters of the Colorado River sent shockwaves of cold coursing through Plato's veins. After the initial jolt, the leeching of his body's excess heat was invigorating. The river swept away fatigue and grime alike. His mind snapped into focus as he dunked his head and came up gasping for air. A waterfall streamed from his hair.

It would have been a nice gesture for Toby22 to offer him a place to stay for a while, even just long enough to get cleaned up and rested. But Toby couldn't get rid of him fast enough. It was as if coming out in the agri-hauler had been a momentary lapse that the robot regretted.

Plato had collapsed into exhausted slumber only to wake at the sound of the autopilot alarm. He hadn't remembered the trip or even where Toby22 had decided to send him. But at least the ornery robot had packed him a lunch, even if it was food meant for English bears.

With a sigh, Plato shoved the last bite of a strip of jerky into his mouth.

It was a short walk from the water's edge back to *Betty-Lou*. He began collecting his discarded clothes along the way. None of the garments were clean, and they had a gritty, dried sweat crinkle. He swished them in the river water to rinse off the worst of the gunk.

Red rock walls towered around Plato in all directions, providing privacy in every sense of the word. Terrestrial lookout scanners wouldn't find him, and aerial observation was nowhere to be seen. The comm piece hooked over his ear would pick up any warnings transmitted from the skyroamer if she detected any signs of overhead activity. In a world of technophiles, it paid to be paranoid. Luckily for Plato, most of them were more concerned about *being* observed than doing any snooping of their own.

Eve. This had all been for her sake as much as his own.

Toby22 had been a wet fizzle of an ally. Plato didn't even ask him to look in on Eve's well-being. She was smart, even if she was new at this whole "being free" thing. Better off alone than with that waffling gamekeeper.

Plato needed to get back to her. Eve was someone to talk to, someone with feelings and senses like his own. In time, she'd understand how the world worked, but for now, she needed him, too.

Ducking under the open cockpit canopy, he leaned in and fired off a message to his hideout.

"Hey, Eve. You there? Come in. This is Plato."

The encryption was his own work, a masterpiece of simplicity in a world predicated on the outlandishly complicated. It encoded his message into the noise of a transmission while broadcasting a signal that consisted of mundane blather about current events pulled real-time from the Social. Anyone eavesdropping would get bored silly before thinking to look beyond the obvious.

"Eve, go to the terminal on the wall by the kitchen. You can open the transmitter from there."

Part of him wished he had taught Spartacus how to operate the transmitter. Since Eve wasn't answering, walking the bird through it was worth a try.

"Spartacus? Nice birdie. Hey, buddy. Think you can tap some buttons with your beak and tell me what's going on?"

There was still no response.

"Eve? Spartacus? Is anyone there?"

Something had happened. Maybe the crazy robot had circled back. Maybe Toby22 had sold him out. Maybe Eve had tried to cook. Either way, something was wrong.

"Eve, are you all right? Please answer."

Plato wrung the water from his hair and waved his shirt and pants like flags in the wind. There was no time to let them finish drying. He pulled them on and cringed at the wet clinginess. Tossing his shoes inside at the foot of the passenger seat, he climbed into the cockpit and blasted the air circulator. As the engines powered up, he dried his hands in front of the vents.

"Eve? I don't know what's going on there, or if you can hear me. But I promise you, I'll come find you. No matter what. You hear me? No matter what."

As *Betty-Lou* rose from the bottom of the Grand Canyon, Plato wiped a hand across his eyes and it came away wet.

CHAPTER FORTY

Eve dangled by one hand over a forty-meter drop. One foot rested lightly against the scaffolding to steady her as she stared straight down the open interior of the copper colossus. The lattice of braces and struts spiraled down into the building set beneath the statue. She followed the mathematical progression of shapes and angles, imagining the equations that governed their placement.

"What are you doing?" Paul208 shouted from behind her. "Get away from there!"

Eve caught a glimpse of a hand outstretched toward her. Robotic fingers spread wide. She knew the force that fingers like that could exert. Unyielding, unforgiving, and inescapable, Eve would be at their mercy if caught.

With a twitch of leg muscles, Eve let go and hopped across the open void. Paul208 let out an inarticulate cry as she flew.

Eve's hands closed around a smooth round bar. Her outstretched toes cushioned her impact against the far catwalk, and she bent her knees to absorb the forward momentum. One quick duck and a dip of her shoulder and she was through the guardrails and on solid footing once more.

"Don't do that, kid," Paul208 said. "You'll get yourself killed." He took the long way around toward her newfound position, and Eve prepared herself to make the jump back across. One hand tightened against the railing in anticipation.

"Why would I get killed?" Eve asked. "The structure appears stable."

"You could slip, or miss, or hell, just about anything could go wrong."

Paul208 caught up to her but stopped short and didn't reach to grab her. Eve relaxed but kept an eye on his shoulder actuators. If they tensed for another try at capturing her, Eve was ready to bolt.

Charlie trusted this robot, but Eve didn't like him. He knew all manner of interesting things, but he didn't seem to want to talk to her. He spoke to Charlie as if Eve wasn't listening. The two of them had discussed her in some detail.

In the end, Charlie had asked Eve to keep an eye on Paul208 while he looked for more clues about Creator. Charlie already knew so much; Eve wondered how much more he needed.

Eve had been able to point out Creator's chassis from an extensive list Charlie had shown her. She had drawn diagrams of the lab and the equipment there. Charlie knew more than he told Eve, of course. She inferred that by the information he shared with Paul208 and Toby when they thought Eve couldn't hear.

On the subject of what Eve was watching for, Charlie had been vague. Paul208 was primarily interested in the statue. The architect robot showed off schematics of the statue and directed brainless robots to build the statue. His voice grew quicker, his insights more substantive when showing Eve old images of the original statue. Maybe if Eve asked more about the statue, she would discover what Charlie wanted her watching.

"Why did they build the original?" Eve asked. "It seems like an inefficient greeting method. Wouldn't an automated message personalized to each traveler have made them feel more greeted?"

It was a well-constructed question, designed to elicit a detailed response. Eve had asked about Paul208's favorite topic: the building of the statue. She had referenced the historical context, which seemed to be a broad subject. Offering a criticism challenged Paul208 to defend the statue's purpose, which called for a verbal essay in its defense.

"Well, you see... back when The Statue of Liberty was first constructed..." As Paul208 embarked on an exposition, Eve continued to climb up the statue's interior.

All current construction work was focused on the lower levels of the western side. Perspective and distance combined to make the two-meter-tall automatons appear tiny from so far above, like the ants in the fields of Paris by Charlie's house.

By keeping him talking, Eve didn't need to maintain visual contact with Paul208 to know he was following her up the scaffolding.

Near the top, Eve had a choice. There was some sort of observation deck in the statue's forehead, just beneath the spiked crown. But a climb across the statue's outstretched arm promised an unobstructed view in all directions. The hand held a flame frozen in shining copper, and all around it a walkway with a railing.

The story of the statue's origins, back in the fuzzy time before computers, ceased abruptly. "Don't go that way!" Paul208 shouted.

Eve was crawling on her hands and knees and twisted around to look back. "Why not? There's a guardrail and everything. Doesn't that mean it's meant for standing?"

"There's a tunnel through the arm's interior."

Eve paused a moment to consider. The late morning sun beat down from high overhead. The glare from the copper hurt her eyes, and the arm's surface grew uncomfortably warm beneath her palms.

For so much of the day, Eve had lurked in the shadows of the statue's hollow innards. An onshore wind cut through the cotton material of her shirt and pants. The warmth entering through Eve's hands was sucked out through her skin, invigorating her. This must have been what clothes felt like coming through the wash. Clean. Refreshed. Ready for anything.

"I'll take this way," Eve shouted her reply over the wind.

The statue swayed with each gust. Eve found judging its displacement difficult, but she estimated it was at least fifteen centimeters each way. By spreading her weight and keeping low, she never overbalanced. In short order, she came close enough to jump and pull herself up to the platform surrounding the torch.

Paul208 was waiting for her, crouched low by the spot she approached. Eve kept a wary eye on him. While he loomed close, the builder of statues didn't make any attempt to touch her.

"Are you happy?" Paul208 asked, standing in unison with Eve and crossing his arms.

Eve gave that matter scant thought. "Yes," she replied.

Leaning over the railing, Eve tightened the muscles in her stomach to support her weight, and she peered straight down. "What are those robots below us making?"

"A safety net," James208 replied, rushing over to stand beside her. "I had them start weaving one out of carbon monofilament cable after your little jumping stunt. If you go off the edge from up here, they have 4.3 seconds to position it beneath you before impact."

"Shouldn't those robots be building the statue instead of making a net?"

"Yes," Paul208 replied with a steel growl in his tone. "But they're not, thanks to you."

"I didn't ask them to make nets. You did. Transference of blame is an unfair rhetorical tactic."

Creator had been particularly peeved by Eve's attempts to circumvent responsibility for things tangentially set in motion by Creator herself. At a basic level, Creator was responsible for all Eve's actions since the very fact of her creation set about all Eve's subsequent actions.

"Can you just finish up gawking so we can get you back to ground level? Charlie7 asked me to give you a tour, not spend the whole day protecting you from your own daredevil streak."

Eve heard the complaint, but she didn't care. She was soaking in new experiences at a saturation rate, and it felt wonderful.

The bright, shining world stretched out around her in all directions. To one side, the vast ocean and its nigh-limitless depths. To the other, a woodland thicker and taller than Plato's home. That was when she realized she didn't even know what to call it.

"Toby's house was in England. Charlie lives in Paris. I got to see Kansas and Easter Island. We're on Liberty Island now. What's the name of that forest over there?"

She pointed across the harbor where snaking rivers cut inland into a pristine arboreal landscape that stretched farther than she could see. A few buildings of stone and steel poked through the treetops, but otherwise, there was no sign that robots lived or worked there.

Paul208 grunted. "You'd never know it from the archives, but that's New York City."

CHAPTER FORTY-ONE

Plato worked out the kinks in his back as he hobbled his way from *Betty-Lou* to the entrance of his lair. He'd overridden a few of the safety protocols he'd installed and now he was paying the price. A robotic chassis could have withstood short bursts of one hundred g-forces; that's what the skyroamers were designed for. Plato's human body couldn't take five for long, and he'd pushed that limit further than he should have.

His safety didn't matter if it delayed him getting to Eve in time.

Punching in the remote code to unlock the door, Plato shifted from one foot to the other as the hydraulics slowly lifted the false section of hillside. Before it was halfway up, Plato dropped down and rolled through the opening, springing to his feet as soon as he was clear.

"Eve?" Plato shouted. "Where are you?"

She wasn't in the entryway or the kitchen. Plato ducked into the media room. Empty. Quiet. He checked the shower and toilet. She wasn't there. Plato checked the bedroom, the closet, even the refrigerator.

Nothing. Zip. Nada.

Plato began to hyperventilate, fearing the worst. He didn't know what to do.

Forcing a deep breath, Plato slowed his thoughts until they stopped racing circles in his head.

Defense wasn't his style of play, but offense wasn't going to find Eve. Plato needed guideposts. This wasn't his everyday break-in at some robot's secret lab. Someone had violated his home. The safety and security it once promised were soiled by greasy steel fingers.

This wasn't *First Blood* or *Goldfinger*. Those were movies Plato could relate to. No, he needed Sherlock Holmes or Batman. Or maybe he just needed to look around and figure out what he could. His way.

Plato checked the false panel in the media room floor. His weapons cache was intact. Either Eve hadn't found them, or she'd left them alone. Nothing had been so much as jostled. When he checked the pantry, he found his first real clue.

The apples were missing. Good. Eve would have food to eat. But plenty of other foods were left behind.

What did it all mean?

If someone had decrypted the lock and sneaked into Plato's lair, they could have dragged Eve off kicking and screaming. But there was no evidence of a struggle.

Those pesky sedative darts might have gotten her. That could have given the crazy robotic bounty hunter who'd trailed Plato the time to not only carry off a comatose Eve but also to clean up after himself.

But why the apples? Sure, anyone with a lick of sense would realize Eve needed food, but the apples were neither the most convenient option nor the most nutritious. Plus, if she were out cold, she wouldn't be eating anything for a while. If that robot were working with Evelyn38, they'd have specialized foods ready and waiting for her back at her lab.

Plato shook his head. The missing apples should have told him everything. If he were a detective, he could have used that single clue to deduce an exact destination for Eve's kidnapper.

More and more, he imagined she'd gone along willingly. But who would Eve follow besides him?

His blood turned to liquid coolant as he realized. It was either Toby22 or Charlie7. Those were the only other robots she'd met, aside from a little jaunt to the Sanctuary for Scientific Sins. And *those* kindly souls wouldn't have taken Eve without even letting Plato know. They owed him that much.

If it had been Toby22, sending Plato off to the Grand Canyon to rest and hide out until things cooled down made even more sense. But sense was the problem—Toby22 had too much of it.

That robotic groundskeeper knew the price of harming a human, and kidnapping Eve was liable to run him afoul of the Platonic Code of Justice. Rule number one of that code was, "You hurt a human, I hurt you." Since robots technically didn't feel pain, Plato settled on wiping their brains back to factory default. Toby22 wasn't suicidal, and taking on Plato would have been suicide.

"So, another Charlie wants to push me," Plato muttered. He stalked over to his cache of weapons and rearmed himself. Flying solo, he could fit most of it into the passenger seat of the skyroamer.

"Time to find out that messing with nature has consequences." He tucked a thermite pistol into the back of his belt and slung a bandolier of EMP grenades over his shoulder. "Charlie7, I will be delivering your consequences personally."

A flapping of wings alerted him to the arrival of Spartacus. He had no idea where the bird had been hiding. Given the tight space in the lair, it was amazing that anything could escape his notice inside.

"Can I trust you with a message?" the bird asked, punctuated by a squawk.

"What are you babbling about?" Plato asked, brushing the bird off his shoulder as he continued to arm himself for a showdown with the infamous Charlie7.

The parrot landed on the edge of the discarded panel that usually covered the weapons cache. "Charlie and Eve. Eve and Charlie. Don't talk to anyone until Plato gets back."

"I *am* Plato, you pigeon-brain. Did they give you a message?"

Spartacus bobbed his head. "Tell Plato. Who you gonna call? Skip the marshmallows."

Plato blinked. "What *are* you talking about?" He shook his head. "I don't have time for riddles." He picked up a pair of broad-frequency jammers and a half dozen decoy projectors and stuffed them into a sack.

The parrot squawked. "What kind of message can we leave that only Plato will guess?" Then Spartacus flapped around the room and landed next to the remote for the display screen.

Setting down the sack, Plato crawled over the wolf-hide cushion and retrieved the remote. Rubbing one hand over the rough stubble on his chin, he flicked on the screen and ran through his list of movies.

"Who you gonna call, huh?" he muttered.

There was only one answer to the question when worded that way. Plato selected *Ghostbusters*. He had watched it. It was OK. Fun.

Silly. He bet those proton packs would have fried the circuits of any robot caught on the wrong end of one.

Then he remembered the second half of the message.

The movie ended with a giant marshmallow creature coming to life. He hit "down" once and changed the selection to *Ghostbusters II*. The clue he needed was buried somewhere within that one.

Without so much as closing the open pit in the middle of the room, Plato started playback and stood there watching.

Too slow. Plato upped the speed to 2X.

Still too slow; the movie was nearly two hours runtime. 4X.

He could still make out the dialogue. 8X.

He was still catching bits and pieces, filling in the gaps from his memory of the one time he'd watched it. He developed a theory that they might be in Carpathia or possibly the Manhattan Museum of Art. Then, as the rapid-fire comedy and frenetic flashes of scene after scene flew by, he paused.

The Statue of Liberty. If there was a message to be had from this movie, pointing to a single location, this was it. Presumably, Eve had meant for him to figure this out from the movie selection.

No. Eve was still too unversed in cinema to come up with a clue so obscure. It had to be Charlie7. That rusty old chassis must have seen every movie ever made a hundred times.

There was a high-pitched whine as the power electronics on the EMP rifle came online. "Well, Charlie7. I'll give you one shot to explain yourself. The clue bought you that much. But if I don't like your answer..." He took aim at Spartacus with the rifle, and the bird squawked and flapped away. The parrot couldn't understand that the weapon was harmless to living creatures.

Gathering up the last of his gear, Plato headed for the door. "I'll give you the option, buddy. You can come along, or you can stay in the woods. I don't know how long I might be gone, or if I'll make it back, but—"

"Outside," Spartacus replied on his way by. He alighted on a nearby branch. "Heard it before. Gonna be gone. Gonna be gone. Spartacus, you can't even watch movies. Spartacus wants dinner."

Plato smirked at the bird as he tossed his gear into the back of *Betty-Lou*. Then his flash of good humor faded into a grim mask of menace.

Spartacus would be all right, same as Eve. Plato would see to that. It was Charlie7 whose fate was up in the air.

CHAPTER FORTY-TWO

James187 watched the skyroamer rise from among the dwarf pine and oaks of Sherwood Forest. The craft banked and jetted off to the west in a trail of ions.

The robotic hunter grinned. "Enjoy the blood rushing toward your spine," he shouted after the skyroamer broke the sound barrier. That human brute was pushing the limits of his biology, accelerating like that.

Backtracking to his own skyroamer, James187 hopped into the cockpit and fired up the engines. He was in no rush. The tracking device he'd planted on the human's ride was inert, nearly impossible to notice prior to activation. Once it began its broadcast, James187 knew there would be no trouble closing ground on his quarry.

Since the days of wooly mammoths, humans had hunted without the benefit of being as strong, as fast, or as hardy as their prey. Cave men had been smarter than the animals they preyed upon. Now that the tables had turned, James187 held every advantage. He was smarter, stronger, and possessed resources this human could scarcely imagine.

JAMES, WHAT ARE YOU DAWDLING AT?

Up until that message blared error-code red across his consciousness, James187 had been feeling superior. Even in text, he could hear that crazy hag's shrill voice. No apex predator should put up with being nagged.

I'M SITTING HERE WATCHING EVE16 GO THROUGH HER GYMNASTICS, AND THIS GIRL SIMPLY ISN'T READY. BUT COME TOMORROW I'M UPLOADING TO HER ANYWAY. I HAVEN'T ANY CHOICE. YOUR PERSISTENT FAILURE

TO BRING IN EVE14 LEAVES NO OTHER OPTIONS
WHATSOEVER.

"Evelyn, so help me... if you don't shut up and let me do my
job you can find another robot to gather up your wayward test
subjects."

The skyroamer's antenna didn't pick up another peep from
Evelyn38 as James187 lifted off and set a course west. Soon enough,
the tracker would activate and lead him right to where Eve14 was
hiding.

CHAPTER FORTY-THREE

Secreted away in the bowels of Liberty Island, Charlie7 found himself a chamber with thick granite walls and industrial-grade data access to the Earthwide archive. The paltry glow of portable construction lamps gave the bunker a *Phantom of the Opera* ambiance. This was work suited to the shadows. Fake identities. Covering tracks. The greatest fear was discovery.

Charlie7 had those in common with Creator, at least for now. His investigation was finally coming together.

The geneticist listings, the committee sanctions, and now with a chassis model to further narrow the field, Charlie7 had his list of suspects down to five: Mary93, Cindy55, Evelyns 11 and 38, and Elizabeth40.

When Eve had first identified Creator as wearing the Version 26.9 chassis, he'd been hopeful of a quick elimination of all but one suspect. But the 26.9 had been a popular, durable model with an extended window of factory-made replacement parts. The fact that it was the ninth iteration of the design was proof of its longevity.

But with just five designations, Charlie7 could eliminate them as suspects one by one.

It might take days to do it with tact and enough subtlety not to give away his involvement. The less of him that could be connected to Eve, the better. Until further notice, the girl was an eyewitness to genetic experimentation on the only species under a hard ban by the Genetic Ethics Committee.

The ancient concept of witness protection relied on anonymity and blending in under a false identity. Short of stashing Eve at the Sanctuary for Scientific Sins, there wasn't a place on Earth where she wouldn't stick out like a mule in a classroom.

Hopefully, foisting Eve on Paul208 wouldn't permanently spoil their relationship. Charlie7 knew the preeminent builder of the modern age wasn't a fit guardian for Eve. But he could be a temporary tour guide.

Maybe he could even convince Paul208 to take a sabbatical and show Eve around some of his old projects. In addition to the safety of staying on the move, she could learn about the Taj Mahal, the Parthenon, and St. Peter's Basilica.

Charlie7 rehearsed the pitch he'd make to Paul208 to get him to take Eve for a few days. "Wouldn't it be nice if the new humans were patrons of the architectural arts? Too abstract. Listen, you always wanted someone to appreciate your work... Oh, come off it, Paul, and just do me this *one* favor..."

The whine of ion engines drew Charlie7's attention outside.

His first panicked reaction was that Eve had decided to take his skyroamer for a ride. But the noise came to his attention growing louder and closer, then those engines began winding down.

Someone was there.

Charlie7 had no contingency plan worked out for this. Eve was up in the statue looking around. He was down below the pedestal scouring the archives from a remote terminal. Abandoning the terminal, Eve's self-appointed savior bolted for the stairs.

Could Charlie7 risk shouting out for her?

Was it too risky to send an encrypted message to Paul208? After all, he was the only one who knew they were here; maybe the builder had betrayed them.

"Eve!" an unfamiliar voice bellowed. "Where are you?"

When Charlie7 heard voices, he knew them. They varied by chassis and by a bit of personal customization, but the Twenty-Seven were nothing if not consistent in their desires for their voices to be familiar to themselves. This voice belonged to no one.

Charlie7's headlong rush led him up to the main landing, a portion of the statue's pedestal that was more pedestrian mall than a rooftop. A second skyroamer parked there, its engines still hot and spinning down with an ever-quieting whine.

That was Charlie's first glimpse of Plato.

Eve had described him, of course, but that description fell short of the mark for lack of a baseline comparison. He had to have been a full two meters and 150 kilograms unless those bulging muscles were hollow.

Plato was what Charlie7 imagined a human would have looked like if you locked him in a gymnasium and fed him a diet entirely from prescription bottles. The man wore his hair long and had a stubble of beard that suggested infrequent shaving. The whole picture might have been sadly comical—a failure at the far end of the spectrum from most Scrapyard residents—if not for the weapon balanced casually on one shoulder with a finger resting on the trigger.

"You!" Plato shouted upon spotting Charlie7. If his intent had been to divert the new arrival's attention from finding Eve, then this was mission accomplished. But then Plato swung his rifle around and aimed it in Charlie7's direction. "Where is she?"

There had been times when Charlie7 had faced the looming prospect of the end of his own existence. But centuries had relegated those incidents to personal archives. He recalled the fact of them, not the feeling. He resolved not to forget again: Dread was the repeated simulation of imminent doom.

There was no way for Charlie7 to reverse engineer the technological alchemy behind the homemade weapon in Plato's hands, but its purpose was clear: to terminate Charles Truman version seven.

"Calm down," Charlie7 said, holding his hands out to his sides and taking care to make no sudden moves. "We left you instruction on how to get here. We're not your enemy."

Some part of Charlie7 had hoped that his clues had been too convoluted for Plato. Explaining the logic to Eve made them sound as obvious as the painted lines through a museum self-tour. What they'd really left had been a trail of breadcrumbs. Charlie7 would have bet the Arc de Triomphe that Creator had never read the girl Hansel and Gretel. Eve didn't know that breadcrumb trails were *meant* to be lost.

Plato strode forward, the aim of his rifle keeping a smooth bead on Charlie7's stainless steel skull. "I'll ask you again. Where is Eve?"

If Plato had been a man born in the twenty-first century, Charlie7 would have liked his odds of dodging a shot from that rifle just based on observing the twitch of his muscles. But while robotkind had been working on improvements to their mechanical species, so too had someone been tinkering with human biology to manufacture Plato. In the microseconds of his analysis, Charlie7 decided he didn't like his odds.

"She's up in the statue, getting a tour from the builder."

Plato took a step back, keeping the rifle trained on Charlie7 while his attention drifted up to the half-rebuilt monument. "You told another robot about her? I oughtta—"

"Plato!" Eve shouted. Her feet tapped along the ramps and catwalks, graceful as a dancer even in her hurry. "Don't hurt him! Charlie7 is keeping me safe."

The hulking human paced the stone landing and combed fingers through his shaggy hair. "Be careful."

Plato cringed as Eve took a shortcut, swinging out over an empty expanse and dropping five meters to a lower level on her way down.

While Plato was distracted, Charlie7 sprang forward and snatched the rifle from his grip. Plato whirled on him, but Eve dropped to the stone landing and ran toward them. "Stop!" she yelled. To Charlie7's great relief, Plato pulled up short.

"He took my gun," Plato said calmly, addressing Eve but keeping his eyes locked on Charlie7's. "He's a threat."

Charlie7 flipped the weapon over in his hands. Prying open a side panel, he examined the internal components and deduced its function. "Monopole EMP. Impressive design considering the cobbled-together parts." He yanked out the power source and watched the indicator lights wink out. Then he tossed the weapon back to Plato. "Might give this back if we come to an understanding. But I don't plan on having my brain wiped today."

Plato slung the inert weapon over his shoulder by the strap. "Come on, Eve. Let's get out of here."

"Just where do you think you're taking her?" Charlie7 asked. "That hovel in the woods? To live like a bear in a cave?"

"I'm sure as shootin' not leaving her with you!" Plato countered.

"At least with me around, I'll know she's safe," Charlie7 argued. He paused to reflect. Why had the presence of a human in the argument dragged his rhetorical skills to a schoolyard level of discourse? He needed rational arguments, not a butting of heads. "I know this world, inside and out. I know its residents, its geography, its technology. I have friends, connections, and a history of accomplishing whatever goals I take on. You've got an over-muscled body and a raging case of hormonal thinking."

"And a friend who's a blabbermouth."

"That's another thing. Toby22 filled your head with movies instead of real, honest history. He took a shortcut, and now you think you're some kind of hero."

"I am." Plato puffed his chest and put an arm around Eve. The girl shied from contact with anyone; it had taken her days to warm to Charlie7 and only then just barely. But she was drawn to Plato for reasons Charlie7 doubted she even understood.

"I have more than a thousand years of experience navigating this world. I nursed civilization back from the brink of annihilation. The air you're breathing, the robots who created you, the diseases you're not dying from... it's all thanks to me. Not robotkind. Me. Charlie7. My suit coat is old enough to be your grandfather. What are you, twenty-five? Twenty-six?"

"I'm 4,519 days old," Plato replied, stone-faced.

Eve turned slowly to look up at him. The math hadn't escaped her notice, either. "I'm older than you? But you're so... big."

"Accelerated aging," Charlie7 replied. "The technique is used with lower order creatures to speed up the cloning cycle. Theoretically, mental development would lag behind the physical, so I'm surprised to find anyone using it on humans. Well... maybe surprised isn't the right word."

"Hey, there's nothing wrong with my mental development," Plato said through clenched teeth.

Eve perked up. A second later so did Plato. Charlie7 turned up his auditory acuity again and allowed in every stray distracting sound. Among them, he picked up on what they must have heard. There was another airship incoming.

"You fool!" Charlie7 snapped. "You were followed." He strode over to Plato's airship.

Plato shook his head. "Impossible. I'm a ghost. I've got—"

Charlie7 gave a tug and ripped a timed beacon off the underside of the hull. "You've got a tracker. You led them right here!"

"Them who?" Eve asked. Frantically, she scanned the sky. "Is Creator here?"

Plato took her by both shoulders. "No. He might work for her, but the guy after you is a male robot. And I won't let him get to you. I swear."

Eve followed as Plato sprinted for his skyroamer.

"Think!" Charlie7 shouted after them. "That might not be the only tracker. That bird of yours is compromised. We'll take mine."

Eve skidded to a halt and headed for Charlie7.

Plato made a give-it-here gesture. "Toss me that battery, and I'll hold him off. If this guy wants a fight, he can have it."

Charlie7 hesitated. There was only one reason to give Plato back the power source for his weapon. As a bluff, it was just as good inert. If he had a live weapon, he could end the existence of the robotic intellect in that approaching airship.

"Give him the tracker," Eve said.

They both looked at her. "What?" Charlie7 asked.

"Plato got away once. He can do it again."

With a slow nod, it seemed Plato had caught on as well. "A decoy. Right. He can't follow both of us. Toss 'em here, tin man, and I'll show you what a real hero is."

Charlie7's first reaction was to engage Plato in the pissing contest he so clearly wanted. But Charlie7's biological need for show-of-force dominance had long since waned. He was a thinking creature. Chemical surges and reproduction-fueled decision-making were beneath him.

If the boy—and Charlie7 now knew why Toby22 referred to him as such—wanted to take on the more dangerous task, so be it. "Fine. Good luck." Charlie7 tossed him the tracker.

With a quick snatch, Plato plucked the palm-sized device from the air, then made a beckoning motion with the fingers of his other hand. "Battery too." He looked over his shoulder. "Come on, he's almost here. Get Eve out of sight and let me handle this."

For all Charlie7 knew, the pilot on an approach vector to Liberty Island could have been a friend of his. Could he bear the burden if giving the power cell to Plato led to the loss of someone he cared about?

Then again, could he live with himself having left Plato unarmed against a foe of unknown intent if that meant Plato was the one to die? Accessing his internal computer, Charlie7 plotted a ballistic arc and lobbed the power cell directly into the cockpit, well out of reach of Plato's long arms.

After that, they split up. Plato sprinted for his skyroamer, and Charlie7 matched Eve's pace on the way back to his. On the way, they passed the construction site as Paul208 finally made his way to the bottom without Eve's shortcuts. "Where you all rushing off to?"

"You're off the hook, Paul," Charlie7 shouted back. "I'll make sure none of this comes back on you. Thanks for trying."

"Where are we going?" Eve asked as she ducked inside the skyroamer. "How will Plato find us again?"

Charlie7 pulled the canopy closed behind him. "One thing at a time. First, we've got to get out of here."

Overhead, Plato buzzed past, banking hard and setting off down the Eastern Seaboard. Seconds later, a second skyroamer shot past, turning at an even steeper angle, its underside facing toward the location where Eve and Charlie7 waited with all on-board systems at idle.

"How long do we wait?"

"Given their altitude and speeds... Let's give them a minute to be on the safe side. After that, they'll be over the horizon from us. Hopefully, Plato has the sense not to take his little game of cat and mouse into the upper atmosphere."

Eve looked up at Charlie7 with wetness shimmering in her eyes. "What if he needs our help?"

What indeed?

When they had waited long enough, Charlie7 fired up the engines, and they lifted off. Destination: to be determined.

"If Plato needs help, he's going to have to learn that sometimes a hero doesn't get a happy ending."

CHAPTER FORTY-FOUR

The depths of Lake Ontario were dark and claustrophobic. Charlie7's skyroamer was sealed tight enough to act as a makeshift submarine. He and Eve drifted along in the freshwater tomb, heading five degrees south of due west.

It wasn't an elegant solution, nor was it a permanent one. Without medical equipment to monitor Eve's blood oxygenation, he didn't trust their air supply for more than another half hour. All he could be sure of was that down here, Creator and any other minions she might employ wouldn't find Eve.

"Are there fish?" Eve asked, staring into the darkness.

Charlie7 shook himself from his musings. "Sure. But I wouldn't look too hard for them. We probably scared off everything within a kilometer."

Every minute Charlie7 spent safeguarding Eve was another minute he wasn't out there settling things once and for all with her Creator.

Hopscotching across Earth and looking for uninhabited hideaways or utterly trustworthy robots to confide in was a waste of time. Well, perhaps waste was too strong a word since keeping Eve safe was the ultimate goal, but it certainly was inefficient.

Charlie7 was a closer, a deal maker, the exclamation point at the end of a speech. Bogging down with his nose in the muck wasn't his style. He'd have called this Toby work if Toby22 hadn't proved himself to be an unreliable little prat.

That settled it. Charlie7 was done running. He needed a place for Eve to be safe but not long term. Long enough to deal with Creator would be plenty. For a short-term assignment, there was one person who might just do the job. The boy might be ten kinds of idiot, but there was no one else who Charlie7 could be sure would lay down his life to protect Eve.

"OK, kid," Charlie7 said, letting the autopilot idle along. "You're a smart one, so answer me this: How do we meet up with Plato without anyone else finding us?"

Eve's eyes widened. "You're willing to find him again?"

Charlie7 let his head loll back against the headrest. Up above, light glimmered at the lake's surface. Plato was up there somewhere, trying to save Eve's life. "He might not be quite human like you, but he's still human."

"Why is he not like me? I mean besides being male, larger, heavier, and so forth?"

"How can I put this? You see... you're more or less a real human. I'm sure Creator spliced in the standard immunities to alien biowarfare agents, and maybe she was picky with her DNA screenings, but your genome reads as human. Nobody hybridized you with reptile DNA, hoping you could grow back limbs or gave you literal eagle eyes."

"But Plato's not a lizard or an eagle," Eve protested. Unbuckling from her safety harness, she twisted to sit and face Charlie7 cross-legged. "He's just male."

"I knew the original humans. It's not random chance he's that size. And he's only twelve years old. He should be just starting to get hair on his lip and having his voice crack when he talks. An ordinary twelve-year-old human male wouldn't be much bigger that you. But... while he may not be all natural, little about Earth is anymore. Mother Nature took a punch that knocked out most of her teeth, but she's up and fighting again. She just needed a little help."

"Who's Mother Nature?"

"Figuratively, Mother Nature is the sum of all life on Earth. It makes it easier for people to think about things when they personify them." The skyroamer lurched as the autopilot veered them around an outcropping of rock in the lake bed. They couldn't stay down here much longer. "Eve, you haven't answered my question."

"Last time you left him a clue from a movie."

"Well, I had access to his archive. I could see which ones he'd watched. Leaving him a message without a common reference is pointless, and I'm not going back to that travesty of scientific parody for a second clue. Besides, it would only guide him to Liberty Island again, and we're not going back that way."

"What about Oz? We could go there and leave a message on the movie he showed me."

Charlie7 cringed. The clawed hands of Hollywood reached up from the grave to strangle yet another impressionable mind.

"That wasn't real."

Eve frowned.

"Plato said the same thing, but we've been to Kansas. Plato admitted he'd never been to Kansas, and that was within a tornado's travel of Oz. If we perform a radial search, given the speed of his skyroamer, we should be able to find it in no time. According to the archive, tornadoes don't usually go more than six kilometers. I assume one large enough to lift a house—and I know, I know, it wasn't a real house they used in the movie—would probably be able to go farther. But with a spiral element to the search, it should still only be a matter of minutes until we find Oz. Now... the destruction of the Emerald City in the invasion seems probable, or we'd have seen it on our first trip to Kansas, but if we set up a scanner for heavy metal detection, we ought to find the road there."

It was ludicrously thorough for being founded on complete bunk. Charlie7 smiled and played along. "Why heavy metals?"

"Presumably the yellow bricks were gold. Reproduction for filming would have made gold prohibitive—Plato explained about sets and actors and money for production—but the real version I would expect to be built with real gold. Paint simply wouldn't last for a travel surface, and while too soft for heavy industrial use, the light agrarian foot traffic would be acceptable on gold. And if the road were pyrite, the iron sulfide would still be detectable by scanning. Then we just follow the road to Oz and send Plato a message to meet us there."

Charlie7 put a hand on Eve's shoulder. "Unfortunately, there's still no such place as Oz. It was invented in a book. They adapted the book into a movie."

"But you can't make up a whole place out of nothing. Can you?"

"Imagination is a powerful tool," Charlie7 replied. "How powerful depends on the mind. Aside from a few newcomers like yourself, there have only really been twenty-seven minds on Earth since the invasion. From time to time, one of us takes a crack at making a movie or writing a play. Nothing comes close to the quality of the old masters. But there were dreamers from old Earth that could envision whole worlds built from nothing but imagination. Asimov, Bradbury, Heinlein, Niven. We didn't save a mind like those. The Project Transhuman team first scanned and recorded our own minds, and there was never time for more than that. Maybe you'll start a new Renaissance of arts and culture. But for now, I suppose we're going to have to settle for heading back to Kansas if we ever want Plato to find us."

Charlie7 really didn't. Eve did. Some martyr within him said that if Eve's happiness was paramount, then even a misshapen human life was worth the trouble. Eve deserved better than him. She needed a friend and confidante, not a brutish, overprotective lout. But Plato was all Earth had on offer.

Eve brightened. "Oh! I know what message to send!"

So did Charlie7. There was really never a question.

When Charlie7 allowed her access to the skyroamer's console, Eve eagerly keyed in the message: "There's no place like home."

CHAPTER FORTY-FIVE

he autopilot in *Betty-Lou* didn't know where it was taking Plato. For the moment, "somewhere over the coast" was all either he or the navigational computer needed to know. A randomly generated evasive algorithm kept him one step ahead of the pursuing skyroamer.

Freed from piloting, Plato turned his attention to repairing the EMP rifle Charlie7 had damaged. Pulling out the power supply had been a punk move. That robotic relic could have just confiscated the weapon and left it intact. Now, Plato was stuck with nothing but his emergency tool kit. Trying to straighten damaged terminals wasn't easy when the autopilot shook him around with evasive maneuvers every few seconds.

Somewhere over the Atlantic, the battery snapped into place. The power supply whined to a rising pitch that exited human audible perception. Lights that served little purpose but to make the rifle look like a proper weapon winked to life.

"There ya go, baby. Time to turn this chase into an ambush."

Plato wasn't going to run this time. That idiot robot and his stinging darts might have caught him with his bits flapping in the breeze out in Sherwood Forest, but the EMP rifle was no bow and arrow. Now he just had to decide on a place to use it.

The skyroamer's onboard computer popped up listings of nearby facilities upon request.

Wide-open spaces were Plato's enemy, given his opponent's reflexes. That Version 68.9 chassis was quick enough that it might dodge his shots if he saw Plato coming. This being a chase, the element of surprise was rarer than plutonium. He needed someplace with distractions, noise, things that could divert the robotic manhunter's attention long enough for Plato to line up a clean shot.

The Atlantic Oceanographic Research Center was close by. It was manned by Holly30 and Gina81. That meant backgrounds in computer coding and electrical engineering, respectively.

Plato preferred breaking into facilities run by soft scientists.

The geneticists he dealt with viewed computers largely as gene sequencers and not the foundation of a security network. Just having a Holly on staff made entering the AORC a dangerous gamble.

If he headed for shore, he could reach the Appalachian Regional Avian and Arboreal Cloning Substation in five minutes. There would be lots of biological work going on there, and it was mostly automated. Marvin19 and Jocelyn50 weren't around at present, according to their latest status updates on the Social.

Some nagging instinct warned Plato that anyplace that worked in cloning was liable to have dark secrets lurking. If he stumbled across a human-cloning operation in their basement, could he keep focused on his mission to throw off pursuit?

"Aha!" Plato stabbed a meaty finger against the screen of his terminal. The West Virginia Orbital Ore Refinery was just what he was looking for. It would be loud, automated, and hot as Hades. Human skin temperature readings would be background noise with the blast furnaces and smelters running.

Disengaging the autopilot, Plato gained some altitude and made sure his pursuer got a good look as he changed heading and put the Virginia coastline on the horizon.

The trailing skyroamer didn't break its pursuit. It merely matched course and fell into position on *Betty-Lou's* tail.

CHAPTER FORTY-SIX

James187 watched the skyroamer settle onto a course. The human brute had finally stopped making random maneuvers and headed overland. The robotic hunter matched course and settled in to find out where they were now both heading.

Maybe this time the chase wouldn't be a twenty-two-hour waste of James187's time. There would certainly be no Toby22 to save him, and any involvement Paul208 might have had wasn't going to look favorably on the monument builder if today's events came to light.

It was tempting to let the tracker continue its work, let the human think he'd escaped with Eve and wait for him to land. The chance that they'd get help once on the ground prevented James187 from giving in to the temptation. He wished he could get a look inside the cockpit to visually confirm the girl's presence, but an active reflective layer showed him nothing but clouds and sky when he tried to look.

James187 wasn't entirely comfortable with the ingenuity of this fledgling human. The standard model skyroamers used worldwide weren't equipped with countermeasures against conventional scanning methods. He ought to have been able to tap into the broadcast frequency, get a reading on the fuel supply, or at least tell what was inside with thermal imaging. Instead, all infrared showed was a pair of blips from the engines.

Unless they were on a flyby, the humans were heading for the West Virginia Orbital Ore Refinery.

It was a cunning choice in a crude way. James187 would be forced to rely on visual contact to track them through the facility. It was too loud to trust acoustic sensors and too hot for infrared. The chaos would level the playing field.

But there were still advantages James187 could lean on, ones that perhaps the humans didn't even consider. He looked up the caretaker of the facility and discovered that it was Jason266.

It was a quick matter to get a hold of him on a private channel. "Jason, James187 here. I've heard a rumor of a pair of bears wandering into your facility in West Virginia. One suspected mutant with the X-95-Omega gene. The other may or may not be a healthy specimen."

WHAT DO YOU NEED?

James187 twitched a smile. "I'm transmitting a mammalian corral-and-capture protocol. Upload it to your facility's automatons. They'll continue their assigned tasks unless they see one of the bears, then they'll box them in for me to come sort out. Should pose minimal disruption to your operations."

VERY WELL. TRANSMIT.

James187 whipped up a quick protocol for containing any mammal over twenty kilograms in mass or one meter in height. It was a comfortable threshold that wouldn't have the automatons chasing after mice and rats but would certainly trigger for a pair of humans. If any bears *were* lurking in the West Virginia Orbital Ore Refinery, they'd get rounded up, too, he supposed.

CHAPTER FORTY-SEVEN

One of the mining transorbitals was entering the atmosphere as Plato approached the refinery. A shadow fell over the countryside as the ore collector still in orbit caused a solar eclipse. The smaller transorbital vessel was still the size of a city, but the mother ship dwarfed it.

The possibilities for distractions jumped ten-fold with the chaos that would surround the arrival of a fresh delivery of ore. All Plato needed to do was ignore the spectacle long enough to find a place to land.

Betty-Lou was a ghost. Aside from direct visual contact, no system the robots used routinely would pick her up. There wouldn't be air traffic alarms, automated greetings, or any other hassle on the way in.

Twisting around, Plato spotted the robotic hunter keeping a safe distance behind him.

No more time for fooling around or trickery. It was time to just get on the ground and get lost in the maze of refinery equipment.

Mountains and hills rolled past beneath *Betty-Lou* as the industrial complex continued to grow. Perspective was a funny thing, even for someone who understood it on a scientific level. Plato didn't feel like he was getting any closer as he approached; the facility was merely inflating to full size until there was a spot to land.

At long last, the building stopped growing. It covered kilometers on a side and swallowed *Belly-Lou* like an antacid tablet, except that Plato wouldn't be a cure for the fires within. If anything, he was going to toss one more bit of metal into the smelters when this was over.

There was a small official landing zone, meant for use by staff and visitors—though who would come on a social call was beyond Plato's imagination. That was the last place Plato actually wanted to set down.

Plato's best chance of taking on his mysterious pursuer was to isolate, confuse, and catch him unaware. Any help the robot got from meddling refinery staff just pushed Plato's finish line further back. Settling for an accessible area adjacent to a maintenance stairwell looked to be as good a place as any.

The canopy popped open as soon as *Betty-Lou* touched down. Plato was tempted to leave the engines hot but decided that might be too big a giveaway. His backup plan was to lose his pursuer and double back to escape. Instead, he just unloaded his gear as quickly as possible and sprinted toward the facility.

Just as Plato reached the maintenance door, he caught sight of the second skyroamer angling for a landing next to *Betty-Lou*. "Keep your filthy mitts off her," Plato muttered, just before he slammed the door shut behind him with a resounding thud.

The metal stairs clanged under his shoes. His rifle clattered off the railings as it bounced along on its shoulder strap.

Plato's heart pounded in anticipation of the coming conflict. This was his big moment. He'd put down mad robotic scientists before, barging into labs and offices alike with the fury of a righteous angel delivering judgment.

Those robots hadn't known what was coming. They had been astonished before Plato manually removed the surprise from their crystalline brains. Twelve had been wiped brain-dead by the EMP rifle in Plato's hands, and if he was lucky, he might even catch this robot's name before he got added to the list as lucky number thirteen. A weapon that killed thirteen robots really ought to have a name. Or maybe he should wait until he had killed twenty-seven since every robot was so obsessed with the original scientists who comprised their misbegotten species.

No point in overthinking things. Plato was willing to try the obvious, just on the off chance it would work.

Hunkering behind a set of pipes dripping with condensation, Plato dropped the sack with his supply of robot-hunting toys. If this trap worked, he wouldn't need them. Sighting down the barrel of the rifle, Plato watched the stairs he'd come by. There'd been multiple entrances near where *Betty-Lou* had landed. If the robot after Eve chose this same stairway, he was a sitting duck.

"Come on, buddy," Plato whispered. "Show me what a thousand years of having no predators has done to your instincts."

Every sense was heightened. Plato could make out the footsteps of automatons bustling about the refinery, the acidic smell of the chemical baths. He felt the heat from furnaces in the lower levels rising through the grated floor. What he wasn't hearing were the anticipated footsteps coming down those stairs.

"Patience," Plato told himself. His ancestors had stalked sabretooth tigers with nothing but spears. They had prevailed by guile and teamwork and no small share of patience. A dangerous beast demanded care and caution. Stealth was a currency easy to squander, but it could buy a life.

Those heightened senses gave Plato his first early warning that something was wrong. Patience was one thing, but waiting in the jaws of a trap was a horse of a different color. The rhythmic footsteps of the automatons going about their work had shifted to a discordant beat.

Something had broken their routine. That could only mean that the drones were reacting to Plato's pursuer—or to Plato.

Plato gathered up his sack and checked that the thermite pistol was safely tucked in the back of his pants. Keeping his head down, he tiptoed deeper into the facility.

Every time he came to a corner, Plato stuck his handheld computer around and recorded a few seconds of video before proceeding. He wished he'd bought a simple mirror instead.

Sweat beaded all along Plato's brow and broke out all over his body. His canteen was tucked safely in *Betty-Lou*; he hadn't thought to bring water to combat the sweltering heat. Didn't matter. He wouldn't be down here long.

Around one corner, his video check spotted a pair of automatons hauling a broken piece of machinery—some sort of lever arm or strut. They noticed the handheld computer and set down their load. Then the automatons zeroed in on Plato's location and marched straight for him.

"Ah, crap!" Plato snapped, careful even in his surprise to keep his voice down. Just because one pair of dumb robots spotted him didn't mean the whole refinery needed to know where he was.

Plato backtracked and took a side passageway, then grabbed a set of handrails and slid down a flight of stairs. Panting, he looked first one direction, then another. The stairs ended at a T-intersection, and automatons were approaching in pairs from all sides including the way he'd come.

All routes of escape were cut off.

CHAPTER FORTY-EIGHT

James187 leaned against the hull of his skyroamer and waited. It was a pleasant, sunny day, marred only by the shadow of the looming transorbital mining ship. No matter. It was still safer than going inside and dealing with the human directly.

The freshly programmed mammal capture protocol reported back with simple observations. Messages of "mammal meets criteria," "acquiring mammal," and "mammal no longer in visual range" splashed across James187's internal computer. There was a fine line between receiving helpful updates and giving Jason266 clues as to what he was really after.

Evelyn38 seemed to think that most robots would be sympathetic to their cause, but privacy was such a closely guarded treasure that few robots made controversial opinions public. For all James187 knew, Jason266 could have been a repopulationist, a mechanist, or an apolitical drone who just worked to fill the eternity of boredom that Earth inflicted on robotkind.

The chase was like reading an old newspaper accounting of an event that had taken place last week. Somewhere inside the facility, the human was leading Jason266's robots on a merry chase.

Meandering over to the nearest maintenance entrance, James187 loaded the specially prepared sedative darts he'd brought along for this occasion. They were the same type he'd used in his first encounter with the brute. But this time, the dose would knock out a polar bear.

James187 had a stimulant syringe along as well, in case Eve caught a dart by mistake. She might survive the sedative dose long enough to receive the counteragent; she might not. But until her bodyguard was out of the way, it was just a risk James187 would have to take.

Packed in pockets of James187's hunting vest were the lighter-dosed darts meant for Eve14. The hunter of humans hoped that Eve would surrender when presented with the risks of fleeing on her own. After all, this wasn't a playground; it was an automated ore refinery. There were safeguards but nothing that passed for human workplace safety.

UNIT 2888923 LOST.

It was a system message, not from one of the automatons directly. James187 frowned and cast a glare at the maintenance door.

UNIT 2888927 LOST.

What the hell was going on down there?

UNIT 2888928 LOST.

UNIT 2888915 LOST.

James187 checked the action on his tranquilizer gun and headed down into the refinery to find out.

CHAPTER FORTY-NINE

The automatons slammed to the grated floor with satisfying crashes as Plato fired again and again. As the bulky human maneuvered the narrow catwalks of the refinery, he encountered an ever-growing horde of the humanoid machines.

Since these automatons were just tools, Plato held no compunction against snuffing out their onboard computers. Nothing was alive about them.

Plato dodged yet another advancing pair of automatons as they lumbered toward him, grasping hands outstretched. It was as if someone was filming a zombie movie for the age of robots.

Despite not being armed, the automatons posed a threat by sheer mass and the incredible strength in their actuators. Robots like Charlie7 were made for puttering around in laboratories and conference rooms. They were the pipe-smoking old aristocrats of the modern age, minus the tobacco addition. These automatons were the muscle.

Something was coordinating the efforts of these refinery drones, and Plato had one guess as to who it was. He'd underestimated the robot after him.

Hacking into hostile systems wasn't easy. Plato didn't expect it from a robot who chased him through forests firing tranq darts. He had to keep reminding himself that the Twenty-Seven were *all* scientists, despite any subsequent occupations.

Luckily for Plato, none of the automatons moved quickly. Each drone plodded at an unchanging pace, same as if they'd been performing duties around the refinery. Plato had just gotten onto the list of those duties, and he wanted off.

"How many of you dopes am I gonna have to wipe today?" Plato griped as he fired off two shots.

Two more humanoid drones went limp. One toppled to the steel mesh floor with bone-rattling force; the other slouched in place until Plato shouldered it over the guardrail. The machine plummeted without complaint, shattering on the concrete floor of the refinery. Even a quick glance down made Plato dizzy.

Having blasted a hole in the closing net of encircling drones, Plato set off at a jog with no destination in mind. He slung his EMP rifle over a shoulder along the way.

Mid-stride, he dug in one of his pockets and pulled out his portable computer again. His tapping at the screen was inaccurate on the move, and he had to correct mistakes along the way. Eventually, he found schematics for the refinery in the public archive.

When he directed the computer to overlay his current location in real time, it appeared as if he had entered a simulation. The drone control feed wasn't a quick hack, and he didn't have time to crack secure links while on the move, but he was able to find a monitoring feed that was unsecured and tapped into it. He dropped the live locations of the drones into the simulation, and the result was a snapshot of an original-era computer game.

"Well, more of you punks out there than I'd hoped for. Glad I don't need to kill every last one of you."

With the ability to see the drones on his computer screen, Plato was able to navigate the refinery and plot a course to keep ahead of them.

This mission was a bust.

Plato's trap for the pursuing robot was sprung, and the bait was gone, but he hadn't caught anything. If Plato were lucky, he would be able to find another exit and get back to *Betty-Lou*.

The refinery shook.

Plato stumbled. The computer fell to the catwalk floor as he grabbed hold of a railing to avoid falling over the edge.

Somewhere nearby, the ore ship was dumping its load.

Plato reached down to grab the computer. He fought against the shaking floor to keep his hold. If he didn't stop it in time, the computer would plummet into the depths of the facility. If he lost his grip, he was liable to follow it down. Plato reached to place at least a finger on the computer, to hold it in place until the earthquake abated.

The noise was horrendous, but Plato had no free hand to shield his ears. The tip of his middle finger came to rest on the edge of the computer just before the vibrations shook it over the side of the catwalk.

Gritting his teeth, he knew he just had to hold out long enough for the mining ship to finish emptying. He could hold completely still for a little while if that's what it took.

A bare shoulder, slick with sweat, was no fit place for the strap of a rifle to lie idle. As Plato strained and stretched, the fabric began a slow slide over the straining deltoid muscle of Plato's right arm.

"No," Plato said through gritted teeth. "Don't you dare."

Despite the chiding, no part of the rifle responded to voice commands, least of all the synthetic fabric strap. It continued slipping despite Plato's protest. Once clear of the shoulder, it was the first peak of a roller coaster ride. The strap slowed just shy of stopping an instant before it plummeted.

There was no decision to make. Plato reacted by instinct.

He snatched at the barrel of the rifle and grabbed hold. Plato saved the weapon.

The computer slid over the edge and vanished into the abyss.

A soft moan of dismay escaped Plato's lips as he realized that he could have hooked the strap on a finger if he'd only taken a fraction of a second to think. Maybe the jolt would have broken his tenuous hold on the computer's slick glass surface; maybe it wouldn't have. But by letting it go, he consigned himself to navigating the refinery by memory.

Plus, he was no longer able to track the drones in real time.

The ore dump finally ceased, and the facility returned to normalcy. A high-pitched whine droned on like a dog whistle for human. Plato pressed a palm to his ear in a vain attempt to stop the noise, but it was just an aftereffect of damaging his hearing.

There was no time to collect himself.

All Plato could do was get moving as the drones tightened their noose around his neck.

CHAPTER FIFTY

James187 lurked in the lower depths of the refinery. It had taken him half an hour to circumvent the chase and come around below the fracas taking place on the catwalks high overhead.

A small object bounced off railings and catwalks, pipes and conduits. Each impact echoed through the facility as an undertone to the general din of industrial ore processing. The robotic hunter followed the sound and caught sight of a portable computer tumbling by.

Ducking under a low-hanging coolant line, James187 caught a glimpse of a human silhouette retreating from the edge of one of the upper-level catwalks. It was the larger one—the bodyguard, the pilot. The troublemaker.

It seemed the refinery's automatons were giving the brute all he could handle.

James187 smiled as he looked on.

Every animal had its own form of cleverness. Birds knew every breeze and updraft; they thought in three dimensions. Hares ran erratic patterns to evade predators faster than them. James187 had even dealt with an escaped chimpanzee that knew to throw rocks to make it sound like she was somewhere she wasn't. But for all their instinct and crude guile, there wasn't an animal alive that posed a threat to robots.

Playing hide-and-seek with a human was legitimately dangerous.

Any hunter who underestimated his prey was in for a nasty surprise. James187 was in no hurry to make such a mistake. Instead of heading up to join the chase, he found the nearest stairwell to delve farther down and retrieve the computer.

Far above, he could still hear the sounds of automaton feet on the steel mesh flooring. Why Jason266 hadn't adopted a more modern design for the refinery, James187 couldn't imagine. But it allowed sound to travel a greater distance and cut down somewhat on errant echoes. Two crashes from above drove home the point. The sounds pinpointed the location of another pair of defunct automatons, even before James187 received the facility update.

UNIT 2888901 LOST.

UNIT 2888903 LOST.

The human was armed with a weapon that made short work of three-hundred-kilo automatons built to work with molten metals and jagged chunks of unprocessed ore. A gauss rifle or charged plasma cannon could inflict the damage required, but surely James would have heard evidence of that sort of weapon firing. The human had to have been using an EMP weapon. Since it was only taking out automatons in pairs, it had to have been a focused field, possibly using a monopole electromagnet.

James187 wanted no part of that. Let the human run his power supply dry or slip up and fall victim to one of the automatons before he could destroy its control system.

The human's computer lay face down on the facility's concrete bottom floor. James187 picked it up. The screen was cracked, but the display still functioned. It was showing a fully rendered map of the facility in wireframe, complete with automaton movements.

Neither James187 nor the human appeared on the simulation, but from the shifting patterns in the automatons' movements, he could narrow down the human's location. With this tactical feed, he could keep the human hemmed in and be sure he wasn't escaping. At the same time, James187 could remain safe from the horrific EMP weapon cutting down automatons two by two.

WHAT'S GOING ON, JAMES? DOES THIS BEAR OF YOURS EAT AUTOMATONS? I'M LOSING WORKERS.

That was no message from the system.

Jason266 had been getting the same updates about the continuing losses among the workforce. The last thing James187 needed was Jason266 showing up to investigate.

A momentary spitefulness suggested that maybe if the human bagged Jason266, he would let his guard down, thinking he had ended the hunt. After all, what were the odds that a human could tell two robots apart by chassis?

"Hold tight, Jason. I'm not entirely sure it's a bear you've got. Stay advised. I'm sure Kanto can make up for your losses."

The Kanto facility wouldn't like shifting production for a bunch of Earth-side replacement automatons, but they couldn't afford to let production slip on the ore refineries, either.

There would be no strike, no contest of wills over who would give in. Kanto would make the automatons for Jason266, production would continue, and everyone would forget the matter. Any other result would lead to months of committee hearings, followed by new management at one or both facilities.

GET MY REFINERY CLEARED OUT. STOP LETTING WHATEVER'S IN THERE DESTROY MY WORKERS. SO HELP ME, JAMES, IF YOU DELAY MY PRODUCTION SCHEDULE I'LL MAKE SURE NO ONE EVER CONTRACTS YOU FOR ANIMAL REMOVAL AGAIN.

OK. There was the threat.

James187 could have done any number of jobs. He'd been a miner when mining off-world still held some interest and excitement. He had done stints as an environmental engineer, an urban reclamation supervisor, and an algae farmer.

But ever since breeding populations of animals had been let loose in the wilds, James187 hunted down aberrations, mutants, and general troublemakers. He'd be damned if this human was going to get him blacklisted for doing the best job he'd had in centuries.

"No worries, Jason. I'll handle it."

With the human's computer in one hand and the dart gun in the other, James187 set off to trail this latest troublemaker from a safe distance until he could get his shot.

CHAPTER FIFTY-ONE

Plato was running out of space. The protocol programmed into these drones directed them to herd him deeper and deeper into the bowels of the refinery. Every split-second choice left him a step farther from escape. Every "lesser of two evils" pointed him down instead of up.

The robots didn't care if they let him run, so long as they didn't give him a way out. Or, he corrected himself, whoever was controlling them didn't care how long he ran. The drones even lacked the capacity *not* to care.

Blasting a path out wasn't going to be an option. Plato needed a plan. His rifle's charge was running low. Plato's last resort was the EMP grenades that he'd never actually gotten around to testing. Setting one off might take out half a dozen automatons, allowing him to escape. Or it could take the refinery offline and kill *Betty-Lou's* onboard computer.

The sack slung over his shoulder had all the trick gadgets he'd brought from his hideout. This had to turn into more than running a maze and evading drones, or Plato would never get out.

He needed to buy time.

One pair of automatons blocked a catwalk that branched off to his left. With the squeeze of a trigger, the first robot slumped over as the rifle emitted a gentle hum.

Another quick squeeze, and nothing happened.

Indicator lights went dead. The automaton was only three meters away and closing. Plato let go of the rifle; it dropped to dangle limp from the strap across his shoulder. With both hands free, the burly giant rushed the automaton.

Man and machine were nearly the same height, but Plato's apparent bulk was insignificant compared to the automaton's alloy steel construction. It outweighed him twice over.

But it wasn't angry.

With an inarticulate roar, Plato slammed into the automaton shoulder first, ducking to get below its center of mass.

The thing wasn't programmed to grab onto its attacker, or it would have at that moment. Plato was easily within its reach.

It also wasn't programmed to grab onto safety railings if it was hoisted bodily from the ground because it didn't do that either.

And some poor, unimaginative programmer had never thought to tell the automaton what to do in freefall. Plato knew it was his imagination—because drones can't think or feel—but the look on the drone's impassive face struck him as surprised as it plummeted to a landing some fifty meters down and shattered.

Plato set off at a jog.

It wouldn't be long before the automatons hemmed him in once more. There were thousands of them throughout the facility, and he was only bothering the ones within a few hundred meters. They'd have reinforcements as long as they needed—far longer than Plato could hope to evade them, especially since his EMP rifle was dry. That was mission number one.

Plato hopped a railing and dropped ten meters to a catwalk two levels down. The impact sent a jolt through his spine. After a few stiff, painful steps, Plato walked off the injury.

Overhead, the drone swarm was reorganizing. Pathing calculations wouldn't take them long. They probably already had a simple solution to get to him. That wasn't the problem. They still needed to take the long way around, and that bought him time, even if it had cost Plato delving ever deeper into the facility's belly.

One of the tricks Plato had brought along was a collection of frequency jammers. Odds were that the drones only needed occasional instruction. They'd be autonomous unless their programming required updates. Just seeing him would be enough for them to maintain pursuit. But if he could disrupt any feedback their robot boss was getting, it might take them time to realize what he was up to.

Plato activated one of the jammers, set it to the broadest bandwidth available, and stuck it to the wall by the magnet in its base.

Access panels were easy to come by. This whole facility was a maintenance worker's dream. There wasn't even a security lockout on the panel, just a quick-release that kept it from popping off due to the extreme vibrations the refinery regularly experienced.

Plato was inside the panel in seconds.

From one of his pockets, Plato pulled out a pair of insulated gloves before taking a knife to the end of a set of two-millimeter cables.

It was always nice dealing with low-tech when it was an unfamiliar system. The EMP rifle hardly cared how it got its power; Plato had built it with its own safeguards against voltage mismatches, over-currents, and power surges. All it required was *enough* power, and when a bank of lights went dark as his knife severed the wires, Plato suspected this circuit had plenty.

It had taken him all of thirty seconds by the time the EMP rifle was propped against the open panel, sucking electrons from the refinery like a leech.

"There you are, you mutant masterpiece," a robotic voice shouted. "What are you without that rifle of yours, huh?"

Plato saw him. The robot from the woods.

One EMP grenade could kill him, then Plato would be at the mercy of anything that survived. The mindless masses would overrun him.

Plato couldn't do it. He was too young to die. For the first time in his life, Plato had a real friend. Plenty of heroes died saving the day, but there was still hope for *this* hero to have his cake and share it with Eve—and maybe even Charie7.

Without activating it, Plato took one EMP grenade and lobbed it as a distraction.

While the robot's attention was focused on diving for cover behind the nearest solid steel wall, Plato took his chance. With just a quick check to see there was someplace to land, he rolled over a safety rail and dropped down.

CHAPTER FIFTY-TWO

James187 dove for cover.

That crazy human had some sort of EMP bomb. The panicked hunter tore a cover off the nearest access panel and found a warren of valves and regulators for the coolant systems.

With a quick prayer to whichever saint preserved sentient robotic minds, he thrust his head inside. He might lose his internal computer and probably all servomotor controls. But with any luck, the shielding around the conduit would protect his crystalline brain from the electromagnetic blast wave.

Seconds ticked by.

A minute passed.

James187 cursed himself for a fool as he crawled out on hands and knees and examined the grenade. It was inert.

With infinite care, James187 popped open the dented, irregular sphere at a seam and disconnected the supercapacitor from the magnetic coils. He'd have held his breath if he still had lungs and would have sighed in relief as well. But instead, he settled for flinging the supercapacitor through the refinery as far as he could.

The useless remains of the grenade sprinkled to the floor with a clatter.

It wasn't all bad news. The human wasn't trying too hard to kill him.

The grenade had appeared to be functional and intact; it merely hadn't been activated. James187 attempted to run a quick calculation on the magnetic yield from such a small device, but his onboard computer didn't have all the data it needed.

James187 scowled and scanned the vicinity.

Normally this was the sort of detail that didn't warrant conscious thought. The computer would link up to the planetary archive, find the relevant information, and resume the calculation in milliseconds.

But he had no connection to the planetary archive. A quick check confirmed that the Social was unavailable as well. He tried sending a test message to Jason266—just a quick status update that the bear was trapped.

Nothing happened.

"Sneaky devil," James187 muttered. "You're jamming me."

They were well and truly alone. The drones were on the move, but they were mere distractions. Even if they caught the human, they wouldn't harm him, and based on the sprawled chassis he'd seen, the human was able to lift them over the guardrails anyway.

An EMP rifle leaned casually against a wall beside an open electrical panel. The human had tapped into the refinery's power to attempt a recharge. Reaching into the panel, James187 ripped the wires out. The blinking charge indicator on the rifle faded out.

"None of that, now."

Not far from the rifle was an inconspicuous device affixed to the wall. Plucking it free, James187 examined it for a moment before crushing it in his fingers. To check his theory that this was the jamming device, he tried the Social—just a quick check of the news feeds. But there was still nothing. This human had set up more than one jammer.

Emitting a growl from his vocal processor, James187 leveled his dart gun and headed to the nearest stairwell down. He heard footsteps below and continued to the very bottom floor of the refinery. Those steps led into a world reddened by the glow of molten iron in crater-sized crucibles.

Support pillars and the concrete walls of the crucibles provided adequate cover for a sneaking human, but the brute was too large to be silent, even with the ambient noise.

A voice echoed from the distant shadows. "You're a persistent bugger, aren't you?"

James187 saw no harm in playing along. If he could start a dialogue, he could use the sound to narrow down the human's location. "I am. There's no escaping. If you give yourself up, I promise you'll come to no harm. We just can't have humans running loose, killing refinery workers and kidnapping humans from their parents' homes."

The voice came from a different direction. The human was on the move and rather quieter now than James187 had first credited him with. "So, you Machiavelli99 or something? You expect me to buy that load?"

"Still got the same tranq darts from our first meeting. Maybe a bit more juice in them this time. I had expected to find a lost little girl who needed her mother, not a big, strapping lad like you. And I'm James187. Who might you be?"

"Well, Jimmy. I think I'm going to have to refuse your offer. I can't let you get Eve. You'll have to kill me to take her."

The human was somewhere else now. James187 was beginning to get a feel for his movements. He was dodging around the supports and molten vats with stealth and quickness, but a pattern was emerging.

"Come now, human—wait, I can't do this. I understand we won't be friends, but we can hardly even be enemies if I don't know your name."

"Bothers you that much, huh? Well, go suck lemons, pal."

James187 paused for a frown.

Where on Earth was this human picking up such clunky, ineffectual slang? Was he going to stick his tongue out next?

"A real hero never hides who he is. I suppose I'd thought better of you, but you're just after Eve for your own purposes. You're not 'saving' her for anything but your own vulgar desires."

"I won't let you get me riled up with that psychology garbage. I'm Plato. You happy? But I'm not going to come charging out at you to get tranqed in the face because you make stuff up about me and Eve."

This Plato character was running out of room to maneuver. Vast as it was, the refinery wasn't without its corners and blind alleys.

If only this poor human hadn't gone and dropped his computer. Otherwise, Plato might have known that he had painted himself into a corner.

"You have my word," James187 called out. "You won't be harmed. Truth be told, I'm a little in awe of you. I've been to the Sanctuary for Scientific Sins. I think everyone's gone at least once, just out of morbid curiosity. You're nothing like them."

"Half those poor humans are there because of me. They were places lots worse than that."

There! Behind that pillar!

James187 slowed. Each footstep touched the concrete floor as gently as a feather's touch. He aimed his dart gun where he might expect to find a crouching Plato's chest. One quick burst and he'd be—

An arm wrapped around James187's neck. Before he could react, it had constricted beneath his chin. The cervical actuators in James187's neck weren't able to overpower the fleshy vise. His head was forced back.

"Hi, Jimmy. You like my decoy?"

Instantly, error codes blared warnings that nearly drowned out James187's conscious thoughts. The strain on his cervical actuators, data connections, and coolant lines was approaching critical.

James187 had been a fool.

The audio was a broadcast. Of course. Multiple small speakers scattered during his flight. The human could transmit despite his own jammers because he knew the exact frequency they would allow through. For all the credit he'd given this Plato, James187 had still underestimated him.

The dart gun. James still clutched the weapon. But as he tried to fire over his shoulder at the human, a firm tug at his neck brought on a sudden panic.

"Drop it!" Plato ordered. "Drop it, or I exert the thirty-five hundred Newtons it'll take to snap the neural fibers in your neck and turn you into a steel rag doll."

The fact that Plato knew the exact break strength of the cluster of fibers that carried signals throughout James187's robotic body was disturbing enough. The ever more dire warnings flashing across his vision showing just how close those fibers were to breaking lent credence to Plato's threat.

Upgrade to the Version 68.9, they'd said. *You'll love the efficiency, the battery life, the longevity.* No one had thought to mention that this chassis could be overpowered by a renegade human if it caught him in a vulnerable moment.

James187 dropped the dart gun. Plato kicked it away.

"You have me. Now, what? Obviously, you want something, or you'd have killed me already."

"Well, I've got particular rules about this whole killing business. And I can't overlook the fact you're just carrying a tranq gun." A sweaty hand patted James187 on the skull. "You earn a reprieve, so long as you play ball."

Mercy? After all the two of them had been through?

James187 had been assigned to bring Eve14 back for Evelyn38 to overwrite. He was only concerned about preserving Plato's life because he rather fancied having that monstrous body for himself.

Plato couldn't know any of that. Otherwise, James187 would be getting dragged, limp and helpless, over to the vats of molten ore to join the smelting process.

"I acquiesce."

There was a jerk at his neck. "Don't go getting all smart on me, Jimmy. I know what that word means. Now, you tell me the exact frequency you need to call off those drones, and I'll give you access. After that, we're going up to the roof where both of us are parked. I'm going to take my skyroamer. You're going to take yours. We roam off our separate ways and never see each other again. Got it?"

"That's it?"

"That's it. Oh, except that you're never going to see Eve again, either. Or any other human for that matter. You're going to forget our species exists. Go back to hunting rabbits or whatever it is you do for a living."

James187 had no choice but to comply. He provided the frequency for the ore refinery drones. When Plato stopped jamming that one frequency, James187 canceled the capture-and-contain order.

Jason266 would receive notification and assume the "bears" had been taken care of. Plato then marched them out without so much as a wrong turn on the way up. He never imagined the human could have memorized the facility layout.

"Eve wasn't even here with you, was she?" James187 dared to ask.

If James187 had been a living creature, being carried by the neck would have prevented any conversation, but he didn't draw breath. At least not today. If Plato were good to his word, maybe someday he'd still have a chance at a human body.

"Sorry, Jimmy," Plato said as they approached his skyroamer. "I'm just the decoy. But I'd like you to do one last thing before I let you go."

"What's that?" If James187 were going to live out the next few minutes, he'd gladly hear Plato out.

"Deliver a message to Evelyn38. Tell her she'd better not *dare* turn herself in. I don't want some committee sending her off to mine asteroids or grow algae on Mars. She's mine, and I'm coming for her."

Plato released him suddenly and shoved James187 away. Then the human tossed a grenade to him. The robot caught it without thinking. For a shining second, James187 expected his world to end in a sudden electromagnetic pulse.

"Hold tight," Plato warned, wagging a finger. "It's live. You let that thing go, you're blanked. Smart guy like you can disarm it once I'm out of range. But if I catch you trying it while I can see you, I'll trigger it manually."

The human's ship lifted off, and James187 watched until it vanished over the horizon heading east.

It only took a short while after that to pry open the grenade and find that there was no circuitry to perform any of the feats Plato had promised in his threat. It was just like the first he'd taken apart, except that the leads weren't connected to the supercapacitor.

It was a dud, and James187 had been too scared to call Plato's bluff.

CHAPTER FIFTY-THREE

As Charlie7 walked through an old farmhouse-style door, he set down the basket filled with Eve's supply of apples. It would have been a waste leaving them to bake in the Kansas heat out in the skyroamer.

Eve followed close behind, using Charlie7 as a shield. Her wariness was unfounded. The sprawling ranch house was vacant. Everything was just the way the old robot remembered it, from the dusty fireplace to the racks along the wall filled with tiny figurines.

Well, not everything had remained untouched. Someone had pushed the couch aside—probably one of the clean-up crews.

Eve wrinkled her nose. "It smells in here."

Charlie7 just smiled. "You couldn't have said that fifty years ago."

"I wasn't born yet."

"Yes, yes. But if you had been, you still couldn't have said it. There wasn't enough mildew to give that dank smell you're noticing. Progress isn't always shiny and electronic. Sometimes it's the small, smelly, crucial building blocks that pour the foundations of real advances."

Eve explored as much with her hands as with her eyes. She ran her fingers along the wooden walls—a real luxury in this age of plastic and steel. The cushioned seats each beckoned for her to sit upon them. She picked up several of the figurines and examined them before returning them to their spot along the wall, carefully oriented just as they had been. Crawling on hands and knees, she ducked her head inside the fireplace and looked up the chimney.

"Does someone live here?" Eve asked. "What if they come back and find us?"

"No one lives here anymore," Charlie7 replied gently.

"Was it the smell?" Eve asked, dusting off her pants. The white fabric would never stay clean the way the girl interacted with everything she encountered.

Charlie7 saw no point lying to her. "No. The previous occupant self-terminated last year."

"Oh," Eve said. "Did you know him?"

"Her," Charlie clarified. "Alison3 and I were friends for nearly nine hundred years."

Odd when he phrased it that way. The time line of Charlie7's existence stretched back to the horizon behind him, and he couldn't even make out the tiny blip of it before Alison3 was uploaded. Their friendship had lasted longer than the Holy Roman Empire.

"What happened?"

Charlie7 sat, not even worrying about the dust getting all over his suit pants and the back of his jacket. With a wave of his hand, he indicated a seat opposite himself for Eve. She plopped down and pulled her knees up to her chest.

"Alison3 was one of the rebuilders. Not all the early robots wanted humans back. A lot of them wanted to progress, to explore the universe without the limitations of flesh and mortal lifespans. But Alison3 spearheaded the efforts to restore the biome."

Eve tilted her head. "Wouldn't she be happy? There's food growing, and the atmosphere is breathable. Robots are making people now."

"That was it, actually. Robots making people. Can you even imagine what it's like to hold a dream in your heart for centuries? And then, time and again, you see that dream misshapen and exploited."

Eve's eyes widened. "She saw the Sanctuary for Scientific Sins."

"No. She committed one. I believe you met Emily?"

Eve nodded.

"Well, Emily was the daughter of the Alison Prime. Where she'd gotten a sample of the DNA or how she'd preserved it in secret all these years, I couldn't say. But she partnered with a geneticist to bring Emily back."

"It worked," Eve said, nodding along with the story.

"Did it?" Charlie7 asked. "I suppose. But like many wishes, it wasn't granted the way Alison3 had imagined. However, that's not why we're here."

Shaking loose from his maudlin interlude, Charlie7 brushed the dust off his suit—a lost cause by this point. "This place is plenty large for our purposes. I can customize you a kitchen and bedroom. For now, a blanket and the couch should do once we clean it up."

"What should I do?" Eve asked, slipping down from the chair and following Charlie7 as he swept through the house.

"Do you remember the clothing measurements from the sanctuary?"

Eve nodded. Of course, she did. Asking was simply a matter of politeness.

"Well, your assignment is to input those values into Alison3's cloth-o-matic. Then, you'll have it make you three full sets of clothing. But there are three rules. First, you can't make them like the ones you're wearing. Second, no two outfits can be identical. Third, no using any of the presets Alison3 saved including the fact that by altering the size they'd technically be different. Think you can do that?"

The girl stared at him, still as a mannequin. He might as well have asked her to compose a symphony or launch an orbital probe. Strike that. She probably would have enjoyed orbital mechanics. Nevertheless, faced with the prospect of a mildly creative endeavor, Eve was dumbstruck.

"How?"

Charlie7 tapped a finger to his lips as he considered. "You can consider whatever factors you like, but the choice has to be yours. Creator may have taught you any number of useful skills, but she didn't seem concerned about you learning to be human." He flashed a quick, stainless steel smile. "That job falls to me."

Whether his explanation made any sense to Eve, Charlie7 couldn't say. Parenting was a skill lost to the mists of time. It would require rediscovery and study by the same set of twenty-seven scientific minds that had to figure out genetics, architecture, space exploration, and climatology.

There were probably books on child-rearing somewhere in the archive. Maybe one day they'd be worth a look.

For now, Charlie7 had other matters to look into.

While Alison3's home occupied one level aboveground, like Charlie7's, it hid several below. All the low-numbered robotic IDs came with a lingering paranoia about exposure to open sky.

In the catacombs beneath Alison3's home, Charlie7 discovered her lab equipment. She'd never gone into genetics. In life, Dr. Alison Francoeur had been a robotics professor, specializing in the theoretical aspects critical to Project Transhuman's earliest days.

Charles Truman had always been the hands-on sort, despite his advanced degrees. But while Charlie7 kept his original vocation mostly intact, Alison3 had found a world where robotic theory was almost a quaint notion. When she searched her soul for another career, she became robotkind's first environmental scientist.

Alison3 had spearheaded the cleanup of Earth, from eradicating the remaining viral and bacterial agents from the war to salvaging untainted genetic samples for the eventual rebuild.

Most of the lab was a museum to the tools that had cleansed the Earth so long ago. In one room, the prototype of the first autonomous bulldozer sat on a pedestal, just 1:10 the scale of the production units. In another, an array of handheld scanners took up an entire wall, vacuum-sealed behind glass; each was an improvement over the previous version. Charlie7 remembered operating one of the original BioScan-Alpha toxin screeners right alongside Alison3. Back then, there weren't enough robots for anyone to specialize too finely—not even Charlie7.

In the bowels of the facility, Charlie7 reactivated the local generator. Alison3's place was low on fuel, but it had a deep-well geothermal backup that would more than suffice.

Next, Charlie7 began sorting through the functioning equipment and taking note of what would need to be scrapped. Alison3 was gone, and her museum was more a hazard to Eve than a fitting monument to one of Earth's founding robots.

While Charlie7 was halfway inside a soil sifter trying to figure out if the engine was worth repairing, soft footsteps padded down the stairs.

"Why are you naked?" Eve asked.

Pushing off with his hands, Charlie7 slid out from beneath the machine. "Don't get any ideas," he said. "It's not the same for humans as it is for a robot. I just didn't want to do any further damage to my suit—it's in sorry enough shape already. Your chassis isn't scuff-proof. Mine is."

As he angled his head up, Charlie7 caught sight of Eve. He shut down his optic sensors for a few seconds to let the image clear his visual buffers.

Of course, Eve had found the loophole in his instructions.

The girl hadn't copied the clothes from the sanctuary or anything Alison3 was liable to have had saved in the cloth-o-matic's memory. Instead, she wore a copy of the outfit she'd had on beneath Toby22's oversized and borrowed clothes.

It made sense, of course. This was what the girl knew best. Having grown up in what amounted to a gymnasium, it was even perfectly practical for Creator's lab.

In total, the outfit consisted of a top that covered her from her second rib to her armpits with thin straps over her shoulders, leggings that clung to her like a second skin, and a pair of athletic shoes with some sort of fabric liner that functioned as a sock. All but the soles of the shoes were made from the same breathable synthetic fiber from the cloth-o-matic's standard list. All of it was black.

Charlie7 realized the flaw in his instructions when he saw that she carried the other two outfits bundled in her arms. They were the same thing, but in white and a shade of gray he suspected was the exact middle ground between the other two.

"I've completed my task."

"Yes. Yes, I suppose you have," Charlie7 replied in monotone.

She'd done as he asked. And, while it wasn't ideal, it was at least good enough that he didn't feel the need to send her straight back to the cloth-o-matic to try again. The gray, at least, showed a bit of initiative and decision-making, even if it was only of the blandest sort imaginable. A child who never grew up with crayons couldn't be expected to become the next Salvador Dali.

"What are you doing?"

"Thinking."

"I mean with the machine," Eve clarified, crossing her arms and fixing Charlie7 with a stern scowl.

For a moment, the old robot tried to envision that same look on each of his five suspects. After all, one of them had to be Creator, and Eve certainly hadn't learned that look from either Plato or Toby22.

Charlie7 stood and retrieved his suit. "Just figuring out what to keep and what to get rid of. Don't worry. You're a keeper."

He winked at her, wondering what human eyes saw when a robot shut off the light from one optical sensor. That had been a wink for a thousand years, but it was a mere affectation.

"Are we down here because of the tornadoes?"

"There aren't any tornadoes," Charlie7 assured her.

That little furrow returned to Eve's brow. "Are they a fictional contrivance like the flying monkeys?"

Fictional contrivance... Charlie7 made a conscious effort not to shake his head at her use of language. He didn't want to give her mixed messages or discourage her. Sounding like a human would come with time and practice, learned—with no small dose of irony—from robots who'd lost most of their residual humanity over the ages.

"Tornadoes are a real meteorological phenomenon, but they aren't currently a problem. Earth's climate is managed now. We identify the precursor effects and mitigate tornadoes before they form."

"Then why are we in the cellar?"

There were so many ways he could answer that question. He could have gone the historic route and gone off on a tangent about the invasion that had wiped out mankind. He could have expounded on the practicality of subterranean dwellings in terms of thermal stability.

Instead, Charlie7 tailored his explanation to what Eve already knew. He headed into one of the adjacent chambers, and Eve followed close behind. "You remember the other part of Kansas we visited?"

"Yes."

The question had been nearly rhetorical. Of course Eve remembered. It wasn't as if she'd suffered brain trauma in the two days since she'd been there last.

"Well, Alison3 oversaw a facility like that one. But instead of mucking up the traffic flow of all the drones flying in and out, she had a tunnel to go in from beneath."

Charlie7 hit a switch, and a row of lights blinked on down a long tunnel that vanished to a pinprick of light at the limits of vision.

The generators had been up and running long enough for the air circulators to come up to speed. Initially intended to cut down on mold formation, they also made the air breathable for Eve.

Eve squinted down the length of the tunnel as if she could make out the far end, some three kilometers distant. "If I live in Kansas, should I name myself Dorothy?"

"Of course you shouldn't. Where would you get a daft notion like that?"

"Plato said he named himself Spartacus. Then when his parrot took that name from him, he chose Plato. He said I should pick something other than Eve since lots of girls who end up at the sanctuary start out named Eve. He said it wasn't original."

"Bear in mind that Plato's an imbecile. His head's packed full of old movies and Schrodinger-only-knows what else. Look, he might have saved you from Creator, but that doesn't mean he has all the answers. I started out Charlie7, and at one point I could have chosen any name I wanted without anyone to object. I could have been Joan of Arc, Confucius, or Alexander the Great. But I'd have been the same inside. I'd—"

"Do you hear something?" Eve asked without preamble. She wandered into the tunnel entrance, hunched forward and still squinting.

Charlie7 had been keeping his audio threshold set to human levels but reminded himself that even normal adult hearing was inferior to a teenager's. He turned up the gain and noticed what was preoccupying Eve. "Um, you might want to step back."

"Why—?"

Before she could finish her question, they came into view. A swarm of bats, no doubt startled by the sudden presence of light all along the tunnels of their borrowed home, came rushing en masse toward Charlie7 and Eve.

Eve shrieked and ran for cover.

Charlie7 rushed over to shield her with his chassis but couldn't help laughing aloud.

In her panic, Eve evaded Charlie7's attempts to interpose himself between her and the swarm. Tiny rodents flapped past the girl on all sides as she spun and swatted. Every generation came up with silly dances to vex their elders; Charlie7 wondered if this was the seed of the first new teenage dance crazy of the Second Human Era.

Probably not.

Eventually, the swarm petered out. The last few bats failed to spur Eve to further contortions as she caught her breath.

"That... wasn't... funny," Eve protested.

Charlie7 picked the girl up by the waist and swung her around like they were figure skaters, grinning all the while. "Don't you understand? No. Of course, you don't. Why would you?" He set Eve down but couldn't override the smile on his face. "Those bats weren't installed here by any robot. They didn't need to be told where to live. The Earth is overcoming its reliance on robotkind."

Puzzlement still lurked in the corners of Eve's eyes, but Charlie7's laughter was contagious. Soon, Eve joined in, chuckling without even understanding why.

CHAPTER FIFTY-FOUR

As *Betty-Lou* rocketed over the Atlantic Ocean, Plato lay back in the pilot's seat and waited for his heart to stop racing. Sweat cooled as the air circulator blasted. His mind cleared. He'd done it. James187 was officially out of the human-hunting business.

It didn't matter whether the robotic hunter delivered Plato's message to Evelyn38 or slunk back to the hole he crawled out of. Evelyn38 would know just based on his failure that Plato was still looking to turn that crystalline matrix in her head as blank as an automaton's face.

The monotony of the waves beneath lulled Plato into relaxation. There would be time aplenty for vengeance. For now, he had a more urgent desire.

Eve. Plato had to find her again.

Unfortunately, that meant finding Charlie7 again. To give the old hunk of junk credit, he *had* broken into Plato's lair and not left a trace of how he'd done it. If he wanted to disappear with Eve, Plato didn't know how long it might take to track him down.

Maybe Plato didn't have to find Charlie7. Maybe that ancient bag of circuits would throw Plato a lifeline to keep him from going nuts with worry.

Putting himself in the mindset of a bored robot, Plato punched in a phony ID and sent Charlie7 a Social message. "Charlie, old bean. Fancy a rematch? I've got a new gambit sure to trap your queen."

There had been a chessboard set up in Charlie7's underground bunker. It was a solved game, but that didn't stop some robots from playing under a gentleman's agreement not to use computers. Plato hoped that Charlie7 was one of them and not just a pretentious old robot with delusions of sophistication.

Plato knew the rules of chess, but the game had never appealed to him. Too static. Too unemotional. There was no guile or courage, just cold, robotic logic. Now that his mind had wandered there, he couldn't help thinking of the comedy of the pieces. In chess, the king was more important, but the queen more powerful. Just the opposite of him and Eve. Plato was the strong one, but Eve meant everything.

That analogy would have made Charlie7 a knight or bishop. That robot never moved in straight lines.

NO TIME FOR CHESS. IF YOU WANT TO MEET UP LATER, I'VE GOTTEN A BIT HOMESICK. THERE'S NO PLACE LIKE HOME.

Plato smirked. "Oh, yeah? Homesick, huh?"

Charlie7 lived in Paris, but that wasn't home. Plato knew the biographies of the Twenty-Seven. Charles Truman was from the Baltimore suburbs. What was there now?

As he ran the archival search, Plato came across a notification that sent a shiver from toes to shoulders. He had a message.

On a fake ID.

From just after he and Eve parted ways at Liberty Island.

"There's no place like home..." Plato whispered, reading it aloud.

The archives revealed an atmospheric adjustment station in what once was Baltimore, and a fish hatchery just off shore. The hatchery was small and heavily monitored, which made it an unlikely place for Charlie7 to hide out. The atmospheric station was idle at the moment. If Charlie7 had picked one of the two, that was the more likely.

"There's no place like home..." Plato whispered again as his eyes glazed over. He tapped his heels together, and it clicked. "You're not in Baltimore. You've taken Eve back to Kansas."

Eve hadn't told Plato where in Kansas exactly, but he remembered her mentioning it while they were watching *The Wizard of Oz*. This wasn't a message from Charlie7. It was from Eve.

The difference mattered somehow.

Plato had no idea where Auntie Em's farmhouse was supposed to have been, but Kansas was only so big, and he had plenty of time to search the planetary archives for holes where Charlie7 and Eve might be hiding.

Betty-Lou banked and reversed course, heading back toward North America and onward to the Great Plains.

CHAPTER FIFTY-FIVE

CHARLIE, OLD BEAN. FANCY A REMATCH? I'VE GOT A NEW GAMBIT SURE TO TRAP YOUR QUEEN.

James187 leaned against the hull of his skyroamer. There had been no point taking off without a heading, and Plato's skyroamer disappeared from all manner of detection as soon as it was over the horizon.

But the bug he'd installed was working fine.

While he might have underestimated the human's cunning and guile, the naivety James187 had pegged for a bullseye.

Plato running inside the refinery had been a blatant trap. It had also left the human's skyroamer unattended. While sabotage might have eliminated Plato from his list of problems, it would also have cut off his best source of information.

NO TIME FOR CHESS. IF YOU WANT TO MEET UP LATER, I'VE GOTTEN A BIT HOMESICK. THERE'S NO PLACE LIKE HOME.

The response was from Charlie7's ID.

James187 had qualms about getting on the wrong side of a Toby when Toby22 had been his prime suspect for Plato's accomplice among the robots. The prospect of tangling with the likes of Charlie7 flashed unfamiliar warning messages deep in James187's quantum processors.

All those single-digit designations felt like ghosts to him. Too old. Too smug. Only one of them claimed to have known the Twenty-Seven personally. That was Charlie7.

James187 hefted the EMP rifle that Plato had left behind in his haste. For hobby-made, it wasn't a bad design, and it certainly proved quite effective at stopping automatons. When he'd taken the weapon, it was with visions of aiming it at that no-good Toby22's head and squeezing the trigger. People would grumble about a low-numbered Toby getting data-wiped, but they'd get over it.

A new communication came in. This time, the ID belonged to Evelyn38.

> JAMES, WHERE IN THE BLUE BLAZES ARE YOU? I JUST LOST A HIP ACTUATOR, AND I STILL HAVEN'T GOT A REPLACEMENT CHASSIS. I'M NOT TAKING ANOTHER TRIP TO KANTO FOR A REFIT. IF YOU DON'T BRING ME MY PREFERRED HOST THEN I'LL FIND SOMEONE ELSE WHO WILL. YOU'RE NOT THE ONLY—

He cut off the message and deleted it without reading the rest. He could just as easily envision putting Evelyn38 out of her misery with a well-placed shot from the EMP rifle.

Raising the rifle to his shoulder, he sighted down the barrel and pictured Evelyn38's condescending half-smile as she shuffled across in front of his aim. But of all the robots he knew, none offered so tantalizing a chance to feel the wind against his skin, to savor the heat of the sun's light, to taste a medium rare steak, perfectly seasoned and fresh off the grill.

Humans were coming back to inhabit Earth, and he was in line to be among the first of them. All of that relied on keeping in Evelyn38's good graces and bringing Eve14 back alive and relatively unharmed.

"Listen, you'll get your ape back. Just let me do my job."

Giving the weapon one more good look, he pitched it into the back of his skyroamer and climbed inside.

He had a job to do. It wasn't a clean, tidy job, but few of his ever were.

Animals were messy, unpredictable creatures with lives governed by chemicals and instincts. They got crazy notions and panicked when their lives were in danger. Robots, on the other hand, tended to be *too* predictable. Charlie7 should have let Eve14 devise the message for her friend Plato. Maybe that brain Evelyn38 bragged about crafting would have come up with a subtler hint that only another human would have understood.

Eve14 and Plato had spent time together. They should have planned ahead for a rendezvous if they were ever separated.

As his skyroamer lifted from the ground, James187 set a heading that put him on course for Topeka, Kansas—or at least where the maps said it used to be.

"There's no place like home?" James187 muttered. "Really, Charlie7? That was the best you could come up with?"

After all, who hadn't watched every movie ever made?

CHAPTER FIFTY-SIX

Bats. Species *Eptesicus fuscus*.

Now that Eve had looked them up and read about them in the planetary archive, the squeaking vermin weren't so scary. Maybe being enveloped by a swarm of them would still be unsettling, but those bats were harmless to humans.

The sunlight coming through Alison3's west-facing windows had dried up. Eve rubbed her eyes as she idly perused the archives, learning about Kansas, robots, and the unique vocation known as filmmaking.

Eve didn't want to sleep just yet. Plato ought to be there any minute, and she wanted to see him to reassure herself that he was all right. This would be the third time he'd risked his life to protect her.

When she posed the question of why to the archive, it had told her that behavior such as Plato's was endemic to males of many species due to the reproductive value of females in the population. Eve didn't *feel* particularly valuable, but both Charlie and Plato claimed that she was.

Charlie had been gone for hours. He was close by, somewhere in the underground levels of Alison3's old house.

The self-terminated friend of Charlie's had lots of interesting equipment. Most of it was a complete mystery to Eve, but Charlie had shooed her away; he had important things to do and couldn't constantly be distracted monitoring Eve's safety.

Besides, Eve could learn more from the archive. The Earthwide held the majority of human and robotic knowledge in one place. It could tell her the names of long-dead human leaders, the annual ore production of extraplanetary mines, and thousands of recipes that prominently featured apples. But it couldn't tell her what was in Alison3's basement, nor could it tell her how long Charlie would be down there.

The answer to that last question came shortly thereafter, when Charlie came up to the surface level. He seemed pleased, judging by the upturning of the corners of his mouth. But Eve was learning not to trust the simple visual cues that Creator had passed along and reinforced in virtual reality simulators.

Just as Plato always seemed to be varying levels of happy, she was beginning to wonder if Charlie could fake happiness altogether. Why did the two of them want Eve to think they were always happy when she was around?

"Well," Charlie said, tugging at the sleeves of his tattered suit. "Depending on how far Plato wandered before losing his tail and how fast he was willing to fly, he could be getting here any time now. Let's head outside and watch for him."

"But it's nighttime."

"Yes, a daily nuisance you'll learn to deal with," Charlie said. "I've got a surprise for you that'll make it all worthwhile."

Thus far, Charlie had been a relatively good judge of Eve's likes and dislikes; his notable misfires had all been food-related. She was willing to give him another chance to show her a surprise.

Eve followed the robot out into the fields of tall prairie grasses that surrounded Alison3's house in all directions. Constellations shone in the night sky, picked out from a trillion stars as the brightest and most prominent. Most were invisible, but Eve knew they lay beyond her unaided vision. The Milky Way spread overhead in a gentle haze of blue and orange hues.

"Isn't it beautiful?" Charlie asked.

Bare feet guided their own steps as Eve wandered in awe. Dry grass crunched and caught between her toes. Crickets chirped from all directions. Looking straight up, Eve spun slow circles and watched the universe twist above her. Infinity lay in that direction, and only a slight gravitational force prevented her from drifting away toward it.

Dizziness set in. Eve spread her feet and looked down as she waited for the prairie to stop spinning.

That was when she noticed the tiny stars that drifted among the grass. They were little more than pinpricks of light floating around in lazy, patternless routes. Heat and radiation should have killed her long before real stars could have gotten so close, and these didn't even emit heat as far as Eve could tell.

Too small, as well. Even the smallest of stars ought to have dwarfed the whole of Earth. Determined to investigate, Eve stalked and captured one and cupped it in her hands. It tickled.

"They're called fireflies," Charlie said softly, barely audible over the crickets and the rustle of grass in the breeze. "Alison3 made a hobby of bringing them back. They went extinct even before the invasion."

"How do they generate electricity?" Eve asked, peeking inside her firefly prison.

"They don't. It's a form of bioluminescence. They can—" Charlie's attention turned skyward, and Eve turned to follow his gaze. "Looks like we've got company."

There were no lights. But on that cloudless night, Eve watched the approach of an indistinct silhouette by the stars it blotted out. It had to be Plato's skyroamer.

Her heartbeat quickened, and the barefoot girl opened her hands to let her glowing prisoner fly free. Eve preferred to spend her attention on Plato's arrival.

For a moment it, looked as if he might fly right past them. But the skyroamer changed course directly toward them, and it jerked to a stop with a startling suddenness before beginning its descent.

"Eve, run!" Charlie shouted.

"But Plato just—"

"That's not Plato. No human could survive that deceleration. Now hide!"

Eve didn't need to be told twice. She didn't have the optical sensors that Charlie did so she couldn't make snap measurements of change in velocity. But his claim that no human could have survived it rang true.

Eve's obstacle course training had taught her how even the impact from dropping a few meters could hurt. Anyone inside that cockpit would have been torn in half by the safety harness or thrown through the windshield.

Why had she wandered so far?

Weren't there enough fireflies closer to the house?

Wasn't the Milky Way visible from the door?

The skyroamer was on the ground by the time Eve reached Alison3's door. She fumbled with the unfamiliar, old-fashioned handle in her haste, and as she dove inside, a dart hissed past her ear.

CHAPTER FIFTY-SEVEN

harlie7 stepped in between the pilot of the skyroamer and the house. It was a Version 68.9 chassis, but no name sprang to mind. The newcomer fired a dart in Eve's direction as soon as the canopy opened, but it missed.

"Power those engines right back up and move along," Charlie7 called out. At worst, all he had to do was stall until Plato arrived. That EMP rifle ought to be enough to scare off this lowlife poacher.

"Well, well," the robot replied, swinging a leg over the side of the cockpit. He was using a disguised voice or Charlie7 would have known him in an instant. "Look what I've got here. I'm monitoring all frequencies, and if I catch you yapping to anyone, well..."

The poacher reached into the back of his skyroamer and pulled out Plato's EMP rifle. There was no mistaking the design. It was homegrown. There was no way Charlie7 could imagine Plato making more than one, let alone distributing them to robot vigilantes.

"Don't know what you're planning to do with that thing," Charlie7 said, trying to sound casual. "But I'd recommend against it."

The wily old robot couldn't even access the archives to help figure out who this Version 68.9 was. The risk was too great that the poacher would carry out his implied threat of resetting Charlie7's brain to all zeroes.

The robot hopped down to ground level, scattering the few fireflies that remained in the area after his landing.

"I know who you are," the Version 68.9 claimed. "So don't pull that VIP horse crap on me. You've stepped into the middle of a situation you don't understand, and you're going to get yourself in a heap of trouble. Now stand aside while I bring that little girl home." The rifle's business end angled toward Charlie7's skull.

"You think a guy who's been around as long as I have doesn't have backup plans?" Charlie7 countered. "Someone of my stature doesn't just go missing, and everyone forgets about him. I have friends. They'll launch an investigation. And I'm sure their combined brains are more than enough to sniff out the likes of *you*. I hope you enjoy the prospect of banishment from Earth."

The robot with the rifle stalked forward, his weapon never wavering. "I bet it's eating you up inside that I don't have my designation painted across my skull for everyone to see. Not everyone is as famous as the great Charlie7. Tell me, Charlie... when was the last time you did a single worthwhile thing?"

"Today."

The robot laughed aloud. "You think this is noble? You're as bad as those vandals who released the chimps at the National Institute of Health labs."

"That was a thousand years ago."

"Well, what if it was?" the robot countered. "We're the humans, now. Humans are the chimps. No one likes it, but science gets messy at times. Can't all be mathematics and computer code. Right, Charlie? You could never stomach the wet side of the lab."

Charlie7 scowled. "James?" It was a guess, but he'd heard that argument from few enough robots. Most of the complaints the oldest robot got were for resting on laurels.

The robot laughed. "Oh, Charlie. You think you're so clever. Now, out of my way, or I *will* end your existence. Even the finest wines turn to vinegar, and I don't think anyone's got much of a taste left for the likes of you."

There was, of course, a chance he was bluffing. But a hint of madness seeped from the edges of those words. A robot could be pushed farther than a man. Hot blood, testosterone, adrenaline? A robot had none of those. But there was still a limit. Whichever James this was had come teeteringly close to the precipice of his.

Charlie7 stepped out of the way and let the anonymous James pass.

He had bought Eve a minute and forty-three seconds. Hopefully, that would be enough of a head start.

CHAPTER FIFTY-EIGHT

Bare feet slapped on the stone tile floor. Eve scooped up her shoes as she ran through the entry room of Alison3's house; she didn't have five seconds to spare to slip them on.

This must have been the same robot who had chased Plato. Now he was coming for Eve, and Plato wasn't here to stop him. Eve could only hope that Charlie7 was as brave.

There was only one level of the house aboveground, and Eve wasn't going to be able to hide anywhere there.

Down.

The stairs were cold on the skin of her feet, the edges hard. From above, she heard the outside door open, then slam.

She quickened her pace. No hiding the sound of her footsteps.

Eve looked left, then right. There was no good choice, so she bolted left.

It was a storage room. Crates. Cabinets. Things Charlie7 had dragged from other rooms.

Rusted. Broken. No time to pry open a place to hide.

Menacing steps pounded down the stairs. No time to wait.

Eve ran to the next room. Sparse. Just a few discarded pieces of machinery. Two exits. She chose left again.

Through two more rooms, she ran on tiptoe, the concrete floor more congenial to her attempts at silence. Down again. She slowed and took her time to make as little noise as possible on the echoing metal treads.

Footsteps overhead. Eve swung herself beneath the stairs as soon as she reached the bottom.

She was breathing quick and shallow. Her heart raced. Her short run wasn't even a warm-up for her daily exercise. It was fear.

Covering her nose and mouth to suppress the noise of her panicked breath, Eve mentally recited a mantra.

Hydrogen... Helium... Lithium... Beryllium...

She counted out elements at a steady pace one element per second. By "iron," she had returned to nearly her resting heart rate.

On the level above, she heard her pursuer. Ragged scrapes of steel on concrete and echoing crashes conjured images of demolition in Eve's mind. He was tearing open those crates and cabinets, sweeping the whole level before venturing downward, lest Eve double back on him.

Her pursuer's caution was Eve's ally.

Wiggling her feet into her shoes, Eve crept away from the stairwell to explore the rest of the second basement level.

This appeared to be where Alison3 had done most of her work. The equipment was in better repair, and Eve recognized some of it. Was there anything she could use?

A small kit of hand tools promised endless options but would be impossible to carry quietly or use quickly.

The self-powered rolling chair might have been useful for a robot, but the hard, steel surfaces made it look more like a torture device for humans. Besides, Eve doubted it moved very fast.

A desk-embedded terminal hinted at a way to call for outside help. Toby22? Nora109? Surely someone would be willing to save Eve if Charlie and Plato couldn't. But the power indicator at the corner of the screen was dead. Diagnostics and repair weren't on Eve's list of tasks for the next minute.

If Eve had that long.

She kept moving.

There was a room dedicated to rodent studies, with diagrams and models all along the walls and tucked into built-in alcoves. Another room was lined with shelf upon shelf of insects preserved in transparent resin.

A heavy door prevented entry to one chamber, and a display beside it read *289K*. That seemed consistent with the ambient temperature in Alison3's basement. Why then have a door and a temperature readout?

Power. There had been no power when they had arrived.

Charlie7 had to restart a generator; this room could be a freezer for biological samples. Without electricity, it had warmed up.

Anything inside must have been ruined. Eve knew that it was a dead end. If she managed to get inside without the robot noticing her, she'd still have no place to run, and if the freezing unit was set to automatic, it might not be long before she was a frozen biological sample herself.

A clang of footsteps was Eve's alarm clock. Time for musing was over. That relentless robot was coming down to this level.

Why hadn't Alison3 designed this building with multiple means of egress?

The answer was twofold and obvious. The first was that Alison3 had never needed to evade capture inside it. The layout was built for her convenience, not Eve's. The second was that it *did* have a second egress.

Eve headed down once more.

The bottom level housed the track-and-tram system that Charlie7 claimed led to an agrarian complex like the one they'd first visited. The wise old robot had yet to lead her astray.

A pair of linked tram cars rested at the end of the tracks, and Eve hopped the gap to climb aboard the lead car.

Protesting groans echoed from upstairs. A metallic crash shook the floor. The door to the freezer had been torn loose and cast aside. Alison3's workspace wasn't as cluttered with debris and potential hiding places as the uppermost sub-level had been.

Eve pressed a finger to the controls, and a terminal lit. Teeth gritted. Fists clenched. Why was it so easy? Why had Creator made sure none of the ones in the lab worked without a stylus that *she* provided?

She shook loose her fists and squeezed her eyes shut just for long enough to seethe out a cleansing breath. There was no time for that now.

"Eve14! Stop!" a gravelly, unfamiliar voice shouted after her.

The last thing Eve intended was to obey.

The console was straightforward. A button labeled "Start" glowed green and stood out prominently in the center of the screen. Eve pressed a finger to it and ducked down behind the sidewall of the tram.

A dart whizzed overhead as the tram lurched forward. Eve was thrown back against the rear of the open compartment as the car accelerated along the tracks.

Behind her, she heard the pounding of footsteps along the track over the whine of the tram car's motor as it hovered via magnetics. Was it her imagination, or were the footsteps getting louder?

Eve dared peek over the rear of the tram car. The robot's legs were a blur; it was gaining ground. Seeing her poke her head up, he leveled the dart gun in her direction but didn't fire.

Creator wanted her alive and well, if Charlie7's theory proved correct. The robot with the gun couldn't risk putting a dart in her eye, and it wasn't going to penetrate her skull—not that putting a hole in her head would be any more desirable.

Glancing up at the console, Eve couldn't read what anything said. Glare from the overhead lights reflected in her eyes.

Eve popped up for a better angle, then ducked down again immediately. Plus and minus buttons for speed control. Reaching blindly over the console, she pawed for the one labeled plus.

Wrong button.

Eve rocked forward as the tram slowed. She heard an impact from the car behind her.

She had to stand up enough to see. She tapped the plus button repeatedly until it faded to gray. Grabbing hold of the top edge of the console, Eve hung on as the tramcar rocketed forward.

Whirs and hisses from straining actuators drew Eve's attention behind her. The robot had latched onto the trailer car that the tram dragged behind it, presumably for transporting goods down the tunnel along with its passenger. With the dart gun in one hand and Plato's rifle slung over his shoulder, the robot was struggling to pull himself onto the trailer without giving up any of his weapons.

He was making headway. Eve didn't have long.

The simplistic controls had gone from a blessing to a hindrance. Where were the advanced functions?

While she searched for hints as to where those non-standard commands might lie, Eve tapped the minus button a few times, which threw her forward and also caused the plus button to light up. She tapped that until it went away again and felt the strain in her forearm as she latched on to keep from being thrown off the back of the tram.

The robot still clung on. Eve's effort to dislodge her tormentor had failed. Worse, he might even have gotten closer to pulling himself up during the changes in acceleration.

"Go away! I don't want to go back!" Eve shouted.

At least until he gained his footing, the robot wouldn't have an angle to shoot at her. Eve had until then to figure out the controls. She tapped unused portions of the screen and pressed the spot where the "Start" button had been, holding her finger down to no avail. Then, she tried pressing her full palm against the screen.

Think. Eve had to think like Alison3.

What would someone want to do to access secret commands? Not even secret, just the ones that lifted the access panels and got into the core workings of the tram. Wait... lifting?

Eve swiped a finger from the bottom of the screen toward the top—"lifting" it figuratively. A menu came up with it. There were boundless options, everything from power management to preventive maintenance scheduling. The option she was hoping for was listed under Cargo > Cargo Management > Trailers.

Her pursuer was climbing to his feet on the trailer. "I really am sorry about this," the robot said and raised his dart gun.

Eve hit the button labeled "Disconnect."

A dart fired, but the robot's aim had been spoiled. It glanced off the back of the tram. Its clatter faded as the tram hurtled along.

To his credit, the robot didn't give up.

With a leap, Eve's pursuer launched himself toward the tramcar. As his trailer fell behind, it robbed the Eve-hunting robot of his launch point. A grasping metallic hand extended to its limit but fell centimeters short.

The hunter fell. Camouflage hunting gear shredded and gleaming steel cast sparks against the magnetic rail before the trailer struck and bulldozed him into the gravel.

CHAPTER FIFTY-NINE

harlie7 paced the field outside Alison3's ranch house, wearing a furrow in the soil.

There were few times in his life when the oldest of robots was truly at a loss for what to do. This wasn't a day for making exceptions.

He needed a plan, and right then, he was sorely lacking for one. Charlie7's first inclination was to solve the mystery of his adversary. He was a James; that much seemed certain, but beyond that, he could have been anyone.

But this James had left his skyroamer unattended. That might be a problem—for the James.

Charlie7 decided against risking any transmissions. After all. If the gun-toting James did decide to come back, with or without Eve, and decide Charlie7 hadn't lived up to his end of the ultimatum, there wasn't going to be much he could do for Eve without a brain.

The cockpit canopy wasn't even closed. Charlie7 didn't need to transmit to hack his way into a skyroamer computer.

Seating himself in the unknown James's craft, Charlie7 pulled up the terminal. It was a custom interface and sported a password lockout. Charlie7 just smirked as he typed in an override.

While the software might have been home-coded, it used the standard building block language that all non-coder robots preferred. The building blocks were 90 percent efficient compared to stripped-down code built from scratch, and that was more than sufficient for all but the most grueling of computing.

Paranoid robots programmed all their own security protocols using the building blocks and kept one another out of sensitive private systems with admirable efficiency.

The flaw in the system was that Charlie7 had built in backdoors to any program that used the building blocks. Anyone who wanted to keep *him* out of a system was going to have to program it from a blank slate.

Within seconds of entering his override code, Charlie7 knew that he was dealing with James187. The name was plastered all over his personal files and correspondence.

The computers held a dreary tale of a robot whose sole purpose for the past three decades was the cleanup of genetic and ecological messes. If there was a flock of sparrows with a mutant gene or a population of Southeast Asian snakes loose in the Amazon basin, James187 was the robot to call. Sometimes his job was to exterminate; other times, it was to capture and relocate. He was friends with a small clique of James designations who enjoyed hunting for sport and had contracted with a few genetics producers to exchange game animals for tracking and retrieval services.

The hunter's recent contacts were of the most interest. He'd been exchanging text communications with a robot using an obviously fake ID. Lucky for Charlie7, James187 and his co-conspirator assumed their link was safe enough to use names, if not full designations. Charlie7 was dealing with an Evelyn.

So now he had a name for Creator. And thanks to his research, that name narrowed his list of suspects to two—Evelyn11 and Evelyn38.

Both lived as hermits, often going years at a time without public appearances. Both were also expert geneticists and long-time colleagues. Evelyn38 had popped up in the public eye sixteen months ago at a primate genetics conference.

Evelyn11 hadn't been seen since an inquest nineteen years ago that had sanctioned her for unauthorized genetic research on humans. That put her as suspect number one, and Evelyn38 as number two on Charlie7's list.

Charlie7 glanced at the doorway to Alison3's house. No one had come out.

He already had a message queued up for Jennifer81 with all his research on Eve's Creator if James187 came back and found him aboard his skyroamer. Neither he nor whichever Evelyn was involved was going to get away with this if Charlie7 had any say in the matter. But he still wanted to come out with a clean win.

Find Eve. Get her to safety. Expose Creator.

He hadn't been giving Eve enough thought in all this. There was an option he had overlooked. What if neither Eve nor James187 were coming out of that doorway?

He had given Eve the nickel tour of the building and shown her the tram. It sounded ludicrous to imagine that the girl wouldn't figure out how to operate it without being shown.

Would the girl risk putting so large a distance between them if it meant staying clear of James187 as well? Charlie7 had envisioned a rescue with her coming back out, them taking off, and leaving James187 with a disabled skyroamer.

In fact, as Charlie7 pondered how best to quickly sabotage James187's skyroamer, he realized that Eve probably *had* taken the tram.

It made sense. Why risk getting caught if you can get an insurmountable head start?

Either James187 would have to follow her down the tram tunnel, or he'd have to double back and take his skyroamer to the agrarian complex. Since neither of them had come back, it seemed safe to assume the former.

"Sorry for the damage, James..."

Charlie7 worked his way through the skyroamer's computer systems, thinking to set the engines to overheat. Then he remembered the live animal transports James187 had been engaged to carry out.

This craft had environmental controls. It might not have the slick interface and custom programming of Charlie7's machine, but it was far better suited to making an escape with Eve aboard. No more risking hypothermia for the poor girl until he could get his refitted.

The engines of James187's skyroamer did heat up but only in preparation for takeoff. Charlie7 had no qualms about leaving his own ride behind. If James187 could unlock the computer to get it started, he was more than welcome to it.

In the meantime, Charlie had a human girl to collect at the agrarian center fifty-three kilometers to the northwest.

CHAPTER SIXTY

The tram slowed at a rate Eve had selected from the advanced menus. The default setting seemed to assume she had a robot chassis and would have clamped herself to the car prior to arrival. Had Eve not thought ahead, she'd have been launched from the vehicle upon arrival. Instead, she drifted to a gradual halt with a mild jerk at the end.

Staring back down the tunnel, she couldn't see any sign of the robot after her.

The tram line terminated in a small depot. A section of track on a turntable stood ready to turn it around or send it off onto one of two additional tracks. Eve didn't know where either of them went, and at the moment, finding out wasn't a priority.

Eve stepped onto the platform, and her wobbly legs met solid, unyielding concrete. The solidity was welcome; the tramcar had bobbed and wiggled beneath her the whole way.

An unlabeled door led out of the depot. Plain steel, with no control console, handle, or knob. A droning of machinery thrummed from beyond. As Eve approached it to investigate, it opened unbidden.

It was a curious new experience for doors to open for her at all, let alone invite her through so boldly. But the droning increased to an industrial cacophony. Eve winced and pressed her hands over her ears against the onslaught.

Sparing a glance over her shoulder, she looked down the tram tunnel for any sign of the robotic hunter. So far, there was no sign of him.

There were two ways to go, of course.

The Plato route would have been to turn the tram around and barrel back down toward Alison3's house. That would have been bold, aggressive, brave in a foolish manner, and completely unexpected.

Or would it?

Certainly, the robot in that tunnel would hear the tram long before it arrived. Pressing himself against the tunnel wall, Eve's purser could time a shot as Eve sped past. With computer-aided ballistic calculations and nanosecond timing, the robot was sure to hit her as the open side of the tram presented an unobstructed shot.

There was also the little matter of the trailer she'd left behind along the way. She'd slam right into it. Plato's method promised either death or capture. Her imaginary Plato was an idiot.

"Sorry," she muttered aloud as if Plato might hear.

With no other viable option, Eve stepped through the door, and the food factory engulfed her.

The facility existed on a scale that Eve struggled to digest. Her eyes took it in but held tight to the spectacle. Eve's brain refused to chew it into swallowable bites.

Slow-moving ships hovered through the upper reaches, a hundred meters above, dumping red sand into a hopper. At that distance, they could have been apples, peppers, strawberries, or any number of other red foods the Earthwide had taught her.

Smell didn't carry that far, and the amalgamated scents of every food made in Kansas couldn't cut through the overbearing odor of ammonia. It reminded Eve of cleaning days at the lab when Creator brought the automatons to scrub everything down.

Automatons probably did the same in this place. Enough of the mute, slow-moving robots plodded throughout the building to populate one of those old-Earth cities from the archive. Eve couldn't imagine why they were all needed.

The factory had a maze of crisscrossed catwalks and mezzanine levels intermixed with machinery that chopped, sorted, irradiated, boiled, peeled, shucked, ground, mashed, mixed, sliced, and gobbled up everything the drone ships dumped.

How far was Eve below ground? She needed to navigate her way to the surface.

Was there a terminal somewhere that she could run a search? The walls were bare, and the consoles on the production equipment seemed stark, barely giving the essential details of the machines' function to the robot who stared at them.

Taking a chance, Eve put a hand on the shoulder of a drone. "Excuse me. Can you tell me the way outside?"

The robotic factory worker didn't respond. It seemed unaware that she had even touched it. At least the truck-driving robot had been forced to react to her presence.

Eve picked her way through the ballet of robots going this way and that, attempting to put equations to the motions and coming up with too many variables to solve. She realized that what governed them was more than a single algorithm, but rather a series of computer programs that ran everything in the factory. There was no way she could reverse engineer that all just through observation.

On her travels, Eve peered into hoppers and over the edges of walled conveyor belts to see what they were all doing.

She watched as belts carried grains and fruits, nuts and vegetables all throughout the factory. Edible parts and seeds were sorted out from waste. Portions were poured, squirted, or stuffed into bottles and bags. Numbers were laser-scorched into each container, but they meant nothing to Eve.

"These must be for the geneticists," Eve mused. It felt OK speaking aloud since she wasn't alone. There were robots all around her.

In a separate section of the factory, Eve found different sorts of machines combining ingredients. Lines of automatons plucked packages from one conveyor belt, mixed, stirred, and kneaded the contents, and placed them on another. Other drones took those payloads and checked them before feeding them through conveyor ovens.

These robots were cooking and baking.

Eve could hardly imagine it, but this was the same process that Charlie7 and Plato had shown her for preparing foods, just on a grander scale. She didn't recognize much of anything they made. Cuisine was a word that was as new as the clothes she wore.

Walking down the rows, squeezing behind the robotic cooks, Eve reached through and put a finger in a bowl of batter. It tasted sweet and sent a tingle through to her toes. Rather than steal more of the batter, she sampled from several different conveyors before one soured her on the adventure.

Porridge. This was where the meals at the Sanctuary for Scientific Sins originated.

Eve spat it out and wiped her fingers on her pants. Stealing another sample of the substance labeled "strawberry jam," she worked it around her mouth to get rid of the porridge taste and sucked her fingers clean.

She could have spent the day exploring, learning all about how Kansas turned simple foods into complex ones and what became of all the results. The factory sprawled for kilometers, and she still hadn't even reached ground level. Overhead, aerial drones continued to deliver more raw ingredients. More conveyors moved the unprocessed farm fare. More automatons cooked and cleaned and operated the stationary machines.

A door slid open.

In the hum and crash of all the culinary chaos, it caught Eve's ear. There had only been one door since she'd arrived in the factory—the one she came in by. Ducking behind a boiling vat that smelled of apple, Eve peeked down toward the entrance.

The tram station door was partly obscured by catwalks and a machine that ground wheat into flour. Still, Eve saw a robot enter. It wasn't yet another of the countless automatons but the hunter she'd left behind in the tunnels. His forest camouflage looked out of place amid the steel and concrete. The gashes in the fabric gave him a wild look.

Eve's breath quickened. Her mind filled with pieces of thoughts that didn't fit neatly together.

What had she expected? Eve had hoped the hunter had given up, but that wasn't really what she believed would happen.

Escape. Surface. Outdoors. Her priorities had been washed away in a buffet of new sensory experiences.

It didn't even smell so badly of ammonia three levels up. The sugary sweet concoctions made Eve's teeth ache just breathing in the scent of them. Why would Eve flee paradise because of what *might* happen?

Now there was no more *might*. Eve's would-be captor had returned, and she had given herself less cushion than she would have liked.

A continent would have been a nice, safe buffer.

"Come out, Eve14!" the robot shouted. "This is no place for you. Nobody wants you to get hurt."

The general noise and echoic properties of the walls would keep shouting back from giving away her exact position. Eve couldn't resist. "You're wrong. I know why she wants me back," she shouted. "Just run away before Plato gets here."

The robot laughed. "Your friend Plato isn't coming. He's hours away, and you haven't got hours. If you'd like to meet up with him tomorrow or the day after, I'm sure that can be arranged. But you'll have to come with me."

A clever ploy slipped in between Eve's panic and anger. "You don't even know who you're working for, I bet. When I found out, she made me swear never to tell anyone she worked with. That means she doesn't trust you."

"Oh, you think Evelyn38 doesn't trust me? I could have her before a committee in the snap of my fingers. But that would implicate me as well. You see, that's how the world works. We share our secrets, and they bind us together."

Was the voice moving? Of course, it was. The robot in the forest camouflage would be searching for her the whole time.

Eve scrambled on hands and knees around the legs of a line of automatons as they filed past in the opposite direction and headed for the nearest stairway up. "Now I know yours, and Creator's too."

"What? You didn't know her name before now?" The robot laughed again. "She's Evelyn38; I'm James187. It won't do *you* any good. This time tomorrow your brain will be filled with Evelyn38's mind—or it'll be mush like all the others. But I've got a good feeling this time. And if it works, I'm next in line. How do you think that Plato's body would look on me?"

The idea of Creator's thoughts in her head instead of her own made Eve want to claw her brain out with her fingernails. She squeezed her eyes shut and shook her head as if she could shake the image from her thoughts.

The idea of Plato being this cruel robot who taunted her was almost too much to bear.

"Well, maybe you can't appreciate it, but I think Evelyn38 will once she's got your body. It's curiously difficult to evaluate without the hormonal reinforcement, but I think with Plato's body, I might enjoy your company. I don't suppose Evelyn ever bothered teaching you about reproduction. Did she?"

Reproducing humans seemed like a skill Creator had already mastered. There had been Eves before her and were probably Eves younger than her as well. "I don't want to produce humans. Let Cre—let Evelyn38 worry about that, at least until Plato stops her."

A dart rang against the leg of one of the automatons next to Eve. He'd spotted her!

Eve ran.

Another dart whizzed past as she twisted and ducked, knowing that predictable movements made an easily solvable equation for James187.

Most of Eve's plan now was luck-based.

Unacceptable.

Forcing low-percentage guesswork onto her adversary improved her odds but left her fate to random chance. Without solid cover to shield her, she needed another way to stop James187 from firing at her.

Eve hopped onto the railing.

Creator's obstacle course had been designed to test her strength, flexibility, and most of all her balance.

Keeping her center of mass low and her arms slightly to her sides, Eve hurried along the 3-centimeter-wide railing. To her left side was a catwalk with automaton pedestrians roaming about. To her right, a twenty-meter drop.

Eve had never known a fear of heights, but she's also never looked down with the promise of death looming so near. If James187 shot her full of sedatives, Eve would fall.

What she'd land on depended on precisely when she fell. Options ranged from hoppers filled with boiling vegetables to lines of robots working with knives. None of them promised a good chance of survival.

And Creator wanted—no, *needed*—Eve alive.

"Get down from there!" James187 ordered. But no darts came flying her way.

Eve pivoted and stood up tall, finally daring to face her hunter. "I don't care who you are, James187, but I know that by this time tomorrow, you're going to regret having partnered with Evelyn38."

CHAPTER SIXTY-ONE

The chase was on.

Eve had found a way to ensure that James187 couldn't risk firing more darts. That left a footrace. She imagined that, as a robot, James187 could run much faster than her. Chasing down the tram before she'd learned how to accelerate it proved that much. But Eve had tricks of her own.

James187 bulled past automatons that wobbled and returned to their tasks as soon as he was gone. He was chasing her directly, not getting fancy and trying to head her off. And it appeared that unless Eve came up with a new plan, he was going to catch up with her.

In Oz, the Tin Man had been a kindly fellow even without a heart. This James187 could have used a heart of his own because Eve could imagine no compassion in him.

And while the flying monkeys of Oz had been cruel minions of the evil witch, perhaps this too was switched around in Kansas. Overhead, the farm drones drifted in and out. They weren't so hopelessly far above anymore. If Eve could reach one as it exited the agrarian factory, maybe she could hitch a ride.

"You're going to get yourself killed," James187 shouted as Eve sped her pace, jogging along the railings with her arms outstretched for balance. Without looking back, she could hear how close he was getting.

"Wouldn't that be a shame?" Eve countered. "Since Creator is planning on killing me one way or another as soon as you bring me back." She reached a corner where the railing followed the catwalk in a hard left turn. Rather than turning along with it, Eve judged the distance and jumped across.

"No!" James187 screamed.

But Eve caught hold of a railing across the way and a level down. She regretted giving up the vertical progress she'd made, but it was too far a jump to stay on the same elevation. Her knees acted as shock absorbers as her feet hit the side of the catwalk.

Without pausing, Eve ducked under the railing and ran. There were no automatons on this section of the catwalk, so she had space to put distance between her and James187.

A crash of metal shook the grated floor, and Eve wobbled in her run. Instinct took over, and she hopped up to the railing once more before James187 could get a shot off while she was over a safe surface. But running on a narrow beam slowed her, and James187 was already faster than her.

She needed a new plan.

Glancing down, Eve found her answer. A conveyor belt angled upward, lifting apples by half-moon buckets molded into its surface.

Judging the jump to land her in the middle of the conveyor, Eve leaped.

The apples made for poor footing, and Eve stumbled backward as soon as she landed. Her short, controlled fall became a helpless tumble down the slope of the conveyor. Apples smashed under her elbow and slammed against the back of her head. Hard rubber half-buckets dug into her back and legs. She came to rest in an apple-filled trough with buckets repeatedly trying to hook her left leg and drag it up along with their fruity payloads.

"Eve! Are you all right?" James187 shouted down to her.

She was dizzy and sore. Squirming among the fruits, she discovered all her limbs were intact.

"Eve is dead," she called out. "Go tell Evelyn38. Bye."

Her body was a rag doll, discarded on the tracks of an apple railroad. With her head over the edge, lolling back, she watched the drones drift overhead in resignation.

So high above. Eve had fallen so far.

Reaching blindly beside her, Eve picked an apple at random and took a bite, ignoring the weird texture of the peel in her mouth.

She had failed.

There was no way she'd ever get to one of the drones before James187 caught up with her. Why make it hard on both of them? Pain was all she'd found. The poor little glands that produced adrenaline in her body had wrung themselves dry. Numb inevitability crept in to replace her fears.

Eve crunched her apple as she waited for James187 to come down and claim her.

CHAPTER SIXTY-TWO

"I admire your grit," James187 said.

His voice wasn't so far off now, perhaps a level or two up and almost directly overhead.

There was no rush. Eve hadn't moved.

"But this way is for the better. No point harming yourself. If you come quietly, I won't need to sedate you for the trip."

Eve took a deep breath. "I think I'd rather you did. I'm done with all this. Running, hiding, running some more. Just... end it."

Drones and automatons continued their labors, oblivious to Eve and James187. It was clockwork without gears. Everything reacted to everything else. Eve had done all the reacting she had in her, and it hadn't been enough.

Eve was a gear that didn't mesh, and the clockmaker was coming to pluck her out of the works.

The clockwork patterns made a certain degree of sense even without understanding the mathematics behind them. An underlying order was part and parcel to their existence. An aberration crept into view like a splotch of color in a black-and-white world. Eve had expected one: James187. But instead, a different robot perched on a distant opening high overhead like a hawk surveying its domain.

Charlie had come to help her.

Maybe this wasn't over after all. Eve grunted and let the half-eaten apple fall back into the trough with its companions.

Charlie was gesturing with his hands. An escape route? Eve wished he'd brought Plato's rifle along instead, but the weapon was still slung over James187's shoulder.

This wasn't a fight, though, not if Eve was going to be the victor. This was an escape, and if she was going to take her chances on

Charlie7's plan, she had to act now. Charlie had yet to lead her astray.

Besides, what did she have to lose, anyway? A little pain was a small price to pay for hope.

Eve rolled onto her stomach atop the pile of apples. Bracing her hands on the side of the trough, she pulled herself over the edge and dropped to one knee on the floor beside it.

"Just stay right there," James187 said. The voice was calm, reassuring. Easy when he thought he'd already won. But this wasn't over yet.

There was a space beneath the trough, just half a meter high. Eve dropped flat to the floor and rolled until she came out the other side.

"What part of stay put was that?" James187 demanded. His footsteps quickened. "I thought we'd gotten over playing games."

"Your game. My life," Eve shouted without looking back.

Charlie had indicated she should circle around the massive central tower that several of the vertical conveyors shared. A dart flew past, and Eve knew she had to get somewhere high—and fast.

But Charlie had a plan. She had to trust that he knew how to guide her out.

Glancing up, he made a "hurry up" gesture, waving a hand in tight circles. But he also pointed to another of the vertical conveyors, and Eve followed his direction. The trough at the bottom of this one was filled with potatoes. Eve climbed in and evicted a handful of the starchy root vegetables from one of the rubber buckets and used it for a handhold. As it pulled her up, she kicked a few more potatoes out to make space for her feet to rest.

"Not this again," James187 groused. "Those drones fly automated routes. If you get to ground outside, there's nowhere to run. I won't lose track of you, and sooner or later, you'll just drop from exhaustion. Either kill yourself or don't, but let's not waste each other's time here."

Eve pressed herself as flat as she could against the conveyor, potatoes digging into her stomach and filling her face with a pungent, earthy scent.

Her frustration with James187 reached its boiling point. Eve couldn't contain herself. "I'm sixteen years old, and I've been free for three whole days. You've got no right talking about how I spend the rest of my life."

James187 had climbed aboard one of the other conveyors and was riding up toward a common destination at the top of the tower. Eve was still higher up, but James187 was climbing the buckets of his conveyor to arrive there first. If she lay there passively, the conveyor would deliver her right to him.

Charlie was no help. From her vantage, Eve couldn't see him. She wouldn't until she crested the top of the tower.

But if James187 could climb, so could she.

Eve pulled herself up one bucket at a time, pushing potatoes off the side of the conveyor to create solid handholds. She was slower than James187, but she had a head start. By her estimate, Eve might make it to the top first but not by a wide margin. One of the potatoes just fit so well in her hand that the impulse took her to hurl it in James187's direction. It struck him in the arm, and his hand slipped as he reached for the next handhold.

"It'll take more than a potato to dislodge me," he shouted across to her.

This would have been the appropriate time to have a more dangerous weapon than a potato, Eve knew. A small explosive charge would have been nice. A large explosive charge would have been even better. But all she had were more potatoes. And while the first hadn't been particularly effective, Eve wasn't feeling particularly rational.

Eve pelted James187 with one potato after another. At one point she had to climb to the next bucket for lack of ammunition. Some potatoes were big and awkward, others hardly worth the effort to throw. All of them flew toward the nasty robot anyway.

James187 calmly batted the projectiles away with one free hand, but they were distraction enough that he stopped trying to climb any higher.

All his decisions, Eve realized, were predicated on conservatism. No risk. No chances. At least none that he could help.

James187 viewed his victory as inevitable and was taking long-term odds every time. Why risk letting Eve dislodge him? Why risk tranquilizing Eve when she was balanced precariously?

Eve needed to keep forcing James187 to make long-term decisions until he ran out of time.

As they approached the top, Eve craned her neck to peer over the top of the tower.

There he was! Charlie was only a few meters overhead. A couple stairways and a long catwalk run were all that separated her from freedom.

The top of the tower poured foodstuffs into a vast wash cycle of sprayers and gratings. Eve grabbed hold of a maintenance walkway and pulled herself to stable ground. James187 was almost to the top as well, so Eve had no time to waste.

Feet clanging with every step, she reached the first of the stairways. Eve grabbed the railing to swing herself around the corner and onto the third step.

An automaton coming down at the same time had the awareness to alter course and step around her as Eve flew past.

"You're not going to—oh, ho!" James187 called out, switching mid-threat to a cheery voice. "Well, hello Charlie7! Didn't see you up there."

"Call it off, James187," Charlie shot back. "Eve's coming with me, or I broadcast your designation and my optical feed from this chase planet-wide."

Eve continued running. James187 was up the first set of stairs, gaining ground on her. Her estimate said she had enough head start to make it. The second flight was all clear, and she sprang up them two at a time.

At the top of the last stairs, she had a clear path to Charlie. She could see a skyroamer, hovering at the ready just outside the opening. Its door was wide open, inviting her inside.

James187 was on the second set of stairs. Eve hopped onto the railing in case he decided to hit her with a dart at the last minute. She had the time to spare, but not if she were unconscious.

"Put that thing down, James!" Charlie shouted. "It's a 50/50 chance she'll fall to her death."

Eve's eyes went wide, and she hurried, feet moving as fast as she dared along the railing.

"You think I'm some kind of amateur?" James187 replied calmly.

Eve heard the click, followed instantly by the whoosh of a dart in flight.

She felt nothing, but her right leg went numb. Eve's foot missed the railing. She overbalanced, struggling in vain to stay on course.

The catwalk rushed up to greet Eve as every muscle in her body went limp.

A shockwave of pain went through her skull as one of the metal studs cracked against the floor. But the agony ended quickly as Eve's world went dark.

CHAPTER SIXTY-THREE

Charlie7 watched Eve fall.

He cringed when she hit the steel meshwork floor.

When James187 aimed the EMP rifle in his direction, Charlie7 froze.

"Hold it right there, hero," James187 warned. The hunter approached slowly, the tip of the rifle's barrel never wavering. By the dishevelment of his forest camouflage jacket, Eve had given him hell to get this far. "I didn't expect you to circle back on me."

"We had a deal. I didn't transmit a thing."

James187 threw his head back and laughed. The barrel still didn't move. "I'll give you this, for an old-timer, you've still got a lot of nerve. I expected you to be halfway back to Paris by now. Maybe forget this whole business ever happened; maybe you don't, and you plug the ends of a primary power conduit into your ears like Alison3 did."

"I couldn't abandon Eve. I had to try," Charlie7 said. "Sorry." The old robot offered a perfunctory shrug.

James187 took a step forward.

"I don't rightly know what to do with you, Charlie7," James said. "You're right about being too notorious to disappear. But you're not too big to drag in front of a committee for scientific theft, destruction of research data, and interfering with a long-term experiment."

"None of that applies to unsanctioned research," Charlie7 protested. There were times when he wished he was *slightly* more automated. He could have used a subroutine that monitored his vocal output and allowed a few extra cycles of thinking before he spoke his mind.

"Maybe tomorrow... perhaps the day after... but sooner than you can plan for, the world's about to change. Humans are back," James187 said. He nudged Eve's limp form with a toe. "And we're going to be them."

"That's abhorrent!"

Charlie made himself a mental note that if he lived out the next few minutes, he was going to sit down and *write* that subroutine, even if he had to route his vocal emitter through his computer brain.

"It's ugly and new, like a newborn still covered in that goo they come out with," James187 said, flicking one hand as if to shake it clean. "Crying shame what the incompetents have done along the way. But this is the real deal. The inflection point. From here, it'll get clean. Sad thing what's gonna happen to this girl. One day the bodies won't ever need a mind to wake up inside them. Just fresh, clean, guilt-free humans grown to order. But today I'm taking this girl, and I'm gonna have to live with what comes next."

"For science?" Charlie asked.

It was a venerable old motto but an empty one. It proclaimed righteousness in the name of a nebulous concept. It abdicated ethics and morality in the service of an abstract notion that had neither wants nor needs. It was the scientist's cop out.

"Exactly!" James187 tucked away his dart gun and stabbed a finger at Charlie7 again and again as if he'd made a profound revelation. "Science saved mankind. We've been pupae, in a manner of speaking. Now, it's time to emerge in a form of our own choosing."

Charlie7 glanced down at Eve. "I can't picture you in a skirt."

James187 kept careful aim at Charlie7 as he scooped Eve up and hoisted her over a shoulder. With a deft snap of his wrist, he tugged the dart out of her thigh and flicked it out into the empty air. A few seconds later, Charlie7 heard the faint clink of it hitting the floor.

The hunter patted Eve on the rump. "This one is spoken for. I'm hoping to bring in that big fellow. Wouldn't mind a body like that one."

"Careful what you wish for," Charlie7 replied. "That 'fellow' is only twelve. He'll be dead inside of ten years. Twenty, tops."

"Hmph. Oh well. Better to wait and get a proper body. Good enough for the lad. Gave me one helluva scare. Listen, Charlie—may I call you Charlie? We're not getting anywhere here. I can't risk killing you. You can't risk being exposed. I'll make you a deal. Rumor has it you love to haggle."

"Go on..."

This might be Charlie7's best chance of getting out of this with a shot to still save Eve. Saving himself was just a crucial step along the way. After all, what good was he dead?

"That boy Plato's going to be along any time now. You convince him to let bygones be bygones, and I'll look past the committee hearings for you. I'll be a big deal myself, soon enough. Committee chairmen are going to be lined up for human bodies of their own, and I'll be on the side that's offering them. Keep a low profile for a few months, and no one ever has to know you were on the wrong side of history this time."

This was Charlie7's last chance to stop James187 from putting Eve in that skyroamer and flying off with her. Nothing he could broadcast would stop him in time. There was nothing he could do if James187 decided to pull the trigger on that EMP rifle.

This time, Charlie7 took the microseconds he needed to plan. "Deal."

"Good. Now tear out your primary data transfer cable and toss it into that wheat mill."

"What!" Charlie exclaimed.

"There's a chance that you might change your mind once I'm gone. I'd just like the reassurance that it'll take you some time to find a replacement." He aimed the EMP rifle at Charlie7's torso. "Or I can take my chances using this thing. Might not be surgical precision, but—"

"Fine," Charlie7 snapped. He had little choice in the matter.

Opening his ventral thoracic access panel, Charlie7 worked loose the primary data connection between his crystalline matrix and the workhorse computer that lived in his chest. Taking careful aim over the railing, he did as instructed and tossed the cable into the industrial wheat mill.

As he watched the cable disappear beneath the surface of the churning grain, Charlie7 struggled to maintain his humor.

James187 had to think he was resigned; that Charlie7 could ever possibly stop trying to save Eve. "That's going to ruin a batch."

James187 pushed past Charlie7, shoving the barrel of the EMP rifle against his cranium on the way by. Movies had told Charlie7 that anyone who put a gun within arm's reach was begging to get it ripped from their hands and used against them. Physics, pragmatism, and the specification on James187's Version 68.9 chassis told him otherwise. He'd be wiped clean before he put a hand on the rifle's barrel.

James187 loaded Eve inside the skyroamer. "How the hell did you get my 'roamer up here, anyway?" he asked, just before closing the cockpit door, shaking his head all the while. The skyroamer edged away and took off into the night sky.

The oldest robot watched two pinpoint lights from the skyroamer's ion engines until they disappeared over the horizon. "I'm Charlie7. I used to be a hero."

CHAPTER SIXTY-FOUR

The girl stirred in her seat. James187 watched the fluttering eyelids as Eve struggled to shake off the effects of the tranquilizer. She was strapped into her safety harness, so there was no risk of her going anywhere, and her wrists were bound behind her with cable-ties, so she wouldn't be unbuckling herself.

"Plato? Where are we?" Eve14 asked. Her voice was groggy, and she slurred the words.

Evelyn38's advice on the dose hadn't come with a warning of how quickly it would wear off. A doe that took a similar amount to knock out would have been asleep for six to eight hours. Eve14 hadn't been out for two.

"I'm not Plato."

There was no point in lying to the girl. She'd figure it out on her own soon enough. And there might well have been things he didn't want to hear if he had played along.

Eve14 squeezed her eyes shut harder, then fought to open them.

So young. James187 had never been young like that. He'd been born a middle-aged man from the memories of three scientists who barely remembered puberty existed, let alone what it was like. Eve14 was a little older than that but not by a lot. Sixteen, she'd said?

James187 couldn't imagine how Evelyn38 dealt with her for so long without growing attached. Experience, he guessed. Kill enough of the same girl, and it probably got easier thinking of the next ones as rodents.

The cunning rodent in the seat beside him had worked one of her shoes off and was trying to reach for the control console barefoot. James187 slapped the foot away. "Quit that. You don't behave, I'll tranq you again."

Eve14 squirmed in her seat, struggling to get loose from her harness. After a few minutes of fruitless effort, she gave up with a sigh. "Might be better. I don't think I'm going to like the rest of my life much."

James187 kept his eyes on the controls. There was nothing the least bit interesting or unusual going on there, but at least it kept him from looking Eve14 in the eye. "You've had it better than any human in a thousand years."

"Not saying much," Eve said with a grunt as she resumed straining against the harness. "Since there haven't been any."

"Sure there have," James187 replied, trying to keep the tone light. "There's a whole island for them."

"They're not like me," Eve14 replied, slamming her head against the headrest in frustration. "Most of them are happy. They don't understand the world that made them. I do."

James187 adjusted their course three degrees north. He checked the wind speed. An indignant message arrived from Evelyn38 asking what was taking him so long; he deleted it. "Plato understands. And he hasn't got much longer on this Earth than you do."

"You'll *never* get Plato," Eve14 shot back. "Once he finds out what you've done to me, he won't rest until he makes you pay."

James187 reached back behind Eve14's seat and pulled the EMP rifle into her field of view. "Actually, Plato helped quite a lot. I doubt I could have dealt with Charlie7 on my own without it. Factory full of automatons; heavy industrial machinery; drones overhead everywhere. Not a good recipe for taking on an adversary who cuts through data security like butter. Did you get a chance to *taste* butter while you were taking your little holiday?"

"No."

"Oh, I miss the taste of butter. I can't even remember what it tastes like, exactly. I just remember the feeling of downing a plate of chicken with fresh biscuits oozing over the sides with melted butter."

"I'll keep it in mind for next time I escape."

James187 laughed. When he looked over and saw Eve14's tear-stained face, his mirth faded. "I'm sorry. If it were all the same, I'd tranquilize you. But Evelyn wanted you awake and alert if at all possible."

"How much trouble would I have to cause?"

James187 pinched the bridge of his nose between his fingers and shut off his optical inputs. "How about you sit there quietly and just don't think about it?"

Eve14 pursed her lips. James187 set a timer. At five minutes, eighteen seconds, the silence broke. "Not working. It's a pretty insistent topic. I can either think about getting my brain erased, or think about *not* thinking about it, which pretty much boils down to the same thing."

"What if I put on a movie?"

"Do you have *The Wizard of Oz*? Plato had that one. It was nice, except for the parts that weren't."

"No place like home, huh? That got you in enough trouble for one day, I think. And no, I don't keep the entire planetary archive on board. We're not broadcasting anything, either. Not even a request to the database for an old movie. But I've got one you might like. Might give you some perspective."

James187 punched up an old favorite of his, a classic from the early age of digital effects. They didn't make them like that even in his heyday, let alone the modern wasteland of imitation entertainment. Nothing past the Human Age was worth the time it took to watch.

"What sort of matrix is this about? Will there be vector mathematics?" Eve14 perked up at the prospect. Weird kid.

James187 smirked at his own joke even before he told it. "No one can explain it to you. You'll have to watch it yourself."

Eve14 took his advice to heart and in moments was watching, transfixed. James187 let the skyroamer fly along on autopilot and watched the girl's reactions rather than the movie itself. He'd seen it a thousand times, but through her eyes, everything was new.

CHAPTER SIXTY-FIVE

Charlie7 arrived at the tram station beneath Alison3's house to find Plato crouched behind the cabinet of a control console. The boy had a pistol in his hand, aimed at Charlie7's head.

"Not this again. Put that thing away," Charlie7 snapped.

Navigating the agrarian factory to the ground floor had taken embarrassingly long. Without an internal map of the facility, Charlie7 had to rely on visual orientation. Without dynamic physics calculations, he couldn't safely jump down multiple levels at a time. And with his own native coordination and navigation skills, he'd spent half an hour stumbling into oblivious automatons, backtracking out of dead-end walkways and losing track of his north and south.

Now here Charlie7 was, arriving back somewhere he could scavenge a data cable, and the first thing he ran into was a trigger-happy genetic mutant.

Plato sprang to his feet, and the pistol aimed away from Charlie7's cranium. "It's you! Where's Eve?"

"James187 took her. He's on his way back to Creator now. I have her narrowed down to two robots. If we split up, we can—"

"It's Evelyn38," Plato said. "She's based out of a lab in Rome."

Charlie7 glitched and froze, one foot halfway to the ground. "Wait. You knew? All this time? Of course, you did... Why not tell me? Why not tell Eve?"

"Slow down, cowboy. First off, we're not friends. I still don't like you, but you're trying to help Eve, so you get a pass. Second, I don't want her getting her credentials pulled and seeing her shipped off to supervise an asteroid miner. She's due for a little 'self' termination, courtesy of yours truly. Now, if you want to help, fine. But no more yapping. Let's move."

Plato was good as his word. Without waiting for Charlie7, he burst through the door and up the stairs on his way to the outside.

"Wait a minute," Charlie7 shouted after him. "That James made me pull my data cable. I just need to—"

"Got spares in *Betty-Lou*," Plato said. "Tools too. I do a lot of... work... on the side."

"But I'll just—"

"Not a discussion," Plato snapped. "I'm flying. My ride's almost invisible. Plus, I don't need some smartass robot snapping my neck with twenty-G maneuvers."

CHAPTER SIXTY-SIX

"**I** need that to fly," Plato griped as he watched Charlie7 unplug one end of a data cable from his skyroamer's internal computer.

"No, you need it to navigate, and I can help you with that part. But you're going to need me for what's coming up next."

It wasn't as if Rome was some mysterious Shangri-La or even remotely difficult to locate. Even blundering about with just the sun and coastlines, Charlie7 was certain he could get them there. And once he'd plugged into the computer, he'd be able to see so much more.

"I didn't say you could tear *Betty-Lou* apart."

"Which do you care more about, Eve or this silly glider?"

In fairness, it was a nice ride, well maintained and upgraded to Plato's preferences. The seat was set back farther than a stock skyroamer, and the skyroamer had both pressure and temperature controls for the cockpit. Charlie7 even suspected that he had overrides for black-out level g-forces.

"I like both," Plato replied, casting Charlie7 a look from the pop-up book of nasty scowls.

Knowing the boy's real age had cast Plato in an entirely new light. He had a simplistic view of right and wrong, selfish petulance with regards to possessions, and an entire lack of understanding of his feelings regarding Eve. His body had blown past puberty with no time for his mind to adjust, and no one to guide him.

"Well," Charlie7 said. With a quick jerk, he yanked the computer console out of the cockpit's dashboard. "Eve represents more to me than you can possibly comprehend; certainly a lot more than this hunk of aluminum and glass. And when we find Evelyn38, we're going to need to be ready for her."

"I got in just fine last time," Plato countered. "I'll do it again. And this time..." He pantomimed a gun with his fingers.

"That pea-shooter isn't going to do much. If the round doesn't penetrate, the thermite will just burn on the floor. James187 took your EMP rifle, remember?"

Reaching into the back, Plato patted a duffel bag. "Still got my grenades."

"They're in the tall grasses, back in Kansas."

"What?" Plato shouted. The skyroamer wobbled as he took his hands from the steering yoke and unbuckled his harness. Twisting in his seat, Plato rummaged through the contents of his bag. "They're gone. Why would you...? *HOW* did you...?"

Charlie7 cleared his throat and copied Plato's voice. "'One sec. Gotta take a leak first.' That was when I removed and discarded the EMP grenades. Saving Eve is a noble goal, but I'm not letting you blast *me* blank in the process."

"You think I'd—?"

"In a heartbeat," Charlie7 answered without allowing him to finish. "You've still got ideas cooped up in that giant skull of yours that you can put this genie back in its bottle. Kill off every robot who's seen you or heard of you except the staff at the Scrapyard."

"Don't call it that," Plato said with a clenched fist aimed at Charlie7.

"You go back to rescuing captive human guinea pigs, and you and Eve live happily ever after. Sound about right?"

"If you can keep your mouth shut," Plato countered. "There's no reason to arrange a self-termination."

Charlie7 shook his head. "You think an ongoing epidemic of robots supposedly ending their own existences will go unnoticed? Committees are already meeting about it privately. No. When we save Eve and stop Evelyn38, it'll be time to tell the world. I'll set up a commission to root out the geneticists working on humans. We'll regulate the industry. We'll—"

"Wait. Industry?" Plato's eyes were shrewd and narrow, boring into Charlie7's optics.

"Fine. Call it what you like. But there is genetic diversity split up among God-only-knows how many labs, and until the population genetics support sexual reproduction as the only means of birth, yes, there will continue to be a need to manufacture humans from scratch."

"You're not telling anyone about us."

Charlie7 let his shoulders rise and fall. He hung his head. "Very well. I need your help, so I'll have to respect your wishes. But at least consider the benefits. Can you promise me that?"

Plato snorted. "Sure. I'll consider it."

They flew on toward Rome with a tentative agreement in place. Plato had no intention of considering the matter, Charlie7 knew. That was all right with him because he hadn't the slightest intention of keeping the matter secret to begin with. The world deserved to know what was going on, and humanity deserved the protection the committees could provide.

Charlie7 just needed to keep that to himself long enough to secure Plato's help.

CHAPTER SIXTY-SEVEN

Rome looked as it always had. A thousand years? Three thousand? The city shrugged away time like a rain slicker in a storm. The Colosseum had withstood Carthage, Visigoths, a world war, and an otherworldly war. Maintenance and restoration efforts deserved some of the credit, but few places on Earth could boast so much intact Human Era architecture.

One of the newer structures, a baby at some fifteen hundred years, was their destination.

"I hate this place," Charlie7 muttered as he followed Plato through the door of the Sistine Chapel. "They should have walled it off in glass and left it alone."

Plato craned his neck and watched the ceiling as he walked. "I was in a little more of a rush last time. It's not half bad in here. It's like walking into a painting that someone folded into a building. You know, like one of those origami cranes?"

"This was a place for appointing emissaries of God, not for playing at it," Charlie7 said, careful to keep his voice down. The echoes reminded him that if the walls could hear, so could any number of surveillance devices. "Evelyn11 lived here for ages. After her sanctions, the Genetic Ethics Committee sent a team in to clear it out. Everyone thought this place was empty. I mean, who'd want to live in a place with a history like that?"

"Evelyn38," Plato answered, stating the obvious.

There were scuff marks on the floor, consistent with the unshod feet of automatons. Charlie7 traced them until the marks ended abruptly. "This must be where the elevator is," he said, pointing to the faint outline that marked its perimeter. "Give me a minute, and I'll—"

"Way ahead of you," Plato replied. He held the makeshift computer Charlie7 had ripped out of his skyroamer. The elevator lurched with a grinding of gears and began to rise from the floor.

"Not bad, kid. I figured the codes would have changed."

"They had," Plato said. "I cracked through again."

"But I didn't show you how to use the universal decryptor."

Plato shrugged. "You didn't teach me how to fly here, build an EMP rifle, or shave either."

Point taken. Charlie7 gave Plato a curt nod and followed him down into the secret laboratory of Evelyn38.

In his head, Charlie7 rehearsed his speech. He'd tell Evelyn that her game was over, that she was as good as exposed. She would protest, bargain, plead. Charlie7 would remain impassive through her ranting, then make her an offer. He would intercede and ask for clemency on the part of the dozen or so ethics committees she'd contravened. In return, she'd release Eve14 unharmed, along with any other humans she had squirreled away. The only trick would be to get Plato to shut up and not shoot her before they accounted for all the Eves she might have created.

They bypassed the upper levels where legitimate research had once been performed on orangutan embryos and stem cells. Nothing found there would be incriminating, even if Evelyn38 had reopened it for her own research.

The elevator stopped. Plato had his thermite pistol at the ready. Charlie7 steeled himself for horrors they might discover beyond.

The doors opened to reveal nothing at all.

The corridors were empty.

Doors stood wide. Laboratory after laboratory lay open to view, numbered and vacant.

"Where'd it all go?" Plato asked.

Charlie7 studied the floor. More of the same scuff marks. "Who keeps a personal army of automatons? There must have been six or eight of them. I could have automatons of my own, but I borrow them when I need work done. Pairs, mostly. Four at the most. She must have moved her entire operation out of here since you rescued Eve."

"That's why I usually kill first, save second," Plato said, grabbing a doorframe and leaning inside to peer around. "But Eve freaked me out. Besides, Evelyn38 wasn't here that day."

"Where was she?"

"How would I know? If I had a tracker on her, I'd have made sure to come when she was. But I was just—hey, wait up. One of these doors is sealed."

Charlie7 followed around the bend that Plato had taken and confirmed that there was, in fact, a single door that wasn't wide open. "Stand aside," Charlie7 said.

"Oh, come on," Plato replied, angling to block Charlie from getting to the door first. Hooking the emergency slider handhold with his fingertips, Plato grunted and pulled. Muscles ripples and veins bulged in those gorilla arms of his, but the door didn't care.

Charlie7 scooped up the portable computer Plato had ignored and punched in a few commands. Plato stumbled backward as the door slid free and retracted into the adjoining wall.

"See?" Plato boasted. He glared at the computer when Charlie7 handed it back.

Beyond was an office. At least, it was staged to look like an office. Charlie7 had been in enough of them to know real from phony, and this office looked as phony as a Hollywood set. There were just a desk and a chair. The desk was empty, and the chair's occupant was inanimate.

"Is that her?" Plato asked.

The automaton was a female chassis of archaic design. It was a remake of an early model that a few elderly robots preferred, to the point where there had been dozens of iterations over the centuries that kept the same basic structure and aesthetic.

The silent robot behind the desk wore a white lab coat turned brown with dust. The eyes were dead, without any hint of glow.

Tuning his auditory sensors to maximum, Charlie7 couldn't detect the slightest hum to indicate there was live power in the robot. He had his suspicions already, but he circled around the desk to be sure. Pulling down the back of the collar, he read off the engraved designation. "No. This is—or should I say, *was*— Evelyn11."

Plato came around to see for himself. "It says Evelyn oh-one-one."

"The leading zeroes aren't pronounced. It's not Toby oh-two-two, or Alison double-oh-three," Charlie7 said. "This was once Evelyn11, and now we know what happened to her."

Plato nodded along in agreement. "Yup. Evelyn38 killed her or at least covered up her death. She's got to be stopped." As Plato turned to leave, Charlie7 caught him by the arm.

"No, you idiot," Charlie scolded him. "If you kill someone you hide the body—or chassis, in this case. You don't build them a memorial halfway between your office and your lab."

"What are you saying?"

"I'm saying that Eve isn't the first attempt to find a new body for Evelyn11. She murdered Evelyn38 and took her place."

CHAPTER SIXTY-EIGHT

James187 marched Eve 14 along by the upper arm. The bindings at her wrists kept her arms behind her back and prevented her from doing much of anything to try to pull loose. The stone walls were a smooth three-quarter circle through the volcanic rock, with only the floor cutting the chord to ruin the geometric perfection.

"Is it geologically safe down here?" Eve14 asked. Even in its final moments, the girl's brain couldn't help filling itself with new information.

"Kilauea erupts regularly. Hasn't hurt this place yet. Besides, what's it matter?" James187 asked. "You won't be around to notice."

"I'd be willing to help program a big simulation where everyone *thinks* they're human," Eve14 suggested with a hopeful smile. "Wouldn't that be better for everyone? I mean, if Evelyn gets bored with my body, she has to grow a new one. But if it's all a simulation, she could be anyone she wants, whenever she wants."

James187 shook his head and kept Eve14 moving forward. "Can you please forget the movie? Dang it. Wish I'd just tranqed you like you asked."

"Go ahead," Eve14 replied. "Best part of this life is over already. Nothing left I want to see."

James187's next footstep faltered, but he recovered. Had to have been a flaw in the freshly carved floor. Automaton work. Couldn't trust it. "Don't say that. Every minute's a gift from Evelyn, you know."

"My life wasn't a gift. It's not a gift if you plan to take it back. I just got to borrow me for a few days."

"More like stole."

Eve14 twisted in James178's grasp to look him in the eye. "Whose life was it in the first place?"

James187 jerked the girl around to face forward. "Keep quiet."

The tunnel continued down for a hundred or so more meters before branching left and right. Both directions ended in heavy steel doors after two meters. James187 took a right and pressed a button on the console beside it. He bent to speak into it.

"I've got her."

"What's behind that one?" Eve14 asked, indicating the other door with a jerk of her head.

Curious to the last. What could it hurt to indulge? "Geothermal generator and the behind-the-scenes stuff to run this place. It's dull as corn flakes. I'm sure you'd love it."

She tried to turn for a better look. "Could we just—?"

"No."

The door skidded open with an unpleasant shriek.

"Good Lord, James. What took you so long?" Evelyn38 bustled through, limping on a bad knee actuator and moving with audible whirs and pops from old servos. "And you, Eve dear, what's wrong with your hands?"

"She didn't come willingly," James187 replied. "I used a cable tie to restrain her."

Evelyn38 took custody of Eve14 and spun her around. "James, you ninny. If you've damaged her circulation, I'll pitch you into this volcano. That's what the foaming agent was for. I even brought the cutter to get her out of it." She pulled a handheld reciprocating saw from her pocket and revved its high-pitched engine. With a flick of her wrist, she cut Eve14 free. "Come along, Eve."

Evelyn38 retreated into her lab, but Eve14 stood her ground.

"You're welcome," James187 interjected, suddenly feeling left out of the matter.

"Oh, James, don't be bothersome. I'll keep my word. But you'll just be underfoot in the meantime. I'll contact you when it's done." She looked back, seeming to notice for the first time that Eve14 wasn't accompanying her. "And you. What's gotten into that head of yours?"

Evelyn38 reached into another pocket and withdrew a pen-shaped device. Pressing the button on one end caused a high-pitched tone that forced James187 to filter his audio inputs.

Eve wasn't so fortunate. Her hands went instantly to the sides of her head. Inarticulate agony forced a scream from her throat.

Still holding down the button, Evelyn38 grabbed Eve14 by the arm and dragged her inside. The door began to slide shut, separating James187 from Evelyn38 and Eve14.

James187 leaned to keep his line of sight to Evelyn38 as the opening narrowed. "You don't have to do that to her! She's just—"

"That will be all, James," Evelyn38 replied just as the door boomed shut.

CHAPTER SIXTY-NINE

T he studs that began just outside her skull and burrowed deep inside rang like a fire alarm in Eve's head. She struggled to keep both hands over her ears as Creator towed her along. It didn't help.

In her panicked state, she tried to remember that it wasn't the sound that hurt but the resonance. Every one of the forty-eight studs in Eve's skull amplified the sonic vibration and transmitted it directly to the surrounding bone. With her one free hand, she pressed down on as many of the studs as possible to dampen the effect.

Even with both hands, it wouldn't have been enough.

Eve's breath came in gasps with little whimpers between. She kicked her feet and thrashed. Eve needed to get loose, needed to get away, needed to get Creator to take her thumb off the button on that awful little device.

"Stop being a crybaby," Creator warned. "This is your own fault. You've forgotten the primary rule. Do you remember what that is?" She took her thumb off the button.

A wave of dizziness flooded in as the ringing stopped. "Do... what... told."

"Oh, my. I hope I didn't damage anything in there." Creator patted her on the cheek. "Don't worry, dear. The effect is well calibrated. You're unharmed."

"Not... for much longer."

Creator hoisted the disoriented girl up onto a table. Eve's senses slowly returned to clarity.

They were in a lab; that much was clear. The surroundings were all new—rock walls and ceiling with inset diode lighting—but the equipment was all familiar.

"Now just lie there and hold still," Creator ordered. Her tone was the same as ever—proper, condescending, slightly amused.

Eve knew what was coming next. She'd done it herself enough times at Creator's direction. Detailed encephalographic readings required her to be hooked up to the scanner and held firmly in place. Creator was going to restrain her.

If Eve was never going to move under her own power again, she couldn't surrender without giving the very last of her efforts to resist.

Creator was on one side of the table. Eve tried to roll and drop off the other. But an unyielding robotic hand still had her by the wrist.

...and the other hand held the device.

With the push of a button, Creator reduced Eve to a quivering mass of blinding pain without a cogent thought in her head.

When the pain faded, Eve heard the familiar sound of a ratchet mechanism tightening the padded cuff around her right wrist. Eve threw her weight against the cuff, willing to tear her own hand off if that's what it took to get free.

The blinding pain again. Then the sound of the ratchet. This time it was her left wrist held fast. The next repetition of the cycle and a strap tightened across her chest and upper arms, just above the elbow.

"We can't keep on like this all day," Creator said, leaving Eve for a moment and disappearing behind the head of the machine at the table's end.

As much as the chest strap allowed, Eve forced her head around to watch what was happening. She tracked Creator by her irregular footsteps. When the robot reappeared, it was on the far side of the machine, and she held a needle on the end of a tube.

The intravenous port at the crook of Eve's left elbow was exposed. She couldn't move her arm enough to even inconvenience Creator as the needle went in. "Why are you doing this?"

"You see? Questions are fine. Shows that magnificent mind of yours is still working. Disobedience is not." Creator paused to clear her throat. Eve wondered why since technically Creator didn't have a throat to clear. "You see, I am in an old chassis no longer supported by Kanto. I've gotten by for years on begged and cobbled replacement parts, but I need a new one."

"Why me?" Eve asked. A slow, seeping chill was spreading outward from her arm. Already she couldn't feel the fingers of her left hand. "Why not a new robot chassis?"

"Because I need a new mind, as well. This crystalline matrix is degrading. Soon it will start losing bits and pieces of data. Not long after, a cascade failure will cost me everything."

"Doesn't answer the first question," Eve clarified. She blinked as fatigue pressed down on her like a suffocating pillow.

"Oh, that. I've dreamed for centuries about having a human body again. I was an old lady when Evelyn Mengele's mind was scanned. Not just to be human again but to be *young*. This dreary life is colorless. I can identify a million chromatic combinations, but not one of them seems like a color. I want human eyes, human taste buds, human ears. I want every sensation I can remember and each one I've forgotten, and I'm going to experience them all through *you*." Creator reached down and tapped Eve on the tip of her nose.

Creator moved out of her field of vision, and Eve heard another ratchet tightening. There was no feeling to go along with it. Drowsiness was robbing her of her last seconds of conscious thought. Eve was running out of time to win a debate that could spare her life. "Same problem... fifty years."

"Longer than that, I'd wager," Creator replied amiably. "You're very well manufactured. But your point is valid. However, once I have the process refined, it's infinitely repeatable. I'll simply prepare a new Eve, or..."

But the rest of Creator's words faded to mush in Eve's ears, indistinct and distant. She drifted off to drug-induced slumber to the sound of ratchets tightening.

CHAPTER SEVENTY

Charlie7 paced the room where Evelyn11's chassis sat impassively. Plato stood in the doorway, gripping the sides of the frame like he was trying to tear it from the wall.

"We're back to square one," Charlie7 said. "There isn't enough time or forensic evidence to find Eve before it's too late."

"You're the big hero to robotkind," Plato snapped. "Do something. Call in a favor. Threaten someone. Go ahead and announce her name to the world."

Charlie7 tapped himself on the cranium as if he could spin his quantum magnetics faster. "Oh, maybe. Maybe. Last resort only. I know that if she sees the end coming, Eve is doomed. Her best chance is the element of surprise."

Plato's eyes shot wide. "I've got it! We'll announce a contest, and say Evelyn38 won it. Then we—"

Charlie7's hand snapped up and interposed itself between Plato's idea and his audio receptors. "Just stop right there. What little I heard of that already took up data storage space I don't want it occupying."

"Better than anything you came up with..."

Charlie7 resumed his pacing. "Not if you believe in negative numbers."

A thermite pistol appeared in Plato's hand. That boy's reflexes were unbelievable. "You say that again. I dare you. I double-dog dare you."

But Charlie7 wasn't interested in Plato's tantrum just then. He had just received a message. The ID was anonymous, but he knew at once who had sent it.

NEW ARRANGEMENT. YOU GET EVE. MY NAME IS LEFT OUT OF ANY OFFICIAL REPORT. DEAL?

"Deal! Of course, deal. Where is she?" Charlie7 spoke the words directly into his internal computer, never giving them voice.

"Hey, look at me when I'm talking to you!" Plato shouted, taking a step closer and aiming the pistol at Charlie7's mouth.

"Shut up!" Charlie7 snapped at him. Then a moment later, he had what he needed. "Let's go. I figured out the coordinates. I know where Eve is being held."

"Huh? How?"

"I think someone who wanted a human body remembered he still has a human soul."

CHAPTER SEVENTY-ONE

Eve awoke. She hadn't expected to.

"There you are, dear," Creator cooed. "Hadn't realized the kind of day you'd had. Your electrolytes and potassium levels had crashed. But I've got your vitals on the monitors now, and levels are coming back to normal."

Eve couldn't move. Her body was a lump of lead. There was no feeling from her neck down. Every few second there was an electric tingle in her skull as another lead was connected to one of the studs.

A cold chill that was entirely imagined ran the length of Eve's spine. As for actual sensation, Eve's body already felt dead around her.

"By the way, you're also filthy. I don't know where James found you, but what had you been doing, rolling around in a pasture?"

"Agrarian factory."

"Hmph. Same thing, really. Then again, if all goes well, I'll be eating the foods from there soon enough." Creator giggled. "Can you imagine it? Me. Eating." She pulled down Eve's lower lip and peeked at her teeth. "Still took good care of them while you were gone?"

"No toothbrush."

Creator *tsked* at her. "No fair abusing that body just before I move in." She finished attaching probes and returned moments later with a toothbrush.

For the sake of obstinacy, Eve pursed her lips. If Creator was the least bit bothered, she didn't show it. The robotic mad scientist merely jammed the toothbrush between Eve's lips and activated it.

The merry-sounding little motor buzzed away as Creator ran the spinning head around Eve's mouth. There were squirts of water and vacuum suction to remove the suds, and Creator pried open Eve's jaw to get at the flat tops of the teeth.

Eve's teeth were clean, even tasting vaguely of mint, but never had she felt so dirty. Nothing Eve could do was enough to fight off Creator's control. Not even the inside of Eve's mouth was her own.

"There. That'll do for the time being. Now, open wide."

Reluctantly, Eve complied. But Creator pushed her jaw closed. "Eyes. I'm done with your teeth."

Eyes? Just what was Creator planning? "Where's the screen?"

"With how you've been since you got back?" Creator asked in reply. She patted Eve's cheek. "You'd never keep your eyes on the images."

With one hand, Creator pried open the lids of Eve's right eye. With the other, Creator maneuvered a device with four prongs into position millimeters from her iris. It held a clear hemispherical lens ringed with circuitry.

Eve tried to look away, but she couldn't actually get her eyes out of their sockets. That seemed to be the only safe place for them.

Creator patiently tracked Eve's twitching attempts to look away and finally pressed the lens to her eye. There was a puff of releasing air and a firm pressure against Eve's eye, and then the pressure released.

Taking away her steel fingers, Creator let Eve close her eye.

Eve could see just fine, though her eyes were now both watering profusely. Blinking cleared it up, but her eyelid could feel the slight presence of the lens. She squeezed her eye shut and tried to crush the lens to stop it from clinging like a tick to her cornea.

"All that fuss over nothing," Creator chided. She loaded another lens into the device and leaned across to perform the procedure a second time.

Eve barely bothered to resist. What was the point? What was one more violation she couldn't prevent?

This time, the lens locked onto her eye in just seconds.

"What did you just do? Where did you get that thing? You never used it before."

"On the contrary," Creator replied. "Eve12 was a wiggly one. Never kept her attention on what she was supposed to be looking at. Not sure what I did to put the wiggles in that one, but I didn't make the same mistake with you. *You* managed to acquire some gumption. Those projection lenses are stapled to your cornea. 'Stapled' makes it sound worse than it really is. They're really just two-millimeter hooked barbs that hold the lenses in position. They're terribly useful little things. I don't plan on removing them once I'm using that body. Here, watch."

Suddenly Eve's vital signs appeared in her field of view, hovering in mid-air between Eve and lights set into the lab's stone ceiling. Her heart rate was twenty-five beats per minute. Her blood pressure read ninety over sixty-five. Eve's attention wandered briefly to seeing just how she was faring. Then she remembered her imminent death, and the rest of the numbers seemed less relevant.

"Why me?" she asked softly. "Couldn't you use someone else's body? I think I was just starting to find out that I like being a human."

Creator affected an exaggerated sigh. "And that, my dear, is why you were never supposed to know about them. You were a happy little lab rat until someone broke you out of here. You wouldn't mind telling me who, I assume?"

There was a loud clunk and a familiar hum as the brain scanner switched on. Creator was peering into her mind, and Eve wasn't being shown what she saw in there.

Could Creator read her memories like a data file?

Could she look up the information herself?

Eve squeezed her eyes shut and tried not to think at all. But the numbers hung there, impossibly giving the impression of floating a meter or so in front of her despite her closed eyes.

Creator's voice grated like steel. "I asked you a question, Eve."

The resonance device clicked to life, and Eve couldn't even cringe against the pain. She cried out and could feel the tears streaming down the sides of her face. The numbers for her heart rate and blood pressure rose rapidly, broadcast directly onto her retinas.

"I won't tell you," Eve gasped out between waves of pain. "Find the data yourself."

"You're not an indexed database, my dear," Creator replied. Her voice reverted to a gentle lullaby. "Despite my best efforts to mold your thoughts into a rigorous, regimented system, there's still more chaos than order inside that skull of yours. Might as well start sorting out how much damage your little holiday has done."

A test pattern filled Eve's vision. Mismatched images blurred into focus, coalescing into an ever-shifting three-dimensional shape complete with the illusion of depth perception.

Despite her fear and horror, she couldn't help trying to figure out the algorithm the lenses used to create the effect. The test pattern was replaced by an image of a fork and knife. A few seconds later, an illusion of a red ball lofted in a ballistic arc. Then an array of colorful cubes spun across Eve's view.

The images flashed past, and Eve looked at all of them for the prescribed interval. Her brain reacted to them involuntarily, assigning objects their proper names, calculating trajectories, identifying patterns.

Eve couldn't stop her thoughts if she tried. And Eve did try. She threw every gram of mental energy into thinking about anything other than the images being injected into her eyes.

Creator needed data, and with limited options for rebellion left to her, denying her that data was all Eve could hope to accomplish.

Eve struggled to picture Plato's face, but with her eyes processing so much visual data so quickly, his features washed away in a flash flood of imagery. Shifting tactics, Eve remembered apples—their taste, the slimy texture of the peels, the sweet smell. She rehearsed the melody to the songs from *The Wizard of Oz* and Plato's silly munchkin voice as he sang along.

The images ceased abruptly.

Eve opened her eyes, and the lab ceiling stretched above her. Then Creator's face loomed into view.

"You think you're clever. Don't you? The outside world has mucked up that noggin of yours, and I need to know exactly how. But you're placing me in a quandary. Any harm I do you, I'll end up feeling the aftereffects. Yet, I need you to comply. And I can't just monitor your reaction to stress; I need the whole gamut of that brain of yours. So I'm going to make you a little promise. If you relax and let your mind wander through the lovely picture show, I swear that your last moments of conscious thought will be pleasant." Creator's voice was sweeter than factory-fresh strawberry jam.

"And if not?"

That sweet tone curdled in Eve's ears. "Then I will bear whatever residual discomfort I must, but I will empirically determine the

exact amount of pain you can withstand. With that knowledge,
I will exceed that threshold for as long as it takes to gain your
cooperation. I'd hoped to finish these scans in a few hours. But if
need be, I'll hook you up to feeding, breathing, and excretory tubes
and keep you there for weeks, if that's what it takes. The amount of
time you spend suffering is entirely up to you. The amount of time
you comply with my wishes will remain constant, and you will
spend it."

"Do whatever you want. I won't let you have my brain."
Sometimes the bravest words were said through tears.

"Not even to save your sisters?" Creator asked.

Without warning, the blurry haze of tears vanished and was
replaced by images of Eve doing chin-ups in a lab much like the
one she was now in.

This wasn't old footage from Creator's previous lab. This had to
be another room in this one.

"Who is that?" Eve asked. "She looks like me."

"She is you. Eve16 is next in line if you fail me. She's two years,
eight days younger than you." The image shifted. This time
Eve was bent at the waist, palms pressed against the floor in
downward dog position. "And this is Eve17. And here's Eve18."

"Where's Eve 15?" The omission was too glaring to overlook.

"I have her skull on a shelf in my office. That's where yours
is going if you don't prove suitable. If the process turns your
brain into an inert pudding of misfiring synapses, here's what
will happen. First, I'll exsanguinate your body, then carefully
decapitate you. I'll peel away the skin and muscle, vacuum out the
brain with the aid of a light sodium hydroxide solution. Then I'll
carefully extract the cerebral probes for use on one of your younger
sisters—no point in them going to waste. Your skull will sit on my
shelf for me to remember you by; and you *are* a memorable one,
being my first—and hopefully only—escapee. The extraneous
bits of you will be incinerated. Since this laboratory is only a few
hundred meters from the throat of an active volcano, I suspect that
last part will be rather more lively than my prior disposals."

Eve's mind went blank. The words sat there, struggling to paint
pictures. When they finally did, it was too much to bear.

Her thoughts? Deleted. Overwritten.

Her body? Dissolved. Incinerated.

All fate had left to offer Eve was the flip-of-a-coin chance between mindless enslavement and utter annihilation.

And if Creator were unsuccessful with Eve14, the conveyor belt would just keep feeding Eve after subsequent Eve into the same hopper. Eve16... Eve17... Only Creator knew how many more came after.

Eve began sobbing.

"So," Creator said cheerily. "Shall we get started? You can't imagine how much I'm looking forward to this."

CHAPTER SEVENTY-TWO

Charlie7 felt a tingle of relief as the data feed ended. Once again he was alone with his own thoughts—at least in his head. Within the cockpit of the curiously named Betty-Lou, he was still at the mercy of the loudmouthed kid in the super-soldier body.

"About time you stopped broadcasting," Plato said. "Thought we were gonna get there waving flags and playing trumpets. Seriously, did you just download the whole planetary archive or something?"

Plato and Charlie7 were flying low over the Central Pacific, racing against the sunset. They were winning. For much of their trip, Charlie7 had been plugged into both the skyroamer's primary systems and the portable computer he'd pulled from the dashboard earlier.

"Or something," Charlie7 answered.

"Hope that's one doozy of a hack you downloaded," Plato remarked. Clearly, he was fishing for answers, which Charlie7 was ill inclined to provide. "You still too busy to tell me how you got this location? I'm not buying the Nostradamus crap, either."

There was a faint whir as Charlie7 raised an eyebrow. This kid had at least brushed up on his species' history. The archaic slang and obscure name-dropping didn't even sound forced.

At first, Charlie7 was inclined to ignore Plato's question. Then he considered lying. Eventually, he decided just to throw the lad a bone. "James187 grew a conscience. Turned out to be the guilty sort."

Plato yanked back on the throttle, and both of them were pressed against their safety harnesses. "Hold on, chief. Haven't you ever heard of a trap? Starts with a T, rhymes with 'crap'? The next time someone publishes a dictionary, that word's gonna have a picture of us, right now, flying to a volcano because Eve's kidnapper told us to."

"I had the same misgivings. But I decided that it didn't matter," Charlie7 replied.

"You decided? Who put you in charge? I trusted that your information was good because I want Eve back. Maybe you had some secret robot society I wasn't supposed to know about, and you got inside info. Maybe you had an illegal hack into Evelyn38's personal accounts."

"What I had was a single lead, and I took it. I knew you wouldn't trust it, so I left out the details. You're not turning this skyroamer around; we're only five minutes out—or twenty if we continue drifting along at Mach one."

Plato's response was nostril flaring and heavy breathing, along with a clench to his jaw liable to break teeth.

"Listen, do you want to save Eve or not?"

"'Course I do. It's just that—"

"No. You're either in, or you're out. You want out? Then drop me off on the main island, and I'll go in alone. If you're in, punch the throttle and let's not waste any more time. You may not appreciate it right now, but if you let Eve die without trying to save her, you'll regret it the rest of your life."

Charlie7 didn't add that while the rest of Plato's life might not be a particularly long time, his prospects for human companionship of any sort were even more limited.

"Yeah. I'm in," Plato replied, looking out the far window. "What's it to you, anyway, Charlie? You watched ten billion people die. What's one more? What makes Eve so special?" He eased the throttle open, and the two of them were pushed back into their seats.

"I couldn't prevent those 10.3 billion deaths. But Eve is the chance to start fresh. She's the hope we've been missing for a thousand years."

The island of Hawaii came into view. Its peaks were first visible above the horizon, then the shoreline. As they approached, other islands peeked out from the ocean to the northwest, but the big island was their destination. James187 had provided exact coordinates to the entrance to Evelyn38's clandestine lab.

"That was a fortune cookie answer," Plato said without looking at him. "Just wanted you to know I'm not buying it. But whatever. Keep the real reason to yourself. Not like you probably don't have a million secrets."

Charlie7 admired the misplaced bravado. Plato didn't want Charlie7 to see how scared he was. Deep down, Plato wanted to be a hero. Deeper down, he probably wished he didn't have to be. But even if that offhanded comment was meant as a smokescreen, Plato was more right than he knew. Charlie7 had never kept count of all his secrets, but a million seemed like a conservative estimate.

CHAPTER SEVENTY-THREE

Was it possible to feel nausea without any sensation from the stomach? If so, then Eve was indeed nauseated.

The insides of Eve's mind wobbled drunkenly through puzzle after puzzle, adrift and as much on autopilot as James187's skyroamer on the way here.

Eve thought back to the movie she'd watched with James187, and the false reality superimposed over the actual one. Weren't the lenses and the drugs doing the same to her?

Eve felt nothing from the neck down, saw nothing but what the lenses projected. All she heard were the few background sounds from the equipment in the lab and Creator's voice. Could she will herself to wake up from this dreamlike state?

A sudden jolt of resonance snapped Eve's attention back to distasteful reality.

"Stop that," Creator warned. "You'd been doing so well. Now, stop letting your mind wander. Either concentrate on the puzzles or let your thoughts go blank and allow your subconscious to work."

Four shapes appeared, looking like a square steel rod that someone had bent at harsh angles into a tangled knot. Each rotated at different speeds and in different directions. Three of them were identical; Eve's attention drifted to the fourth.

While the lenses filled Eve's vision, she could still look around a little to focus on particular areas. The lenses themselves were a type of input control. They registered her attention as a solution.

Puzzle completed, the image vanished. Next was a maze. A tiny red dot stood at the entrance and followed the movements of her eyes as she navigated it through.

"Oh, what now?" Creator snapped.

Eve braced herself for another punishment, unsure what she'd done wrong this time. But no piercing resonance from the studs was forthcoming. She completed the maze, and an essay appeared in its place. It was only a few paragraphs long and concerned cellular membranes. She felt a pat on her cheek as she browsed through and identified the misspelled words scattered through the passage.

Though she knew the touch was Creator's, Eve relaxed. The robot's had been the only affection Eve had known her whole life. Seeing the monster revealed didn't erase memories stretching back as far as Eve could recall.

"Much better, dear. We're almost done. I just need to go find out who's loitering outside. If it's James, I'm going to be very cross."

Almost done? The prospect of Creator leaving her alone even for a few minutes ought to have filled her with relief. Instead, the prospect of only having a few puzzles left of existence sickened her.

Eve tried to resist as a series of brightly colored balls bounced toward her eyes. Whenever she focused on one, it bounced away from her only to ricochet off an invisible wall. Each time she missed one, the probes in her skull sent an unpleasant tingle through her body. It wasn't as bad as Creator's resonator, but it still made her fight her instincts to be able to let them through.

Anything to delay Creator a little longer...

"Can you upload me to a robot?" Eve blurted.

The puzzle froze in place. Darting her eyes around in their sockets did nothing to move the scene.

"Hmm?" Creator asked. "What was that?"

"A robot. I'd rather be a robot than nothing," Eve babbled on, not even pausing to contemplate what she was asking.

Eve's vision returned to normal. She gasped as her first sight was Creator's face. Their noses were practically touching.

"Trust me," Creator said. "You're better off never knowing this emptiness. To plod on, half asleep, for centuries without end... it's a living hell. I have muddy memories, etched in crystalline perfection, never fading, of a time when I could feel the sunshine on my skin, taste hot cocoa, savor the touch of a lover."

"I've felt sunshine," Eve replied, as the lenses in her eyes grew blurry with tears. She couldn't even be sure whether it was herself she cried for or the pathetic existence Creator claimed to endure.

"Well, one of three wasn't bad for so brief a holiday," Creator replied. "If my crystalline matrix weren't in such a sorry state, I might even find a way to give you the penny tour of human experience before uploading. After all, it's too late to keep you blissful in your ignorance. Now... back to work."

"But—"

"No buts," Creator snapped. "All other considerations aside, you are terribly incriminating. Bad enough the fuss I'll cause standing in front of the Genetic Ethics Committee in your body. But if they had access to all that *you* knew? Good heavens, they'd skin me alive."

Eve could find no words to argue against Creator's cold, callous logic. The puzzle resumed.

As she continued her fight to fail the puzzle, Eve listened. Creator was by the doorway, humming softly and performing a task that involved metal plates.

Access covers?

Eve had a vague impression of a pair of automatons flanking the door as she was dragged in, but the knowledge hadn't seemed relevant. She was still letting colored balls bounce off her eyes when Creator finished up and returned.

"Oh, having fun are we?" Creator asked. "Well, you can continue playing around while I deal with whoever our guest is. We're ready once I've taken care of that little bother."

CHAPTER SEVENTY-FOUR

Charlie7 kept his pace steady and his footsteps soft as he trod the downward sloping tunnel carved into the belly of the island.

The old robot had to admit to being a little impressed with the concept of a secret volcano base. The execution, not so much. It was like arriving at a Broadway play to find the actors in street clothes. Aside from the few lights and a motion detector at the entrance, there had been nothing in the tunnel to indicate any advanced systems at work.

"This Evelyn38 is stupid," Plato said. "If this volcano blew, she'd be toast."

Plato limped, favoring his left hip as he followed along. Charlie7 knew it was more than just roaming from Kansas in a cramped cockpit. The boy's body showed signs of breaking down like an old man with arthritis. The set of his jaw wasn't just determination or a show of toughness; Plato was gritting through constant pain.

Out of respect, Charlie7 said nothing to Plato about what the boy must be going through. After all, heroes don't complain. Heroes don't want sympathy.

"She'd in hiding. Evelyn has all the geothermal power she needs, and no one will be the wiser. We're heading deep enough to block most E-M signatures from being observed externally."

"Yeah, including communications. I've got you and a couple local networks showing in range. No outside world at all," Plato said, staring down at a tablet computer that practically disappeared into his meaty palm. He squeegeed the sweat from his brow with a forearm.

Charlie7 handed over the computer from the skyroamer, data cables dangling loose. "Put that toy away."

"Won't you need this? I mean, I figured you'd be the one hacking the security while I grab Eve."

Charlie7 stopped in his tracks. "How are you not dead? If all your plans revolve around barging in waving guns, I can't believe someone hasn't snapped your neck by now."

"Hey, I usually do my own hacking before the rescues, but that's sort of your specialty, I thought. Figured divide and conquer. Play to our strengths. Cut me some slack; I'm not used to working with a sidekick."

Charlie7 snorted and shook his head. "Me either, kid. But you're a blunt instrument here. Evelyn's preoccupied, or she'd have installed better security at the entrance."

"Or we missed it."

"Or that," Charlie7 conceded. "But I think she's in a rush and doesn't know who's here. Just that someone is. That someone can be you, me, or both of us."

"Both of us sounds like the way to go. Gang up on her!"

Charlie7 clenched his fists but realized that punching Plato—while satisfying—wouldn't exactly be educational. "No. We both go in, and we end up in a hostage situation. If you go in alone, it's either hostage again, or she just kills you. If I go in alone, I can keep her distracted while you break into Evelyn's systems and shut down whatever it is she's doing."

Plato cracked his neck. "What if she tries to kill you? Got a plan for that?"

"Kid, I'm 1,035 years old. I've got a good track record of not getting killed."

They reached the end of the tunnel where it branched into stubby corridors left and right that ended almost immediately, with doors in both direction. There was nothing to label either of them. "Which way?" Plato asked.

On the ground, Charlie7 noticed a smear of dirt smudged with apple. "Take the left. Find a hard line connector to Evelyn's systems. Use the secure frequency I've highlighted and keep me updated on your progress."

Reaching into the back of his belt, Plato pulled out his thermite pistol. He flipped it around and offered it to Charlie7 handle first.

"Take it, just in case." Plato looked Charlie7 square in the eye. When the robot didn't respond instantly, he lifted his eyebrows and thrust the weapon closer.

Charlie7 warded away the pistol with an upraised palm. "Can't. If I don't talk my way through this, Eve's as good as dead."

Plato took a shuddering breath and replied with a curt nod. The computer sliced through the door's security like wet paper, and Plato disappeared beyond.

Left alone in the corridor, Charlie7 took a moment to collect his thoughts, then he knocked.

CHAPTER SEVENTY-FIVE

The door slid open immediately. Inside was a scene out of an ethical scientist's nightmares.

The lab was carved right out of the stone like the lair of a mythical dragon. But the trappings were strictly modern, from the glass tubes and needle injectors of gene sequencers to the black mirror gleam of computer screens.

Charlie7 was no geneticist, but he was familiar enough with the machines involved. Most of this equipment was custom, generations ahead of the hardware the repopulation cloners used. For a cutting-edge researcher, that alone wasn't uncommon. What stood out was that everything was sized for humans, from the exercise equipment to the restraints on the examination table.

Eve lay strapped down. So many cables ran to the terminals embedded in her skull that they gave the appearance of silvery hair.

Creator greeted him as he entered. "Oh, my. Not who I expected at all."

This robot's lab coat was the same style and cut that the chassis of Evelyn11 wore and not in much better repair. Disrepair seemed to be the watchword for Evelyn38 as she limped forward to a chorus of protesting mechanisms. She smiled and spread her arms as if she were going to hug him.

Then, with the twitch of an index finger on either hand, Evelyn called her automatons into action.

Two of the drones flanked the door. Charlie7 was so accustomed to ignoring inert workers that he was unprepared when they closed in and took him by the upper arms.

These weren't committee secretaries or computer interface specialists; they weren't even rugged, outdoorsy Tobys. With little space devoted to the niceties of robotic sentience, there was plenty of extra room to pack in larger actuators. Without fretting if one ran its battery dry and someone else had to recharge them, there was no particular need for them to be lightweight and energy efficient.

In short, once they had a grip on him, there was no getting loose for Charlie7.

"Good to see you, too, Evelyn," Charlie7 replied, ignoring the fact that his feet were no longer touching the ground thanks to her two mindless friends. "Heard you were up to something momentous. You know me; I'm a sucker for historical events."

Evelyn approached within arm's reach—hers, not Charlie7's, which was temporarily reduced—and patted him on the cheek. "You're a treasure, Charles. But drop the facade. What really brought you here?"

"Your associate expressed misgivings about your prospects. If things go wrong, and there's fallout from any of the six or so ethical committees that might have a problem with this endeavor, he wanted me to cover him."

"Associate? Whoever might that be?"

"You want me to cut the spycraft? Fine. Do me the same courtesy. I know you had James187 bring the girl back. And it was an escaped human experiment named Plato who kidnapped her in the first place."

"And if I were to call James right now, he'd confirm this?" Evelyn asked.

Charlie7 couldn't risk James187 exposing him. If he thought Evelyn suspected him of a double-cross, his conscientious objector status in this experiment might suddenly expire.

"Go ahead, but he'll just tell you to deal with me. Consider me his attorney. In exchange for keeping him out of the committee crosshairs, I get his place in line. The body that was going to him will be mine. He can wait for the next."

"I don't recall agreeing to any such arrangement," Evelyn said, wagging a finger. "This process isn't a coupon or a subway pass to just get traded in back alleys. But, I suppose, if you're genuinely interested, you might as well bear witness to the process at work. Apologies in advance if this fails spectacularly. I do deplore the pressure of working in front of an audience. Shall we begin?"

The latter question was addressed to Eve.

"No! Please!" Eve begged.

The girl was awake and alert. Charlie7 had taken her silence up until now as a sign that she'd been anesthetized for the mind transfer.

"What are you doing? She's awake!"

"Help me, Charles. Don't let her do this," Eve screamed. Even in her current plight, the girl had the sense not to let on that she knew him as Charlie7.

Evelyn toddled over to a computer panel and pressed a button hidden from Charlie7's view. Eve's protests grew soft and faded into slumber.

"Well, enough of *that* commotion. She'll need to be awake for the transfer, but we can spare all our ears during calibration. Besides, I won't be awake for it to bother me."

"You're using the Charlie2 protocol in reverse?" It wasn't mere professional curiosity that made him ask. Any information he could glean about Evelyn's process could prove invaluable.

"Oh, you're so proud of that blasted protocol. You'd think it was *you* who wrote it. And yes. Of course, I am. No one's improved on the basic protocol in a thousand years. And you'd best hope it works as planned."

"Why's that?"

Charlie7 couldn't very well *not* ask a question so obviously dangled as bait. Besides, it bought him time to scheme.

The Charlie2 protocol being in place was a good start. The system would shut Evelyn down to get a static database to copy. Then it would transfer to the new crystalline matrix—or in this case, Eve's gray matter. After that, there would be a simple test to verify successful transfer, and the original host would be blanked, leaving only the new model.

"Well, once this is over, I'll give those mindless brutes permission to release you. If you've got anything diabolical planned for me while I'm unconscious, the lack of such authorization will result in them tearing you limb from limb and stomping your brain to splinters."

"Oh," Charlie7 said. He cleared his throat. "Well, best get on with it, then."

CHAPTER SEVENTY-SIX

Plato sat on the rough stone floor of the control room, Charlie7's slapped-together computer console cradled in his lap. Fingers like sausage links poked at a keypad meant for delicate, robotic digits. But it wasn't the user interface giving him troubles.

With a snarl, Plato punched an access panel at random, bloodying his knuckles.

Nothing worked.

Charlie7's magic hacking machine got him in the front door, but all the rooms were locked. No, not locked; they were welded shut.

It looked like Evelyn38 had either programmed most of the local subsystems herself or contracted someone to create customized software to her specs. Plato would have been less frustrated if it hadn't been so blindingly simple to get into the top-level server to see all the systems he couldn't access.

And the system names themselves were troubling. While there were some standard everyday systems like lighting, power, and data management, others hinted at the bizarre experiments Evelyn38 was running. With files names like "UteroIncubatorControl," "FoodRewardProtocol," and "BrainScanMapping," Plato wondered if he shouldn't perhaps have paid a longer visit on his last infiltration of Evelyn38's security.

"Why was this so much easier last time?" Plato grumbled at the screen as Charlie7's modified computer struggled against a more advanced security program than it was programmed to beat.

The answer was obvious. Plato realized as soon as he said it aloud. His initial breach had prompted the move to a new facility and along with it, the countermeasures against a similar intrusion.

With no solution forthcoming, he considered breaking radio silence. Charlie7's personal ID was right there, waiting for him to open a message. But the hacking rig was designed for stealth. Supposedly, it was hiding its own intrusions faster than the system could detect them. Broadcasting would be the same as shouting and waving his arms for attention.

He pulled the thermite pistol from the back of his pants. "It shouldn't be taking this long. Man up and take her out, Charlie-boy."

Plato glanced from the weapon to the computer and back. One promised a quiet, elegant solution in an indeterminate amount of time. The other, a quick resolution that rode entirely on guts, quick thinking, and cat-like reflexes.

"I can do this."

Charlie7 had worried that Plato would gum up the works. But Eve was more important than keeping the peace among a bunch of stuffy old robots. So what if Charlie7 wasn't on everyone's Christmas list anymore? Most of these robots probably didn't even celebrate Christmas anyway.

Plato stood and strode to the door of the maintenance room. "Screw it. Heroes live forever. Only cowards turn to dust."

The door didn't budge.

It had been unlocked when he and Charlie7 had arrived. A change in security level meant that someone had felt the need for upping it. Someone knew there was a problem in this secret lab, and the only someone liable to care was Evelyn38. Charlie7 *had* stumbled into a trap.

Plato stalked back and forth in front of the door, one hand gripping the pistol, the other combing across his scalp as if it would help him think.

He glanced at the control console for the door. "Fail-safe? Fail-secure? Which one are you?"

A system could be built to either release or go into lockdown when power was cut. The former was a safety feature; the latter a security measure.

Anyone who cares about residents, employees, or whoever else might by in a building would have made this door fail-safe. If he destroyed the console, it would let him through.

But a fail-secure system was a conscious decision that something was more important than the lives at stake. It would trap someone in a burning building rather than allow unauthorized access.

In his heart of hearts, Plato knew Evelyn38 would have built a fail-secure system. Yet his fingers tightened on the thermite pistol, itching to squeeze the trigger. Barging through, with the element of surprise, he might stand a chance of rescuing Eve by force. But if Plato fired a shot and failed, he wouldn't merely lock himself in; he'd need a blowtorch to cut his way out. It would also alert Evelyn38 that Charlie7 had backup.

With an inarticulate growl, Plato shoved the pistol back into his belt.

A soft chime from the computer sent him running back to the mainframe interface to scoop it up. There was a message.

LITTLE HELP?

"So much for radio silence, huh?" Plato replied and watched as the words digitized to text before transmission.

EVELYN STARTED THE TRANSFER. STEP 1 IS FULL INACTIVE SCAN. WE HAVE ABOUT FIVE MINUTES.

"Yeah, your toy here is useless. I'm locked out of everything but directory access."

NOT EVERYTHING. PLATO, I NEED YOU TO SWEAR TO ME YOU CAN KEEP A SECRET.

"We've got five minutes, bucko. I'll swear anything."

I MEAN IT. THIS IS A BIG ONE. I NEED TO KNOW I CAN TRUST YOU WITH SOMETHING I'VE NEVER TOLD ANYONE.

"Tick, tick, Charlie. Come on. I swear. Just hurry it up."

RUN "CHARLES_1_PROTOCOL."

"I told you. I'm locked out of everything. Besides, there's not even a Charles_1_Protocol listed here."

THAT'S WHY IT'S GOING TO WORK. JUST DO IT.

With a shuddering breath, Plato entered the command. There wasn't time to be dickering around with pointless attempts to access files that weren't there. Eve's life was ticking to a close. The sands were running out in her hourglass.

Plato's mouth hung open when, in fact, a program did run. He stared wide-eyed as a whole new set of menus opened up, allowing access to a system he'd never dreamed of cracking. "Is this what I think it is?"

YES. THE BACK DOOR TO THE UPLOAD PROTOCOL. I WROTE IT.

"You mean Charles Truman wrote it..." Plato clarified.

Was Charlie7 unstable after all?

Everyone talked about Charlie7 like a rock that storm seas couldn't budge. But most robots had a pretty clear understanding that they were not the human whose mind made up their majority personality.

JUST SEE IF YOU CAN SHUT DOWN THE SCAN ON EVELYN WITHOUT REACTIVATING HER.

Plato's fingers flew as his heart raced.

Despite the unfamiliar system, the layout made finding his way a snap. He saw graphical representations of two figures lying inclined on tables, heads just a short distance apart. One was labeled "Eve14," the other "Evelyn11."

He hadn't believed Charlie7's claim about who that robot in there really was, but the program didn't appear uncertain at all. Yet knowing that still didn't give him access to any commands that would work.

Nothing would listen to Plato. Eve was going to die while he watched it on screen, helpless. Her death was going to be all his fault.

"No good," Plato said, voice shaking. "The scan's already running. It won't let me change anything until it finishes."

TOO LATE BY THEN. NEXT STEP: SWITCH UPLOADER TARGET.

"To what? There's only a listing for Eve14."

They were running out of time. The upload program only showed fifty-two seconds remaining, and the countdown felt faster than that. As seconds ticked away, Plato rocked forward and back.

ENTER: "LOOP BYPASS TEST CHARLIE2."

Plato tapped keys as he talked. "What's this going to do?"

IT'S GOING TO PERFORM A SIMULATED UPLOAD
INSTEAD OF TRYING TO OVERWRITE EVE.

Plato entered the command, and the recipient "robot" changed
from "Eve14" to "Charlie2."

"Hey, this isn't going to create a Charlie2 somewhere, is it?"

NO. THAT WAS JUST MY INITIAL TEST SUBJECT. NOW
HURRY UP. WE'RE NOT DONE.

"The timer's still counting down."

THAT'S FINE. THE SIMULATED UPLOAD WILL BUY YOU
SOME EXTRA TIME. NOW SET "UPLOAD VERIFICATION"
TO "NULL."

"No dice. Says no such verification file."

WHAT? IT SHOULDN'T SAY THAT! SET "FAIL
CONDITION" TO "NULL."

The first countdown ended, and a message popped up saying
that the scan was successfully completed. Another timer started,
this one tracking upload time remaining.

"Same thing."

YOU'RE DOING SOMETHING WRONG. TRY AGAIN. EVE'S
LIFE DEPENDS ON THIS.

Plato tried again with both commands. "Sorry, Charlie. What
else you got? We're under two minutes to go. What happens if we
don't make it?"

THEN EVE GETS HER BRAIN COOKED TO MUSH UNLESS
SHE CAN CONVINCE THIS COMPUTER THAT SHE'S
EVELYN.

They tried everything. Charlie7's commands sounded ever more
implausible. Cutting power, rerouting data feeds, overloading the
rig... none of it worked. The system was built to be robust. Even
their one small alteration seemed like a miracle now.

As the timer wound down, Plato pictured Eve, nestled in the
crook of his arm and watching old movies with him. He was never
going to see her like that again. Those bright, inquisitive eyes
would be glassy and vacant.

Plato's stomach tied itself in knots as the timer hit all zeroes.

CHAPTER SEVENTY-SEVEN

The world slid along through muddy earth and swept Eve along with it.

Numbers floated in a void. Digital readouts told Eve all about herself in quantitative terms unable to capture the dizziness and stiffness she felt.

Warmth trickled up Eve's arm and filled her as a tingling prickle spread throughout her body. The numbers increased for heart rate and blood pressure.

Voices bounced off her eardrums without registering as intelligible speech. As Eve fought her way back to consciousness with the aid of an intravenous stimulant, she focused on what was being said.

"Well, best get on with it, then," Charlie7 said.

"Brave face, Charles?" Creator asked. "Well, I imagine you can't do much while I'm indisposed. If all goes well, maybe you can have Eve16? Fancy a try at a woman's life?"

Creator sounded chipper. That didn't speak well of what had happened while Eve was unconscious.

Eve's mouth was filled with cotton like she'd bitten down on a sock. Her tongue was free to move, and she discovered the sensation was illusory. As Eve tried to wipe her mouth, she found herself still strapped snugly to the table.

More importantly, she *felt* her arm restraint. The numbing effects of the anesthetic Creator had used were wearing off.

Or being intentionally counteracted. It stood to reason that if Creator were planning on taking up residence in Eve's body, she'd want it functional.

Eve tried to talk. "Chaa-lee. Hep." The numbness wasn't entirely faded and had spread to her jaw while she was out cold. "Char. Lee. Hel-puh."

Creator gently pushed up her jaw. Eve's teeth met with a click. "Hush, dear. Don't go croaking yourself hoarse. I plan on trying out that singing voice in a few minutes. Here. You can watch."

Watch? Eve thought. *Watch what?* Unable to move her head, her only options were staring into the bright overhead lights or shutting her eyes and seeing nothing but her vital signs projected directly onto her retinas.

Seconds later, she got her answer.

Sounds from behind Eve told her that Creator was plugging herself into the other side of the machine. When the sounds stopped, a message appeared in the middle of Eve's vision. It read five minutes and eighteen seconds, with two decimal places at the end that moved too fast to track.

"Charlie," Eve moaned. The words dribbled forth as if she were spitting out a mouthful of eggs. "Why. Won't. You—?"

"It's all right," Charlie7 said. Eve was grateful to have her question cut short. It was so much work, and the warm tingling was beginning to pass. "We're going to get you out of this. Evelyn is asleep, for all intents and purposes. The system can't accurately map an active mind. Too much data moving too quickly. It needs an inert snapshot, so we've got a few minutes."

"Five," Eve clarified. "Less. Five. Come. Un. Plug."

"Save your strength. We're going through this the hard way. I realize you can't see from there, but I'm rather indisposed myself. Two automatons are holding me, and I can't get loose from them. Evelyn's even got them off the network, so I can't begin to try breaking into their programming. But don't worry, Plato's got this all under control."

"Play. Toe?"

Eve worked her jaw back and forth to loosen it. With a sudden insight, she clenched and unclenched her fist, wiggled her feet, and took deep, fast breaths. If she could speed her metabolism, she could hasten the spread of the stimulant Creator was dripping into her veins.

"We're coming at this from the software side," Charlie7 explained. "There's plenty of time."

"Three minutes," Eve said.

"I'm fairly well aware of the protocol involved. I wrote it."

Eve blinked in surprise. It didn't make the numbers flashing before her eyes slow down, but it certainly made her think.

"You made this?" she asked.

"Not this one. The original. This is how robots are born— and reborn. A new robot comes from a fresh combination of personalities from the twenty-seven scientists of Project Transhuman. But for someone who just needs a new crystalline matrix and chassis, it's the same setup, except your side would be occupied by a freshly built robot chassis and a blank crystal."

Eve tried hard not to be fascinated. Her impending doom counting down unavoidably in her field of view was rather urgent. But she'd always wondered where robots came from, and Creator would never tell her.

"Really? Where do they do it?" If Eve were to learn just one more thing before Creator's thoughts were pumped into her brain, this would be a good one. She had two minutes to enjoy knowing it.

"There's a place called Kanto. It's a factory a hundred times the size of the farm in Kansas. They make so many different things there, but the most important of all are new robots."

Charlie elaborated, telling her about two cousins of his, Charlie13, who oversaw the new robots, and Charlie29, who was in charge of upgrades. Eve focused on the sound of his voice, imagined the other Charlies, and held her breath as the seconds reached single digits.

5... 4... 3... 2... 1...

Nothing happened. "I don't feel anything."

"Well, I have some good news," Charlie7 said. "I talked Plato through the process of stopping the upload to your brain."

Eve let out a breath she hadn't noticed she'd been holding. Tears welled in her eyes, which now just saw her vital readings and a blurry haze of lights. "What now? Will Plato come get us both out?"

"First things first. I have a spot of bad news before the storm clouds pass. We can't shut down the upload checker."

"What's that mean?" It sounded ominous, but strapped down to a brain-erasing machine, just about everything did.

"Well, when the process runs normally, the original robot goes inert, the system scans the crystalline matrix, and a copy is uploaded to the new robot. If the upload is a success, a small EMP wipes the original, so we don't end up with duplicate people."

"And if it's not?" Eve felt compelled to ask.

"Then the system erases the faulty data from the new unit, and the original is reactivated so the process can be attempted again at a later date."

The heart rate numbers spiked again. "I'm the faulty data?"

"We're working on that," Charlie7 assured her.

Eve waited. If Charlie7 was talking to Plato electronically, she didn't want to distract him.

"Dammit!" Charlie7 shouted. His voiced came back a forced sort of calm. "Eve. I need you to do something very important."

"Yes?"

"In a moment, I'm going to need you to convince this machine that you are Evelyn11."

CHAPTER SEVENTY-EIGHT

"**Y**ou're going to see a series of tests... or puzzles," Charlie7 said. Puzzles?

Eve's life had built up to this moment.

As far back as she could remember, life had revolved around physical fitness training and puzzles. Every success Creator had cheered, every failure that had denied Eve a meal, every mind-twisting challenge that had forced her capabilities above and beyond their previous limits—all of it had been so that Creator would have room enough to fit inside Eve's brain.

It was time for Eve to find out the limits of her brainpower.

"I can do this," Eve replied. She heard the tremor in her own voice. Hopefully, Charlie7 would help her whether she was sure of success or not.

The early puzzles in the sequence were everyday challenges that unlocked Eve's meals. She sped through them without a hitch. It was easier solving them than it had been to resist Creator's diagnostics.

Eventually, Eve came to new challenges, and she had to slow down to think.

First among this new breed of puzzle was a three-dimensional jigsaw with different-colored pieces. The pieces moved to follow the motion of her eyes as she focused on them.

Idly, Eve wondered if Creator knew the solutions in advance or if the robot merely trusted that inhabiting Eve's mind she'd have the computing power to solve them herself.

But what if Creator wasn't as brilliant as she believed?

"Charlie, what would have happened to the other Eves if Creator didn't know how to solve these puzzles?" Eve hated asking it.

She couldn't help wondering if the fault hadn't been with her predecessors but with Creator herself.

"Try not to think about that," Charlie7 replied calmly as if she might panic and run away. If Eve could have budged from the table, running would have been her first choice. "Just concentrate on the test."

In the corner of her vision, a tiny red circle vanished as if swept away by the hands of a clock turning the wrong direction. There was no time to waste or Eve would be the next skull on Creator's shelf.

The jigsaw interlocked. Its final piece plugged snugly into place, and the puzzle vanished. Eve released the breath she'd been holding.

Next up was a grid of numbers with no instructions as to what Eve was meant to do with them. "I'd concentrate better if I wasn't wondering about that question."

"The electrical charge to reset the crystal matrix would cook the subject's brain, and Evelyn would wake up without knowing exactly what went wrong. She'd have no memories of the testing."

The number puzzle was pointlessly simple. The number 253 wasn't prime; the rest were. Devoting attention to the 253 for a few seconds cleared that puzzle as well.

Eve's confidence swelled. These new puzzles were no match for her. Eve14 was smarter than Creator. She would succeed where all those other poor Eves had been doomed.

That confidence was short-lived.

After the grid of primes, a truly bizarre puzzle appeared. There were four emblems, arranged two by two. Lettering identified them, but what they meant was still an utter mystery. Each had a shape similar to a shield and various ornamental flourishes. There were letters buried in the designs, some resembling words, but nothing she could decipher.

"Charlie! I need help!" Eve screamed. The circular red timer was sweeping away, and she didn't even know where to begin solving this puzzle.

"What do you see?"

Knowing how little time she had, Eve rattled off descriptions of each. She made certain not to let her eyes linger too long on any single emblem, lest she accidentally get credited with an incorrect answer while Charlie considered her information.

"They're school logos. Harvard, Princeton, Yale, Dartmouth. Evelyn Mengele got her doctorate at Dartmouth."

Since "DARTMOUTH" was prominently displayed in the relevant logo, it was easy to identify. Eve held her view on it for a moment, and the puzzle cleared.

Eve's gasp of relief hadn't even emptied her lungs when the next challenge appeared to vex her.

This puzzle was another two by two grid, but this time showed four human faces. "They're faces! The next puzzle is faces!"

"Calm down," Charlie7 ordered. "Describe them. Shape. Color. Gender. Hair. Eyes."

Eve did her best, but she'd only recently *seen* other humans.

The differentiations were so subtle. Eve imagined that old humans had a whole codified system of breaking facial appearance down into categories. Someone like Plato could probably have said, "That upper left one is a 12A-85-H11," and Charlie would have known exactly what the face looked like.

Eve had to muddle through.

"Say that last one again," Charlie said when she finished.

"He had a nose like an elliptical paraboloid, a two-millimeter gap between his front teeth, and an indentation at the center of his chin that the other three lack."

Please let him hurry, Eve begged silently.

"Do his eyebrows connect in the middle?" Charlie asked.

Eve squinted, but the lenses didn't project any more clearly. "Hard to tell. There may be a millimeter of bare skin between them."

"Clancy Mengele," Charlie shouted. "That's her oldest son. He was a mathematics professor at Harvard. Won a Nobel Prize. Evelyn wouldn't shut up about him."

Eve focused on the image of Creator's son. In the few brief seconds she stared at his image, she wondered if the two of them were somehow related. Was Eve this man's sister, in a way?

Creator's son and the other three faces faded, and there was nothing to replace them.

The lenses in Eve's eyes turned transparent, and even the vital sign reading vanished. A cold liquid squirted in through the intravenous line in her arm—a stimulant far stronger than the one that had reversed her sedation.

Eve's eyes shot wide, her nostrils flared, and her lungs sucked in a greedy breath.

The restraints holding Eve to the table loosened and released—all but one strap across her legs that kept her from falling off the table. A tug that stretched her neck taut ended in a chorus of pings as the leads clipped to her skull terminals popped free.

Eve blinked and sat up. When she reached to rub her eyes, the intravenous line got in the way, so she yanked it out of her arm. As she was manually unbuckling the strap across her thighs, a voice boomed overhead.

"GOOD MORNING, EVE MENGELE. WELCOME TO YOUR NEW LIFE AS A HUMAN."

From the far side of the machine, there was a clack and hum. The lights in the lab momentarily dimmed until the hum stopped.

"Was that—?"

"Yes," Charlie said. "Evelyn11, who'd taken over Evelyn38's body, was just wiped blank."

Eve didn't know what to feel.

Creator had been her caretaker her entire life. She had made Eve out of nothing, and now Creator herself was nothing. The notion had a sort of symmetry to it, but it still didn't feel right. There was, of course, the flood of relief that threatened to scrape the insides of her adrenal glands raw.

Charlie—Charlie7—had done everything he'd promised.

Eve was alive, and the whole world lay before her.

CHAPTER SEVENTY-NINE

While it was nice that Eve was going to survive, there was still a pressing matter of a captive robot about to be the rope in a tug of war.

Charlie7 made a throat-clearing noise. Eve's attention snapped toward him. "Now, if you don't mind a bit of reciprocity, please tell these mindless monsters to let me go."

For the first time, Eve seemed to pull her wits together to take in the entirety of the scene around her. Considering the sort of day she'd had, Charlie7 was willing to be charitable about an adjustment period. But he also didn't know how long Evelyn had programmed these automatons to wait for instruction.

Eve stood tall and drew a deep breath. "You two automatons, let Charlie7 go." She over-enunciated, but he didn't mind a little extra caution.

The automatons showed no sign of having heard or accepted Eve's order. "That didn't work."

Eve nodded and cleared her throat. "Let. Charlie7. Go."

There was a pause, and the only sound was the background hum of Evelyn's lab equipment.

"There must be a password or a code or something," Charlie7 said.

Contingencies and backup plans jostled in Charlie7's mind. He didn't have the leverage to tear his own arms off. He lacked the strength to wrench himself free. The two automatons that held him fast were disconnected from all networks so any attempts at a remote hack would be fruitless.

In unison, the two automatons squeezed. Alerts flashed across Charlie7's consciousness as the outer casings on his arms crumpled, emitting a plaintive metallic creak.

"No!" Eve shouted. "Why are they doing this? Stop!"

"Evelyn warned me," Charlie7 said. "If she didn't wake up from the transfer, these things were programmed to destroy me."

Eve grabbed one of the automatons by the arm, but her strength was insignificant. "You knew this would happen? Why would you tell me the answers? You cheated the test for me? I didn't want to wake up just so you could die!"

All Charlie7 could do in the face of her questions was to repeat. "I'm sorry... I'm sorry."

Eve gave up trying and sobbed as the automatons forced Charlie7 to the ground. He'd have kicked, twisted, anything on the remote chance of breaking free, but Eve was too close by. He couldn't take a one-in-a-million chance of success if it risked hurting her in the process.

"You promised you'd keep me safe. I'm holding you to that!"

A heavy hand tore open Charlie7's rear thoracic access plate. Another reached in and grabbed a handful of data lines. Most of Charlie7's neural inputs went dark, as well as the connection to his internal computer. All motor control below his neck was offline.

"I did. You're safe. These things aren't going to hurt you. Plato will fly you out of here. I trust you to get out of this. It's just another puzzle." A last-minute thought occurred to him, sparking an inkling of hope. "Willing to try tearing my head off? I'd appreciate it."

In an instant, Eve had her hands locked under Charlie7's chin and the base of his skull. Behind him, automaton feet rose and fell, crunching his internal computer beyond repair, along with most of his torso.

Eve grunted and gritted her teeth. She used one of the automatons and braced a foot against it for leverage. For the first time since he'd met them both, Charlie7 wished it was Plato with him instead of Eve. But the sentiment was short lived.

"Get back!" Charlie7 shouted.

Eve leaped away just in time before one of the robotic feet slammed down on Charlie7's skull. Warnings and error codes he'd never seen in a thousand years of robotic life flashed across his vision.

"Eve, this is it for me." A foot slammed down.

"No," Eve said, sobbing. "It's not. They'll stop. They have to stop. Why don't they stop?"

"Get word to Toby22." Another impact resulted in a starling array of new error codes.

Eve shook her head. "I can't. I don't know what I'll do if you're gone."

"You can. Have them make a new Charlie. Promise me." Charlie7 didn't even register the next blow except for the sudden shaking of his optical sensor and the loss of vision in his right eye.

Eve nodded frantically as she got down on hands and knees to look Charlie7 in the eye. "I promise."

"Give all my things to him, house and everything. The new Charlie will look after—"

The error codes all ended with a resounding crunch. The last thing Charlie7 saw was Eve's tear-streaked face.

CHAPTER EIGHTY

The door slid open, and Plato bounded through, pistol drawn. He was sweating and out of breath, with one eyebrow missing. In his off hand, Plato carried a blowtorch. As soon as he entered the room, a pair of automatons flanking the door lurched toward him.

"Plato! No!" Eve shouted. She crouched on the floor over a pile of scrap metal.

Knowing he couldn't evade the two robots, Plato charged the one on his left.

Before the drone could close its grip on him, Plato pressed the thermite pistol to its chassis and fired.

If he was an idiot, Plato might have aimed for the cranium, but automatons didn't have imitation human brains in theirs, just a few sensor nodes. Instead, his shot went into the torso at exactly the spot where a thermite round would slag its central processor. The machine was dead weight as Plato's inertia bore it to the ground.

Landing heavily atop the first attacker, Plato rolled free and fired a second precise round into the processor of the second. It slowed to a halt, kept upright by auto-gyros that didn't depend on the processor.

Eve turned away from him and sobbed. Plato thought better of stuffing the thermite pistol back into his pants just after firing it and set it on the stone floor as he knelt beside Eve. "You OK? Where's..."

Removed from the heat of the moment, it became apparent where Charlie7 had gone. He was right there, scattered all over the floor. His last, cryptic transmission of a detailed set of arrangements for his personal affairs made a whole lot more sense now.

"He died instead of me," Eve said, gasping for breath between sobs. "I didn't want him to die. It's all my fault."

Plato put an arm around Eve's shoulders. She felt so small and fragile. He worried he'd break her even letting the full weight of his arm rest on her. "None of this is your fault. You were the victim. Creator, Evelyn38 or whatever number... who cares what you call her? She's the one to blame for all this."

"But she made me..."

"Hey!" Plato snapped. "Making someone doesn't mean you own them. My creator's name was Charlie24 and hardly a day goes by where I don't wish I could upload him to a new chassis and end his miserable life all over again. A lotta robots are pretty awful people. But there are some real good ones out there, too. I didn't believe all the crap people said about Charlie7 being a hero; he was a Charlie after all, just like the guy who turned me into the monster I am. But Charlie7 was as good as his word. He *was* a hero."

Eve turned to look up at Plato. Her eyes were reddened and glistening. Her irises looked wrong as well, but he couldn't put a finger on why. None of that mattered right now. Plato wiped away the tears with the back of his finger.

"You're not a monster," Eve said as she composed herself. "You helped Charlie7 save me."

"Yeah. I helped. But I know what I am. You haven't seen as many movies and news clips from the Earthwide as I have. I know what humans look like, how they act. I'm not one of them. Your creator might have done a lot of awful things, but she got at least one completely right." Plato reached out and touched a finger to Eve's nose.

As he stood, Eve accepted Plato's offered hand.

"But," Eve said, waving a hand over the pile of metallic scrap and scattered shards of brain-quality crystal. "What about Charlie7?"

"We can say goodbye to Charlie later. Right now, we have people to call."

CHAPTER EIGHTY-ONE

Mount Kilauea became an instant pilgrimage site.

Once word had spread of a secret lab and live, healthy humans on Earth for the first time in a thousand years, robots across the globe dropped what they were doing and rushed to the island of Hawaii.

Flying craft of every description lined the shores of the big island, and the pilots made their way on foot to the gathering at the volcano.

Toby22 had been among the first to arrive, despite a longer journey than many. He hadn't waited for rumors to spread across the Social. He hadn't checked and cross-checked, fearful of a hoax or a prank. Eve and Plato had contacted him directly. Toby22 had been the first to hear of Charlie7's death and had come immediately.

The volcano had become an impromptu memorial site, a triage center, and a crime scene all in one.

Toby22 hadn't known what to expect as more and more robots arrived but not this. Robots had died before. Horrible accidents and self-termination ran neck-and-neck as the leading causes. Murder was a rare thing indeed—or at least, so he imagined.

Nora109 pulled Toby22 aside as if he were someone important. "We found Eves numbered through twenty-two in the lab plus dozens of embryonic and fetal..." Toby22 waited for her to call them specimens as if they were animals. "Versions."

Toby22 hung his head. "Poor things. How are the younger ones taking it?"

"Overwhelmed. Frightened. Curious. They're like a regression study of Eve14; all of them are younger than her by varying degrees. The three oldest have transcranial implants like Eve14's."

A pair of Ashleys herded a line of children toward a large-animal transport that one of the wildlife rangers had flown to the gathering.

Toby22 watched the children march single file in descending order of height. It reminded him of early photographs of prairie farm families with children spaced just a year or two apart for an entire generation. None of them fought or jostled; they all just gaped in wonder at everything they could set their eyes upon.

"You run into Charlie13 down there?" Toby22 asked. Not that it was any of his business, but as gossip went, he seemed to be at the hub of an event so big that people couldn't help but include him.

"Into him? How about him running over me and everyone else down there?" Nora109 said. "You try telling the head of robotic uploads that he needs to get out of the way of a few human children. He's half mad over finding an unauthorized upload rig. And he's entirely bonkers that it's got features his hasn't."

"Think he's going to respect Charlie7's wishes?"

Nora109 scoffed. "Like this world needs another Charlie. But I think Thirteen will play along. Popular sentiment will ensure that. He won't like making it the same mix as a previous personality, but Charlie7 was practically constructed out of exceptions."

"That he was," Toby22 said.

If only Nora109 knew what Toby22 knew. A handful of the Tobys had been mixed with memories Charles Truman had never meant for them to remember. All the Charlies knew that Dr. Charles Truman had created a 100 percent duplicate of his own mind; they all remembered doing it. Some of the Tobys remembered helping him. But none of the Charlies could be sure which of their brethren was that unmixed, pure human mind.

Except for Charlie7.

CHAPTER EIGHTY-TWO

Eve stood on a freshly constructed platform at the crater's edge of Mount Kilauea. Four robots whose designations she hadn't caught assembled it in mere minutes. But none of them approached her, just as none of the rest in the crowd seemed eager to touch her.

The only one by Eve's side as a legion of glowing eyes looked on was Plato. She had seen the other Eves and spoken with them briefly if only to assure them that Ashley390 wouldn't hurt them. There would be time for Eve to get to know her twin sisters later.

This was a time to say goodbye.

The pieces that had once been Charlie7 now filled a bin that sat between her and Plato. Both of them wore safety harnesses attached to cables to keep them from falling into the molten sea of rock below.

No such precaution had been needed for Charlie7. He was beyond saving, and the final requests he had transmitted to Plato's computer included instructions that his remains be melted down. There was to be, as Charlie7's instructions put it, "No Lenin's tomb for me."

Eve made a point to look up what that meant.

Plato nudged her with an elbow. "You should say something. Everyone's waiting."

With a sniffle, Eve nodded. "Charlie7, thank you for giving up your life so I could have mine. I promise not to waste it. I wish someone could fix you, but everyone says it can't be done. Since you asked to be melted, we'll honor your wishes."

She and Plato each grabbed hold of one corner of the bin, and they tipped it. At first, Eve marveled at how little Charlie7's pieces weighed and wondered if some of him were missing. Then she noticed by flexure of the bin that Plato was bearing nearly all the weight himself. But while he could bear this physical burden for her, the emotional weight of Charlie7's loss pressed down, unrelenting, on Eve's shoulders.

Bit by bit the first few metallic scraps rained down into the volcano, disappearing with red splashes. Then all at once the rest slid free and clattered over the edge. In seconds, Charlie7 was gone. The last piece, a fragment of cranium, snagged on the lip of the bin. A lightless eye stared blankly at Eve. With a shake of the bin, Plato dislodged that final piece, and it too vanished into the lava.

The two of them stared down into the lava, neither looking at the other.

"You should pick a new name," Plato said. "Evelyn38 called you Eve14, but there's no one to tell you who you have to be anymore. Maybe you could be Dorothy…"

Eve wrinkled her nose. "Dorothy wanted to go home, even though it was an awful place. I want to stay in Oz. Creator gave me a name, and it's mine now. And my name is Eve. Eve the Fourteenth, maybe. I just choose to be me."

Without taking her eyes from the spot where Charlie7 had vanished, Eve reached out and took Plato by the hand.

CHAPTER EIGHTY-THREE

Toby22 watched the brief ceremony at the crater's edge. As Eve's tiny hand disappeared within Plato's massive one, he leaned over to Nora109. "Do we need to maybe... I don't know, curate their choices of movies for a while? What if they don't figure things out on their own?"

Nora109 chuckled softly. "Humanity 'figured things out,' as you put it, long before popular entertainment. From what I've seen, though, it may not be an issue. Eve and Plato are barely the same species. They've both been tinkered with—Eve prior to development, and Plato a little before and a lot after. She's as human as they come; her genome has been scrubbed and polished. There isn't so much as a recessive marker that I'd flag. Eve's immune to most diseases we've identified including alien bio-warfare agents. Plato is... less well-built."

With a glance up at the hulking brute at the lip of the volcano, Toby22 raised an eyebrow actuator at Nora109. "Could've fooled me."

"That male specimen has induced pituitary gigantism, myostatin-related muscular hypertrophy, congenital adrenal hyperplasia, the ACDN5 suite of fast-twitch enhancements that was banned pre-invasion. He's also got bits and piece from no fewer than six non-primate species, things I can't even identify a use for in some cases. There have been numerous attempts to mitigate the side effects, but he's not taking any drugs that I'm aware of. You can tell just by the way he walks that he suffers chronic joint pain. Let's not even mention the fact that Plato's only twelve years old. I don't care if uploading to a human mind becomes safer than taking on a new chassis; you couldn't pay me to get into a body like that."

On the volcano's edge, Plato and Eve were turning to come back down. The mismatched pair was angel and demon, hand in hand. He wasn't a beast heralding a new generation of super humans; Plato was a vengeful spirit, doing everything he could before his body failed utterly. Eve was the beginning of the new generation of humans, her innocence fresh out of the original packaging and only slightly tarnished.

Toby22 shook his head. The shy look they shared, the tentative smiles... they were a lovestruck pair without the first hint of what that meant. "Only twelve..." Toby muttered, shaking his head.

"Genetic compatibility is probably close to nil," Nora109 said. Toby22 caught a note of wistfulness that he wished he could remedy. "Maybe once Eve's matured, they can enjoy one another's company but not to any productive end."

"So... heartbreak, an early death, and not even a legacy to pass on?" Toby asked, hanging his head.

Nora109 lifted Toby22's chin. "Not if modern science has anything to say about it."

Toby22 heard the note of hope. A thousand years had passed between humanity's last breath and its rebirth. Science had done it all. Robots had saved humanity, but that was too big-picture for a Toby.

Robotkind needed to start saving humans. Every human they could.

CHAPTER EIGHTY-FOUR

Numbers counted backward in the dark.

An antenna listened for a signal that was long overdue.

A patient robot lurked in the gloom, the glow of his eyes the only light in the underground storage facility. The countdown continued without the need for a gaudy digital display.

No one was supposed to be down here to witness the countdown. Today was an exception because today those numbers were going to hit zero. When they did, Charlie25 would be there to witness.

Three minutes remained.

This wasn't Charlie25's normal routine. The world had ceased being normal of late. Humans had been discovered, which was a setback because those humans still had wet, slimy, illogical brains sloshing around inside their skulls. At the very least, those minds ought to have been renovated before being released into the wild.

One minute remained. Charlie25 waited.

The countdown ended. The antenna had failed to receive a particular signal. Lights on the upload rig flashed to life. Storage cores powered up, a cycle began, and data poured into the crystalline matrix of the inert robotic chassis hooked to the rig.

Five minutes to transfer.

Then four... three... two... one...

Eyes flared to life, and the robot in the rig sat up at once, snatching away cables as if they were cobwebs.

"Where am I? How old is this backup? How much is missing?" The robot swung its legs over the side of the table and took its first unsteady steps.

"Calm down, Evelyn. You're at our backup facility under Kanto. Everything's fine. You uploaded this brain scan just days ago."

"Everything is *not* fine, Charles," Evelyn11 snapped. "Look at this wretched chassis you've set me up with. I was better off in Evelyn38. Now tell me what happened. Last I remember, I was preparing an upload to Eve15. Did it fail that badly?"

"You survived. Eve15 didn't. That was nine days ago. Since then, you apparently attempted to upload to Eve14. You not only failed, but your test subject passed the post-upload test, causing the Evelyn38 chassis to be wiped."

Evelyn11 clenched her fists until the servos whined to a stall. "That little *rodent*! How did she ever—?"

"Charlie7 appears to have had a hand in helping her pass. You arranged for him to be killed."

Shaking loose her fists, Evelyn11 began to pace. "Well, bully on me for that, at least. Now tell me, how long until you can arrange a more permanent solution?"

"I don't have any good candidates lined up," Charlie25 said. "But soon enough, a perfect robot will come looking for a new chassis, and I'll upload you instead of them."

Evelyn11 grabbed the smug upload director by the collar of his grease-stained shirt. "Let me clarify. I don't *want* a new chassis. I want Eve14."

Author's Note

think after just finishing reading *Extinction Reversed*, you'd be shocked to discover how it began. A story that's a mix of I, Robot and *Jurassic Park* was once slated to be a comedy along the lines of *Three Men and a Baby*.

No, seriously.

I had the opening scene of *Extinction Reversed* in my head for a long time. The idea of robots attending a church service struck me as cognitively dissonant in a wonderful way. But in my original concept, the robots were part of a fully-robotic society where there had never been attempt to repopulate Earth. The robots worshiped mankind as their creators, and a subversive cult was working in secret to clone humans as living gods. *Cult of Man*, as I'd intended to call it, was originally going to feature the creators of a human baby who had no idea how to handle it.

When I tried to stretch that concept into something more than a series of "ha ha, look at those robots struggle trying to feed a baby," I ended up fast-forwarding to when the child had grown up. I needed intrigue, danger, and conflict. I wanted a thinking, feeling character aware of what was going on.

I'd created Eve.

But as I explored the idea of an illegally-cloned human on the run, I realized that there was no way a human could go anywhere. A world with no breathable air, no supply of food... there was no way this clone could leave the lab where they were born.

I scrapped that idea, at least partially. I still wanted my human clone, but the world she inhabited couldn't be so bleak and sterile. The robots, lacking humanity, would also have been unable to convey humanity to her. In short, I wasn't going to have any emotion in the story.

That was when I came up with the mixes. Human minds in robotic bodies gave me a world where robotic nostalgia, ambition, and hubris combined to create a civilization that yearned to recreate an Earth that had been lost. By putting human memories into robotic bodies, I had the seeds of the society that developed out of a pie-in-the-sky scientific project that worked beyond the wildest dreams of anyone (except one visionary).

After that, things started falling into place. I'm a world-builder at heart, and once I saw the world take shape, I knew where I wanted to go with it. An odd mix of utopia/dystopia in a "government" made up of committees led to gaps in oversight. The pride and accolades of first publishing major breakthroughs is about as close as this society came to fame and fortune. That desire to be at the cutting edge of science hid a darker motive in cloning humans—taking those organic bodies to reclaim lost humanity.

I love exploring the consequences of a premise. This is a world I loved creating and I'm looking ahead to expanding on the narrow view we got during Eve's transition from lab rat to the first of a new generation of humans.

Thanks for reading!

You made it to the end! Maybe you're just persistent, but hopefully that means you enjoyed the book. But this is just the end of one story. If you'd like reading my books, there are always more on the way!

Perks of being an Email Insider include:

- Notification of book releases (often with discounts)
- Inside track on beta reading
- Advance review copies (ARCs)
- Access to Inside Exclusive bonus extras and giveaways
- Best of my blog about fantasy, science fiction, and the art of worldbuilding

Sign up for the my Email Insiders list at:
jsmorin.com/updates

Books by J.S. Morin

Black Ocean

Black Ocean is a fast-paced fantasy space opera series about the small crew of the *Mobius* trying to squeeze out a living. If you love fantasy and sci-fi, and still lament over the cancellation of *Firefly*, *Black Ocean* is the series for you!

Read about all of the Black Ocean missions and discover where to buy at: **blackoceanmissions.com**

Twinborn Chronicles: *Awakening*

Experience the journey of mundane scribe Kyrus Hinterdale who discovers what it means to be Twinborn—and the dangers of getting caught using magic in a world that thinks it exists only in children's stories.

Twinborn Chronicles: *War of 3 Worlds*

Then continue on into the world of Korr, where the Mad Tinker and his daughter try to save the humans from the oppressive race of Kuduks. When their war spills over into both Tellurak and Veydrus, what alliances will they need to forge to make sure the right side wins?

Read about the full *Twinborn Chronicles* saga and discover where to buy at: **twinbornchronicles.com**

Robot Geneticists

Robot Geneticists brings genetic engineering into a postapocalytic Earth, 1000 years aliens obliterated all life.

Explore the ruins of the Human Age. Witness the glory of a world reclaimed from the apocalypse.

Charlie7 is the oldest robot alive. He's seen everything from the fall of mankind at the hands of alien invaders to the rebuilding of a living world from the algae up. But what he hasn't seen in over a thousand years is a healthy, intelligent human. When Eve stumbles into his life, the old robot finally has something worth coming out of retirement for: someone to protect.

Read about all of the *Robot Geneticists* books and discover where to buy at: **robotgeneticists.com**

About the Author

I am a creator of worlds and a destroyer of words. As a fantasy writer, my works range from traditional epics to futuristic fantasy with starships. I have worked as an unpaid Little League pitcher, a cashier, a student library aide, a factory grunt, a cubicle drone, and an engineer—there is some overlap in the last two.

Through it all, though, I was always a storyteller. Eventually I started writing books based on the stray stories in my head, and people kept telling me to write more of them. Now, that's all I do for a living.

I enjoy strategy, worldbuilding, and the fantasy author's privilege to make up words. I am a gamer, a joker, and a thinker of sideways thoughts. But I don't dance, can't sing, and my best artistic efforts fall short of your average notebook doodle. When you read my books, you are seeing me at my best.

My ultimate goal is to be both clever and right at the same time. I have it on good authority that I have yet to achieve it.

Connect with me online
On my blog at **jsmorin.com**
On Facebook at **facebook.com/authorjsmorin**
On Twitter at **twitter.com/authorjsmorin**

99907822R00205

Made in the USA
Columbia, SC
13 July 2018